Artistic Licence

KATIE FFORDE

Artistic Licence

Century · London

First published in the United Kingdom in 2001 by Century

1 3 5 7 9 10 8 6 4 2

Copyright © Katie Fforde 2001

Katie Fforde has asserted her right under the Copyright, Designs and Patents
Act, 1988 to be identified as the author of this work

Century
The Random House Group Limited
20 Vauxhall Bridge Road, London SW1V 2SA

Random House Australia (Pty) Limited
20 Alfred Street, Milsons Point, Sydney,
New South Wales 2061, Australia

Random House New Zealand Limited
18 Poland Road, Glenfield
Auckland 10, New Zealand

Random House South Africa (Pty) Limited
Endulini, 5a Jubilee Road, Parktown 2193, South Africa

The Random House Group Limited Reg. No. 954009

www.randomhouse.co.uk
A CIP catalogue record for this book is available
from the British Library

Papers used by Random House
are natural, recyclable products made from wood grown in
sustainable forests. The manufacturing processes conform to
the environmental regulations of the country of origin

Typeset by SX Composing DTP, Rayleigh, Essex
Printed and bound in Great Britain by
Mackays of Chatham PLC, Chatham, Kent

ISBN 0 7126 6972 8 (hardback)
ISBN 0 7126 6973 6 (trade paperback)

Acknowledgements

To Sue Wilson, photographer, Gilli Allan, writer and travelling companion, (who isn't bossy and doesn't snore), Jane and Alan Ford for an idea. To Pam and Julian Swindell for taking us to Hollow Cottage in County Mayo. To Aix-en-Provence and New York for being so wonderful. But mostly to Lyn Cluer-Coleman for creating The Stroud House Gallery and letting me watch.

To Lyn Cluer-Coleman and to
The Stroud House Gallery.
With much love.

Chapter One

Thea was standing in the rubbish bin, trying to crush its contents enough to get the lid on, when she heard people approaching down the hallway. They were talking.

'Come into the kitchen and excuse the mess, it's always a tip,' she heard as she crushed a pizza box beneath her heel.

Petal, her youngest and most demanding lodger, followed by a man Thea had never seen before, entered the kitchen.

'Hi, Thea! What *are* you doing in there?' Petal said, curious but not interested enough to hear the answer. 'This is my Uncle Ben. Oh, that's my phone.'

While Petal searched in her bag for her fifth limb, Thea tried to step out of the waste bin without falling over. There was nothing to be ashamed of in compacting takeaway cartons, cereal packets and Pringle's tubes, thus reducing landfill, but she could have done without witnesses. Petal, having dived on her mobile phone like a gull on a fast-food leftover, went out of the room, talking hard.

Thea, unreasonably annoyed, reached for the wall to balance herself. The bin teetered and her foot penetrated the layer of cardboard to the substratum of detritus beneath. Trying to pull herself free, the heel of her shoe caught round the loop of a drinks can holder and Thea began to lose her balance. For an instant she had an image of herself lying prostrate on the floor, surrounded by eggshells, banana skins and coffee grounds. She put out a hand, groping for something to hold on to, but couldn't reach the wall.

The stranger, seeing her predicament, crossed the room and caught the flailing hand and then her body, steadying the bin and holding Thea upright.

Maybe, if she hadn't been in such a bad mood, she could have seen the funny side and laughed up at him. As it was, she just blushed furiously while he supported her, unwilling to see if he was laughing at her. 'Thank you so much,' she muttered to the bin, as she rammed the lid back on. 'What a ridiculous thing to have happened.'

Petal quite often managed to make Thea feel more disagreeable than the most caricatured seaside landlady and she felt very tempted to tell her so-called uncle that it was all Petal's fault; she had promised to get some new bin liners, having used up Thea's entire roll. But although this was the truth, it would be extremely petty, and it was bad enough to appear bad-tempered and ridiculous in front of strangers without being small-minded as well.

'That's OK,' he said. 'It could happen to anyone.'

To anyone foolish enough to climb into a rubbish bin, she thought, but didn't say. To direct his attention away from the tea bag that had got trapped down the side of her shoe, Thea nodded towards Petal. 'That girl burns the telephone at both ends. I hope it doesn't fry her brain.'

Petal's uncle, who had been surveying Thea and her surroundings with a sort of mystified concentration, said, 'Possibly it already has.'

Thea struggled to get her usual good humour back, but it was difficult. He was tall and dark, with deep-set eyes, and it was easy to take his quiet, serious demeanour as disapproval. She wished she could tell him to go and wait for Petal in the hall, but unfortunately she was chronically hospitable, unable to have people in her house, however unwelcome and uninvited, without offering them food or drink. 'Would you like a cup of coffee? Tea?' She slid the kettle over to the hot part of the Rayburn. She was desperate for a cup herself and didn't feel she could have one if he didn't join her.

'I don't think we're staying. I just came with Petal to collect some things.'

'Does that mean Petal is taking her artwork home at last?'

This was such good news that Thea couldn't help a feeling of benevolence breaking over her. She smiled widely at the thought that she would soon be able to get into the attic, her bedroom and the bathroom, without tripping over the component parts of a dragon, a princess and a castle, all made of papier mâché and covered with Thea's bin bags. 'You might as well have some tea. She'll be ages.' And it'll give us something to do, so we won't have to talk, she thought.

Perhaps her glee was rather too much of a contrast from the grumpy woman he'd helped out of a dustbin because the man frowned. 'I can't stay long. I've got to get back tonight.'

'Suit yourself, but if I don't have something my tongue will cleave itself permanently to the roof of my mouth.'

'Then, thank you,' he said, looking somewhat surprised.

Her euphoria faded a little. Petal's Uncle Ben appeared to have no social skills. Why didn't he comment on the filthy weather or something?

'Do you have far to get back to?'

'Well, after I've dropped off Petal's things, I've got to get back to London.'

That would take him at least three hours at this time of day. Thea found an unchipped mug and put a tea bag in it.

At that moment the phone rang. Thea manoeuvred her way across the kitchen and picked it up. It was an old and dear friend who liked a good half-hour per phone call, and that was if she was in a hurry. Thea talked to her for a couple of minutes, then took evasive action. She picked up a box of matches and a candle, kept there for the purpose, and lit the candle. Then she reached out into the hallway and held it under the smoke alarm. It shrieked obligingly. 'Darling,' she told her friend. 'I've got to go. Something's on fire!'

'Sorry,' she said to Petal's uncle, who was looking at her with stunned amazement. 'That always works. Although I do worry that I'll have a real fire one day as a punishment. Now, where were we? Tea!'

'I really mustn't be long and I was supposed to call in on Molly – er – Petal's aunt, too.'

'You don't have to have any, but I'm gasping.'

The man sighed. 'Actually, so am I.'

As she poured boiling water into mugs, she glanced over her shoulder. 'Is that Molly Pickford? I know her. It's through her I got Petal.' It was Thea's turn to sigh as she wondered why she'd let herself in for having Petal as a lodger. She hoped it wasn't because she was too feeble to say no to Molly, but she feared it was. Molly had insisted that her god-daughter and niece would be quiet and reliable, and able to pay the rent. While the last bit was true, which was important, Molly had forgotten to mention that Petal was extremely demanding. Thea often thought that even if she paid twice as much, she still wouldn't be worth it.

'Milk? Sugar?' She handed her guest a mug, with suitable additions. 'Are you related to Molly, too? Petal referred to you as her uncle, but it doesn't necessarily follow that you are.'

Usually, by this time, Thea would have got over her feeling of awkwardness at being caught with her kitchen at its worst, but as he kept looking around him like a character in a science fiction movie beamed down into a strange land, she felt obliged to distract him with questions she didn't want to know the answer to.

'We're some sort of cousins. You'd have to ask Molly

4

about how many times removed we are. She loves that kind of detail.'

Thea warmed to him a little. She picked up a pile of papers from a chair and indicated he should sit down. 'Sorry, I didn't catch your surname?'

'Probably because Petal didn't tell you it. It's Jonson, without an "h". Ben Jonson.'

'Like the poet?'

'Yes.'

His slight surprise that she should have heard of one of the sixteenth century's most famous poets annoyed her. 'I love his poems, especially the one he wrote about his son.' She bit her lip. 'His best bit of poetry . . .'

His glance made her feel she was strangely almost human, and yet not quite. 'He said "piece", actually. *His best piece of poetry.*'

Thea's moment of sentimentality evaporated and her irritation returned. 'Well, I knew it was something like that. You'd better sit down; Petal might be hours. Now, I hope you don't mind if I get on with my cooking? In a moment of madness I agreed to give my lodgers an evening meal.'

'Every night?'

'Not Fridays or Saturdays, as they're usually out, or home for the weekend, but I always do a big meal on Sunday night.' It was Sunday now and Thea had been making a bolognese sauce for the lasagne on and off all day. She silently urged Petal to come back before she felt obliged to invite her uncle to supper. The lasagne might stretch, but the salad and French bread wouldn't. 'Please sit down, you're making the place look untidy.'

She didn't turn round to see if he realised she'd made a little joke; she was almost sure he had no sense of humour, but she didn't want it confirmed.

Petal came back into the room, still talking: 'Must go, see ya, doll.' Almost the moment she had disconnected, the house telephone went. 'Oh,' said Petal, breezily confident, 'that'll be for me.'

Thea took a gulp of tea, wishing it were red wine. Now Ben was seated, she couldn't get past him to the fridge. 'Would you mind very much passing me a bottle of milk? And the lump of cheese? The fridge is just behind you.' He had already seen her kitchen, so the inside of her fridge should be no shock to him, although Thea wouldn't let anyone very nervous look in it. 'The semi-skimmed, in the door.'

He handed her the milk and cheese. Petal was still on the phone, making arrangements. Soon, Thea's other lodgers would begin to arrive back from their weekend haunts, and the kitchen would be more crowded and cooking would be more difficult.

'I do wish Petal would get off the phone,' said Ben and Thea together. They looked at each other and Ben smiled.

It transformed him, but as Petal hung up the phone at that moment, Thea looked away before she could work out why. When she looked back again the smile had gone.

'Oh, by the way, Thea,' said Petal. 'Aunt Molly's coming over later.'

'Oh, God, why?' Too late, Thea realised that this must have sounded extremely rude to Molly's relatives. 'I mean, I'm just so busy at the moment.' Thea tipped the milk into the pan. 'Do you know why?'

'Some art appreciation tour or something. On Wednesday.'

'Well, it's my day off on Wednesday, so I can probably go. I'll give her a ring later. Save her the trouble of coming over.' It was more to save Thea the trouble of sanitising the kitchen. Ben Jonson might look about him disapprovingly, but at least he kept his thoughts to himself. Molly would be voluble on the subject of Thea's standards of tidiness and hygiene.

Petal frowned. 'I may have got it wrong, but I'm sure she said something about France.'

'France?' Thea, whisking hard, was wondering if she'd made enough sauce and wasn't really listening.

'Yeah. I think Aunt Molly wants you to go to France with her. On Wednesday.'

Thea put down her whisk, leaving a smear of cheese sauce on the worktop. 'Try and think, Petal. What did Molly say? She can't possibly be asking me to go to France with her on Wednesday.'

'Yes! Molly's mate's broken her leg, or her hip or something, so she needs someone to go with. I told her you were probably up for it.' Petal, bored with a subject that didn't involve her, turned to her uncle. 'Oh, Uncle Ben, I'm glad you've got some tea. It'll take me ages to find the stuff in the attic, it's so full of junk.' She looked at the crowded table, the crockery-covered worktops, the Welsh dresser buried under paper. 'This house is always so untidy.'

'So would yours be if it were full of lodgers who can't put a mug in the dishwasher, let alone run a tap and wash it,' said Thea. 'And I hope you're going to take everything off the landing. At least the stuff in the attic is out of sight most of the time.'

Momentarily abashed, Petal said, 'Sorry Thea, but you don't nag us enough. If you don't nag people, they just don't clear up. When I move into a flat people are just not going to leave their stuff all over the place!' Petal marched out of the room, stiff with resolution, leaving Thea limp and without it.

'So Petal drives you mad?' asked Ben.

'Is it that obvious? Well, only sometimes.' She tasted the sauce and reached for the nutmeg grater. 'I mean, I love her really. She's very decorative, and great fun and great to go shopping with.'

She was aware that if only she were a firmer and less indulgent landlady she wouldn't be so walked on by her lodgers. But she was new to the trade and hadn't learnt how to make rules and stick to them. 'You wouldn't be a sweetie and grate some cheese for me?' she asked and then had to hide her giggle with a smile as she realised how inappropriate her endearment had been.

He raised an eyebrow. 'Since you ask so nicely, how can I refuse?' He took the cheese and the grater, and set to work.

'I wonder what Molly wants? I can't believe she really wants me to go to France on Wednesday. Even she . . .' she paused, suddenly realising she was about to criticise his second cousin once removed or some such.

'Couldn't be that unreasonable?' he suggested, not giving anything away on how he felt about Molly.

'Not at all. I just meant that she's usually very organised. I hope she doesn't arrive just as everyone's sitting down to eat.' This was likely. Molly, with only a husband to organise, was likely to have got her evening meal cooked, served and cleared away before nine o'clock. Thea, whose supper was a feast made moveable by the punctuality or otherwise of its guests, rarely achieved this happy state.

Petal came back just as Thea had levered the completed dish into the oven. Preceded by a large number of plastic sacks, Petal said, 'You really should clear out the attic, Thea. I can't believe you've got so many cardboard boxes. What on earth have you got in them?'

In fact, they were full of Thea's photographs and negatives, carefully indexed and catalogued, from when she was a student to the moment she gave up professional photography. But she had no intention of telling Petal that. 'The attic's probably a lot clearer now you've taken your work out of it, Petal,' she said, mentally trying to locate the corkscrew.

In a minute Petal and her uncle would go away, and she

8

could open the bottle of red wine which was hidden behind the bleach in the cupboard under the sink, the one place her lodgers would never look, however desperate for a drink they were. She wouldn't offer any to Molly when she appeared. Molly was of the 'life's too short to drink cheap wine' school of thought. Thea felt that life was too long not to.

Petal, oblivious to the acid in Thea's tone, looked anxiously about the kitchen. 'Don't you think you should tidy up a bit, if Aunt Molly's coming?'

Thea would have liked to commit murder, but thought she'd better not. It would only add to the mess. 'I'm in the middle of cooking a meal, Petal. And I take it you're not eating with us?'

'Oh, no! Didn't I say? Sorry.'

At that moment the doorbell rang. 'Answer it, will you?' Thea implored.

'But it'll be Aunt Molly, for you.' Petal was surprised Thea could ask such a thing of her. 'I'm really busy.'

'So am I!' said Thea who was swooping round the work-tops with a cloth.

'I'll get it,' Ben offered.

This was kind and, if he wanted to be even kinder, he would involve Molly in a lot of time-consuming chat upstairs in the hall, giving Thea valuable extra seconds to clean up.

Molly, whom she had met on her first day in Cheltenham, had been introduced by some distant relative of Thea's mother's. It was a very tenuous connection but Molly, who could be very kind, had followed it up immediately by inviting Thea for coffee. Thea, delighted to get away from the removal men, walked round in her old jeans and torn shirt. Molly, as always, was immaculately groomed and dressed, and had given her sherry, not coffee. She assumed that Thea's dishabille, meant that she was 'arty' and had taken her under her wing. In the two and a half years that Thea had lived in Cheltenham the two women had spent quite a lot of time together. Now she entered Thea's kitchen, all benevolence, a good five minutes after she had rung the doorbell.

Thank you, Petal's uncle, thought Thea.

'Thea, sweetie!' Molly was fond but brisk. 'I hope this isn't wildly inconvenient, but I wanted to come and tell you in person.'

'Tell me what, Molly?' asked Thea, after they had kissed each other.

'About the trip.' Molly pulled out a chair, regarded its seat dubiously and sat down. 'To Aix. In Provence. Should be lovely at this time of year. Petal did give you my message?'

'She said something about you going to France on Wednesday.'

'Darling, Provence is *in* France. Surely you knew that? But not just me, you too.'

Thea, who had been getting more of her surfaces wiped than she usually achieved in a week, turned round. 'What?'

'Thea, do pay attention! I said I want you come to Provence with me. On Wednesday.'

'This Wednesday, coming?'

'Yes. I was going with my friend from my pottery class, but she's broken her leg. If I go on my own I'll have to pay the single room supplement. Come on,' she went on bracingly, as if Thea were refusing to go swimming because the water was cold. 'It's only for six days.'

'Take Derek.'

'Derek hates art and sightseeing, and all that stuff. He is such a Philistine.'

'But Molly – it's terribly short notice.'

'Oh, I know it's a bit sudden, but think how heavenly it would be. Early April is just my favourite time for

Provence, before all the tourists get there.' Molly obviously hadn't noticed she was a tourist herself.

'I can't afford it, for a start.' This was a guess, but Molly was, by Thea's standards, enormously rich and had probably booked a very expensive tour. 'And really . . .'

'Oh, come on, Thea, be a bit spontaneous. Don't worry about the money, Derek'll pay. It was his idea that I ask you, actually. He said you probably deserve a holiday for looking after Petal.'

Thea gave Derek a mental 'thank you' for understanding that his niece was not all joy. 'But Molly, it would be far cheaper to pay the single room supplement.'

'Oh, I know. It's the company I want you for, really. You never know who you'll get on those trips. I like to go with someone I know. Someone I can talk to.'

Personally, Thea liked to go on holiday with somebody she liked and although she did like Molly, even the very best of friendships could founder in such conditions. And she wasn't sure that Molly qualified as 'very best'.

Thea decided to risk losing Molly's good opinion of her by producing her hidden wine. As Petal probably had the only decent corkscrew in her room, she had to prise the cork out with one that hurt her fingers. 'It's terribly generous of you, Molly, but I can't possibly accept. Have some of this. It's only a "bogoff" but really quite OK if you warm it up a bit first.'

'Bogoff?' Molly looked at her glass as if it contained very nasty medicine.

'You know, buy one, get one free.'

Molly was a member of a wine club and this notion appalled her, but she didn't comment. '*Of course* you can come to France,' she said decisively. She picked up her glass, thought better of it and put it down again. 'Really, Derek can afford it and he's right, you deserve a break for looking after Petal.' She looked up at the ceiling. The sound of banging and crashing indicated that Petal's

11

artwork was nearing the front door. 'Can you get away at such short notice?'

Suddenly the thought of exchanging her lodgers and her boring part-time job for Provence in the spring was terribly attractive. And even if Molly was bossy and overbearing, she was fun.

Thea took a large sip of her wine and decided that Molly was right: it wasn't very nice. The wine in Provence was bound to be better. Then she pulled up a chair and threw her cloth into the sink. 'We're not particularly busy at the moment and I don't get holiday pay or anything. I don't think it would be a problem.'

'Super! You'll need comfortable shoes, an umbrella and a sunhat.'

Just then, Petal opened the kitchen door and shouted through it, 'Ben said thank you for the tea and sorry he can't say goodbye, but he's loading the car. And Aunt Molly, he'll give you a ring as he hasn't time to call in now. 'Bye!' The kitchen door closed and then opened again. 'By the way, Thea, there are some clothes of mine in the tumble-dryer. If you could be an angel and hang them up for me?' Assuming that Thea would be an angel, Petal removed herself.

Thea regarded Molly. 'A sunhat?' The cold spring rain was lashing against the window and the tumble-dryer was full of Petal's clothes. 'I'd love to come, Molly.'

Thea's part-time job at a high street photographer's was not one which was ever going to bring her much in the way of job satisfaction. Sending off other people's holiday snaps and handing them back twenty-four hours later was not intrinsically interesting. She had realised that going for that particular job was a mistake the moment she had first made coffee for everyone. But because in a previous life she had been a photographer it had seemed natural, although she now knew that selling cheap imported clothes to bo-hos and second-time-around hippies would have been much more fun.

But while she often inspected cards put up in other shop windows and turned to the jobs page in the local paper, she couldn't quite summon up the energy to find anything more challenging. It was to do with the lassitude that had begun to affect her lately; she wasn't happy with her life, but hadn't the initiative to do anything much to change it. Perhaps an art appreciation tour in France would give her the necessary prod.

It would have been an overstatement to say that Thea's 'life' and the 'love of it' had both deserted her at the same time, but she had hoped the man in question would turn into a partner – or even a husband.

She had been a photojournalist, just making her name, and what had happened was hurtful and humiliating, but the worst part was that her female photographer friends all told her it was her fault.

They had bullied the story out of her three days after her arrival at the door of one of them, late one evening, asking if she could stay the night. After three days of seeing Thea in her pyjamas watching Channel 5, the friend, who wanted her sofa back, called in reinforcements. Ordered to get dressed, she was frogmarched to a local pub where they could straighten her out in peace, accompanied by tequila slammers.

After they'd heard that she and Conrad had broken up (which they'd guessed), they moved on to the reason why. And, to a professional, hard-boiled woman, they condemned her as a naïve amateur.

'I know,' she admitted, finishing her slammer. 'I've got so much egg on my face I can hardly see out.'

'I could do with egg like that,' said Zelda, a model who had moved round to the other side of the camera. 'How much did you get as a thank you present?'

Thea repeated the amount, although they all knew

perfectly well by now. 'I feel bad about accepting it, but Anna insisted. She told me that I'd given her much more than money could ever buy and that being generous involved receiving as well as giving. I thought it was rather sweet.'

The women's collective expression told Thea they found it rather nauseous, actually, but they didn't comment.

'So now what? You can upgrade your shoebox to a boot box. When you've got the bastard out, that is,' suggested one.

'What you should do is get some really fancy equipment, something that will earn you proper money.'

Elizabeth was career-minded and made Thea feel tired at the best of times. 'What I really want to do', she said, preparing to duck from what was about to be thrown at her, 'is to buy a large house in Cheltenham and fill it with students.'

Chapter Two

❧

They were all too shocked to throw things.

'Why Cheltenham?' asked Elizabeth, in case there was something Thea knew about it that she didn't.

'Because I don't know anyone in Cheltenham. I can have a completely new start in life. Do something entirely different. Earn my living without having to hustle for work and lug half a ton of equipment around the place to do it. I've done a lot of thinking during the last few days and I've made up my mind.'

'But it's so stimulating! Not knowing where you're going to be working each day,' said Magenta. 'And the equipment's getting lighter all the time.'

'But not fast enough for my back, alas.'

'And you could always do studio work.'

'I could,' Thea agreed, 'and perhaps I might set up a studio, after a while, but just for now I want to hide away and lick my wounds.'

'You must have been hurt badly if you want to retire to the provinces.' Zelda said with a shudder. 'Have you ever been there?'

Thea nodded. 'I did some work at the Literature Festival once. There's a lovely parade of shops, with caryatids. I really fancy it. And yes, I was badly hurt. I don't think Conrad ever loved me.'

'What did you say? Did you have a huge row?'

'No, not really. I just couldn't make him understand what he'd done wrong. There was no point in rowing. I don't think you do quarrel with people you don't care about. He never cared about me and I suddenly stopped caring about him. Put me right off men, though.'

'Don't they have men in Cheltenham?' asked Elizabeth.

'No, I don't think so. It's partly why I chose it.'

Everyone laughed, but they didn't manage to change her mind throughout the course of the evening and they did agree that she was way too naïve for photojournalism.

'Well,' said Magenta, 'you can always come and stay if you want to come back and rejoin the world.'

'And you can come and stay with me, if you want to get away from it.'

'Thank you, darling. It sounds heaven,' Magenta replied, completely unconvinced.

For a while she enjoyed her change of lifestyle. She worked extremely hard doing up her house, making friends and making it clear to the world that she didn't want a man, thank you, ever. Now, nearly two years on, her house was decorated and full of lodgers, and the lodgers were driving her mad.

Mostly, she enjoyed the kids. She was easygoing, didn't really mind hanging people's washing out, or taking it in if it was raining. And only a real cow could object to ironing something when someone was 'really, really late' and desperate for a white blouse, especially if it was 'for work'.

But she was only thirty-five and was surrogate mother to people far too old to be her children. Those people, often away from home for the first time, were only too glad to find such a kindly, helpful person to listen to their problems and sew on their buttons in an emergency. If she occasionally nagged them about not leaving their dirty crockery all over the house, they mostly ignored her. At least she didn't grill them about who they were going out with.

Thea felt she had gone from potentially successful

photojournalist to mother of teenagers too quickly. She should have had a life in between. But hindsight is a perfect science and when she had arrived down from London, exhausted and emotionally bruised, 'a life' was the last thing she wanted. She had wanted retirement, order and to wake up every morning without having to wonder which town her hotel room was in. She no longer wished to spend evenings fighting off advances from photographers who had drunk their mini-bars dry and wanted to take advantage of the double bed.

She hadn't intended to give up on men completely – at least, not for ever. She knew perfectly well that while Conrad was a shit, a lot of men were honourable and trustworthy. She had even gone out with a few of them since she'd moved out of London. It was a shame that these cardinal virtues seemed to go hand in hand with dullness and a love of obscure classical music.

Much to Petal's dismay, she had ended her relationship with one such just recently. Petal had been horrified: 'But Thea, I know he's not very exciting, but he's *someone* and you shouldn't finish with one boy – I mean, man – before you've got another one. Otherwise you're on your own, manless and dateless! I mean, derr! How sad are you?'

Thea bit back a smile at Petal's indignation. 'I thought I'd play the field, like the women on *Sex and the City*.' This particular American entertainment was one of Petal's favourites.

'Thea! You're not like those women! You couldn't screw around like they do!'

Thea was relieved to hear this. While she knew perfectly well that she couldn't 'screw around', the fact that Petal was equally shocked at the idea meant that perhaps Petal couldn't either. Thea knew that Molly thought she should keep an eye on Petal's morals, a task Thea felt completely unequal to. 'Well anyway,' she said.

'I couldn't stand another evening of early music in a freezing cold church.'

'Tell him you don't want to go! You don't have to finish with a bloke because you don't share the same taste in music. Just bring him round to what you like!'

While Thea was certain that Petal could convert the most dedicated classical music scholar to 'techno', or 'drum'n'bass', she didn't feel she shared Petal's skills in manipulation. Molly, on the other hand, might even be able to teach Petal a thing or two about getting her own way.

Molly's husband Derek, well-trained and with the prospect of a week without Molly organising his life, had agreed to drive the two women to Gatwick. Molly took an elegant suitcase on wheels and a fitted vanity case as hand luggage. Thea took a battered holdall, borrowed from Jerry, one of her lodgers, and a large, flowery cotton handbag into which she could fit a huge amount. Molly would have made a list, and packed an outfit for every day and every evening, and numerous pairs of shoes. Thea had stuffed her bag with everything she owned that was navy-blue, so there was a hope of it blending in, if not exactly matching, and a pair of slightly less tatty shoes for evening than the trainers she was now wearing.

Derek and Molly arrived at Thea's house at eight o'clock in the morning. Molly was in full make-up and looked marvellous. She regarded Thea with her lips pursed. 'Oh,' she said. 'Trainers.'

'You said I'd need comfortable shoes,' Thea reminded her.

'I know, but I meant – oh, well, never mind. Have you got a light mac and an umbrella?'

'I've got a cagoule but no umbrella,' said Thea firmly. 'I don't get on with them.' She hadn't got an E111 either, or personal travel insurance, but she knew if she told Molly this she'd have a fit.

'Well, it's up to you. So, where's your case?'

'This is my case.'

Molly looked horrified. 'I wouldn't be able to go away for a night with only a bag that size.'

Thea shrugged, hoping she hadn't forgotten anything really vital, like her one pair of tidy trousers.

'Oh, well. You do know we eat out at restaurants every night?'

'I'll be fine.' Thea closed the front door behind her, wondering if agreeing to go on holiday with Molly hadn't been a dreadful mistake. Molly was already making her feel harrased.

'We won't put our badges on until we're in the departure lounge,' said Molly after Thea had insisted that Derek be allowed just to drop them off at the entrance, and not park his car and assist two able-bodied women through the check-in process. 'We don't want people identifying us too soon. You did get an identifying badge, didn't you? They promised they'd send one?'

'Oh, yes,' agreed Thea, 'it's just that I've lost it. But it doesn't matter. If you've got yours, I can stand by you.'

Molly regarded Thea crossly. 'Honestly, Thea . . .' Just before Thea could respond Molly remembered that Thea had only had two days to get ready for this trip. 'Of course, it was terribly short notice and I'm really pleased you could come . . .'

Thea smiled. 'And I'm really pleased you asked me. I haven't been abroad for ages.'

'Oh, my goodness! You did check your passport hasn't expired, didn't you?'

'I must say,' said Thea, weak with relief that nothing was found wrong with her passport and that the last-minute

19

changes to her ticket were all in order, 'I'm looking forward to not having to think for a bit and just follow our tour guide like a sheep. It's been so hectic lately. It'll be restful to be told what to do.'

Molly never did anything like a sheep and wasn't good at being told what to do, but she did like a good fortnight in which to pack and have herself coiffed, waxed, plucked and beautified, and couldn't possibly have got ready in the time available to Thea. 'It was a dreadful rush for you. But don't worry, I can probably lend you anything you've forgotten.'

'Thank you,' said Thea meekly, knowing she hadn't brought toothpaste and there would probably be other things.

'Shall we have coffee now, or after we've done the perfume?' suggested Molly.

'I do need to buy a book . . .'

'Oh, no. You never get time to read on these holidays, you're kept far too busy.'

'So you've been on this type of tour a lot?'

'Yes and our guide's such a nice man. You could say I was a bit of a Gerald groupie.' Molly giggled alarmingly.

Thea flirted with the notion of developing a previously unsuspected medical condition and going home, but it seemed both cowardly and churlish. Besides, Molly would find out she didn't have travel insurance. 'Oh, well, if you like it enough to come back, I expect I'll have a good time too.' She was trying to convince herself. 'What's the lecturer on Cézanne like?'

'I've no idea. I've never heard of him. I don't think he's a Tiger Tours regular.' This definitely marked him down in Molly's book. 'But I dare say he'll be all right. They're very careful who they get. Now come along, I want to get some cream for my eyes.' She peered at Thea. 'I expect you could do with some too. It's no good waiting for the wrinkles to appear to do anything about them, you know.'

Thea, whose idea of duty-free shopping was spraying herself with a lot of free scent, smiled. 'I think I'll just cut along to the bookshop and meet you back here.'

Molly had put on her distinctive, stripy Tiger Tour badge as they stood by baggage reclaim at Marseilles airport. Thea began to spot other badges, and they were all attached to women of a certain age and type. Thea began to feel that she was going to be the baby of the party. Even Molly, though over fifty, was younger than most of this crowd. A few men appeared wearing badges, and people began to smile tentatively at each other.

'You see why I wanted you to come.' Molly's stage whisper was guaranteed to reach the back of the stalls. 'Most of this lot are geriatric. I might have got latched on to by some old dear with incontinence pads who couldn't keep up.'

Thea hoped that the old dears were all stone deaf. She felt that anyone who had enough gumption to come on a foreign holiday must have something about them. She smiled at a few people to detach herself from Molly's unkind remark.

'Right, troops,' said a tall, dark-haired man in his early fifties. 'Gather round while I give you a few instructions. I see some familiar faces, which is good, because you can help me keep the newcomers in order.'

Thea glanced at Molly and saw her smiling benignly. There were several other smiling faces too. They were obviously all Gerald groupies. Well, if he could keep Molly under control he must have something going for him. Poor old Derek was well under the thumb.

'And why aren't you wearing a badge, young lady?' Gerald asked Thea with an oily smile.

'I've lost it,' she told him somewhat defiantly, knowing

she and Molly would never fight over men if Gerald was her ideal.

'It's all right, Gerald, she's with me,' said Molly. 'You remember me? Arles, last year? Molly Pickford?'

'Molly! Good to have you aboard again. And you've brought a chum. Jolly good. Now, the *toilettes* are over in that direction, people, and the trolleys are over there.'

Thea could see people debating which was their greatest need and said, 'Shall I go and get a few trolleys and bring them over? Otherwise they'll all disappear.'

'Good idea. I'll stay here until we're all together again. Then we'll get on to the coach.'

The holiday had begun. Thea wondered if it wouldn't have been better to take herself off to a cheapo hotspot for a few days, but realised that if Molly hadn't frogmarched her on to this tour she would never have upped and left everything. If Molly drove her mad, she comforted herself, she could always latch herself on to an old lady – there were plenty to choose from.

As Thea lay on the bed, watching Molly unpack, she realised that she hadn't shared a room with another girl since she had been on a school trip, when everyone had just lived out of their rucksacks. Molly made unpacking an art form.

'Only about a dozen hangers. I don't suppose you brought any with you, did you?'

'No,' said Thea. 'But twelve hangers should be plenty, shouldn't it? That's one each per day.'

Molly sighed. 'Perhaps I should have got us single rooms. I'll never get all my things in half this space.'

'It's all right, no one . . .' She was just about to tell Molly that no one under fifty ever unpacked, when she realised it wasn't kind. 'I'll just drape my things over this chair.'

'But we'll need to sit on that while we make up our faces.'

'Couldn't we do that in the bathroom? Standing up?'

'Well, you may be able to, but I need a chair, a magnifying mirror, a good light and a good half-hour. I'm not as young as you are.'

Having used up all the hangers, and put her travel iron, her hairdryer and her heated rollers into the drawers, Molly began to unload her beauty products. These she distributed across the table, having first moved it under the window. This did involve Thea in doing without a bedside cabinet and getting in and out of bed halfway down it, but having lost ground over the wardrobe, she was in a weakened position. Besides, she was fascinated by the number of patent creams and serums that Molly had brought. Molly did look very good for her age and, if it was all those bottles that did it, Thea thought perhaps she should try to upgrade her own beauty routine.

At last Molly was ready. Her many clothes were neatly stacked in the wardrobe. Her underwear was in the chest of drawers. Her bath oil, shower gel, shampoo, conditioner and hairspray were lined up on the shelf in the bathroom. Bags of cotton balls and cotton pads and tissues were hung on all the available hooks, and her special linen cloth for her face was draped over the towel rail.

'Darling, where will you put all your stuff? Is that all you've got? Love, I know you are a lot younger than me, but you need a bit more than just a pot of Astral, surely? What about cleanser and toner?'

Thea, who was amazed at how much it took to make Molly look like Molly, felt she might as well come clean. 'I don't do much in the way of cleansing and toning. I just smear on some cream, wipe it off with loo paper and put a bit more on.'

Molly was horrified. 'I can't believe *anyone*, in this day and age, doesn't cleanse and tone.' She peered at Thea. 'Well, you seem to have got away with it so far, but it could rebound on you horribly. You have to take care of yourself, Thea . . .'

Before Molly could finish her thought, which Thea knew from experience was something on the lines of 'or you'll never find yourself a man', Thea broke in, 'I do have deodorant with moisturiser in it. It makes my armpits wonderfully soft and manageable.'

Molly pursed her lips. She was a natural matchmaker and, sensing this, when they first met, Thea had given her a very graphic and well-dramatised account of her break-up with Conrad. Otherwise, Thea had felt at the time, and had no reason to change her mind since, Molly would be dragging single men out of the woodwork until, maddened by boredom, Thea put herself into a convent.

Now, Thea looked at her watch. 'We've got three-quarters of an hour before we have to meet downstairs for dinner.'

'Really? Oh, my God! Do you mind if I have the bath first? What are you going to wear?'

Thea didn't have a lot of choice. 'Something navy-blue, I expect.'

Gerald was impatiently striding up and down the hotel foyer, waiting for the last of his flock to arrive when they got down the stairs. He wanted to march them briskly off to dinner. 'Late again, Molly! I thought I'd taught you a bit of punctuality when you were with me before.'

'It was my fault,' Thea began, sacrificing truth for her friend. But then she saw Molly bridling happily under Gerald's stern admonishment and realised she liked it. In any case, no one would believe that she had spent more than ten minutes doing herself up, when her hair was still slightly wet and her navy-blue skirt distinctly crumpled.

'Oh, Gerald, you're such a bully,' said Molly. 'I don't know why I come with you.'

As the party processed down the narrow street to the

24

restaurant, Thea wondered if Molly would like it if Derek were as masterful as Gerald and decided not. It was one thing to enjoy being bossed about by Gerald for five days on holiday, but quite another actually to live with someone you couldn't control.

'Well, I thought the bath was awfully small, for one,' said a woman who'd brought her husband with her and so had a natural advantage over those who hadn't.

'What was it like for two?' asked Thea under her breath.

Another Home Counties accent drifted across the clink of glasses. 'I looked and looked, but although they had everything else, they didn't have cards with "to my cleaning lady" on, so I had to just get her one with flowers.'

Thea was hypnotised and didn't at first hear her neighbour's kindly enquiry. 'Is this your first Tiger Tour?' She was certainly the wrong side of seventy-five but had a definite twinkle.

'Yes,' Molly answered for her. 'She's come with me.'

'I see,' said the old lady, sizing up Molly immediately. 'It's nice to have a younger companion when you're getting on.'

Molly opened her mouth to protest when the old woman went on, 'Just teasing, dear.' She gave Thea a roguish wink.

'Right, everyone,' Gerald called, from the head of the table. 'You old hands know the Tiger Tours rules. From the left, we each tell our neighbour our names, and then they introduce you to the person on their left, so we get to know each other's names.'

'I hate this,' said the old lady. 'I'm Doris, dear. Tell me your name but don't bother to tell me anyone else's because I won't remember.'

'You didn't warn me there'd be parlour games,' Thea reproached Molly when the ritual had been gone through. 'I wouldn't have come.'

'Nonsense,' said Molly, 'it's just a little exercise to help us get to know each other. Oh, good, here comes the wine.'

By the end of the evening Thea was feeling tired, but generally much more optimistic about the holiday. Not everyone was elderly, and the few that were seemed to make up for their years by their interest in each other and life in general. She yawned widely as they walked back to the hotel, didn't join in the chatter and was asleep before Molly had finished her bedtime beauty routine.

After about an hour she woke up again. Molly snored, loudly and irregularly. Thea burrowed down under the covers, wondering if she'd ever be able to get back to sleep. Tomorrow she'd try to buy some earplugs, although how she'd manage without speaking much French she didn't know. It wouldn't be fair to Molly to ask the fluent Gerald to help her buy earplugs when he knew they were sharing and Molly had such a crush on him.

Thea loved Aix-en-Provence. It was a charming town of manageable size, and stuffed with beautiful fountains, old buildings and delightful cafés. It was a shame that she slept so badly at night because it meant she was prone to falling asleep on the coach. If Molly caught her with her eyes shut, she would dig her in the ribs and order her to look at the view. It wasn't that Thea didn't want to see yet another view Le Mont St Victoire – she loved the mountain and fully appreciated Cézanne's apparent obsession with it – but she was *tired*.

On the fourth day the party gathered in a beautiful room in one of the ancient *hôtels* which had been taken over by the university. Portraits of Aix notables stared down disapprovingly at the plastic stacking chairs which were put out for the students, old Tiger Tour hands got out notebooks and pens. It was time for the lecture on Cézanne.

Thea sat at the back, well away from Molly, with some of the older guests who might well nod off and not criticise her for doing the same. That afternoon was designated 'free time' and Thea knew Molly wanted to go shopping. It wouldn't be free time for either of them: it would cost Molly a fortune and Thea would be longing to escape.

The lecturer came in. At first Thea thought he must be someone called in to move chairs or something, for he was far too young to have anything to do with a Tiger Tour. Younger even than Thea, he was tall, dark and delicious. Thea sat up straighter and decided not to fall asleep after all – ancient monuments had a beauty all their own, but so did well-built young men with blue eyes and curling eyelashes. He was, in Petal's parlance, 'well-fit'.

Thea kept her attention on him for some moments, but then realised that his good looks did not make him a good speaker. He mumbled, he didn't smile and, unlike the masterful Gerald, he didn't bring his subjects to life with his brisk enthusiasm. Thea decided to nap after all. His voice, what she could hear of it, had an Irish lilt to it, which was pleasantly soporific.

After about ten minutes, Thea woke up and decided she wasn't going shopping with Molly; she was going to have lunch instead. Thea liked shopping as much as anyone, but not with someone who had a gold credit card and an urgent need for a fiftieth handbag. Besides, she was still not getting much sleep and she didn't have the energy.

She spent the rest of the lecture planning what she would say to Molly – 'I'm going to return to my room and read a little Proust.' That would shut Molly up for a good ten seconds. Would that be time enough for Thea to leg it down the road, up an alley and into a little café? It might be, she decided, but later she would have to buy a copy of Proust and be able to explain to Molly her sudden passion for culture. She could, of course, just admit she was tired because she couldn't sleep and only wanted to sit outside a bar in the sun, but that would be unkind. Besides, Molly probably wouldn't believe she snored. She and Derek had separate bedrooms, but Thea have been given the impression it was because of Derek's bodily functions rather than Molly's.

By the time the lecture had finished Thea still hadn't come up with a story she thought Molly would wear. When she saw her edging along the seats towards her, Molly was already saying, 'we won't have lunch as such, just coffee later . . .'

What wasn't immediately obvious was that Molly wasn't talking to Thea, but the woman behind her, who Thea remembered was a rather nice person from the Home Counties. She was nearer both in budget and age to Molly, and now it seemed Joan wanted someone to shop with.

'Are you set, Thea? I was just saying, we'll skip lunch and have coffee and a cake later.'

'Actually, Molly, would you mind frightfully if I didn't join you? I'd like to take some more photographs and I've got postcards to write.'

Molly took this almost without protest. 'Are you sure? Well, that's fine. Joan and I will have a lovely time.'

Thea felt like skipping as she waved goodbye to Molly, and set off on her own. Molly, at close quarters twenty-four hours a day, made her long for solitude.

She found an enchanting *place*, with an intimate little fountain and a charming-looking café with outside tables. She collapsed into a seat, ordered a beer and a salade niçoise, and took her book out of her bag.

'May I join you? I don't speak a word of French and I've a thirst on me which makes . . . my stomach thinks my throat's been cut.'

Thea looked up to see the beautiful, boring lecturer. He looked so much less boring close up that she smiled. 'You could ask for a beer, couldn't you? I don't speak much French either.'

He helped himself to a chair at her table. 'I could, and I could probably order a cognac, but I should eat as well. I know that if you're not careful you can end up with entrails all over your lettuce. What are those?' He peered suspiciously at Thea's salad, which arrived at that moment. 'They put gizzards on salad here, you know.'

'Anchovies. It's a salade niçoise. Have it, it's delicious.'

'*Pour moi aussi*', he said to the waiter, pointing at Thea's plate and glass. '*S'il vous plaît.*'

'You see, you can manage perfectly well.' Thea was beginning to enjoy herself. There were worse fates than sitting in the sun with an attractive man, eating and drinking.

'I can, but when I saw you sitting here, I thought, "Why walk past an attractive women and eat on my own, when I at least recognise her and could inflict my company on her."' He held out his hand. 'Rory Devlin.'

Thea gave him hers, hoping he would put her blush down to Provençal sunshine. 'Thea Orville.'

'So what is a lovely young woman like you doing on a Tiger Tour?'

'Lapping up the culture and listening to lovely young men tell me about Cézanne.'

'I was shite, wasn't I? I've forgotten more about Cézanne than most of these people have ever known and I can't make him sound interesting.'

'And what most of the people listening knew about Cézanne could be written on the back of a postage stamp . . .'

He gave her a rueful smile. 'You're a wicked, heartless woman, telling me the truth like that. Have another beer.'

'Well –'

She was about to say that beer, sunshine and lunchtime were a dangerous combination when he broke in, 'Don't tell me, if you have another beer you'll need the lavatory. That Gerald, you'd think he was potty training this lot, with his obsession with toilets.'

'I think you'll find his obsession is shared.' She smiled at him. 'It's a policy of mine to always travel with people who need the loo slightly more often than I do.'

'Well, you were right to pick Tiger Tours, then. What else do you have in common with this bunch?'

'I came with Molly – the tall, handsome woman?'

'Oh, yes.'

'But actually, the others are dears. You wouldn't come on a tour like this if you were too stuffy or set in your ways.'

'I wouldn't say that. I gave a lecture last week to a bunch from another company. There was a woman there who was so damn bossy the others tried to bribe the coach driver to leave her behind.'

'You do these talks quite often, then?' She was surprised, since he was so bad at it.

He shook his head. 'I was offered my expenses and a bit of a fee, so I came early and took the opportunity to do some painting.'

'So you're an artist?'

'Yeah. What do you do?'

He obviously didn't want to talk about being an artist. It was unfortunate that she didn't much want to talk about being a landlady, or having been a photographer, either. 'The good thing about being on a tour with retired people is that on the whole, no one asks you what you do, because they mostly don't do anything.'

'Is that a brush-off?'

'Not at all. I just don't want to bore you.'

'I'm sure you couldn't do that if you tried. I, on the other hand, can do it at the drop of a hat. I saw you nodding off during my talk.'

Thea laughed. 'I'm dog tired. Molly snores like a grampus.'

'And I'm shite at talking – we won't go into that again. I'm a much better painter.'

'I'm glad to hear it.'

He frowned. 'To punish you for that unkind comment I will make you tell me what you do.'

'OK, but here's your lunch.'

'Deux bieres, garçon, s'il vous plaît.' He picked up his knife and fork. 'Well?'

Thea sat back in her chair. 'I have a house full of students and a part-time job in a photographer's.'

He frowned. 'You're not your typical landlady, are you?'

'What is a typical landlady? Nora Batty? Arms folded? Out of the house by nine and not in again until tea and rock cakes at five?'

'Don't get edgy. You know what I mean. You're too young to be a landlady with a part-time job.'

'No one fits into the stereotype, you know, and I like young people.'

'And the part-time job in the photographer's? That's some camera you've got there. You should be taking photographs, not putting them in envelopes.'

She looked down at her Leica M4. She had bought it for fifteen hundred pounds, second-hand. She loved it. 'Yes.'

'You're holding out on me.'

'Why shouldn't I? I don't tell my story to just anyone, you know.'

'I'll tell you mine if you'll tell me yours.'

He gave her the sort of smile which caused a reluctant awakening in the region of her libido. Thea had almost forgotten she still had a libido, it had been so long since she had allowed herself feelings like that. 'OK,' she said eventually, 'you go first. But if it's not very exciting, I reserve the right to pike it.'

He frowned. 'Pike it?'

'Back out, give up, go home. Or in my case, back to the hotel.'

'I suppose you got that dreadful expression from one of your student lodgers.'

'That's right. Now – I'm listening.'

Chapter Three

He insisted on ordering cognac for them both before he started. Only when it had arrived and he had taken a large sip did he finally begin. 'Well, I was an art school whizz-kid. I went early, taught myself to draw and, at first, followed the party line. At that time anything representational was considered naff. Only abstract or conceptual work was thought worth anything. Do you know what I'm talking about?'

'I *am* on an art appreciation course. I have heard of Tracy Emin.'

'Sorry. I was forgetting. Where I come from people mostly think an unmade bed is an unmade bed.'

'Go on.'

'Well, I did the conceptual stuff, the dustbins full of road kill, the giant aquarium with amputated limbs suspended in jelly. And I did the abstracts, great swirling balls of fuck-all, which I made out represented "anger" or "grief". And I wrote statements about why I did what I did that would make you sick. Come the degree show, I did what I wanted. Paintings, drawings, of things you could recognise. I thought I'd be slated, but no, that came later.'

He took a sip of brandy and Thea sensed that there was a certain amount of pain in what he was about to tell her.

'My degree show was a fantastic success. I was hailed as the next big thing and I met a beautiful woman who introduced me to the owner of a Cork Street gallery. So far, so fairy tale.'

He regarded Thea directly and she knew she had been

right about the pain. 'Go on,' she said gently, her curiosity too much aroused to spare him.

'To cut a very depressing story short, I got offered an exhibition, accompanied by as much hype as you like – far more than I liked – and I blew it. I got completely wrecked before the show even started and didn't stop drinking until I passed out. In the morning it turned out I'd insulted every major critic in the business and vomited over a major gossip columnist.'

'Oh, dear.'

'Yes. So the bastard critics trashed my work, and said I'd never come to anything and would end up painting greetings cards.'

Thea winced. 'What did you do?'

'Buggered off round the world. I travelled for a bit and then settled in Ireland. Now I make a bit of a living painting people's dogs and horses. Sometimes their children. I like the dogs best. But I don't do frigging greetings cards.' He said this last so bitterly Thea could tell it all still hurt. She put her hand on his wrist; there was nothing she could say make anything better.

'I wouldn't have minded them telling the world I was a drunken slob, because that was true enough. But they liked my work well enough before I got drunk. The work didn't change because I'd a few too many – OK, a lot too many. Now, what about you?'

She chuckled gently. 'I'm afraid my story hasn't got a happy ending either.'

'Oh, God, do you need another drink.'

She shook her head. 'It's not that bad although it isn't very much more cheerful. I was a photographer, just making my name, getting enough commissions to pay the mortgage and justify having an accountant.'

'What sort of work did you do?'

'I was a photojournalist, really. I took shots of famous people, sometimes I went abroad. I was just getting somewhere when – well, the shit happened.'

'What sort of shit?'

She took a breath. She really didn't like telling people this story, it made her feel so stupid. 'I had a boyfriend – a journo I'd met out in Africa. I thought he was a hero, risking his life to bring the stories of the oppressed to the world and I thought we were . . . well, you know. I was about to sell my flat and move in with him –'

'And? He cheated on you?'

'Yes, though not with a woman.'

'Oh, my God! A man!'

Although these memories were still tender Thea had to laugh. 'How like a man to think you can only betray people with sex.'

He accepted her censure with a twinkle. 'How, then?'

'He stole something from me, an image, and tried to sell it and use it without my permission.'

'Would that have been the end of the world?'

'Yes. It was a very . . . a very sensitive one. I was only allowed to take it because the clients trusted me and it wasn't for the general public to see.'

'And he didn't give you the money?'

'Honestly! Sex, money, isn't there anything else in the world that's important to you?'

'Sorry. So he didn't take the money and run off with another woman?'

'You're not taking this seriously! This is my life story, my sordid past, the reason I'm the embittered woman you see today –'

'You don't look embittered.' His tone implied that she looked something a great deal more pleasant, but she ignored it. This was no time to be distracted. 'So if he didn't take your money, or cheat on you, what was the problem?'

Thea sighed. She'd never been able to convince Conrad it was because he had tried to sell her honour that she was so furious. 'It was him selling – or trying to sell – some-

34

thing so private to people with the morals of tomcats and fewer scruples. He just disregarded the fact that it was my integrity that was on the line.'

Rory frowned, trying to understand. 'So what was the picture of?'

'I don't want to tell you. The people involved are extremely famous.'

'So, was it published?'

'No, thank goodness, but no thanks to Conrad, and it took some persuading on my part to convince them that I hadn't had anything to do with trying to do a deal.'

'How did you manage it?'

'I told them what had happened as soon as I found out and advised them to get on to their lawyers straight away. The lawyers got it stopped without too much trouble and fortunately I could prove that the image had been stolen.'

'How did he get hold of it? Did you leave the neg lying around in your darkroom?'

'No, I did not! It was stolen from the recycle bin on my laptop.'

'Shite!'

Thea hadn't talked to anyone about this for a long time. 'I lent him my laptop. I didn't need it. I never suspected he'd look in the recycle bin –'

'Why would he do that?'

'Either because he's a nosy bastard, which is my pre-ferred option, or that the machine was running slowly and he wanted to clear the recycle bin, which is his story. Either way he came across a JPEG, which is a saved image, which mentioned the name of these celebs.'

'You'd never tell me who they were?'

'Quite right. I never would.'

He grinned. 'Go on, then.'

'Well, he double-clicked and got a full-page picture of someone very famous, very commercial, in glorious colour, in a very tasteful but erotic pose.'

'You mean, she was naked.'

Thea nodded.

'And you'd taken the picture?'

She nodded again.

'How'd you get to do that?'

'The family wanted a series of special, intimate shots for their personal family album. I stayed with them for a week, taking shots of them eating breakfast, having a barbecue, that sort of stuff. Then one day the woman, whom I'd got to know quite well by then . . .' Thea paused reflectively. 'I think she was a bit lonely and found me easy to talk to, although I'm quite a bit older than she is.'

'I can understand that part.'

Thea ignored this. 'Anyway, she wanted me to take a picture of her naked, wearing this special antique jewellery her man had given her, in a copy of a pose in an old master they had.' She glanced at him. 'No, I'm not telling you the name of the old master, either. That's confidential too.'

'So you took the shots?'

'Yes. She told me later that she'd found a lump in her breast and was frightened she might have to have a mastectomy. She wanted her husband to have pictures of her in case. The lump turned out to be benign in the end, but at the time she was frightened. Anyway, after I'd had them processed I gave her the negatives. It was very sensitive material and I knew her husband would be worried about them getting into the wrong hands.'

'But she wasn't?'

Thea shook her head. 'She's very young and she was so worried about the cancer that I don't think she gave the negatives a thought. She hadn't told anyone but me and the doctor about the lump.'

'Poor child!'

'Exactly.'

'So how did the image get on your laptop if you were so careful?'

'Not careful enough. She liked the colour shots, but she also wanted one in black and white. She thought I'd have to come and take another, but I told her I could take the colour out on the computer, tone it up a bit and she could say what she thought. When the job was done I deleted it, but forgot about the recycle bin.' She sighed. 'I suppose you could say I was careless, but quite honestly, it never occurred to me that anyone would look in my recycle bin.' She made a face. 'Unlike my clients, I'm not used to people grubbing about in my dustbins, even my virtual ones.'

'So were they furious with you when you told them?'

'Initially, because the husband thought I might be trying to blackmail them, but the wife, who'd had her all clear by then, convinced him that was the last thing I'd do. I was extremely upset and she knew I wanted to give up photography. Anyway, to cut a long and dirty story short, they gave me some money, out of gratitude.' She smiled. 'No, I'm not going to tell you how much. But after I'd sold my flat in town and paid off the mortgage, it was enough to buy my house and set myself up as a landlady.'

'That was decent of them, though I expect they could afford it.'

'Of course they could afford it, but it was very decent of them. An—I mean, the girl, insisted that if I hadn't warned them the picture would have been all round the European press, if not our own. She thought if I felt I had to give up photography, the least they could do was to give me some way of starting again.' Thea looked at her glass for a moment. 'I wouldn't have taken it, but A—she said that they spent millions on people they didn't even like, and that I'd helped her and that she really wanted to give me something. Basically, because my life and career had been ruined because of that creep.'

His expression seemed to demand a little more

explanation. 'I'd realised by then that generosity sometimes involved taking as well as giving.'

Rory was silent for a few seconds. 'Men are bastards, that's the top and bottom of it.'

Thea sighed. 'Well, yes, I won't disagree with you there. But to be fair, I didn't *have* to give up photography. I'd just had enough of traipsing around the country with half a hundredweight of equipment hung round my neck.'

'Oh? So he didn't ruin your career after all?'

'What he tried to do was much worse. But the only thing I regret is that I didn't get a chance to take a Stanley knife to his suits, or anything satisfying like that.'

'Clothing ripped in anger? Now there's an idea. Imagine them, a heap in the middle of the gallery, under a pile of torn-up love letters and photographs, stained with wine and aftershave and less mentionable fluids. It might make my fortune.'

'Feel free to use it. I won't demand a cut.'

He laughed. 'Not my thing at all, I'm afraid. So now you're a landlady?'

'Yup. With a house full of lodgers in a sedate Cotswold town, which has a university. Which reminds me, I should give them a ring.'

'Doesn't sound very fulfilling.'

'Oh, it's all right, I suppose. Mostly I like the kids. And it keeps me, just about.' She finished her brandy with a sigh.

'You don't sound like you've reached the happy ending to your story.'

'Happy endings don't exist in real life. It's all just compromise, isn't it?' She wanted him to agree with her, to tell her to ignore the yearning she felt when she wasn't fully occupied, the feeling that something was missing in her life. Then suddenly she chuckled. If he knew what she was thinking he would assume that what was missing was a man.

'What's funny?'

'Nothing, really, something just tickled my imagination.'

'And you're not going to tell me what?'

'No. Let me get you another brandy.'

'Only if you have one too. My mother warned me about beautiful women who ply me with alcohol.'

Thea really laughed now. 'I don't think it was the likes of me your mother had in mind.' She waved her hand, caught the waiter's attention and ordered the drinks.

He curled his fingers round his brandy glass and regarded her with his head on one side. 'It occurs to me you're wasted being a student landlady . . .'

'. . . with a part-time job.'

'You need a proper life.'

'Like you've got one. Derr!' She sounded so like Petal that she laughed and realised at the same time that she was slightly drunk.

'No, I haven't. But between us we could make one.'

Thea suppressed more laughter. 'That sounds like an improper suggestion to me.'

His smile reflected hers, only much more charmingly. 'It could be, only to begin with I've got a proper one – at least, not one my mother could object to.'

'Which is?'

'You come to Ireland and look after me for a bit, have some time on your own to do some real photography, lap up the scenery, feel the wind in your hair and the sun on your face . . .'

'Do you write poetry in your spare time by any chance?'

'Now you're mocking me. I mean it. I could show you another life.'

'I'm sure you could, but why should I swap looking after student lodgers for looking after you?'

'Because there's only one of me, I'm very undemanding and I have a pregnant dog.'

Thea shook her head. She was drunk, but not incapable. 'Thanks, but no thanks. I'll have my little holiday and go back to reality. You can't run away from yourself, you know.'

'But do you need to? Yourself seems in fine condition to me.'

He really was very attractive. His eyes were clear greeny blue, with maddeningly curly eyelashes. His hair was curly too and his mouth, large and generous, curled up at the edges.

'Well, it's sweet of you to ask me, but I couldn't possibly.'

He produced a battered ring-bound notebook from his pocket. 'Here, I'll give you my address, in case you change your mind.' He scrawled something on a sheet and tore it out. 'You fly from Stansted to Knock, which is an international airport.' He added this bit of information with a sort of mocking pride. 'I'd pick you up from there. It's not far.'

'It's very kind of you, but I won't change my mind.' She took the paper and tucked it into her handbag. She would keep it as a little 'might have been', if ever she got too fed up.

'You never know. People do.'

She smiled a little wistfully. 'I think we should have a cup of coffee.'

'With another brandy?'

'Definitely not.'

He ordered the coffee and she shut her eyes and let the hot Provençal sunshine warm her face and chase away thoughts of lodgers, her boring job and the tail end of winter which could take weeks to turn into a proper spring.

'Oh, it's you!' Molly's voice, strident with surprise, startled Thea into opening her eyes. Molly was frantically

40

trying to disengage her arm from Gerald's, but because of the large bag she was holding she was finding it difficult. Molly had an odd expression, which on anyone else would have been guilt. There was no sign of Joan.

'Hello,' said Thea, 'come and join us. Did you buy anything nice, Molly? Where's Joan?' She was feeling more than a little sheepish herself. Sleeping with a strange man was always wrong, even if it was in full view of the public.

'We're just having some coffee,' said Rory, 'can I order some for you?'

Molly glanced at Gerald, then regarded them both with tight lips, obviously wondering if their sin was greater than her own. 'Joan felt tired and returned to the hotel for a nap. We went back later – to see if you wanted to join us for a patisserie,' she added quickly, in case Thea thought she'd gone to the hotel for any other reason. 'And you weren't there. I thought you were writing postcards?'

Molly's strange behaviour made Thea wonder if she and Gerald really had been up to something when, until now, she'd assumed their flirtation was entirely harmless. 'No, I took a few photos and then felt like some lunch.'

Thea could tell that Molly was longing to ask if she'd arranged to meet Rory, or whether they'd met by chance. She looked from one to the other, and then at Gerald.

Rory helped her out. 'And I was lucky enough to see Thea sitting here and persuaded her to order lunch for me, too. My French is rubbish, isn't it, Gerald?'

'Tiger Tours don't employ you for your languages,' said Gerald, pulling out a chair for Molly. 'Just as well, really, eh?' He laughed heartily.

Molly might have been one of a string of handsome middle-aged ladies he dallied with on these tours. Maddening though her friend undoubtedly was, Thea didn't like the thought of her being used.

Gerald sat down too and held up his hand. '*Garçon*!'

'I'll have a brandy,' said Rory quickly, 'and so will Thea.'

Thea was certain Gerald had no intention of ordering drinks for them as well as for Molly, but as the waiter wrote it down on his pad, before looking expectantly at Molly, there was nothing he could do about it.

'I'll have a lemon tea, please, Gerald,' said Molly, 'if I may.'

'Certainly.' He turned to the waiter and ordered in French. He went on long enough to have ordered them an entire meal, more, Thea felt, to show off than because it was necessary. She and Rory had managed perfectly well earlier.

To stop Rory and Gerald from looking at each other as if they were fans of rival football teams, Thea said to Molly, 'So, what did you buy? Did you get the shoes you wanted?'

'Yes and a matching handbag.' Molly was torn between wanting to show off her loot and tell someone off – Rory for ordering brandy, or Thea for flirting with Rory. Possibly because she didn't know what Thea and Rory had been up to and was in a dubious position herself, she got out a cardboard box. 'There – what do you think?'

Thea thought that another handbag and pair of shoes added to Molly's dozens made no difference to anything, but she murmured politely.

'They were a bargain,' Molly explained. 'Because of the strong pound.' She went on to name a figure which was still enormous, strong pound or no strong pound.

'And what did you buy?' Thea asked Gerald.

'Me? Oh, nothing. I leave the shopping to you ladies. If I bought knick-knacks in every town I lead a group in I wouldn't be able to get into my flat.'

As Molly hadn't bought knick-knacks and Thea personally objected to being 'you ladies' she said, 'But some shoes might have come in useful, don't you think?' She looked down at Gerald's highly polished brogues.

'Those must be awfully heavy to clump around in all the time.'

Molly shot her a furious glance, Rory choked into the last of his coffee and Gerald took a breath to tell her that he had all his shoes hand made in London and that they lasted him for years. Fortunately for Thea, the waiter arrived with the drinks.

Later, back at the hotel, Thea lay on her bed while Molly made up her face. She was still annoyed with Thea, although what about Thea wasn't sure. She questioned her about her lunch with Rory. 'Did you ask him to join you?'

'No, he just did. I think he was lonely. He's been in France painting and he wanted a little English company.'

'But he's not English, is he?'

'No, Irish. Is that eyeliner you're using?' Thea didn't care what Molly was doing to herself, but she was fed up with her questions.

'Yes. You have to be terribly careful with it, or it looks dreadfully tarty.'

'Did you do a make-up course or something?' Anything to stop the cross-questioning – cross in both senses.

'When I was a girl I went to Lucy Clayton and learned how to put make-up on there.'

'How fascinating! Do tell me about it.'

At last Molly was satisfied with herself, sprayed eau de toilette on to her wrists and glanced at her watch. 'Hell! It's nearly half past and you're not ready. Do hurry up. Gerald hates it if anyone's late. Especially for the *dinner adieu* – you know, they have them on ships.'

Fortunately Thea's toilet took mere minutes.

'So sorry, Gerald,' said Molly as they appeared in the lobby, where he was counting heads for the second time. 'I am trying hard to be more punctual.' She glanced at Thea, managing to imply it was her fault.

'Well,' said Gerald, following her glance, 'I think we can agree that the effect was worth the wait.'

Thea smiled stiffly back at him, grateful that they would be going home the next day.

Derek wasn't waiting in the arrivals bit of the airport so Molly rang him on his mobile with hers. 'Oh. You're just parking the car? Well, thank goodness for that, I hate waiting around to be collected.' She punched in another number. 'Traffic, he says,' she told Thea as if she didn't believe his story. 'I'm just ringing my sister to see if there's any news.'

Thea smiled at departing Tiger Tourers as they made their way to their separate destinations. In spite of Molly she had really enjoyed Aix-en-Provence and didn't look forward to returning to winter, a house full of students and a boring part-time job.

Still short of sleep, she tuned out the bustle of the airport and let herself indulge in a little daydreaming, of Provençal sunshine and a certain lunch in a certain *place* in the company of a certain Irishman.

'Oh, my God!' said Molly, ending her call to her sister. 'You'll never believe it! Your lodgers have had a party and they've left the place in a terrible state apparently. It's like that advert for Yellow Pages.'

'Damn! They didn't say anything about having a party when I rang the other night.'

'You'd better ring them, find out what's going on. Poor you, it sounds *dreadful*. A lot of gatecrashers got in and there's vomit all up the stairs.'

Thea hadn't been looking forward to going home anyway; now the prospect seemed utterly dismal.

Molly tried to press her mobile phone into Thea's hand. 'Better to find out now than be greeted with a horrible surprise. It's going to take you ages to clear it up. Apparently you might have to have the whole house redecorated. And, Petal says, the washing machine's broken down. It's so awful for you, I'm so sorry. What a thing to go back to.' She wiggled the telephone helpfully, urging her to use it. 'I know a firm of professional cleaners you could use. They'd only cost a couple of hundred pounds.'

Thea regarded Molly and all her previous indecisiveness fell away. She no longer felt like a sleepy sheep, following dozily along, obedient to every instruction to look up, or look down. Her way ahead seemed clear. It was obvious what she should do. 'Actually, Molly, I'm not going back. I've changed my mind. I'm not returning to a trashed house and a broken-down washing machine – the lodgers can sort it out for themselves. I'm going to extend my holiday a bit.'

'What?' Molly was stunned. 'But how can you do that? How can you know your house is in a state and not do anything about it? Besides, you can't let Petal live in a house without a washing machine. I'm not sure it's even hygienic.'

'They can die of salmonella for all I care. It's *their* fault; they had the party. It's *their* gatecrashers who vomited up the stairs, *they* can fork out the two hundred quid for the professional cleaners. Why the hell should I do it?'

Molly gawped.

'Look, I know Cyril's going to Stansted, I'll go with him. *You* tell Petal to organise the cleaners, or do it herself. You can also tell her she can either ring up the repair man herself, or learn to use the launderette!'

Regretting only the paper carrier filled with dried lavender she'd bought in the market, which she gave to Molly, Thea picked up her other bags and ran after the elderly veteran of ten Tiger Tours. She reached him just as he disappeared through some sliding doors. She glanced back to see that Derek had now arrived, and that Molly was pointing in her direction, open-mouthed and horrified.

'Cyril! Hello. It's me. Thea? Are you going to Stansted? Can I come with you?'

At the airport, having left Cyril's comforting company Thea was forced to face up to her impetuousness. Certain that she would live to regret it, she went to find out about flights. There was no point in ringing Rory until she knew she could actually get there.

It was surprisingly easy. By some fluke she had reached the airport a couple of hours before the flight was due. There was a ticket available and she could get there in daylight. It must be meant, she told herself. I must be meant to run away from my wrecked house and my responsibilities. It's written in the stars that I should have a wild affair.

She rang Rory with a dry mouth. It might not be written in his stars. 'It's Thea, we met in France?'

'Oh, Thea, yes. Nice to hear you.'

At least he sounded as if he remembered her. 'You invited me to stay?' She must be mad! Rushing across the Irish Sea to stay with someone she'd only known a couple of hours.

'And you've changed your mind? You're coming?'

'Yes, if you're sure you don't mind.'

'I'll kill the fatted calf and put out the red carpet for you.'

Relief caused sweat to bead her forehead. 'It would be better if you met me at the airport. Is it miles from where you live?'

'Not at all, I told you. Only about an hour. What time do you get in?'

Elated, she ran to buy a ticket, high on the excitement her impulse had created. As long as her credit card had some credit on it all would be well. To have to crawl home now would be the most dreadful anticlimax, not to mention humiliation – Molly would have a field day.

The smiling, bright-eyed Irish girl who sold her a ticket seemed a good omen. The card cleared, the ticket was handed over, and Thea fairly skipped off to the shops to buy some extra pants and socks. She then spent a long time in the Ladies washing all parts of her uncovered by clothes, wondering if she could wash her hair and dry it under the hand dryer. A girl did like to look her best, especially when she was chasing a younger man.

Taking a chance that her card would hold out for one last purchase, she dithered between buying Rory a bottle of cognac, to remind him of Provence, or a bottle of Paddy Irish Whiskey. She settled on the whiskey because it was cheaper, then bought some film and the latest Jilly Cooper for herself. Then, as clean and calm as possible, given that she was running away from home, she settled down to wait for her flight.

Chapter Four

Rory was standing at the arrivals gate. When he saw Thea, he opened his arms. Good manners insisted that Thea go into them and receive a very hearty kiss on what was nearly her mouth. She wasn't entirely reluctant. He was even more good-looking and attractive than she remembered.

'Jaysus, Thea, it's good to see you. What changed your mind?' he asked, picking up her bags and tucking them under his arm.

'My bossy friend Molly.'

He dropped the bags. 'I don't believe you! She never said "my advice to you is to run away with that handsome Irishman who knows so much about Cézanne".'

Thea laughed delightedly. 'No, she didn't. She rang her sister and found out that there'd been a wild party, with gatecrashers, at my house while I'd been away and told me I'd have to get professionals in to clean it up. Her husband hadn't arrived yet, so I decided to make a run for it.' Thea paused. 'I am so glad to see you, Rory. You're never quite sure if people mean those invitations issued on holiday.'

He made a horrified face. 'I wasn't on holiday. It was the hardest work I've ever done, trying to be exciting about Cézanne, watching them close their eyes and nod off, one by one.' Then he gave her another kiss, this time definitely on her mouth, and although it was certainly pleasant, she did wonder if it meant he expected rather more than she was prepared to give on such brief acquaintance. Running away from home was one thing, but she didn't want to leap into bed with Rory before she'd had time to get to know him. Her morals were a lot harder to leave behind than her lodgers.

Seeing her doubts, he laughed. 'Is this all the baggage you've got with you? Never mind, you can borrow my clothes if you need to. The car's this way.'

As she followed him to the car park, it occurred to Thea, somewhat belatedly, that the clothes she had thought suitable for a week in Provence were unlikely to be the right sort of gear for the west of Ireland. She snuggled into her fleece as he opened the door of a very battered Land Rover.

'Climb in. It's a mess, I'm afraid, but it's a good workhorse. The track down to the house is quite steep and this can do it in most weathers.'

'Do you get a lot of snow here?' It felt to Thea as if snow were imminent, with grey clouds tossing across the sky and flurries of icy rain throwing themselves at her from time to time.

'Not snow, hardly at all, we're too far west, but plenty of rain.' He slammed the door of the boot behind her luggage and walked round to the driver's side. 'It's what gives us the forty shades of green, after all.'

The Land Rover, for all its noisiness, had a very efficient heater, which blew hot air at her like a hairdryer and as the scenery became pretty, she began to feel better. She only had to stay with Rory for a week or so for the sake of her grand gesture and in the meantime she could just enjoy herself. She had never been to Ireland before.

'Mayo's mostly famous for Clew Bay and Croagh Patrick. It's a mountain which looks uncannily like a slag heap, but one day a year it's a place of pilgrimage and people walk up it, some of them in bare feet.' He smiled. 'If you look down to the left as we reach the top of this hill you'll see the bay.'

She looked. The sun, which had been sulking, suddenly pierced the cloud base, turning the sea to silver and tingeing the distant islands with gold. The beauty of it made her catch her breath. Part of her longed to photograph it, but mostly she just wanted to look, take it in and remember it. She sighed so deeply it became a yawn.

Rory glanced at her. 'You must be tired. But we're nearly there now. When you've got settled and had a drink, you'll feel better.'

'I am a bit worn out. It was an early start this morning and I haven't been sleeping well.'

'That Molly snore, did she?'

'I didn't tell you that, did I? How dreadfully disloyal.'

'I just guessed. Well, you've a choice of two bedrooms' – he shot her a look – 'not including mine. You can choose which one you like best.'

'How kind.' Was he tactfully telling her that his bedroom wasn't an option for her, or that she had plenty of choice without having to sleep with him? She suddenly wished for a more misspent youth; she might be better at the subtext. As it was, the social niceties of running away with a man you didn't know were pretty much a mystery to her.

'Well.' He grinned at her. 'You won't be wanting to jump into bed with me until you've had a chance to check out how often I take a bath, or if I snore worse than Molly and things like that. Will you?'

His grin, his sympathetic understanding and the fact that the world was now tinged with pink and gold from the setting sun made her feel her mad impulse was justified.

It was a cottage more than a house, almost on top of the beach. A long green lane ran down to where it hugged the ground, long and low with white walls, grey slate roof and a blue front door. She stood in the garden, looking at a gate framed by two thick, tall bushes, through which she could see the beach and the silver sea.

'The view's even better from my studio, on the hill up there.'

'I can see why you would want to live here. It's so beautiful.'

'Come inside. It's too chilly to be admiring the view from out here, when you get just as good a one from the kitchen window.'

They were greeted by a huge, deep barking.

'Enough to put the fear of God into you,' said Rory. 'But she's a sweet thing, really. Ready to have puppies any day now.'

He opened the front door and a dog the size of a small sofa tottered out, unable to jump up because of her huge bulk. She was definitely smiling and greeted Thea with just as much enthusiasm as Rory.

'This is Lara. She's an English mastiff. You get to know her while I get your bags out of the back.'

Thea cuddled the dog as best she could. 'Are the puppies English mastiffs too?'

'I doubt it. We've no idea what the puppies are going to be until we see them. Probably half collie, although there was something that got in through the cat flap. Come on, let's get you inside.'

The front door opened straight into the sitting room, which was wide and high, with a curved ceiling like a boathouse. There was a fireplace in which a turf fire smouldered in a welcoming manner, and bits of boat and fishing tackle hung on hooks high up, out of the way. There was no wall between the kitchen and the main room, so it had a feeling of space and light. There were windows on three sides.

'Now,' said Rory, when Thea had stared about her,

taking in the pictures, the charts pinned on the wall, and the glass fishing floats and bits of driftwood which were scattered about. 'Would you like a cup of tea or a glass of whiskey, or both? I recommend both.'

Thea laughed. 'Both sounds greedy, but lovely.'

'You stay by the fire while I get that, then I'll give you the grand tour.' She looked about her. The grand tour wouldn't take very long, she decided. The kitchen she could already see, with its huge picture window facing towards the islands and, beyond them, distant mountains. There were three other doors off the main room and she hoped one of them concealed a bathroom.

'Sit down, take off your coat if you feel warm enough.'

She sat on a saggy old sofa, which was so soft that she seemed to sink to Australia in it. It was also covered with dog hairs and was obviously where the dog slept. Sofa and dog did look as if they were related. Thea wondered idly if the puppies would come out half puppy, half cuddly toy, with bits of stuffing emerging from them, an endearing combination of baby dog and worn-out upholstery.

After regarding her balefully for a few moments, with more than a hint of reproach, Lara sighed hugely, and heaved herself up beside Thea, squashing herself into the space that remained. She put her head on Thea's lap, an extremely heavy hint that if Thea sat on her sofa she would have to take the consequences.

Thea quite enjoyed the physical contact. The weight was tremendous, but it was a pleasant feeling, warm, almost comfortable and it made it quite impossible for her to offer to help with the tea.

Rory produced a tray bearing a chipped brown teapot, a couple of mugs, two tumblers and a bottle of whiskey. A packet of sugar, crumpled and tea-stained, and a carton of milk were fitted on somehow. He set this down on the little table in front of the sofa. 'When you've a cup of tea in your hand I'll show you the bathroom and you can choose a bedroom. Do you have milk and sugar?'

'Just milk, please. Do you live here alone?' she went on, when he'd handed her a mug.

'Yup. There's a wee girl who comes in and keeps the house in as much order as she can. Otherwise it's just me. I live in the house and my studio's up the hill. She doesn't go in there, so it's in a pretty desperate state.'

'Will you let me see your work, or do you want to keep it private from me too?'

He opened the bottle of whiskey, poured generous measures into the tumblers and handed one to Thea. 'I haven't shown anyone my work for so long that perhaps it's time I did. Slancha.'

'What did you say?'

'Slancha – it's spelt s-l-a-i-n-t-e, believe it or not.'

'Slancha.' She shuddered as the neat spirit went down.

'Oh, God, did you want water in that? I haven't anything else except some red lemonade.'

'Red lemonade?'

'In Ireland it comes in two colours, red or white. You don't want any in your whiskey?' The idea seemed to horrify him.

She shook her head. 'No, this is fine just as it is.' She took a sip. 'More than fine, actually.'

The whiskey began to relax her almost immediately and she realised it had been a long time since she'd last eaten. At this rate, what with the fire, the dog and the drink, she'd fall asleep where she sat. She thought she'd better make conversation in an attempt to keep herself awake. 'Are there shops nearby?'

'Westport is about five miles away, but there's a little shop in the village which sells everything. Can you drive?'

'Yes, but I'm not sure about the Land Rover. Why do you ask?'

53

'Well, it's just that I'm pretty unsociable during the day. It will be better if you can entertain yourself a bit. The Land Rover's easy enough when you get used to it and there's no traffic here to speak of.'

'Do I have to drive to the shop?'

'It's three miles away. It would be your choice, but you don't have to do anything you don't want to.'

She felt a sudden surge of warmth towards him, probably induced by hot tea and neat whiskey. 'It was so kind of you to let me come at such short notice, when I said I wouldn't.'

'I like girls who can change their minds.'

'I'm hardly a girl. I'm thirty-five.'

She felt she had to tell him. While he could probably guess, she liked to be open about these things. Unlike Molly, who would die before letting anyone know how old she was.

'Thirty-five is the perfect age for girls.'

'Is that so?'

'It is indeed so. I'm an expert on these matters.'

'So how old are you? It's only fair that you should tell me.'

'I'm twenty-eight, which is the perfect age for boys.'

'But too young for girls of thirty-five.'

'Would you like me to prove you wrong about that?'

Thea woke up enough to see the glint in his eye, which told her not to push the point. 'I think I'll take your word for it.' Then, because she didn't want to close the door for ever on something which might be very pleasant, she added, 'For now, at least.'

'Good things are worth waiting for,' he said.

Thea, in an attempt to change the mood and get herself out of her recumbent position, pushed at the dog's head. 'I really should visit the bathroom.' The dog's head moved with a huge groan and Thea fought her way to the front of the sofa. 'If you could tell me where it is.'

'Go through that door.' He pointed, but did not get up himself. 'And it's on the left.'

Thea took a couple more gulps of tea and hauled herself upright.

'While you're there, you could take a look at the little bedroom. You might fancy it. It's got two single beds in it, one each side of the room. Very chaste.'

Thea ignored this remark but did inspect the room, which was much as he described. It was pretty, but felt a bit chilly. It was obviously part of a later extension and the walls didn't have the thickness of those in the main part of the house.

When she got back she found that Rory had refilled the glasses. She sat back down next to Lara, wondering if it was wise to drink so much on an empty stomach.

'I dare say you'll be wanting something to eat,' said Rory. 'Which presents a bit of a problem. I was going to eat at the pub.'

The thought of getting up, making herself look presentable and going out made her feel suddenly exhausted, but she moved her features about as if this were what she wanted to do most.

'On the other hand, you may not fancy a longish drive at this time of night when you've only just arrived.' He grinned. 'If I'd known you were coming, I'd have baked a cake . . .'

'I really am being a dreadful nuisance.'

'Not at all. I wouldn't have invited you if I hadn't wanted you to come. I'm just not that much of a cook.'

Here was a situation she felt at home in. 'On the other hand, I'm an expert in making meals out of nothing.'

'I couldn't ask you to do that,' said Rory, obviously quite keen on the idea.

'Why don't I have a poke around and see what I can come up with?' Thea got to her feet again, determined that Rory shouldn't regret her arrival. If she couldn't promise him a night of hot, imaginative sex, hot, imaginative cooking might be some compensation.

'Excellent plan. I'll make up the fire. Did you want to sleep in the back bedroom?'

'What are the alternatives?'

'Come and I'll show you.' He opened the door to the right of the front door and showed Thea a glimpse inside a large room with a wonderful view of the sea. 'This is mine. It has a double bed, a goose down duvet and goose feather pillows, but I come as part of the package. I don't mind sharing, but I'm not giving it up entirely.'

'Right,' said Thea cautiously. 'And what about the other bedroom?'

It was across the way from his, on the left of the entrance. It had the same high, wood-lined ceiling as the sitting room, two single beds and a couple of wardrobes in it.

'The house belonged to my uncle. He didn't have children of his own, but he used it as a holiday cottage for his nieces and nephews. He left it to me when I told him I'd live in it if he did. He was an artist.'

'Did he do these?' Thea indicated a pair of small seascapes in oil which hung over the beds. 'Or is that your work?'

'His. It's good, though, don't you think?'

'Mm. Did he do them here?'

'I should think so. I tend to work on a slightly larger scale.'

'Will you show me your work tomorrow?'

'Maybe. But now I'm going to show you the kitchen and all that it has to offer in the way of spaghetti, tinned custard and tomato ketchup. If you can find a meal in it I'll show you all the wonders of my kingdom.' He smiled into her eyes and she felt her libido stir again. 'There's also a sack of potatoes and a hunk of cheese.'

*

They ate at the table in front of the fire. The dining table was entirely taken up with books and junk mail, a selection of dirty crockery and a large coil of rope. Obviously no one had eaten at it for a long time.

'You're a grand cook!' said Rory. 'I'm glad I invited you.'

'I'm glad you think so, because I pretty much invited myself.'

'Not at all. I gave you my address, didn't I?'

'You did. Have some more pie.' She had boiled sliced potatoes and made them into a pie with tinned tomatoes, fried onions, eggs and milk, and covered it all with grated cheese.

'I will. I wouldn't have got anything half as nice down at the pub.'

'You're very flattering. Shall I make some tea?'

'Or a drop more of the "crater"?'

Thea was willing to bet he meant whiskey. 'I'd rather have tea. I am quite tired.'

'Tea it is, then. And don't worry about the washing up. Susan will do it in the morning.'

Thea was dead on her feet but she resolved to get up early and sort out the kitchen. She had a feeling that her lodgers didn't bother about clearing up their late-night snacks because they said, 'Thea will do it in the morning.' How were they managing now, she wondered? Tomorrow, if she felt like it, she would ring them and tell them where she was. But only if she felt like it.

Rory and Thea said good night amicably, with just enough teasing flirtation on Rory's part to make it clear how he felt about Thea. Thea went to bed half wishing she were the sort of girl who could just jump under his goose feather duvet and let Rory seduce her. But as much as she would have liked to, she couldn't, somehow. Although, after a couple of nights at this

57

temperature, she might well feel she wanted to snuggle up to someone.

She fumbled in her washbag for her toothbrush, imagining Petal's horrified surprise if she found out what was going on – Thea with a toyboy, and such a good-looking one. Thea had overheard Petal discussing her recent dumping of her nice-but-dull man friend with one of her mates. 'I know he wasn't much,' she had said. 'But who else would she get at her age?'

'Thirty-five is the perfect age for girls,' Thea whispered to herself smugly, as she snuggled down for the night. 'So there, Petal!'

Wee Susan, from down the road, found the house surprisingly tidy when she appeared the next morning at about eleven. She was not overly delighted to see Thea, however, and not, Thea deduced, because the washing up had been done. Susan had a crush on Rory the size of Croagh Patrick.

Rory gave Susan a friendly, easy smile, which confirmed he was not an over-exacting employer. 'Hello, Susan. Thea's come to stay for a bit. She's in the front bedroom, if you'd care to give it a bit of a once-over. Come on, Thea,' said Rory, who was not an early riser. 'I'll show you the studio while Susan gets on with the cleaning. You'd better borrow a coat.'

Thea tried to give Susan a sisterly smile, to show they were united by the oppression of lazy men, but Susan didn't respond. *Perhaps later I'll get her talking*, thought Thea, as she followed Rory up the hill.

The studio was a huge shed with windows from ceiling to floor. In April it was decidedly chilly and must have been really freezing in winter. A wood-burning stove stood in the corner, looking too small to make much impression on the place.

'You can see why I took the opportunity to do some

painting in Provence. Lucky old Cézanne, with his early spring and baking-hot summers. Although the stove is surprisingly efficient. I'll light it in a minute.'

Thea moved towards a vast easel with a cloth over it. The painting beneath must have been the size of one of the walls in the cottage. Rory stepped in front of her.

'That's work in progress. No one sees that until it's finished. Over there are what keep me in bread and butter. And whiskey.' He indicated a medium-sized painting of a horse.

It was an old-fashioned picture, representing someone's huge wealth, but it was beautifully painted. 'And is it a good likeness?' she asked, teasing him.

'Indeed it is. I could spend my life and earn a very good living painting racehorses.' He made a face. 'My aunt, the widow of the uncle who left me the house, often asks me why I don't. The money's certain and after all, painting is painting, isn't it?'

'No,' she said for him. 'One is a job and the other is your life.'

The look he gave her was more than reward for her understanding. She picked up a battered pewter mug and changed the subject, not wanting to have Rory make love to her there and then. 'And so, do you surround yourself with the things in your paintings, like Cézanne? Or was this just lying around?'

He sighed, accepting her decision. 'Women are all the same. Never satisfied until they have poked their pretty noses into every corner of a man's heart. Hell, Thea, you've come a long way to see me. You can see the paintings too. They're in the shed next door. Just don't ask me to show them to you, or to tell you what the hell they mean.'

'I don't suppose my nose is that pretty, just nosy.'

He took her chin and moved her head so the light shone on her fully. 'You do have a very fine nose, but it's your eyes which first caught my attention.'

'Oh?'

'It's their colour, pale, yellowy green with a dark circle round them.'

'Oh.' No one had ever commented on her eyes before, which was probably why she had run away to Ireland with an artist. Possibly only an artist, an Irish one at that, could pay compliments so eloquently.

He kissed her lips, briefly, but firmly. Pleasantly.

'You probably want to get on and do some work,' she said, clearing her throat and glancing at her watch. 'Lara and I will toddle to the beach, but then – would it be all right if I had a look at what's in the shed?'

'Trust me to pick a woman who's more interested in my etchings than in me.'

Thea smiled, glad to feel back in control. 'You don't do etchings, do you?'

'Go and look at my daubs, and don't blame me if you don't like them.'

The paintings were all stacked up along one wall. They were huge and there were no windows or electricity in the shed, so she opened the door to let in some light. She suspected that Rory had only let her see the paintings because he was fairly confident that she would see little or nothing of them.

However, when a shaft of silvery sunshine hit the first picture, Thea knew she would have to drag each one outside to have a proper look. They were stunning: beautiful, painterly works. They were landscapes, enormous rectangular views of the sea, the islands and the mountains. The quality of the light was superb; it glittered, making Thea believe that if she walked into the picture she would feel the brightness of the sun contrasting with the coldness of the air. He had done with paint what she could never quite have managed with a camera.

There were also still lifes and nudes, old-fashioned,

discreet. Thea inspected the women's faces, to see if one of them was Susan, but she realised that these were naked women and Susan was still a girl.

The painting was masterly, with hardly a brush stroke visible, the colours so intense they seemed liquid. She felt that if she stepped into their viscous depths she would emerge icy with sea water, or blood-stained.

Thea was enraptured. She hadn't seen new work which so moved her for years and nothing so exciting. She felt she was looking at the work of a new Granet. This was not the work of an Impressionist, or a conceptual artist, but a real, old-fashioned painter.

One by one she took each canvas out of the shed to inspect it in the light. There were ten in all and each one was different, each breathtakingly beautiful. In the right hands, they would fetch thousands and thousands of pounds.

'It's one o'clock, haven't you seen enough yet?' Rory, coming up behind her, made her jump out of her skin. She'd been so lost in his work that she'd completely forgotten about him.

'I don't think I can ever see enough of these paintings,' she said, aware that if she weren't very careful she would start to cry.

Rory took her in his arms and held her tight. They stood together at the top of a windy hill overlooking Clew Bay, wrapped in each other's arms, overcome with an emotion neither of them recognised.

'I think you're probably a genius,' she said.

This time he kissed her properly, passionately, deeply, bringing her already alerted senses to a peak of sensation. Her head whirled and swam, and when he drew her down on to the damp grass she let him kiss her more. It was only when his fingers started to fiddle with the toggles on her borrowed duffel coat that she pushed away his hand and sat up. 'Not yet, Rory. You have to take it slower.'

Rory pushed his hand through his dark hair and shook his head. 'No one has seen my work for a long time. I got a bit carried away.'

'So did I. It's wonderful, fantastic work. You're an incredible painter and you could be rich. If you showed those paintings in the right place you'd make your fortune.'

'Are you sure? I tried it once, remember.'

'You wouldn't blow it like that again. And no, I'm not at all sure. I don't know about markets or anything, but I know good work when I see it. You've got to show it, Rory. It's selfish just to keep it here, hidden away.'

They were both dazed, drunk with their discovery. They sat on the hill in silence, he shaking his head, she recognising the view from one of the paintings, knowing she had to make him show his work if it was all she ever did in her life.

'You really think it's that good?'

'You must know how good it is. You're a trained artist, for God's sake!'

'But no one has ever wanted anything from me except a painting of their damned horses.'

'That's because no one knew you could do anything else.'

'It's only you who've liked them, though. You may be wrong. You may just have fallen in love with me and so with my work.'

'Rory, I haven't fallen in love with you, not yet. But I have definitely fallen in love with your work. Let me tell someone about them. Let me take some photographs and send them to someone.'

'But who?'

'I don't know. I know people at the art college where I live. They'll know who might be able to tell you how good they are. This is important. If you don't show them, you'll die without ever selling a painting, like Van Gogh.'

Rory drew himself up. 'You're forgetting my animal paintings, woman. I have sold those.'

She hugged him again. 'I'm going back down to the house. Can I use your phone? You have got a phone?'

Chapter Five

It was rather a shame that, after all her proud boasting about knowing people, eventually Thea had to call on Molly. Molly really did know everyone, who either knew, or would find out, who Thea needed to get in touch with. But Thea and Molly had parted on rather odd terms: Molly on the defensive – presumably about Gerald – and Thea . . . well, Thea had just upped and run away. If she hadn't felt so strongly about Rory's paintings, she would never have dared pick up the phone.

'Molly? It's Thea.'

'Thea! Are you all right? That man hasn't done anything dreadful to you, has he?'

Thea could tell that part of Molly wanted Rory to have loved and left her (even though he'd hardly had time). Molly liked people to get their just deserts – not 'Death by Chocolate' when they deserved cold semolina.

'No, I'm fine. How are things your end?' Thea wouldn't have said this if she could have avoided it, but if she'd gone right in and asked for Molly's help, Molly would have assumed the worst.

Thea held the phone a little away from her ear while Molly went on and on about the state of Thea's house, the washing-machine repair man and a thousand other irritations for which Thea should have taken responsibility. When the recriminations had slowed down she cut in. 'Molly, darling, I know I did a bad thing, but it's all right so far and I'm sure the kids are fine. Petal will sort them out.'

'Petal! Don't talk to me about her.'

As this was the last thing Thea wanted to discuss she complied. 'All right. Now, Molly, I need your help. I can't think of who else to turn to.' Molly loved to be helpful and a little flattery would do no harm either.

'Well?'

'I think Rory may well be an artistic genius. I need someone to look at his work, but I don't know who. If I took some slides, could you think of whom I should send them to?'

Molly was silent for a few moments, a rare state of affairs Thea would normally have appreciated. Now it just made her nervous. 'I'll have to ring you back,' she said eventually. 'Have you got the number there? And the address? I'll get back to you. In the meantime, take some good photographs. Have you got a decent camera?' Molly had been on holiday with Thea's Leica M4, but because it was a quiet, discreet camera, that didn't have a phallic symbol which went in and out, or any other obvious bells and whistles and automatic focusing, Molly didn't think much of it.

'Yes. My Leica's fine. I'll have to buy some colour reversal film to take slides, but I should be able to find that locally.'

'I'll get on to David Knox, you know, Head of Fine Art at the college? He'll tell me the right person.'

'Fabulous. Thank you so much, Molly, I knew I could rely on you.'

'Relying on me is one thing, but Thea, you can't just run off . . .'

'Actually, Molly, I already have. Do you think you could be sweet and collect my rent for me, and pay it into my bank? It's the one on the corner. The account's in my name. You're a doll.' Thea rang off, thanking Petal for her unconscious lessons on how to manipulate people.

Susan came into the room just as Thea got off the phone.

She was about twenty, with clear, freckled skin, curly eyelashes and hair which formed tight little ringlets round her hairline, above her high forehead. Thea thought she would have been divinely pretty, had she not looked at her with such suspicion. 'I hope you don't mind me staying.' She wanted to soften Susan's brittle surface. 'I'll try not to get in your way.'

'It's Rory I'm worried about. He doesn't usually take time away from his work to pick people up from the airport,' she said, her head thrown back. 'He doesn't often have people staying in the house, either. He likes to work undisturbed. Usually.'

This break in routine was clearly all Thea's fault. She tried to look like someone who would never disturb Rory, not even if there was a fire.

'So, what do they call you, then?' said Susan. The 'and why are you here' was unspoken, but just as clear.

'I'm Thea. I came to stay with Rory last night. It was a spur-of-the-moment thing. He didn't know I was coming. And I didn't know he was behind with a commission, or I wouldn't have come.' Thea wasn't quite sure this was true. 'I'll look after myself. I won't expect him to take me sight-seeing or anything. And I'll try not to make more work for you.'

'I don't mind *work*.' Susan gave the word emphasis to make clear it was Thea she objected to, not a bit of extra washing up.

'I did do the dishes from last night.' Thea sounded like Petal trying to placate her landlady.

'I saw. And cooked a meal, I suppose.' She gave Thea a look as near to a frown as she could manage without being too obviously rude. 'I usually cook something and leave it for Rory to heat up. It was my day off yesterday.'

'Oh, well, he said he was planning to go to the pub, but as I was tired I decided to make a meal instead. You know how it is, it's sometimes easier to peel a few spuds than it is to put your make-up on and go out.'

'I don't wear make-up,' said Susan.

Thea half smiled, half shrugged and, feeling condemned as a scarlet woman bent on preventing Rory from so much as picking up a paintbrush, went into her bedroom. Perhaps if she put on all her clothes at once she would be warm enough. She huddled up to Lara and received an affectionate lick.

Before she could start photographing the pictures Thea had to get her film, which would either mean disturbing Rory, thus earning herself a stake through the heart from Susan, or struggling with the Land Rover.

Susan's pretty mouth tightened as Thea came into the kitchen, where she was drying the china Thea had washed last night.

'I'm going into town to get some film. Rory told me I could borrow the Land Rover. Do you want anything?'

'You're going to drive the Land Rover?'

'I was. Is it difficult?'

Susan considered, deciding whether just to let Thea loose with the beast, or give her some pointers. 'It's a bit of bastard to drive,' she said at last.

Thea bit her lip. 'I really need the film. I want to take slides of Rory's paintings. I think he's really, really good.' She gave a rueful smile. 'If I'm right, he may never have to paint a horse again.'

'Honestly? And what do you know about art?' This was a genuine question, not the sarcastic sneer it might have been.

'I haven't been formally trained, but I reckon to have a good eye. I think Rory might be a genius.'

'And you say he could give up painting the dogs and horses?'

'If the right person sees the slides.'

Susan nodded. 'I've got to go in and do some shopping myself. I can take you in my car. When do you want to go?'

'Whenever it's convenient to you. I'd like to take photos of Rory's pictures in daylight, when it's not raining, if possible.'

'I finish here at two. I'll take you in then.'

The town was small but pretty, with a river in the middle lined with trees. It bustled, with a good combination of tourist outlets and proper shops for natives, selling hardware, haberdashery and fishing tackle. One of its chemists also had the film Thea needed.

She didn't get to know Susan a lot better during the outing, but she did feel she was slightly less hostile. She smiled wryly to herself as she looked out of the window on the journey home. So much for getting away from a house full of students so she could have a torrid affair – she would have to be up at the crack of dawn, changing sheets and ruffling her own bedclothes, to avoid offending her. At least the students kept out of her bedroom. Susan, bustling around with her hoover, would be exposed to anything and everything they got up to.

Clouds scudded across the sky, darkening the landscape and making the possibility of taking good photographs slight. Thea decided to get up early – earlier than Rory – to try to get a start on the day. Morning light would be best for the photographs anyway.

'So, how did you get on today?' Rory asked her, as he came down from his studio, paint-spattered but happy.

'I've got the film, but I won't start doing them until tomorrow. The light's not good now, and if I get an early start I might get them done and off by the afternoon. What about you? Did you finish your horse?'

He made a face. 'I tell you what, the thought that I might

never have to paint another one lent wings to my brush. Whiskey?'

'Yes, please.' Thea watched him pour the drinks. 'I'm cold.'

He handed her a glass with a frown. 'I told you to borrow anything you needed. Didn't you ask Susan to find you a jumper or something?'

'No. She did take me into town, though.'

'I'm glad about that. She can be a bit prickly, but she'd do anything for you.'

'I think she'd do anything for *you*, Rory.'

'Really? What do you mean?'

'Nothing.' If Rory didn't know about Susan's crush it was hardly fair for her to tell him. 'Now, I bought some steak in town. Would you like oven chips or baked potatoes? I told Susan . . . I told Susan I would do the cooking while I was staying. I think she might find it awkward, us sharing a kitchen.'

'That's fine by me. Did anyone ever tell you that you're a lovely girl?'

She couldn't help responding to the mischievous twinkle in his eyes, but she tried not to show it. 'Does that mean oven chips?'

'It means whatever you want it to mean. Here's to your fine eyes.'

Thea concealed a little shiver of flattered excitement and took her drink into the kitchen. 'I'll get dinner started, then.'

Rory followed her lazily. 'I'll find a nice bottle of red wine to open, then I'll gee up the fire a bit. Would you like some music on or shall we just talk?'

'I'm easy. What would you prefer?'

'I must admit that after a day with nothing but my own company it's nice to have someone to talk to. And the advantage of having the sitting room and kitchen connected is that the cook need not miss any of the crack.'

'Crack?'

'Irish for chat, gossip, or even high philosophy.'

She chuckled and, having found an onion, began searching for a knife to chop it with. 'Well, speaking as the cook, I'd hate to miss out on any discussion on Nietzsche that might be going.'

Rory stretched and then made up the fire. Lara groaned and shuffled about, finding it difficult to get comfortable.

'Poor old thing,' said Thea, glancing up from her cooking. 'Do you think it's near her time?'

'The trouble is we don't have any real idea about when her time is. I was away and Lara was staying with Susan. I told Susan that Lara was "looking away", as we say in Ireland, but Lara still managed to get out.'

'Well, I got her a nice bone from the butcher's. You could give it to her.'

'Well, missus, is tonight the night we make passionate love under my goose down duvet?'

The steak was eaten, the bits of fat fed to Lara and the plates were pushed back. Rory was peeling apples and handing pieces to Thea, which she ate with the very good Irish blue cheese she had bought in town. This question came with the last section of apple.

Like Eve, she took the apple and, like Eve, she was tempted. Almost everything was perfect. She liked Rory, she adored his work and she found him extremely sexy. Perhaps it was the thought of making love with a complete stranger when she had had slightly too much to eat that was making her hesitate. If she really, really fancied him, she realised, the idea of ripping off her clothes in front of someone she didn't know very well wouldn't cost her a thought. Now, the idea of her nakedness next to his athletic body made her pull her tummy in and worry about the bits of flesh not seen on models. Regretfully she put her hand on Rory's wrist.

'Would you think I was an awful tease and a spoilsport if I said that it's still too soon?'

Rory smacked his forehead with his hand. 'Damn! I knew I should have cooked for you. Women love that.'

Thea laughed. 'They do, but I don't think in this case it would have made any difference. I just don't feel I know you well enough. I'm a bit of an old-fashioned girl, I suppose.'

Rory tipped the last of the bottle of wine into Thea's glass. 'Is that your final answer?'

Smiling gently, she nodded.

'Well, it's a blow. But I expect I can accept it in a manly way.' In spite of his gentlemanly words, Rory was looking at her with a glitter in his eye, which slightly belied them. Thea started to gather to plates. 'Perhaps I just need to get you a little bit drunker.'

'Certainly not! We've had a whole bottle between us, not to mention a couple of whiskeys first. If I don't drink at least a pint of water I'm going to feel dreadful in the morning.' She took the dirty things into the kitchen.

'You know what alcoholics say about people who don't have hangovers,' said Rory. '"You mean you wake up, and you don't feel better, *all day*?"'

Thea offered the apple peel to Lara, who took it gracefully and laid it on the floor. 'Hangovers make me want to shoot myself.' She picked up the apple peel and said briskly, 'Now, I should really have an early night, if I want to get all the pictures taken tomorrow. Can I make you coffee, or tea, or anything?'

Rory shook his head. 'I'll just take my broken heart to bed and sulk.'

'You don't have a broken heart and good things come to those who wait.'

'That sounds very like a promise to me.'

Thea bit her lip guiltily. It did indeed sound like a

promise. 'You don't actually know that going to bed with me would be good.'

'Woman, that seems like a challenge. I've a good mind to carry you off and ravish you.'

Thea laughed. The joy of Rory was that he could be sexy without being threatening. 'Oh, what care I for your goose feather bed . . .' she sang merrily.

'You'll find out soon.'

'I'm looking forward to it, Rory, but I have to feel ready.'

'That's all right. It's just as well I'm not a raw lad who can't control his passions.'

'Away with you and your passions! I'll see you in the morning.'

The photography went well. The weather obliged and Rory took time off from his horse to help her drag the work in and out of the shed. When the major paintings were done, he said, 'I've got a whole lot of drawings in the loft of the cottage. Would you like to have a look at them, too?'

'I'd love to, but I've run out of film.'

'There's no need to photograph them. If anyone's remotely interested they can come and see them for themselves.'

Thea sensed his pessimism. Rory was by no means the first artist she had known who was arrogantly confident about his work one minute, defensive and apologetic the next. 'I know there's a lot riding on this for you and I can't promise you anything, but I do think that eventually cream will rise to the top.'

'God, I hope you're right. Now, would you consider a little dalliance on the sofa in the studio? I've had the stove going all day and it's warm as toast in there. Susan would never know a thing about it.'

Now why, wondered Thea, should Rory worry about that? She smiled and pushed him away. 'I bought the most wonderful lamb chops yesterday. I thought I'd make you a chocolate sponge pudding for afters. Would you like that?'

'You're a hard woman, Thea, but I'll wait for you a little longer if you cook for me in the meantime.'

Thea frowned with mock disapproval. 'There are so many politically incorrect statements in there that I don't know where to start enlightening you. I'll just have to ignore them. Now, I'm going to go down to the cottage and have a quick shower before I start cooking. You go and finish your horse.'

The chocolate sponge was in the oven, the kitchen was filled with a warm, chocolatey smell and Thea had had her shower. For a while she wished she travelled with as many beauty products as Molly did. She could have done with some body moisturiser, perhaps a little Immac and a bigger bottle of perfume than the trial size she had taken on holiday. She had not exactly prepared her body for seduction, but she did wonder if tonight she would have the courage to let Rory whisper Irish nothings to her until she followed him to bed.

Now she was peeling potatoes, when he came in and handed her a glass of whiskey. She looked at it hesitantly. 'I couldn't just a have a glass of wine, could I? I missed a hangover this morning by the skin of my teeth. I don't want to get drunk again.'

'You can have what you like.' He seemed a little taken aback. 'I'm surprised you suffered after sharing a bottle of wine, though. A whole one might give you a bit of a headache.'

'We did have whiskey first, remember.'

'Well, I'm going to have whiskey now, too.' When he had found a tumbler and tipped the required amount into it, he raised his glass to her. 'To you, Thea. Thank you for coming.'

'Thank you for having me.'

'I haven't had you –' The 'yet' was unspoken.

This was showdown time. She thought she might as well come clean about a few things. 'I feel a bit uncomfortable about you being so much younger than me.'

'I've always preferred older women. I love their wisdom, their humanity –'

'Their cellulite?'

He laughed. 'No one who'd looked in the Reader's Wives section in the top row of magazines would ever worry about cellulite. Women's flesh is so much more sensual than men's.'

'I would have thought you'd prefer men's bodies, with their muscularity more defined.'

'I like men to draw, but not to sleep with.'

Thea took a deep breath and made her decision. But just as she was about to announce it there was a strange, high cry from Lara. 'What on earth's the matter?' asked Thea, her heart pounding with fright.

'Oh, my God,' said Rory. 'I think the puppies are coming!'

They both moved quickly to Lara, who looked up at them, confused and distressed. She seemed to be asking what was happening to her.

'It's all right, honey,' said Rory gently. 'You're just having your pups.'

'It's a perfectly natural process,' Thea agreed. 'Dogs have them all the time.'

Lara didn't seem convinced and, secretly, Thea wasn't either. 'Have you had puppies before?' she asked Rory, 'either personally or through another dog? She might need some help.'

A look of horror crossed his face. 'No. Lara is my first bitch. I haven't a clue what to do.' He backed away like a father in a delivery room who'd rather be in the pub.

'Well, where do you think she should have them?' asked Thea. 'I mean, the sofa looks awfully cosy, but there'll be nowhere to sit for weeks and weeks, and they might get lost down behind the cushions.'

'To be sure, everything else does. I suppose we'd better have a box. There may be one out in the shed, though for the life of me I can't think what, short of an elephant, would come in a box big enough for Lara and her pups.'

'And I don't suppose you've had an elephant delivery for months.' Thea couldn't help feeling that Rory should have thought about this before.

'The service is a bit patchy, here in Ireland.'

'Well, let's push the sofa back from the fire a bit and put newspapers and stuff down in front of it for now,' Thea decided. 'We can think where to put the pups later.'

'Sure, she's only a dog, we don't need to fuss too much.'

Thea didn't know if it was the woman or the animal lover in her which rebelled at this remark. 'She's entitled to a little care and attention, isn't she?'

'Of course. We just don't need to go overboard. She could have the pups in the shed if necessary. Then they'd be out of the way.'

Thea barely had time to give Rory a horrified and reproachful look before there was a knock on the door.

'Who the hell is that?' demanded Rory.

As Thea was nearest, she opened the door. Unless it was a vet, or Susan with a giant cardboard box, whoever was there would get short shrift.

Chapter Six

Thea thought she was suffering from some strange sort of hallucination. There on the doorstep stood Molly and, just behind her, Petal. Behind them loomed a large, dark man and a small boy. It was like one of those dreams where people who couldn't possibly know each other all come together.

'At last we've found it,' exclaimed Molly, pushing past Thea who, stunned, could only step out of the way.

'About time too! I'm absolutely starving,' said Petal, following Molly. 'They wouldn't let me play my music in the car. They are *so* not fair.'

'Who the hell are you lot?' demanded Rory as the man, whom Thea faintly recognised, came in with the small boy, who looked so like him that he could only be his son.

'I'm Ben Jonson,' said the man, holding out his hand to Rory. 'I'm sorry to barge in on you like this. I meant to come on my own.' He cast a despairing look at Molly and Petal. 'I've been trying to track you down for years.'

Lara, who'd been silent for some moments, gave another cry and began to move around the room as fast as her bulk would allow.

Thea, stepping aside and pulling Molly out of the way too, demanded, 'Molly! What the hell are you doing here? And why did you bring Petal? I asked you to find a contact for me, not personally escort the Cavalry.'

'*I* came to look after Toby,' said Petal somewhat defiantly and Thea noticed that she wasn't wearing make-up and didn't look her usual confident self.

'We were so worried about you,' explained Molly. 'I realise it probably does look a little extreme, but I felt I had to come and see you were all right. When Ben said he'd heard of your artist, I thought it my duty –' Thea's look made her add, 'Oh, OK. I was *dying* of curiosity.' She made it sound like it really was a fatal disease. 'I *had* to go with him and see what had happened to you.'

'And Toby came because he's dotty about Irish myths and legends. He's read a book about them,' said Petal, half proud, half mystified.

Thea sighed deeply and turned to the little boy. Whoever else was to blame for this fiasco, it wasn't him. 'You must be Toby,' she said.

He nodded. He looked extremely tired and confused. 'Are *you* hungry?' Thea had little or no experience of small boys, but anyone under seventeen seemed to need to eat almost constantly. She wasn't sure when this kicked in but thought she'd take a chance on it being at about seven. He could have the chocolate pudding.

Toby looked around wonderingly. 'Not really.'

'I am. I'm starving,' said Petal again. 'Have you got a biscuit or anything? It's been *ghastly* at home. We got some people to clear up the sick, but the washing machine still doesn't work, although the man came and took a penny out of the filter. It cost ninety pounds, by the way, which you owe us, because he wouldn't go away until he'd got it. So, have you got any food?'

Any thought Thea had of offering Petal chocolate pudding dissolved. 'I've no idea, it's not my house. You'll have to ask Rory. Rory, this is Petal.'

Thea watched Rory make Petal wish she'd put on make-up. 'No biscuits,' he said, 'but would you like a drink? Irish whiskey, it would make a dead man get up and walk.'

'Not a good idea on an empty stomach, Petal,' said Thea.

Petal, having basked in the warmth of Rory's charm for a few seconds, got out her mobile phone, possibly to report this to somebody, before remembering it wouldn't work.

'Why don't we all go off down to the pub?' said Rory who, amused by Petal and interested by what Ben had said, had become a lot more welcoming. Molly he would charm when he had a couple of seconds to spare.

'You can't!' Thea objected, 'Your dog's having puppies. I don't mind not going to the pub, but I'm not going to have Lara's puppies by myself.'

'Puppies.' Petal brightened up. Then she realised what Thea had said. 'You mean, actually *having* them? Oh, yuk!' She looked defiantly at Molly, obviously about to accuse her of dragging her across Ireland to be grossed-out by puppy birth, when she remembered it was Molly, not Thea or her mother, and therefore she couldn't be rude.

'Low blood sugar level,' said Thea, relenting somewhat. 'I heard about it on *Woman's Hour*. Come and find something to eat, Petal.' Petal was enough of a handful when she was cheerful.

'It's so not fair!' Petal said the minute they were through the archway to the kitchen. 'I *did* want to come because home is crap at the moment, with no one there to look after us, and Piers dumped me –' There was a pause and Thea realised this was a first. 'And I didn't want to go out when I was single, because everyone would know.'

Thea's heart softened and she put a spoonful of pudding in a bowl. 'Well, you'll have to go out some time, or you'll never get another boyfriend.'

'I know,' said Petal, with her mouth full. 'But I do think they might have told me that my phone wouldn't work in Ireland.'

'I don't suppose Molly's very phone aware.' Thea suddenly found herself on Petal's side. 'Otherwise they'd have rung and told me they were coming.'

'Oh, they did try, only the code was wrong or something and they couldn't get through.'

A muttered curse from Rory told Thea that something was going on in the sitting room. She left Petal with the pudding and went to see.

Molly was looking tired and horror-struck both at once, Rory seemed impatient and Ben Jonson was squatting down by Lara. Toby held on to his shoulder.

'Is she all right?' asked Thea.

'She's fine, but the first puppy is going to appear at any moment.'

'How do you know?' demanded Thea. 'Have you had them before?'

Ben made a face. 'In a manner of speaking. I've watched a couple of whelpings.'

The thought of trying to look after a dog having puppies with Petal and Molly in the room was more nightmare than bizarre dream. She knew they were both incredibly squeamish and would probably squeal louder than Lara every time anything happened. She caught Rory's eye and signalled 'do something!' with every sinew.

He didn't respond. Either he found the thought of Petal and Molly screaming and getting on chairs amusing, or he couldn't do sign language.

She caught Ben watching her silent panic. 'Perhaps I should warn you, Molly,' he said. 'Whelping bitches can make an awful lot of mess. I don't suppose you'd like it and I expect Lara would appreciate a little peace as well.'

'What sort of mess?' asked Petal with horrified fascination.

'Oh, you know, blood, water, black slime,' Ben went on. 'It stains everything it touches. Oh, look, she's having a contraction.'

Rory, obviously amused by the general expressions of horror, finally took the hint. 'Why don't I take everyone off to the pub? We can get a bite to eat there and Lara could have her pups quietly on her own.'

'You can't leave her on her own to have her pups,' protested Thea.

'Well, make up your mind, woman,' said Rory. 'First she needs peace and now she needs company.'

'No,' Ben said. 'The pub's a good idea. Rory, you take Molly and Petal while Thea and Toby and I see to the pups.'

'That's a good idea,' Thea agreed. 'Can you fit everyone in your Land Rover, Rory?' She moved nearer him so they could speak in private. 'And see if they do B&B – we can't put everyone up here.'

Rory went into his room to get a coat and Thea found herself being edged into a corner by Molly. 'Darling, I had to get you on your own, just for a moment.'

Thea didn't feel on her own, she felt herself in a room full of people, but Molly had an earnest expression which bordered on the worried. 'What is it? Nothing's really wrong at home, is it?'

'Oh, I don't know. What I wanted to say is . . . I mean . . . there's no need for you to . . . you won't mention to Derek that I had a little flirtation with Gerald, will you?'

Thea really did wonder if she was awake – it was all so bizarre. 'Molly, we're in the middle of Ireland – well, on the edge of Ireland – Aix seems a lifetime ago.' A terrible thought occurred to her. 'Don't tell me, you've left Gerald in the car and you've run away from Derek.'

'What utter nonsense you talk! Of course I haven't left Gerald in the car! And I certainly haven't run away from Derek. Why would I do that? And Aix was only last week.'

'Well, I'd completely forgotten about it. Even if I hadn't, I wouldn't dream of telling Derek about something I assumed was perfectly innocent.'

'Oh, it was! Perfectly innocent. I just thought . . . I just wondered if you'd got the wrong end of the stick, that's all.'

Just as Thea realised that Molly had possibly come all the way to County Mayo merely to tell her there was nothing going on between her and Gerald, Petal screamed.

'That's it,' said Ben. 'Rory, Molly, one of you, take everyone away and let this poor dog have some quiet.'

He didn't actually raise his voice, but Molly instantly picked up her bag and her car keys.

'To the pub, then. I haven't had anything to drink, so I'll drive. Come along, Petal. At least they'll have a decent bathroom. Rory, you sit in front and direct me. Toby will want to stay with Daddy, I expect. Are you coming, Thea? Hurry up, Petal.'

Petal, who had been looking round, seemed relieved to be hustled out. The cottage was obviously far too remote and primitive for comfort.

'I'm not going,' said Thea firmly. Glad as she was of Ben's masterful stand, she didn't want him being masterful with her. 'I'm going to help with the puppies. After all, Lara knows me.'

'The puppies will make a dreadful mess,' Ben told her. 'Our last bitch to whelp managed to break her waters on every piece of furniture on the ground floor and left green slime everywhere. It took ages to clear up.'

'Mess doesn't bother me,' said Thea.

Ben suddenly almost smiled. 'Nor it does. I forgot.'

Molly shuddered. 'Well it bothers me. Come along.'

A few moments later the house was almost empty and blissfully quiet. Ben, Toby and Thea were alone.

They watched Lara in silence for a few moments as she paced about, trying to escape from what was going on inside her.

'We'll need some newspapers, and old sheets and stuff,' said Ben. 'And quickly.'

Thea, who had no real idea where to look, went to the

81

airing cupboard and arrived just in time to hear Toby say, 'Dad! Something black and slimy's coming out! It's gross!'

Thea and Ben moved swiftly to inspect Lara's back end from whence emerged a black bag, presumably full of puppy. Ben put out his hand and lowered it gently down. Lara slumped on the ground and immediately started licking and biting at it. There was a crunch as the afterbirth reached her mouth.

Thea suddenly felt like crying. Watching Lara's huge tongue licking and licking, while the shape became more and more like a puppy wriggling under her rough ministrations made her feel very emotional. It even opened its little mouth and squeaked. At last Ben picked it up, latched it on to Lara's huge flank and it started suckling. It was dark brown with a few white patches.

'Oh, wow,' said Toby.

Ben smiled. 'It is a bit.'

'Will the others come now, too?'

Ben shook his head. 'It could be ages.' He looked up. 'Why don't you ask Thea if she can get you a snack, or something.'

Thea wiped away a rogue tear. 'I expect you both need a proper meal. I'll cook the lamb chops that Rory and I were going to have. I put a couple of potatoes in the oven ages ago. They're quite big, we can share them. I've opened some wine, and there's a chocolate sponge if Petal's left us any.'

'Toby's a vegetarian.' Ben's expression seemed to chill slightly at the mention of the cosy meal Thea described.

'Well, I can easily grate some cheese on the potato. Would you like that?'

Toby nodded. 'That would be very kind.'

'And what about you?' Thea asked Ben. 'Are you a vegetarian?' She mentally surveyed the fridge. She'd bought eggs yesterday; if necessary she could run him up an omelette.

82

'No, I eat anything.' He gave her a grin, which was a little startling. She'd thought him totally reserved and suddenly there was a glimpse of what went on behind. 'It's very kind of you to look after us like this.'

'Not at all, I'm used to looking after people and if you look after Lara, it seems a fair deal.'

'Talking of which, did you find any old rags or sheets or anything?'

She was still clutching a lemon-coloured sheet she'd found in the airing cupboard. 'There's really nothing wrong with this, except it's a bit bobbly and an unpleasant colour, but I can always buy Rory another one.'

Ben produced a penknife, nicked the top of the sheet and ripped it in two. While he was draping the sofa as best he could, Thea asked, 'What do you think the father was?'

'There's no telling by looking at the pup, but as we're in the country, I expect it's a collie.' He looked up at Thea. 'Can you imagine, all the intelligence and energy of a collie wrapped up in something the size of Lara?'

Thea opened her eyes wide. 'I'd rather not – a baby elephant on speed.'

'On the other hand they might all take after their mother. The shepherd will say, "Come Bye," or something, and one of these chaps will amble up saying, "All right, all right, where's the fire? I'll be along in my own good time."'

Toby chuckled loudly before shushing himself as he remembered Lara. Thea giggled, not just because the picture he created appealed to her, but because she hadn't realised Ben did jokes.

'And before you ask, no, we can't have one.'

'Aw, Dad!' It was obviously a stock phrase, uttered when something utterly unreasonable was denied.

Ben laughed. 'Don't "Aw, Dad" me. You know we couldn't have a huge dog in London. He patted his son's shoulder. 'And as it might be ages before the next one, we might as well have a cup of tea and you could have your baked potato, Tobe.'

'I'll get it,' said Thea, seeing he was about to do it and not wanting the role of midwife. 'I feel I should make Lara a cup of tea too, as she's just had a baby, and without swearing or anything.'

'Do women swear when they have babies?' Toby asked her.

Thea nodded. 'I'm not an expert because I've never had one myself, but when it's on telly they sometimes use the most dreadful language.' Then, realising that she might have said something she shouldn't, she retreated to the kitchen where she knew what she was doing.

'There's no need to run. Toby won't starve to death, will you?'

Toby laughed and then yawned.

'Would you like tea, or something stronger?' Thea called. 'Ben?'

'Better stick with tea. Lara's probably going to be fine, but if we do have to find a vet in the middle of the night I'd like all my wits about me.'

As Thea grated cheese, mashed potato and mashed tea, she realised she found Ben's attitude to alcohol and driving reassuring. Rory was rather gung-ho about it.

When Toby had eaten his meal but there was no sign of more pups imminently, Thea said, 'I don't suppose you'd like to pop into bed? I could get you a hot-water bottle. There's one hanging up in the bathroom. We could call you when Lara's next puppy starts coming.'

Ben opened his mouth, as if to argue with this arrangement and Thea realised she'd probably made a dreadful faux pas. 'Or whatever Ben thinks is best,' she added, copping out.

'No, that would be fine,' said Ben. 'Would you like to be woken, Toby, or would you prefer to find all the puppies born in the morning?'

84

'I'll see if I get to sleep. If I don't, I can watch the puppies, but if I do, I'll just see them in the morning.'

'I'll do you a hot-water bottle and show you the bed, then. It's very close, so you probably won't miss anything.'

'After you've done your teeth,' added Ben, giving Thea a glance which seemed a reproach.

Once Toby had been tucked up by Ben and Thea they went back to Lara. 'I don't know anything about children,' said Thea. 'Sorry if I said something I shouldn't.'

'Well, Toby seemed to like you.' Ben gave Thea a glance which questioned his son's judgement.

'I'll get on with making supper, then.'

Ben followed her into the kitchen. 'I'm sorry if our arrival spoiled your little tête-à-tête with Rory. You must have been all set for a romantic evening.'

'Well, we were.' Thea pulled out a couple of plates from a cupboard. 'We were going to stare into each other's eyes while Lara had puppies around us.' She wanted to tell him they were going to make mad, passionate love on the floor, because he'd suddenly made her angry. She glared at him. 'I'm going to have a glass of wine. I think I need it.'

Ben's eyebrow flicked upwards, possibly asking what she'd done to deserve wine. 'She seems to be dozing and I can't see any contractions at the moment.'

When the kettle was on for water for the frozen peas and the chops were beginning to heat up under the rather inefficient grill, Thea took her wine and went to join Ben. She had a few questions for him. 'Did I gather that you've heard of Rory and knew his work? He told me he hasn't exhibited since a disastrous time just after he got his degree.'

'I was at his show. It was stunning, though his behaviour during it was even more so and not in a good way. I haven't heard of him since.'

'So what is it you do, exactly?'

'Do you want a CV or just a brief rundown?'

Why was he being so bad-tempered? Then she remembered he'd spent all day in a car with Molly and Petal, and had been forced to deliver puppies almost the moment he arrived. His blood sugar level must be at rock bottom. She forgave him. 'A rundown is fine.'

'Well, now I'm an art director in an advertising agency. Once I was head of an art college.'

'What made you change? The two jobs sound rather different.'

Ben shrugged. 'My life changed. I got married, had Toby. My wife wanted something better than I could give her on my salary as head of an art college so I changed direction.'

'Are you – um ?'

'Still married? No. But being divorced is even more expensive. Two houses, a full-time nanny, the odd little legal argument.'

There seemed to be a fair amount of bitterness attached to this statement. 'So you think Rory's work might be good?'

'It might be. But it's perfectly possible that it's a load of self-indulgent rubbish.'

'I don't think so, which is why I told Molly about it. I thought she'd know who I should send the slides to.'

'But you weren't expecting her to turn up, large as life, with a whole supporting cast?' There was a glimmer of a smile in this.

'No, I wasn't. It was quite unnecessary, when I've taken loads of slides and it wouldn't have taken long to get them developed.' Her gaze narrowed. 'I suppose Molly said something which made you think my slides wouldn't be any good.'

He had the grace to look embarrassed. 'Toby and I had a trip to Ireland planned anyway. He's mad about Irish myths and legends. I think he secretly believes that he'll see a leprechaun, though he'd never admit it. I'd never been to Mayo, so we just went north instead of south. And very far west.'

Thea laughed.

'But I wouldn't have brought Molly and Petal if they hadn't made such a fuss about wanting to come. She said she really needed to see you about something, but personally I think she wanted to catch you and Rory in the act.'

'Huh!'

'But Molly's been very good to me over the years, and Toby likes her, so I indulged her and let Petal come. If she'd known Lara was chaperoning you I'm sure she wouldn't have insisted,' he added palliatively. 'And I didn't know about the slides, so Toby and I would have turned up anyway.'

'Do you have Toby for holidays, then?'

There was an irritated pause. 'I have Toby all the time. His mother has him for the occasional weekend if she can get a babysitter.'

'Oh.' Thea wanted to apologise for assuming Toby's mother would be his main carer, but she didn't know how. Besides, Ben seemed quite capable of jumping to conclusions too.

'It is fairly unusual, even nowadays,' Ben went on, slightly less starchily.

Thea nodded. 'I do think you might have phoned.'

'We tried, every time we stopped, but we could never get an answer. Molly assumed the worst and decided we should press on regardless and save you from making a terrible mistake.'

'For God's sake! I'm free, white and over twenty-one.'

Ben shrugged, absolving himself from responsibility.

Lara, filling in the awkward silence, gave a little moan. Ben and Thea watched as a huge contraction rippled along her body.

'Do you think we should get her gas and air?' asked

Thea, partly to lighten the atmosphere and partly because she needed reassurance that all was going well.

'I think she's managing fine. She's obviously gone to her NCT classes.'

'Humph.' Thea hadn't had children herself but had several friends who, all set for a natural birth, ended up yelling for drugs when it was too late.

Ben glanced at her. 'I don't think it's anything like as painful for dogs as it is for humans, unless one of the pups is breech, or something like that. Toby's mother had an elective Caesarean.'

Thea winced. 'That's *more* scary. But what worries me is that we don't even have a telephone number for a vet, let alone know where one is.'

'We should try and find out about one.' He paused and sniffed.

'Oh, my God! The chops!' Thea fled to the kitchen, turned the chops and poured boiling water on the peas. When she came back she said, 'The trouble is I haven't a clue where to start looking for vets. I don't know anyone to ask, either. Except Susan – she's Rory's "wee girl" who comes in to clean. But I don't know where she lives.'

'Well, we may not need help. Oh. Here we go. Any minute now.' Lara got on to her haunches and strained.

'Should we get Toby?'

'I hope he's dropped off by now. It's been a tiring day.'

'I'll just check. I'd feel mean if he were awake and we'd promised to let him know.'

She found Toby fast asleep in her bed, pulled the covers up over his shoulders and sped back, arriving just as another black bag appeared. 'Toby's asleep,' she said, watching the puppy being shoved about by Lara's huge, rough tongue. 'It's amazing how they're just an amorphous mass and gradually take on puppy shape. It's as if Lara's a sculptor or something.'

'I think it's where the expression "licked into shape"

comes from.' He looked up. 'If it's ready, we could eat. There's probably time.'

While he washed his hands, Thea cleared enough table for two plates and two glasses. She served up in the kitchen, adding a huge lump of butter to their shared potato. 'I hope they found somewhere nice to eat and stay,' she said, refilling her glass and waving the bottle questioningly over Ben's.

He indicated that he would like some. 'Yes. I don't think Molly's used to roughing it. Nor is Petal.'

'Well, after all this, I hope you like the paintings.'

'So do I.'

'What will you do? Buy them all? Do sit down and start. We may not have long to eat this.'

'We've probably got hours and I doubt if I'd be able to buy one, let alone the lot. No, I'll try and talk a London gallery into giving him a show. They're booked up years ahead, of course, but he'll just have to wait.'

Thea thought that while Rory might be prepared to wait a few days to get her into bed, it was unlikely he'd be willing to wait a few years for an exhibition, not when he'd just broken out of his artistic purdah.

'I'm sorry the chops are a bit overdone.'

'They're fine. I eat a lot of crispy chops. The phone always rings when I'm cooking.'

'It's funny, that, isn't it? You'd think they'd tell people selling fitted kitchens that people aren't receptive when their unfitted one is in chaos and they're trying to get a meal on the table.'

'So you use your candle and smoke alarm trick, do you?'

She looked bemused for a moment. 'Now, how do you know – oh, yes, you were there when I did it the other day.' She smiled. 'No, I find it far easier to get rid of cold callers, I just say "no thank you" and put the phone down.'

'You cook for your lodgers, do you?'

'For my sins, and only in the evening, and not if they tell

me they're going to be out. Just like a family with rather a lot of teenagers in it, really.'

'It must be quite tough, taking on teenagers when you haven't had children of your own.'

She shrugged. The fact that she hadn't had babies was something of a sadness for Thea. When she was younger she'd felt you couldn't mix dashing all over the country being a photojournalist with small children, unless you had a really supportive partner. None of the men she knocked around with were partner material. Conrad, she had thought, was the exception, but even before his massive betrayal she had known he wasn't cut out for fatherhood. Now that she had retired from the lists of cut-throat journalism, she was beginning to worry about being too old and had no partner at all, suitable or otherwise.

'These knives are hopeless,' she said a moment after she had shot peas across the table on to Ben's plate. 'I'll go and see if I can find something a bit sharper in the kitchen.'

Ben put a hand on hers as she stood up. 'Don't worry about it. You probably won't find anything and we can use our fingers.'

Thea sat back in her chair, tiredness wafting over her unexpectedly. 'OK. You must be shattered. Did you drive all the way?'

Ben, who had picked up his chop, shook his head. 'Molly drove too. Fortunately she's a good driver.'

'Why didn't you fly from Stansted to Knock airport, like I did? You could have hired a car.'

'We didn't know about Knock airport. Besides, it would have been much more expensive with so many of us.'

'I didn't think Molly worried about things like expense.'

'She doesn't, but I do.'

Thea was stabbed by a pang of guilt for running out on Molly when she had paid for her holiday. 'I do hope she enjoys herself. I really shouldn't have just . . . run away like that.'

'I wouldn't worry about Molly. She's loving this adventure. Is there any more wine in that bottle?'

'I expect I could find another if we needed it.'

'No, I'm sure just the one bottle will be enough, seeing as we're working.'

Thea grimaced. 'What are we going to do about a vet?'

'Hope we don't need one.' He got up and stacked the plates together.

'Oh, let me do that,' said Thea. 'Lara might need you!'

Chapter Seven

He gave her the sort of glance midwives give fathers who look as if they might faint. 'You could go to bed if you liked. I'm sure I can manage.'

'I wouldn't dream of it! I couldn't abandon Lara now.' She didn't add that Toby was in her bed already.

'I think Lara is quite happy with me,' said Ben, not realising that Thea was being flippant.

Thea shook her head. 'I think she'd rather have another woman with her, at this difficult time.'

Ben raised his eyes to heaven. 'Then make us a cup of coffee.'

'And raspberry leaf tea for Lara?'

He frowned. 'Don't you take anything seriously?'

'Not if there's someone there to do it for me.'

'Molly never told me you were like this.' He meant 'warned'.

'Oh, I always behave myself with Molly. Petal does too.' Thea sighed. 'I'd better get the kettle on.'

Having done the washing up, she came back with two mugs and set them on the mantelpiece. There were no more puppies and Lara was looking fed up. 'Poor Lara, I haven't known her long, but I feel she's an old friend.'

'Like her owner.'

This was a statement, not a question and Thea didn't know how to take it. Was it a criticism? Was he, like Molly, infused with moral outrage? Well, if he was, he could go on being infused. She wasn't going to tell him that actually, she hadn't slept with Rory in case he spotted the missing 'yet'. 'Possibly.'

Lara, who had a strong social sense, decided to lighten the atmosphere with another contraction.

'That's a good girl. Just breathe through the pain. Sorry,' Thea said to Ben. 'I'll shut up now.'

The labour went on through the night, with no sign of Rory and the others. Ben and Thea agreed that while the absence of Molly and Petal was definitely a good thing, Rory could at least have helped them find a vet if they needed one.

Lara had had four puppies and Thea had made three lots of tea when a problem seemed to develop. Lara had been straining for some time, with no result. Suddenly she leapt on to the sofa with surprising swiftness and passed a lot of black fluid all over the cushions.

'Oh,' said Thea.

'It's all right. It means the bag has burst inside her. It'll be a dry birth and the puppy might be breech.'

'It doesn't sound all right at all and here's us without a vet.'

'You could look in the Yellow Pages.'

'I don't know where they are, or whether they even exist in Ireland. I don't get through the door of a house and check it out for telephone directories before I've even got my coat off. I see now it's a terrible failing of mine.'

'There's no need to panic.'

'I'm not panicking,' said Thea, who was. 'I'll have a look round.'

'If we have to manage without a vet, we'll have to manage. Ah, I can see something coming. It's a leg. Two legs.'

'Does that mean it's breech?'

'Yup.'

Lara gave a howl, which tore Thea's heart. A bit more puppy emerged and Lara began to panic. She jumped off the sofa and ran round the room, squealing, trying to escape from the pain.

Thea scooped up the puppies already born and got them out of her way while Ben pursued Lara. When Thea had settled the puppies by the fire, where no one, including Lara, was likely to tread on them, she joined Ben.

'Hold her head and reassure her while I try and get this little fella out.'

Thea held the head the size of a bucket, hoping that, in her distress, Lara wouldn't turn vicious and bite. Many a woman would have bitten her husband or the midwife if they'd been able to reach them, going on what she'd seen on television.

She watched admiringly as Ben gently teased the little form through an opening which seemed too small for it. He murmured to Lara while he did it and, although she still whimpered, she seemed calmer. Thea was about to say that Lara knew Ben was helping her when she realised she would probably sound dreadfully sentimental. She felt a bit tearful as it was.

'There we go.'

The puppy landed in Ben's hands and opened its mouth to squeak. Lara flopped down where she was, behind the dining table.

As she watched Ben give Lara the puppy to lick, she had a strange feeling that this moment was significant, as if she had learnt something extremely important, but had instantly forgotten what it was. She shook her head quickly and decided it was something to do with the puppies. Her hormones coming out in sympathy with Lara's.

Lara seemed fine, though. The last puppy, larger than the others, didn't need her teeth to release it from its bag. It sucked strongly when Ben latched it on. 'Definitely a boy,' he said.

Thea mentally gave herself a little shake. 'I think we need more tea. Will the other pups be all right without Lara for a bit?'

'Oh, yes. As long as they're warm.'

Thea had found one of Rory's jumpers for them to nestle in, so they were fine.

She thought about Ben while adding to the pile of used tea bags on a saucer, about how he delivered that little pup. He was so strong and yet so gentle. Lots of women developed crushes on their vets and now she could see why. If they'd brought your beloved cat back to life you'd love them for ever in return. When she brought the tea in he had coaxed Lara back to her place in front of the fire.

'If you can find me some old rags or something, I'll start clearing up the mess.'

He looked up at her and she noticed how dark his eyes were, how they had a hint of sadness in them, as Toby's had. It was something to do with Lara and the pups which made her want to take him in her arms, she realised. She couldn't conveniently cuddle Lara and, having watched the miracle of childbirth, she felt the need to hug someone.

She sipped her tea. She was tired and anxious – all these strange feelings would go away in the morning.

She yawned loudly, making Ben look up. He smiled. Thea smiled back. He had a wonderful smile, rare and special; you had to respond to it, however tired you were. 'How many more do you think she'll have?' she asked.

He ran his hands over Lara's flanks. 'I think there's at least one more in there, but I'm not experienced enough to be sure.'

While there were no more puppies imminent they struggled to get the worst of the greeny black slime off the sofa.

'It'll need dry-cleaning,' said Ben. 'At least, that's what Molly would say.'

95

'Molly would need a whole new suite if anyone dared have puppies on her sofa.' She looked up. 'I expect Rory will just leave it. Where the hell is he, by the way?'

Ben gave her a look which, in spite of being enigmatic, still managed to convey his opinion of Rory. 'We're managing perfectly without him.'

'You're right. He'd probably get in the way.'

'So,' Ben went on. 'Did you and Rory just meet on this holiday you went on, as Molly said? Or did you know him before?'

It sounded dreadful now. 'No, it was only on the holiday. I'm usually perfectly sensible and cautious –' She threw a glance in his direction to see if he believed her. 'But when I found out there'd been a party, with gate-crashers and all sorts of hideous mess, I thought a week's holiday was just too short and I wanted to extend it a little. Apparently the house was just like that Yellow Pages commercial.' Thea stopped, wishing she hadn't mentioned the Yellow Pages. 'It does sound dreadfully irresponsible, now.'

'Oh, I don't know. If you'd just gone home and cleared up the mess I wouldn't have found out where Rory was.'

'Well, no, I suppose not. It was lucky Molly asked you about him.'

'That wasn't luck. Molly has a member of the family to ask about every subject. I'm the art man because of having been head of a college. When the head of the local college hadn't heard of him, I was next in line. The luck was that I'd remembered Rory. At the time I felt it was unfair that his work was slated because of his behaviour. However appalling it was. He was the artist I'd been trying to track down for years.'

'Well, I think he's really good, too.'

Ben glanced at her as if them sharing an opinion was merely coincidence. 'I think Lara's going to have another puppy now.'

'Just in the nick of time, eh, Lara? Shall I put the kettle on?'

'No. I'm awash with tea. There's a good girl, another little bitch. If these were pedigrees they'd be worth a lot of money.'

'Perhaps we could invent a new breed. What would we call it?' For a moment she struggled to combine the words 'collie' and 'mastiff' and failed. 'Something entirely new, like Ponderosos or something. Lara seems quite ponderous.'

'It's not going to be easy finding homes for mongrels this size.'

'I expect I'll have one.'

'Have you any idea of the responsibilities involved in having a dog? They're not toys, you know.'

'I do know that, but I only work part-time – in fact, I may not work at all after taking time off with hardly any notice. I could take care of a dog.' Thea's dormant maternal instincts had surfaced with all the force of a volcano.

Ben's exasperation increased somewhat. 'But what about six of them?'

'Perhaps Molly could be persuaded, if she could tell her friends it's some exotic, rare breed and terribly valuable.'

He shrugged. 'Stranger things have happened.' He turned his attention back to Lara. 'Come on, old lady, we're all getting tired.' He glanced at his watch. 'It's nearly three in the morning.'

'I suppose Rory must have decided to stay at the pub with the others. He had had rather a lot to drink.' Thea thought this was a good thing. It meant she could sleep in his bed and she could put Ben in her room with Toby. His much vaunted goose feather duvet would be heaven just now.

Lara's sides heaved, and both Ben and Thea crouched by her just as another little pup appeared. It was much smaller than the others, and didn't wriggle and squeak.

97

'Is it dead?'

Ben picked it up and started rubbing it roughly with the towel – Thea's towel – which she had produced earlier. 'It may not be, but it is a runt. Come on, little chap, take a breath!'

It did and a cry so small they wouldn't have heard it if it hadn't been the middle of the night emerged from its tiny mouth.

'That's the one I'm having,' said Thea with a catch in her voice.

'It's a runt,' he repeated. 'It may not survive. Don't get too attached to it.'

'Too late.' Thea realised she was crying.

Ben put his hand on her shoulder. 'Wait until tomorrow. See how it gets on. It may not last the night.'

Thea felt like emotional jelly. She was tired, she was overwrought. She wanted to lean into Ben and have him take her in his arms. For a moment it felt like he was going to, when an enormous rumpus developed by the front door. It opened and in walked Rory, followed by Molly and Petal.

'They didn't do bed and breakfast at the pub,' said Rory, slurring slightly, 'and the hotel was shut. So I brought them home. We've been wetting the babies' heads.' He staggered over to where he could see Lara and her pups. 'There, you see? I told you she'd be fine.'

Having no time to kick him, Thea turned her attention to Molly, whom she expected to be incandescent with fury.

In fact, she was also pretty merry. 'We had to get a taxi back,' she said gaily. 'We were all too drunk to drive.'

'I wasn't,' said Petal grumpily. 'But I can't drive. Can I please go to bed now? Irish folk songs just don't do anything for me. The pub was full of old people, singing and dancing. It was gross.'

Thea, startled out of her emotional stupor, realised that

if she didn't do something about finding places for people to sleep, no one else would. She got to her feet. 'I suppose I'd better find some bedding. Have you got any bedding, Rory? Or is it just what I've . . .' She hesitated. If she let slip that Lara had had puppies on the spare bed linen, Molly and Petal would both have tantrums.

'Don't know. Look in that cupboard.' He pointed to one in the corner of the sitting room, the last place anyone would put blankets. 'I'm going to my bed now. It's a double.' Then he opened his door and disappeared through it.

Thea took on her landlady persona. 'I don't suppose any of you brought sleeping bags?'

Molly looked at her like someone who, even if she knew what a sleeping bag was, certainly didn't own one.

Petal – who had a very expensive sleeping bag, guaranteed to keep out an arctic blizzard, but hadn't brought it with her – snapped, 'No!'

'I've got one for Toby,' said Ben. 'But as it's only big enough for him, it won't be much use for anyone else.'

'It'll do as an extra cover,' said Thea. 'I'll look for sheets. If only I'd known about this cupboard before,' she muttered, as she sifted through Ben's dead uncle's old bed linen and blankets. None of it was in very good condition and most of it would have been fine for Lara. Thea began to regret the bobbly lemon sheet she had sacrificed earlier. Petal would have grumbled but it would have covered her bed. Now it was under six little sucking, tube-shaped pups.

'Oh, how sweet!' said Petal, who had discovered the puppies. 'Aren't they gorgeous?'

Lara growled and wagged her tail. She was very proud of her brood but also protective.

Molly looked over the back of the sofa. Her merry glow was fading, fatigue and alcohol catching up with her. 'They do look a bit ratlike and there are so many of them.'

'There are six,' said Ben. 'That's not many at all, for a big breed. They can have dozens – up to a dozen, anyway.'

Molly groaned. 'I've got a headache. I think I've had too much to drink.'

Thea had stolen the hot-water bottle from Toby's bed and put it in Molly's. She had managed to find just about enough sheets and blankets for both beds in the back bedroom to be decently covered. Ignoring their complaints, she herded Molly and Petal into it and, before shutting the door, said firmly, 'No, there isn't any hot water. You'll have to wash in the morning.' Actually, she had no idea if there was hot water or not, but she wasn't having Molly and Petal fighting for the bathroom mirror at this time of night. No one else would have a cat in hell's chance of getting in before Christmas.

That left Ben. While Thea was sorting out worn blankets and sides-to-middle sheets, he tidied up the sitting room as best he could and made up the fire so it would stay in all night. He accepted his instructions about taking the other bed in Toby's room meekly. Thea could see now how tired he looked – a long journey, followed by Lara's puppies, plus a whole lot of baggage Thea could only guess at were etched under and around his eyes. Even his hair looked tired, flopping over his forehead as if it hadn't the energy to stay back any longer.

Alone in the sitting room, Thea was forced to face what she had known all along – unless she shared with Rory there was no bed left for her. Even the sofa was bereft of cushions. 'Which leaves the bath,' she said to Lara, who wasn't listening. 'But not without as much bedding as I can scrounge.'

First, she tiptoed into Rory's room to see what she could scavenge. His bed, huge and comfortable, was very tempting, except that it had Rory in it. Ben, she was sure, sadly, could share a bed with a woman and not lay a finger on her. Rory would pounce the moment Thea's head hit the pillow. But she did find an old horse blanket under a pile of clothes, draped over a chair. She removed the clothes and took the blanket. Then, very bravely, she stole a pillow from under his snoring head and left the room.

A pair of old velvet curtains in the bottom of the airing cupboard were a good find. They smelt of mothballs and dirt, but were quite thick. Then she discovered a double sheet which was almost new and properly laundered – probably ironed tenderly by Susan. Good old Rory, he'd be glad to lend his sheet to a good cause.

Suddenly exhausted, Thea just pulled out all the remaining bedding, which revealed a leaking paisley eiderdown, and carried it into the bathroom.

The bathroom was not a cheery place. It had fading yellow paint and the bath had an iron stain descending from one of the taps. Thea ached and shook with tiredness, and was shaking out the curtains prior to folding them when she spotted a red light above a switch. An immersion heater; on! Her heart lifted. She would have a bath, and then, while it and she were still hot, she would pile everything in and nestle among it.

Neither Ben nor Toby stirred as she went into their room, damp and wrapped in an inadequate towel, to find her nightie and washbag. She didn't allow herself to look at them beyond a quick glance, because she'd read some-where that if you look at a sleeping person it will wake them.

Quickly, so she wouldn't lose the blissful heat of the water, she laid the velvet curtains in the bath, wrapped herself in the sheet and pulled everything else on top of her. The pillow was blissful, the rest good enough. She slept.

*

'Oh,' said Toby. 'I didn't know there was anyone in here.'

Toby, in his pyjamas, was an endearing sight but also a little embarrassing. Thea didn't want anyone to know she had slept in the bath. It was light and she looked at her watch: nine o'clock. As she hadn't got into bed until nearly six, she wanted a few more hours' sleep. 'Hi, Toby, I'll get out and let you have some privacy. Is Ben awake?'

'No. I only am because I needed the loo. I'll go back to sleep in a minute.'

Thea looked at him over the rim of the bath. 'Toby, tell me if you hate this idea, but supposing I just lie back down here and shut my eyes. Could you still pee? Or would you be embarrassed?'

Toby bit his lip and thought. 'That'll be OK.'

Thea burrowed down into her musty heap of cloth and went back to sleep.

She was woken again and realised Susan had let herself in the back door. It was eleven o'clock. There didn't seem to be any indication that anyone else was stirring. She climbed out of the bath and wondered how to prevent Susan from knowing what it had been used for. She settled on piling up everything in the corner and getting it stuffed back into the airing cupboard while Susan was in the kitchen. She went to say hello. 'Hi, Susan. Lara had her puppies last night.'

Susan's expression was radiant. 'Did she? How lovely? Where are they?'

'In front of the fire in the sitting room. Not really a good idea, but where else would there be room?'

Lara banged her tail hard on the floor, pleased to have her puppies admired.

'I told Rory he ought to be thinking about where she was to have them,' said Susan. 'They look so tiny, don't they? I don't suppose the father could have been very big.'

'One still got stuck, though,' said Thea and was about to tell Susan about Ben's gallant midwifery when she remembered Susan didn't yet know about Ben, or any of the others.

'Look at that little one.' Susan pointed to the runt. 'I doubt he'll survive long.'

Thea instantly felt tears prick her eyes. Short of sleep, she was in no mood to be adult and realistic about the chances of tiny puppies. Hopelessly sentimental, she wanted that puppy to live and thrive even more than all the others. 'Are you sure?' Susan was a country girl. She was bound to have experience of these little matters of life and death.

'Not sure. But he is little and you should probably –'

'Lara made a bit of a mess, I'm afraid,' Thea broke in before Susan could tell her to bump the puppy on the head. 'And one of the pups, that big one, with markings like a killer whale, was breech. Ben had to deliver it.'

Susan turned away from the little balloons which lay in a row by Lara's huge side. 'Ben? Who's Ben?'

Perhaps now was as suitable a moment as any to tell Susan about the great visitation. 'Ben's – Ben arrived last night, with some other people.'

Susan regarded Thea as if she'd had some kind of fit.

'Let's make tea and I'll explain.'

'OK,' said Susan getting up and going into the kitchen. 'Oh. There don't seem to be any tea bags.'

'Ben is some kind of relation of Molly's. Molly is a friend of mine and Petal's aunt. And Toby's Ben's son.'

'So Ben is the one who used to be head of an art college and likes Rory's paintings?'

'More or less. They didn't need to come in person and certainly not all of them. I spent ages taking slides.' It was important that Susan didn't think she was particularly pleased by the invasion.

Chapter Eight

While Susan was tidying the kitchen, Toby appeared. He looked sweet and rumpled, and endearingly like his father.

'Hi, Toby. Did you sleep all right?' Thea decided to ignore their earlier meeting.

'Hi. I'm glad someone's up at last. I've been in bed reading for ages.'

'Well, I suppose you didn't go to bed as late as everyone else. Come and see the pups.'

Toby knelt down respectfully at Lara's side. 'Look at that little tiny one,' he said.

Thea swallowed. 'He may not live very long. But he's my favourite.'

'Mine too,' Toby agreed.

Ben came into the room, dressed, but only half awake. Seeing him with his hair adrift made Thea put up her hand to her own. She discovered it had curled into knots at the base of her neck where it had got wet in the bath and badly needed brushing. She clawed at it with her fingers.

'Hello, Thea. Hi, Tobe. Admiring the puppies? The little one's still with us, I see.'

'That's mine and Thea's favourite,' said Toby firmly.

Ben gave Thea a look which told her never to lie to children about the chances of tiny puppies surviving. She looked back, trying to indicate that she hadn't. 'Has Lara been out yet?' he asked, when this silent altercation was over.

'She hasn't stirred,' Thea answered.

'She should get out and relieve herself and she'll need breakfast, too.'

Thea opened the front door and called Lara. She wagged her tail but didn't move.

'You need something tasty to bribe her with,' Ben told her.

'Let's see what we can find in the kitchen and you can meet Susan. Susan, this is Ben and this is Toby. This is Susan. She looks after Rory.'

'Morning, gentlemen,' said Susan. Her smile was equivocal, not enthusiastic, but not hostile either.

'We need some food to make Lara go out,' said Thea. 'What is there?'

'Precious little.' Susan opened the fridge and peered inside. 'Precious little for you folks' breakfast, either.'

'There must be something Lara likes. A bit of cheese, perhaps?' Thea knew there was cheese because she'd bought it herself.

'There's half a rasher of bacon she might as well have, as it won't feed a person.' Susan handed it to Ben.

He went over to where Lara lay. There were five little balloons and a sausage, where before there had been five little sausages. The runt, though still alive, hadn't filled out in the night like the others.

'It's a good sign that he hasn't died, isn't it?' Thea asked.

Ben looked down at her but didn't speak. Thea felt like Toby must when his father had bad news.

'OK,' she went on. 'It's nature's way. If he dies it's for a reason.'

She delivered the lecture to herself in a voice that was brittle with the effort of keeping away the tears. She was short of sleep and nervy, and wondered if somehow she was suffering from some kind of referred post-natal depression, but decided not to mention it in case she found herself locked up for lunacy.

'Come on, Lara, look what I've got for you.' Ben angled

106

the bacon in front of her nose and she reared up to sniff it. Holding it out of her reach, he lured her to the front door, got her outside and only then let her have the bacon. Seeing she was about to bolt back, Thea shut the door.

Through the window she saw Lara squat down, and then have a sniff about before charging back towards the door, demanding to be let in.

'Her food's in that sack, over there,' said Susan.

Ben inspected the sack in the disapproving way parents inspect boxes of cereal which are much advertised on television, with free toys in them. 'She may need something with a bit more protein now she's got pups to feed.'

'You may all need something with a bit more protein in it, if you want breakfast,' said Susan, who had a more pragmatic attitude to animals than Thea and Ben did.

'Is anyone else up?' asked Ben, when he'd fed Lara.

'No and no sign that they'll be up soon.' Thea had put her ear to the keyhole and heard Molly's familiar snore, but nothing from Petal.

'You've got two eggs, one and a half tomatoes, and half a loaf of bread,' persisted Susan, determined to keep Thea's mind on the job.

Thea wanted to creep back to her bath. 'I don't suppose Molly will want a cooked breakfast,' she began.

'Rory will,' said Susan.

Ben turned to Thea. 'Can you drive Rory's Land Rover?'

'I expect so.' But she wasn't keen. If it were a matter of life and death she wouldn't have hesitated, but not if it were just a matter of eggs and cornflakes. Oh, and freshly squeezed orange juice for Petal.

'OK,' said Ben, seeing her lack of enthusiasm. 'We'll walk to the pub and fetch Molly's car. Then you can come with us and show me where the shops are.'

Thea felt unreasonably excited at the prospect of abandoning her sleeping, uninvited guests. Perhaps running away from people was becoming a habit. 'Susan, just tell anyone who appears that we've gone to buy breakfast,' she said gaily.

'You'd better buy lunch while you're there,' Susan told her. 'It's getting on for one o'clock already.'

The air was damp and chill on Thea's cheeks, refreshing and invigorating. It felt wonderful to be outdoors, in the light and air. The sun was a silver disc behind the clouds reflecting silver on the water. It was like moonlight but without the darkness. The islands rose from the sea like benign sea monsters getting the sun on their backs.

She gazed at the view for a few moments while Ben found the keys and then got Toby settled in the back of the car. 'It is a lovely spot,' she said happily as Ben adjusted the front seat for his long legs.

'Yes.'

'Very inspiring for an artist, don't you think?'

Ben shrugged. 'I have yet to see the artist's work so I can't comment on his source of inspiration.'

Thea wanted to click her teeth, roll her eyes and say, 'Oo, la di da!' like Petal and her chums did, in similar situations. Perhaps Ben wasn't a morning person.

Toby sat silent in the back. To Thea, who had no experience of children, he seemed quiet and thoughtful for one so young. She glanced round to look at him, but he seemed quite happy, looking out of the window.

Toby wasn't the only one to be quiet during the drive into town. Thea wanted to enjoy this moment of peace, knowing there would be none when they got back, and Ben was probably tired. He must be a little anxious in case this expedition was for nothing. He'd rearranged his entire holiday. If Rory hadn't fulfilled his potential it would be a dreadful waste of his and Toby's time.

Thea found Toby extremely useful in the supermarket. He knew what he and his father liked to eat, and was good at finding things, like fresh orange juice and Greek yoghurt for Molly and Petal, and croissants for Thea who felt she deserved a treat. 'He's a very efficient shopper,' she said to Ben as Toby spotted the dog food aisle and ran off.

'We neither of us like it much, so we get it done quickly.'

Thea didn't usually like shopping much either, but she had been enjoying this amble round an unfamiliar shop, looking at the different things that were available in Ireland. 'Oh, look,' she said, her spirits dampened by Ben's lack of pleasure, 'cooked chickens. I'll get one for lunch.'

The dog food in the supermarket deemed inappropriate by Ben, they found a shop selling everything any farmer could want, from barbed wire to Barbour jackets. It also sold large bags of dog food, one of which was 'for nursing bitches'.

Toby and Thea found dried pigs' ears, looking pathetically like their undried origins. Suddenly remembering that Toby was a vegetarian, Thea wished she hadn't drawn his attention to them.

'Sorry, Toby, I forgot you didn't eat meat, you probably think these are gross.'

'It's all right. I don't like meat myself, but Dad has explained that if no one ate it there'd be no animals in fields and stuff.'

'Quite right. Shall we get one of these for Lara?'

'Yeah. She deserves a treat. But what if she doesn't like pigs' ears?'

'I expect she will,' said Ben. 'Shall we go? Our parking ticket will run out.'

'And the others will be up and starving,' added Thea.

'And Lara,' Toby reminded them.

Just for a moment Thea wished the others and Lara didn't exist, and the three of them could poke around the pretty riverside town at their leisure. Although Ben would probably hate it.

There had been a slight tussle at the checkout. Ben had got out his wallet, assuming he was going to pay, but Thea had got in first. Her argument was that as they were all there because of her, the least she could do was buy breakfast. Ben had regarded her as if she were a rare species that he'd heard about but never thought to see. While this gave Thea a warm feeling for a moment, she reflected later that he would probably brand her a rampant feminist and cross his fingers whenever he saw her.

They got back just as Rory came out of his bedroom. He was bare-chested and his lean, lightly muscled torso disappeared into a slender waist and flat stomach. A narrow band of dark hair led from his chest to the waistband of his jeans, where it disappeared. His arms were tanned and the hairs on his forearms were bleached by the sun. He yawned and brought his arms up behind his head. Thea saw Petal observe this from across the room and they exchanged glances. Yummy, they both thought.

Their moment of concord was swiftly over as Rory said, 'Hello, everyone. Jaysus, I've a headache!'

'So have I,' said Petal plaintively. 'Has anyone got any paracetamol.'

'Why are there no aspirins in the jungle?' said Toby to himself. 'Because the parrots eat 'em all.'

Diverted from Petal and Rory, Thea turned to Toby. 'I like that.'

'I didn't make it up. I heard it from someone at school.'

Thea nodded. 'Well, I expect Molly's got something for headaches. We've brought fresh orange juice for hangovers and all sorts of other things besides.'

Now, Molly emerged from the bathroom, looking ready for whatever the day might bring. She was perfectly made up and her hair was tonged and brushed. Thea realised she must have got up the minute they left for her to be looking like this now.

'Good morning, everyone, Rory.' Molly averted her eyes from Rory's luscious torso; it was probably too much before breakfast.

'Hello, Molly.' Thea negotiated her way through the people and the furniture to her friend. She felt a sudden rush of warmth towards her, for looking so good and for not complaining about anything. 'Good night?'

'Yes, darling. Of course, I always bring my own pillow with me. Now, who's going to show me these pups which caused so much commotion. Toby?'

Toby seemed to retreat, although he didn't move. 'They're over there.' He pointed to where Lara and the pups lay in front of the fire.

Thea wondered if he saw too much of his cousin. 'They may not want to be disturbed just now. What do you think, Rory?' Belatedly, Thea realised she and Ben had become rather proprietorial about Lara and her pups, when actually they were Rory's.

'Sure, I wouldn't know. But I do know that if I don't get a cup of coffee soon I won't be fit to live with.'

'I'll make it,' said Petal.

Susan, who had been in the kitchen watching the proceedings like a spear carrier in a play, decided to exit, left. 'I'll clean the bathroom then, if you folks have finished with it,' she said, having given Molly a look which told Thea that indeed, Molly had been in it for a long time.

'I'll cook breakfast,' Thea stated. 'Who wants eggs and bacon?'

'I do,' said Rory, 'and sausage and tomatoes and fried bread.' He gave Thea a grin which made her wonder why she didn't want to leap into bed with him. He was so delicious and cheerful. Ben seemed to have trouble finding his smile muscles.

At least in the kitchen, she thought, debating whether to cut off the bacon rind or not, *I'm doing something useful and not taking up space*. There was a jostle for space at the moment, with Lara taking up so much of it. Petal was fiddling with something on the windowsill, glancing sideways at Rory, who was still only half dressed and was reading his post while scratching his belly. Molly was straightening things which weren't designed to be straight, longing to create order where no order was possible.

Ben and Toby had gone for a walk, promising they would be back very soon.

At last everyone was settled round the table, drinking orange juice and eating yoghurt, cereal or a heart-attack-inducing fry-up, according to taste. Thea was just relaxing into a bit of toast and Irish marmalade, when Toby said, 'Thea, why were you asleep in the bath last night?' He didn't speak particularly loudly – he wasn't a loud child – but somehow at that moment everyone stopped crunching and scraping and swallowing, and instead looked at Thea.

'You slept in the *bath*?' Molly found her voice first. 'Why?'

'Jaysus, and there was half a perfectly good bed gone to waste,' said Rory. 'Was I too drunk to sleep with?'

'If you'd said anything I'd have slept on the sofa,' Ben sounded cross.

'I can't believe you slept in the bath,' said Petal.

'The answer to your question, Toby,' Thea told him, 'is that there wasn't anywhere else to sleep.' Then she felt colour creep up her neck and into her face. *I'm too old to blush*, she thought, trying to look insouciant, *and too young for hot flushes. Why is this happening*? Carefully, she loaded her last scrap of toast with marmalade and carried it to her mouth. She was aware of Ben regarding her, but without turning to look at him she couldn't tell what sort of look it was. *Dear Toby*, she thought. *It might actually have been easier for me if you'd just wet the bed.*

'Well, now, Petal, you can give me a hand with the

112

dishes,' she said, and then realised people were still eating, 'when everyone's finished.'

'I'd like to see your pictures, if I may,' said Ben to Rory.

'Of course. I'd be glad to show them to you. Until Thea came I never showed anyone, but since she liked them enough to tell you about them I feel a bit differently.'

'After breakfast, then.'

Damn! thought Thea. *I'm going to be stuck in the kitchen with Petal when I want to be there when Ben sees Rory's work!* 'I'm going to make more coffee,' she said getting up. 'Who wants some?'

There were enough requests for coffee and tea to justify Thea evacuating to the kitchen, taking as many dirty plates as possible with her. *If they dawdle over their coffee and Rory has a cigarette, I'll have this lot done and can go to the studio with them,* she thought. *Petal can dry up.* 'Molly, what are you going to do while Ben sees Rory's pictures?' she called, swooping and dunking her way through the washing up.

'Oh, Molly,' said Rory, reaching his hand across the table. 'Are you not going to look at my work, then?'

'To be honest, Rory, if pictures aren't of anything I can recognise, I really don't understand them. I think I'll do some telephoning and find a hotel as there's not room for us here. We've got the decorators in at home and Derek prefers me to keep out of the way.' Molly smiled back at Rory in a way which told Thea that last night, when they were downing pints of porter, or chasers of Paddy, or Jameson's Irish Whiskey, Molly and Rory had become friends.

'Can I come?' asked Petal, shyly eager.

'Sure, come one, come all,' said Rory gaily.

'We can dry up later,' said Thea.

Led by Rory, Ben, Toby, Petal and Thea trooped up the hill to Rory's studio. He unlocked the shed, and he and Ben began dragging canvases out into the field. Thea didn't comment, but she felt their power again. They were breathtaking, the colours so deep, made of pigments so pure that they could change from almost black to the most intense hue, depending on the light. They were so enormous that no ordinary house could fit one through the door, either. Rory had told her that one of the reasons he lived such a hand-to-mouth existence was the cost of the paint.

When they were all outside, leaning against bits of hill like huge, resting walkers admiring the view, Thea went back down the hill to look at them from a distance. She didn't want to hear Ben's opinion, or Petal's, or Rory's explanations. She just wanted to look at them while she could.

Later, Petal skidded down the hill to join her. 'Ben's very keen, but he says it's going to be hard to find somewhere to exhibit for a couple of years. It's because they're so big. Rory says he's already waited long enough, so he'll take them off to America where they understand "large".'

Thea felt instantly proprietorial. They were British pictures or, at least, Irish. They couldn't go to America to be exhibited.

'Rory says he's got lots of drawings and a few water-colours too. Sketches, mainly. Ben thinks he should get those framed, because at least they're not ten foot square and they might sell.'

'I always like drawings myself,' said Thea, who really yearned for one of the paintings, a wall of coloured light, only she didn't have a wall big enough. 'What do you think of them, Petal?'

'Amazing! They sort of blast you with colour and light, don't they?' Petal rubbed her arms, chilly in her sleeveless fleece. 'I'm cold. I think I'll go back to the house.'

'You could do the drying up while you're there.' Thea, in Rory's coat, wanted to go on gazing at the pictures.

Petal made a face.

'Go on,' Thea urged. 'It won't take you a minute, and it'll –'

'It won't look good on my CV, Thea, if that's what you were going to say.'

Thea was in the habit of encouraging her lodgers to get jobs, even if their parents gave them huge allowances, because 'it would look good on their CVs'.

'I was going to say it'll earn you Brownie points with Molly and Ben.'

'Ben's all right, actually, isn't he? I've never really got to know him before. I was so embarrassed when Mum said he'd offered to collect my work.'

'So you've dropped the "uncle" bit?'

'Yeah. He said he wasn't my uncle and he'd prefer to be just Ben. Molly was a bit shocked.'

'But you're not calling Molly, Molly?'

Petal shook her head. 'Nah. She'd freak.' Petal sighed. 'I'll go and dry up, then.'

'Thank you, Petal. You're a good girl.'

Warmed by the beauty of the paintings, more than the weak sunshine, Thea suddenly felt very fond of Petal.

Thea had stopped gazing at the work and was lying back on the scrub with her eyes shut. The sun had emerged from its cloudy veil and was now quite hot on her face. She was nearly asleep when Ben joined her. She sat up and tried to look intelligent.

'Well, they are good, that's for sure.'

'And you agree with me that they should be exhibited?'

'Yes, but where? I do have contacts in some London galleries, but they're all booked up for years ahead. He says he won't wait, but will ship them off to America. The gallery owner he first showed with has a gallery in New York and might well be keen to show him again, particularly now he's matured a bit.'

'But how will he afford to do that? He was telling me

that even the cost of paint is crippling. He'd have to paint horses and dogs for years to afford to get them to America.'

'Not if he sent slides to the right people. Someone would pay for them to go.'

Thea's happiness threatened to vanish. She'd wanted Ben to like Rory's work, she'd wanted the paintings to be as good as she felt they were, but she did not want them to disappear to America. 'They're my slides. Or they will be, when I get them back. I won't let him have them.'

Ben sighed. 'He can always take more slides, for God's sake.'

'But don't you want Britain to have them? Or Ireland?'

'Rory's not really Irish, he told me. He's just taken on an Irish personality because he lives here. He was born in Liverpool.'

'Oh. Well, what has that got to do with anything?'

'Nothing, really. It just means he'd be happy to exhibit in England, which makes it easier as I have contacts there.'

'But those contacts can't get us a show quickly enough?'

Ben shrugged. 'I can ask around, but it's unlikely. There's been a huge surge of interest in art since Tate Modern opened and they're booked up further ahead than ever.'

'Can't you find a new gallery? One that hasn't got booked up yet?'

Ben looked at her. 'No. I have a job, and a child and a nanny to support.'

'Oh. Sorry.' Thea realised that her enthusiasm was making her unreasonable. She sighed and closed her eyes. 'Well, I'll tell you what. I'll have to open a gallery myself.'

Ben chuckled, assuming she was joking. 'Even you wouldn't be mad enough to do that.'

'No, I'm serious. I want to open an art gallery, to show Rory's work.' It suddenly seemed so obvious that she wondered why she hadn't thought of it before.

'You really are mad! I thought it was just a persona you adopted. Do you know the sort of rents they charge for property in London?'

'Very well, as it happens, seeing as I only moved away a couple of years ago. But who says the gallery has to be in London? If there's no room for Mohammed in London, the mountain will have to move out of town or something.'

'What are you talking about?'

'I'll open a gallery in Cheltenham, or somewhere like that. We'll make the Artylartary, or whatever they're called, come to the provinces!'

Chapter Nine

❧

Ben looked at her as if she were unhinged, but this didn't faze her – she was getting used to it. 'I'll find premises near where I live and open an art gallery to show Rory's work. And if I like it and can make a go of it, I'll keep it open and show other people's work.'

The more she thought about it, the more she realised that this was just the sort of project she needed. For the past two years she'd simply been existing; this was some-thing she could really throw herself into.

'You do realise', he said eventually, having waited for Thea to start eating the grass and tearing her clothes, 'that it's unlikely you'll ever make any money?'

'Money is not the only thing in life.' She regarded him reproachfully. He should know that.

'That's all very well to say if you've got some. Without it life can be pretty desperate. Having a gallery is a fine idea, but you wouldn't be able to afford to give up the day job for years.'

Thea wanted to put her hand on his, where it was crumpled into a fist on top of the short, glossy turf, but she sensed he wouldn't appreciate the gesture. 'I know, but I'll have my lodgers, who keep the house going. My day job earns me very little. I'd do better to run the gallery during the day and work in a bar at night.'

He frowned. 'When would you sleep?'

Thea shrugged. 'In the afternoons, when I'm sitting in my gallery and nobody comes?'

He smiled at last. 'So you have at least been in a small art gallery, then?'

'Yes. And I promise you, before I make any commitment I will visit a lot more, talk to people, find out what's involved.'

His smile extended a little further and she saw he had small indentations in his cheeks, what would be dimples in a woman or a child, or even a different sort of man. 'And all for the love of Rory?'

'It's his work I'm interested in. I just want it to stay in this country . . . continent. If he sends it to the States it'll be lost to Britain for ever. Another artistic brain down the drain. And in a silly way I feel I *discovered* him. Perhaps I want a little of his potential glory.'

'But how are you going to persuade him to hold back from the US? Why should he wait for you to set up your gallery in Long Shufflebottom, or whatever, where nobody may ever see it, when he could have a great, big, grand opening in some wonderful Manhattan loft in a matter of months, not years? I mean, if he has to wait for you to start a gallery from scratch, he might as well wait for a London gallery to have space.'

Thea felt a cloud pass over her enthusiasm and at the same time a breeze got up, making her feel chilly. 'No reason at all. I'll just have to convince him that he must. I know it's all a dream, really, but I've got to try, or I'll regret it for ever.'

Ben got to his feet and held out his hand to pull her up. 'I suppose that's true.'

By the time Thea was standing by Ben's side she felt more cheerful. She'd had a helping hand, literally. It must be a good omen.

Molly walked up to look at the work while it was still displayed outside the studio. Thea went with her, thinking it was possible she might need a rich patron. 'They're very good, aren't they, Molly?' she insisted, after Molly had inspected them in silence. 'Wouldn't you like one?'

'I can tell they're very well painted. Our week in Aix has taught me that much, but they're so large. And I thought landscapes were out of fashion. I thought it was representational art, now. You know, pictures of things you can recognise?'

Thea did know what representational meant, but she wasn't really abreast of the most recent fashion trends of contemporary art. And here she was, planning to devote her life to it.

'I've only got one small space in the hall,' Molly went on, not noticing Thea's little panic attack. 'Where the hunting prints run out, and another in the downstairs loo. Although I would like to help Rory out.'

'Well, I'm glad you think they're good, even if you can't buy one,' said Thea. She could tell Molly her grand plans later, when she'd spoken to Rory.

It was hard to get Rory on his own. Elated by everyone's appreciation of his pictures, he had opened a bottle of Paddy. Petal was his only co-drinker, but it was still difficult to talk seriously about anything.

Molly had found a bed and breakfast nearby and announced that she and Petal would be staying in it. 'That means Thea won't have to sleep in the bath any more,' she announced, giving Thea an ambivalent look. 'And I can have an en suite. What about you, Ben? Are you and Toby happy to stay here?' She didn't actually say that Thea needed chaperoning, but the implication was clear.

Ben glanced at Toby, who said, 'I'd like to be near the pups.'

'If that's all right with Rory, I think we'll stay put. It's only for a few days. We've planned to go down the Burren later.'

Rory, who'd recently lived the life of a hermit, had suddenly become very hospitable. He waved a liberal hand. 'You might as well hang around. I want to talk to you about the work, anyway.'

Having shown no one for years, now his work had been on show, even to such a small audience, Rory wanted to talk about it all the time.

'Will you be having meals at the B&B?' Thea asked, her practical streak diverting her from pleasure that Ben and Toby would be staying, and sorrow that it would only be for a few days. 'Or will you have supper here, with us?'

'They don't do an evening meal,' Molly replied. 'But I thought I'd take us all out to the pub tonight, to save you cooking, Thea.' It was just possible that Molly had looked in the fridge and seen the packet of mince that Thea thought she'd make spaghetti sauce with. She wasn't into student food.

Thea accepted this invitation gratefully. She had managed to get away from her lodgers, or at least most of them, but the huge collection of permanently dirty mugs, plates and glasses seemed to have followed her.

'Well, then,' Rory said, still in party mood. 'Who's coming out in the boat, then?'

'I will,' said Thea. She wanted to talk to him and the cottage was too small for conversation.

Molly and Petal shuddered in unison. Toby looked at his father, who muttered something about 'life jackets'. 'We'll hang on here and look after the pups, and perhaps arrange to borrow some.'

Toby sighed resignedly.

'Suit yourselves. I'll show Thea the seals.'

Rory was adept in the water and the little vessel was soon speeding away towards the islands, its outboard motor buzzing along bravely. Thea would have liked a life jacket herself, but she knew that Rory would think the idea feeble in the extreme.

'There are always seals on this island.' Rory pointed

ahead to a lump of land which seemed completely bare apart from a few rocks. 'See? Those dark shapes?'

Gradually, as they drew nearer Thea watched, fascinated, as one by one the shapes slid into the sea and came swimming towards them, as if warning them off. They all had distinctive markings, and their huge liquid eyes were strangely glamorous in their round faces and shapeless bodies. Only the old grandfather seal, scarred and leathery, didn't bother to move from his patch of sunshine. People in boats weren't much threat to him, especially if they weren't fishermen.

After they had watched until all the seals had got bored and disappeared, Thea said, 'Can we turn off the engine for a while? I want to talk to you. The house is so full of people that we might not get another opportunity.'

He switched off the engine. 'Speak. And tell me why you stole my pillow but didn't share my bed. The bath, indeed. You're not a student, Thea.'

'I know and that's not what I want to talk about. This is serious, Rory. It's about your work.'

'Oh?' Rory seemed on the defensive, as if she were about to tell him off.

'It's fabulous, you know that, and I expect Ben's said the same. I suppose he's also told you that you might have to wait a couple of years at least for a London show.'

'Yeah. Which is why I'm going to send slides to the States. Try and track down the guy who showed my work before. I won't have to wait for so long and the British art scene won't get another chance to thumb its nose at me.'

'It was years ago and even you admitted you behaved appallingly. There's no reason to refuse to show here now. Not when you're so good. They'll all realise they were wrong.'

Rory pulled out the oars from where they lay under the gunnels. 'Fish about under your seat, you should find the rowlocks.'

Thea fished, fearing she'd lost his attention. After a bit she came across a pair of metal things. 'Are these them?'

'That's it, can't row without them.'

'You're not going to row all the way back?' She watched him fit the rowlocks into the holes on the side of the boat and begin to row.

'We'll row until you've got whatever it is you want to say off your chest.' He looked at her chest and she felt suddenly self-conscious, although there wasn't much he could see of it through Molly's borrowed puffa jacket.

'It's difficult to know where to start, but what I want is for you to wait for me to open an art gallery, in the provinces – I couldn't possibly afford London rates – and let me show your work. All of it, together, in one place. And possibly your drawings and sketches too.'

'It sounds a grand idea, but how long will it take you to set up an art gallery? One year? Two? I might as well wait for something to turn up in Cork Street.'

'Do you think a posh Cork Street gallery would be willing to show *all* your work? They wouldn't have the space. I can make sure I get premises that have big enough walls.'

'Sure, but when? Now I've exposed my work to you lot, I want the world to see it.'

Thea realised he was lumping her in with Ben and Molly, Petal and Toby, when before it had been her and Rory. A tiny part of her was sad, a delicious *affair* with a gorgeous Irish artist was such a lovely idea in theory. 'The world *will* see it. With Ben's contacts –' Thea wasn't exactly sure what these were, but that didn't bother her. 'We'll get the art world to come to . . . to . . . wherever my gallery ends up being, to see *your* work. Mohammed coming to the mountain. Or is it the other way round?'

Rory grinned. It was a devastating grin, white teeth in a tanned face, with enough wickedness to turn any girl's heart. 'All right, m'darlin'. You've sold the idea, now give me a time-frame.'

Thea watched him moving easily backwards and forwards as he pulled the boat through the water. 'How long can I have?'

'Three months, or I go to America. I already have a contact over there.' He shook his head as if trying to get water out of his ears. 'I must be mad! There I have a very lucrative bird in the hand and I'm turning it away for some hair-brained chicken portion in a bush.' He narrowed his eyes at her. 'It must be love.'

Thea swallowed. She knew perfectly well that Rory didn't love her, but he did want her and he might, not entirely unreasonably, expect a little something in return for his forbearance. 'Three months isn't very long to get an entirely new project going from scratch.'

'Tell you what, why don't you come to my American show instead and I'll tell everyone you discovered me.'

'But I'm sure I'll manage. We'll need to get the drawings and sketches mounted and framed. Do you know someone who can do that?'

'Do you know someone who can give us a bit of a loan to pay for it? I already owe him money.'

'I'll sort that out,' said Thea, knowing she'd already got in far over her head. With luck she could ask Molly for the 'bit of a loan'.

'Good.' Rory shipped the oars. 'Now, Thea. Just a kiss to seal the deal.'

Thea allowed herself to be pulled into his arms. They were strong and his mouth was cold and firm. Very pleasant, really.

'So you're going to stay here, on your own, with Rory?' Molly was drying up glasses, covering them in bits of lint when they would have been better left to drain. Thea, who wanted to talk to her, didn't stop her doing it.

Molly was suspicious, although since Thea had told everyone of her plans to open an art gallery she had become an enthusiastic supporter. 'But won't that waste a lot of time?'

'I'd like to stay while the puppies are so little and while I organise getting his drawings framed. It's bound to be more expensive in England and besides, I can't trust Rory to do it. He'll just forget and we must have them to show, or no one will be able to afford to buy anything. There's nothing much to lure me back home just at the moment. Just a dirty house. I'm sure they've found someone to replace me at work.'

Thea didn't add that she had to keep Rory focused and away from the notion of sending her slides to his contact in America. She wasn't quite sure how she was going to do it.

'Three months really isn't enough,' said Molly, who'd argued at length and unsuccessfully for six. 'It takes longer than that to get a bathroom decorated.'

'I know, which is why I want you to go to estate agents and find out about suitable properties to rent. You can send details here – perhaps' – this was taking a bit of a risk: give Molly too much responsibility and she'd take over the whole show – 'perhaps check some of them out for me. Please, Molly? I know it's a bit of a cheek to ask you but I don't know anyone else I could trust.' Who lived locally and who had time, she added silently.

'Oh, very well.' Molly hid her pleasure by folding up her tea towel. 'Now, what's Petal doing? We're going to go for a walk.'

Thea raised her brows in surprise. Petal didn't 'do' walking unless she was in a covered shopping mall. When Molly had gone she unfolded the tea towel, so it could dry.

Thea watched the party leave with regret. She hadn't asked them to come, but now she didn't want them to go. It was partly because she didn't want to be left with Rory, but mostly it was frustration. Now she'd decided to open an art gallery, she was anxious to leave her Irish idyll and do it, especially as she had so little time.

Rory stood behind her as they waved the car away. 'Well, Thea?' He turned her round and put his hands on her shoulders.

It was crunch time. 'Rory, you are one of the most attractive men I have ever met,' she began. 'And I must be completely mad not to make love to you right now, in front of the puppies.'

'I sense a "but" coming on.'

'I *am* completely mad. I don't want to make love to you, or for you to make love to me.'

He took it well. He raised his eyebrows, but didn't seem particularly surprised. 'You mean you came to Ireland, to my house, with no intention of giving me what we both wanted? We did both want it, didn't we?'

Thea considered for a long time before she answered. It was important to tell him the truth, but not to give him any false impressions. 'When I came to Ireland I thought I wanted a break from my humdrum life. I was terribly flattered by your interest – my ego will remain inflated for years, just on the memory. But when I saw your work, your paintings, I realised there was something more important than just wonderful sex.'

'Believe me, nothing is more important than wonderful sex.'

'Yes there is. There's wonderful art. It lasts much longer, although, admittedly, it's much more expensive. What I needed, and what I've now found thanks to you, is a mission, a project. I want to make you famous. I want your work to hang in all the important museums. I want the world to see you, through me.'

'You don't need to do that, Thea. There's a fella in America who'll do all that for me, I'm sure. If I can just track him down.'

'No, you're not with me. *I* want to do it. Because I want England, the country that spurned you . . .' Spurned was probably putting it a bit strongly, but the Irish liked poetry. 'I want them to salute you as the talent you are. Surely you want that too? They slated your work, just because you got drunk. You must want them to acknowledge you for the major talent you are.'

He stood looking down at her, chewing at the inside of his cheeks, putting his head first on one side and then the other. 'Well, I suppose I do.' He sighed. 'Thea, now you've made your pretty speech, what about making me some lunch?'

A few minutes later, while Thea was in the kitchen chopping up vegetables for soup, she uttered a silent prayer of thanks to the sea, the islands and the mountains beyond, for having managed to pull it off. Many women, women she would respect and like, would have happily enjoyed Rory with simple animal pleasure, without feeling guilty, or used, or anything except happy. But she couldn't. Was it because she thought it would muddy the waters between them and it was his art she was really interested in? It seemed a sensible solution, but it didn't quite ring true. *You're a funny woman, Thea*, she told herself.

In the following days Thea was very busy. The slides arrived, and guiltily, she kept them to herself. They were wonderful, and if Rory saw them, he'd want to send them to America straight away. She kept a careful eye on the pups, especially the little one, who seemed hungry and active enough, but didn't grow at the rate the others did. Having done that, she organised Rory.

First, they visited his friend who framed the animal pictures. He agreed to mount and frame the huge roll of drawings and sketches only if he was paid a deposit. 'I'm sorry, Thea,' he said with a sad twinkle, 'but this fella, although he's a lovely man, already owes me more money than you can shake a stick at.'

Tight-lipped, Thea observed how picturesque was his use of language and wrote a large cheque. For the first time she regretted putting all her money into her house and not having a mortgage. But maybe she could suggest to Molly that she might like to invest in a fine artist, otherwise she would have to put the rent up quick-smart and put a lodger in her darkroom.

When she was sure that Rory's cheaper works of art would be framed well and made certain that he had a painting on the go, which would take up all his attention and not allow him to think about researching his American (thank goodness there was no computer in the house and Rory had barely heard of the Internet). And when she was certain that Susan knew about Lara needing four times as much food as usual, she decided it was time to leave.

She and Rory took a last trip out to see the seals, a last walk up the hill behind the house and she made sure there was plenty of nourishing food in his cupboards. She would be very sad to leave the cottage. It was an idyllic spot, but real life went on elsewhere, for her at least.

She handed Rory the book she had bought about rearing puppies. 'It tells you when to put them on to solids. In fact, it tells you everything. In eight weeks, which is a month less than the time I've got to get my gallery up and running' – she said this to rub in how unreasonable he was being – 'I'll be back to collect my puppy. The little one.'

'Sure, he'll die, won't he?'

'If he dies, Rory, I'll . . . just don't let him die.'

She'd asked Susan to take her to the airport, giving her money she didn't have to do so. She looked out of the window as they drove, partly excited but mostly terrified.

These are my last moments as a carefree, hand-to-mouth, solvent woman, she thought. *When I get back home I've got to join the real world, arrange loans, find premises, do things that grown-up people do.* She sighed so deeply that Susan noticed and looked at her. Thea smiled quickly. 'Had a bit of a late night last night.'

'Oh. Had you?'

'Susan, you may not care about this one way or the other, but I might as well tell you. Rory and I haven't slept together. I'm only interested in his work.'

'You hadn't seen his work before you came here, but you came anyway.'

'I know. I was suffering from delusions. I thought I wanted a fling with a beautiful young man. What I wanted was a proper job.'

Chapter Ten

When Thea opened her front door she was bracing herself for chaos but the hall was much as usual, dusty, with the pictures hanging slightly askew on the walls, where people had knocked them as they went through, but there were no bags of rubbish blocking the door. Although this was a relief, Thea knew that it was just the tip of the iceberg. The kitchen might reveal the seven-eighths of mess below the surface.

But it didn't. Everything shone and everything was eerily missing. It was either exceptionally tidy, or the anti-clutter burglars had been, taking everything, including the washing-up liquid.

No. There was a note on the table. 'Dear Thea, I made them clear up. Hope you had a lovely time. How are the puppies?'

Thea suddenly felt very fond of Petal. How she'd managed to bully her other lodgers into producing this gleaming result she could only imagine, but she had and it had probably been very unpleasant for them. But for her, coming back after a comparatively long journey, it was bliss, at least until she needed to find anything.

The kettle was crammed into the cupboard with the saucepans, fairly easy to track down, and Thea filled it.

Just then the telephone rang. Thea's heart lurched. She had been thinking about the puppies a lot during the journey from Ireland. Lara was a perfectly good mother, but the little one, known now as 'Little Chap' needed to be latched on for extra feeds. Susan would do it when she was there, but Rory was unlikely to remember, although Thea had taped a large note reminding him above Lara and the pups. She couldn't face the thought of bad news.

The answering machine clicked on. 'It's Molly. I've looked at lots of properties for you, all hopeless. Do you want to do it yourself when you're back, or shall I just carry on? Give me a ring. By the way, Derek's thrilled I've got a new project.'

Thea sipped her tea contemplatively, relieved it wasn't Susan. Having Molly on your side was a very mixed blessing. She had bags of energy and enthusiasm and ideas, which was wonderful, but on the other hand she was so bossy, so certain she was right that she was likely to take over completely. Should she politely but firmly insist on taking the list of properties still to view and tell Molly she could manage on her own now?

The second sip of tea brought her to the conclusion that this wasn't possible. Firstly because she would never have the courage to tell Molly, however nicely, where to get off, and secondly she probably *couldn't* manage on her own now. Even with Molly batting for her it was a vast, probably impossible project.

When the phone rang again she picked up her mug and answered it. It would probably be for Petal anyway.

'Oh, hi,' said a slightly surprised-sounding deep male voice. 'I was expecting the machine. Ben Jonson here.'

'Oh, hello.' Thea felt her stomach give an unexpected little flip, in a way it hadn't since she was at school.

'I've got to be down your way to visit a client. I wondered if I could call in and talk to you? Next week?'

Thea was torn. She knew she would be very busy next week, but on the other hand she was surprised to find how much she wanted to see him. 'Well, of course. But couldn't you talk now?' She was proud of herself. The sensible answer.

There was a pause. 'Well, we could, I suppose. I've got gallery space for Rory.'

'Oh.' This was good news. She wanted Rory's pictures to be shown in a gallery. So why did she feel so deflated? 'How clever of you.'

'Yes.' Ben sounded pleased. 'We were very lucky. A good gallery, with lots of space, has had a cancellation unexpectedly. I heard about it and got in before anyone else did.'

'Excellent.' Really, Thea wanted to say 'oh, pooh', like Petal did, or stamp her foot. What a shame she was a grown-up. 'Will you tell Rory, or shall I?'

There was a pause. 'If you give me the number, I will.'

After a bit of burrowing in her handbag she produced the relevant bit of paper. 'Remind him to latch Little Chap on to Lara, whenever he remembers. Even if he's asleep.'

'Little Chap? Charming. I'll tell Toby and I'll remind Rory.'

'I hope there's time to get all the framing done.' She couldn't help sounding fractious. She'd worked very hard organising the framing and had paid for it herself. Now some posh London gallery was going to sweep in and get all the credit.

'Oh, there should be plenty of time. The space isn't available until early next year.'

'Next year?' A smile spread over Thea's face. She couldn't be certain that Rory would consider this too long a wait, but she was in with a chance. 'He only gave me three months.'

'Yes, but Thea, no offence, there's a slight difference between a major London venue –'

'And a small provincial gallery that hasn't even got premises yet? I know.' She paused for a second. 'Well, let me know how you get on.'

She ended the call, feeling pleased with herself, in spite of Ben's news. She felt she'd handled the call well. Wasn't there something in *The Rules* about finishing phone calls first? Or was that only with men you were dating? She'd better fish out her copy and reread it. For some reason she felt herself flush. Why was she thinking of Ben in terms of dating?

She decided to ring Molly back before she got into the bath. She was likely to be just as disappointed as Thea was and depressing news was better delivered when dressed.

Molly was satisfyingly annoyed. 'After all our plans. And all those dreary buildings! What a waste! And I got so filthy.'

'It's supposed to be good news. We want Rory's work shown in a London gallery, don't we?'

Molly made a satisfyingly dismissive noise. 'Quite frankly, I don't care where Rory's work is shown, or even if it moulders in his shed for ever. I wanted to open an art gallery!' There was a tiny pause. 'Help you open one, I mean.'

Thea sighed. 'I did, too. But we have to be happy for Rory.'

'I suppose so. Damn! I was looking forward to being a working woman again.'

'Well, I must go and have a bath now before the lodgers start coming home and I can't get near the bathroom.' Thea put the phone down decisively, pleased that her brush with great art and her subsequent plans for it, though brief, had made her able to end phone calls without resort to a candle and a smoke alarm.

When the phone rang again, just as Thea had lowered her body into a bath that was the perfect temperature, was doused with some very expensive bath oil left over from Christmas, just as a really interesting programme came on Radio Four, she was very tempted to leave it. But it rang again, just after the answerphone kicked in, which might have meant it was urgent.

It was Ben. 'Bloody Rory! He says he won't wait a year.'

'So it's back to plan A, then.' Thea tried hard to keep the growing smile out of her voice. Even naked and dripping she felt inordinately pleased.

'Yes! He'd rather go with you or send the paintings to New York. He says he's not going give the Cork Street crowd a chance, after they snubbed him last time.'

'Good for him! I knew he was a nice boy.'

Ben's disparaging grunt was even better than Molly's. It must be a family characteristic – an ability to be dismissive without resort to words. 'You, trying to open a gallery with no experience, is a completely hair-brained scheme, if I may say so.'

'Say what you like. Words are free.'

'And how he can turn down the opportunity of a lifetime just because . . .' He took a deep, possibly calming breath. 'I'll be down on Wednesday. About eleven? I'm seeing the client at half past eight, so I should be finished by then.'

'Oh.' Thea felt confused. 'I thought you were coming down to tell me about the gallery in London. Which I know about now and it's all off anyway. So why are you coming?'

Ben sighed. 'I had a feeling that Rory would turn down Cork Street, he's such an eejit. You know he's not really Irish at all? All those quaint little Irishisms are just put on?'

'You mentioned it.'

'So I'm coming to talk you out of this ridiculous plan.'

Thea laughed, feeling suddenly light-hearted. 'Well, you can try.'

'I'll meet you at the house.'

'Fine. I'll make some lunch.'

'Oh, don't do that.' The idea seemed to horrify him. Probably far too domestic. 'We'll go out. See you on Wednesday, then.'

His ending of the call was far brisker than hers had been,

but nevertheless a smile was pulling at the corners of Thea's mouth. She still needed to set up an art gallery and Ben was coming to see her.

She dialled Molly's number. 'I'm going to be very quick because I'm naked, dripping wet and the bath's getting cold, but Rory's turned down the London gallery. We're still in business.'

'Lovely,' said Derek. 'I'll tell Molly; she'll be pleased.'

'Thank you.' Meekly, Thea replaced the receiver and hurried back to the bath as she heard a key in the front door.

The following Wednesday, when Thea opened the door to Ben, who was scarily prompt, she didn't know what to say. Really she should have told him immediately that he was completely wasting his time, she couldn't or wouldn't be talked out of her project. She settled for, 'Do you want to come in?'

He shook his head. 'I called in on Molly and she gave me all these.' He shook a sheaf of papers derisively. 'Apparently they're potential art galleries.'

'Oh.' Thea put out her hand to take them.

He held them out of reach. 'I thought we'd go round them together, so you can see for yourself how totally impossible the whole project is.'

She felt she really should ask Ben why he was helping her, when actually, it was nothing to do with him whether her gallery failed or not. But she didn't. Because she didn't want him to tell her she was absolutely right and turn round and go home. Her vision of him smacking his forehead with his hand as he realised his mistake made her smile.

Ben scowled down at her, wondering why she was smiling and not wanting to ask. 'We can have lunch when we've got these out of the way.'

There was no denying it was fun. The first two were far too small and poky to display anything bigger than intimate watercolours, but the last space was much more encouraging – at least on paper.

It was in a small town about twelve miles away, an area noticeably lacking in art galleries. As they drove through to find somewhere to park it seemed to be lacking in lots of things, being dotted with the plethora of empty shops that plagued many small town centres. She consulted the estate agent's details she had purloined from Ben.

'There's only one property listed to rent here, although if that's not suitable, there seem to be lots of others which might be. Why didn't I think of coming to this town in the first place? I bet property is cheaper.'

'I'm sure it is, but how are you going to get people in? I don't think this town is exactly a mecca for art.'

Thea was indignant. 'You'd be surprised! The surrounding villages are delightful – all sorts of artists and media types live in them, even if not in the town. They'll love having great art on their doorstep.'

He looked at her and sighed. He didn't say he thought she was doomed to disappointment, possibly because he knew enough about her by now to know that she wouldn't listen.

They walked down the hill and cut through a little alleyway.

'They call these laggars,' said Thea conversationally. 'I learnt that at a course on local history when I first came down here.'

'Really? Where I come from they're slips. I suppose it's one of those words that never becomes a general term but just stays local.'

'So, where do you come from?'

'Wimbledon. It's got very smart recently.'

They located the property on a street corner, just by the station. Until recently it had been a building society, but before that it had been a dress shop, prominent in the town, with huge plate-glass windows on two sides.

'It's wonderful,' said Thea. 'It's so huge.'

'Let's go in before we get too carried away.'

While Ben struggled with the key, Thea wondered if he'd used the word 'we' in the patronising way adults did with children, or if he meant 'both of us'. Naturally optimistic, she decided on the latter.

Inside, Thea was just as enthusiastic. There seemed so much space and light. It cried out to be something more exciting than just another financial institution.

Ben followed Thea as she went into the largest room, exclaiming on the building's beauty. He didn't point out the grubby carpet, the dark beige walls or the dirt.

'It is a lovely space, you must admit that,' said Thea.

He nodded slightly, like a man bidding secretly at an auction.

'It's just a pity there probably isn't enough wall space,' she went on.

Ben took a breath. 'You could block out the windows, if you needed to, with fibreboard. You just build a framework and fix the board to it.'

Thea turned to him, delighted. 'What a good idea! You are clever. What's through this way?'

There were two other rooms, also with huge windows and Thea began to feel more and more that this was the right property. 'Let's go downstairs,' she said, when she'd mentally found space for about half of Rory's huge works.

Downstairs was a basement. There were no windows, no natural light and there was a suspiciously damp smell.

'It's the carpet,' said Ben. 'If you got it up and let some air get to it, it would probably be fine.'

'And there are no windows,' said Thea enthusiastically. 'We could put paintings on all four walls and prints in the corridor. We'd just need some good lighting. What's in there?'

There was a little kitchen and another office, again with no windows.

'This would be good for installations.' She indicated the office. 'And the kitchen's got potential.'

'As a kitchen,' said Ben firmly.

'And an office. I could put a desk in there.'

They stood in the dingy passage. He was looking down at her and, while she couldn't see his expression, she sensed that he wanted to talk to her, in the way that headmistresses had often wanted to talk to her when she was at school. In other words, what he was going to say was not good news.

'Thea,' he began, putting a hand on her arm.

'Ben,' she said firmly, taking it off. 'I think I know what you're going to say and I think it would be better if you said it somewhere else. Like a pub. There's one just across the road. I spotted it as we came in.'

'So,' she said, having taken a sip of her lager, still resolutely upbeat. 'You're going to tell me that I'm mad, that I can't possibly make an art gallery work without a private income and that I should just let Rory's art go to the States, which he can do really easily – all he needs to do is look up his contact on the Internet – and leave me to take up a useful hobby. But let me save you the bother – I know all that. I'm going to raise a mortgage on my house, put another lodger in to help cover the payments and give this gallery my best shot. I'll give it two years and, if in that time I've made no money, I'll accept defeat. OK?'

He sipped his drink. 'Well, I *was* going to say a lot of that and I did come down here to talk you out of it, but I suppose I knew there was no point.'

Thea had been hoping for a brisk, impassioned argument. 'No,' she said quietly.

'So, while I think you're completely mad and doomed to failure, I will help you in any way I can. With contacts, stuff like that.'

Thea's mouth twitched. 'Oh, but not with the painting and decorating?'

His mouth twitched too, but was quickly controlled. 'I don't have a lot of time, but I expect I'll do a bit of that too, if I have to.'

Thea smiled properly and put out her hand. 'Of course you don't have to. It's very kind of you to help at all. And the contacts stuff will be really useful – after all, any fool can slap on a few coats of emulsion.'

'Which you'll probably find is a good thing.'

'I'm sure I can get Petal and co. to help out.'

'Really? She's never struck me as the most helpful girl.'

'Oh, yes! She got the other lodgers to clean the house beautifully, before I came back. I don't mean she actually did it herself, but she made the others.'

'Well, good for her. Perhaps she's growing up at last.'

'I think she takes after Molly.'

'Probably.'

'And Molly's mad keen to be involved, too.'

'Thea, I don't know how well you know Molly. I'm devoted to her myself but she is rather –'

'Forceful? Bossy? Yes, I do know, but I need someone like that. She's so *positive*. I think I can keep her in check.' She smiled. 'I'm so grateful for your help as well. Rory will be, too, I'm sure.'

'I'm not doing this for Rory!' He sounded unreasonably cross. 'I mean, much as I admire his work, I know he'll succeed as an artist, especially now he's so keen on showing . . .'

'So?' Thea whispered, when she couldn't wait any longer.

'I'm doing it – or I will be – because I admire you for having a dream and going for it.'

Thea gulped. She didn't know what to say. To be admired by Ben, even for being crazy, was wonderful. And so, she realised, was Ben. Like the last clue in the crossword puzzle, it was so obvious when you knew the answer. Why she couldn't make love to Rory, why her heart beat faster when she heard his voice on the phone, why she wanted him near her, even when he was saying negative things about her project. She was either in love, or had the most almighty crush. Either way, she had to say something, and quickly, or he might guess. 'I thought you thought I was mad,' she burbled. 'In fact, you said I was, in so many words.'

'Yes, I do and you are, but I do admire you for it.'

'Oh.'

'And it will keep Molly out of mischief, too.'

She felt more in control of herself now, but he really did have lovely eyes. 'So I'll get a medal from the rest of the family?'

'Definitely.'

Thea smiled in what she hoped was an insouciant way. Without a mirror she couldn't check that she didn't just look simple.

Afterwards, when they'd called on the estate agents and told them Thea was interested in renting the property, and had arranged for Thea to meet the owner's solicitor, Ben drove her home.

'Do you want to come in for tea or anything?' Thea asked. 'Or do you have to get back?'

Ben took a breath and looked firmly out of the wind-screen. 'Listen, Thea, I feel it's only fair to tell you straight away that although I am attracted to you – I could hardly help it – I'm not into relationships. I don't know what, if anything, Molly's told you about my private life, but Toby's had too many women coming into his life and passing out of it again without me having girlfriends as well. I'm sorry, but that's the way it is.'

It took her a few moments to take in what he said, but she still couldn't quite believe it. 'What?'

'I said, I'm not into relationships.'

A tide of pure anger began to force its way up from Thea's stomach to her face. She knew she was bright scarlet and that she must try to keep her feelings under control. If she let herself betray any emotion at all, she was likely to deck him.

Molly hadn't told her anything about his private life. In fact, it was very odd, when Molly had dragged every single man she knew out of the closet for Thea to meet, that she'd never mentioned Ben. Did she know he 'wasn't into relationships'? It didn't seem a good enough reason for Molly, somehow. More likely it was because Molly didn't want to annoy Ben by offering him women he wouldn't want.

'If you don't want a cup of tea,' she said, rigid with the effort of controlling herself, 'you only have to say no. You don't have to give me a whole lot of information I really have no interest in.' The control had slipped and, now that it had, Thea went with it. 'Why on earth do you think I give a stuff about your dating habits?'

He appeared taken aback and she plunged on. 'But still, now I know, I can file the information away with all the other useless facts we all clutter our minds with. And if ever I have an opportunity to pass it on to any woman mad enough to want to go out with you I certainly will.'

He caught her anger but, unlike her, kept it in check. 'I'm sorry. I've probably said too much –'

'You have. Way too much. Now, if you don't mind, I'm dying for a cup of tea, so I'll go.'

She was out of the car and up the steps to her house when she realised she hadn't thanked him for driving all the way down from London to help her.

She stalked back to the car. He opened the passenger door. 'Thank you very much for helping. Please don't feel obliged to do it again.'

She had found her key, unlocked her door and got through it before Ben drove away. Once in the kitchen she stared at the whisky bottle for a long time before settling for tea. But she was glad she'd made the sober choice because five minutes later there was a knock on the door.

It was Ben. 'I've changed my mind. I would like a cup of tea.'

'Then you'd better come in.' Thea had had plenty of time to regret losing her temper. She followed Ben down the stairs to the kitchen. 'The kettle's just boiled, it won't take long.'

Ben stopped at the kitchen table and turned round to confront her. 'Actually, I don't care about the tea. I came back because I can't bear the thought of you trying to open a gallery without any sort of experience, or contacts, or anything. Whatever you think about me personally, you must let me help where I can.'

Having recently wanted to tear him limb from limb hadn't affected Thea's feelings for him at all. She shrugged. 'Then thank you. I would be very grateful for that.'

He scowled. 'You don't have to be grateful,' he said angrily and strode out of the room. She could hear that he took the stairs three at a time.

Meeting the owner of the property's solicitor was not the boring but easy task she'd imagined. The owner, it seemed, had been let down over matters of rent several times. Thus, he not only wanted Thea to sign a contract undertaking to rent the property for two years, whether the gallery was open or not, but he wanted three months' rent as a deposit. This amounted to approximately six thousand pounds, money Thea had to have before she could sign the contract and get into the space to start decorating.

Thea was certain she could raise the money, and more, from her house, but she couldn't do it instantly. She drove home, considering her options. She could go to the loan sharks, people who would lend her the money with pleasure and probably let her have it immediately in used notes, but at a rate of interest which would require her to sell her entire house to pay them back. There was Molly, who could probably let her have it immediately and would be happy to wait until she'd arranged a mortgage to get it back, but would then feel she was an equal partner in the project, which might be a dreadful nuisance. There was her mother, who would want Thea to ask her for money, but as she lived on very little, Thea wasn't prepared to do it. 'I'll sleep on it,' she decided, knowing she'd sleep on a rail if one were offered. 'And sort it out tomorrow.'

Thea was confident when she walked into the building society the following day. After all, she was a woman of property. It should be a simple matter of borrowing money against the property. The woman she spoke to was young, pretty and efficient. She was also firm. Thea could not have a mortgage, or 'Personal Finance' for however little, unless she had a regular income. And she couldn't say for sure, but she didn't think lodgers would count.

'Once you've got the money, of course, it's up to you how you pay it back. But we will need payslips and things to prove what you earn.' Then, seeing Thea's desolation, she added, 'I could refer you to a more senior member of staff. He might have some better suggestions.'

Thea sighed. 'If I need to see him I'll come in again.'

The woman smiled. 'It would be a good idea to make an appointment.'

When Thea got home she made an uncharacteristic raid on the bedrooms for dirty mugs and glasses. She rescued the corkscrew from Petal's bedroom yet again and decided to buy her one of her own. Then she remembered she had no money, and no prospective art gallery, just because she had been paid cash in hand at the photographers.

143

She thought about going back to them and asking them to write a letter, stating what she'd earned and implying she still earned it, so she could go to another building society, but decided against it. She *had* told them she wouldn't be coming back, but only after she'd got back from Ireland, when she'd already missed rather a lot of her scheduled days.

Instead, she put on the kettle and waited for it to boil. Something would occur to her. Some way of getting a large amount of money, and fast, would come to her. It had to, otherwise she'd have to ring Rory and tell him to take his pictures to America. And she would have to get a job that paid proper money.

Chapter Eleven

❦

Thea was still drinking her tea, or rather, sipping at the now cold liquid in her mug, when Molly rang. She definitely did not want to tell Molly her problems until she'd found a solution, but when Molly asked her how things were going, her 'fine' was a little forced.

'Good,' said Molly, not noticing, 'because I need a little favour.'

Thea would have liked to have told Molly that she was fresh out of favours and was far too busy. But even if this had been true, she wouldn't have said it. As she murmured helpfully, she wondered if she should go on a course called 'How to Say No to Bossy People'.

'Ben's leaving Toby with us this afternoon while he goes to a job interview in Bristol and I'd forgotten we'd got to go out tonight. I was wondering –'

Even Molly had to breathe sometimes. 'If I could pop over and babysit?' murmured Thea, wondering why Ben hadn't mentioned changing his job to her.

'Oh, no, I wouldn't dream of asking you to do that. You must be far too busy with the gallery. I expect you're sitting there now, chewing your pencil, working out which picture to put where.'

This was so far from the truth that Thea let out a sigh. 'If only that were what I was doing!'

This unaccustomed despondency penetrated even Molly's pressing concerns. 'Well, what *are* you doing?'

'Wondering how on earth to fund my gallery – at least, how to get some money quickly. Long term I could sell my house, buy something smaller in Stroud and do the gallery with the change. But I can't do any of that in the three months Rory's given me.' She sighed. 'Do you suppose, if I offered him my body, he might stretch it to four?'

'Oh, Thea!'

Realising she'd said far too much, Thea backtracked. 'It's only a temporary problem, Molly. I've just got to think of a way of raising some cash fast. It'll be all right. And if you want me to come over and babysit for Toby, that's fine. I'm not cooking for the hordes tonight – they're all going to be out.'

'Well, thank you, Thea, but I've already told Toby he's going to your house. I thought you wouldn't be able to come over, you see.'

'Well, I don't mind. I'd love to have Toby here, but what about Ben? Won't he be expecting to pick him up from you?'

'Ben's staying the weekend. It's some sort of team-building exercise. Although he hasn't definitely got the job, they want him to go along to see if he blends in.'

'How grizzly!'

'Mm. Poor Ben. Not his sort of thing at all. But actually he's very good at all that outward-bound stuff, so he'll be all right with that.'

'But it's still a late night for Toby, even if you pick him up.'

'Well, yes, which is why I was hoping you'd let him stay the night.'

'Well – it's not that I wouldn't love to have him, it's just where on earth could I put him? The house is full and so is my darkroom.'

'Toby says he's very good at sleeping on floors,' said Molly after a brief pause. 'And he wants to know how the puppies are.'

'They were fine last time I spoke to Susan,' she said. She'd arranged to ring when Rory was working. If she spoke to Rory, he might find out how badly her plans for the gallery were going. She waited while Molly passed the message on. 'And he'll really be all right on the floor?'

'He says so.'

'Well, I dare say I can sort something out. So you'll pick him up tomorrow morning?'

'That's it.' Molly lowered her voice confidentially. 'I'll have to think of some way of entertaining him over the weekend. I don't suppose there's a new Disney, is there?'

'I haven't a clue, but I'll ask the lodgers when they come back. In the meantime, I'd better sort out some sort of bed.' A horrible thought occurred to her. 'You *have* asked Toby, haven't you? You've asked if it's all right with him to come and spend the night with me?'

'Of course! Honestly, you'd think I'd never had anything to do with children!'

While Thea was sorting out her bedroom so she could find a corner for Toby in it, she debated whether or not she should ring Rory and tell him the whole plan was off, that she couldn't open an art gallery in the time and that he might as well take his paintings to New York and have done with it. Yet, somehow, she couldn't, not yet, not until she'd worried away at the problem a little longer and made absolutely sure she'd thought of everything.

As she found hangers and hung up the many clothes which lay draped about her bedroom, she wondered how much she'd get if she sold everything. Not a lot. Most of her clothes were comfortable, informal and old. Her few smart things she'd given away to her London friends before she'd left, eager to get rid of memories of a life she'd rejected.

Molly would probably have the odd ten thousand lying around for emergencies, but she really didn't want her too involved.

But what was the alternative? The alternative was to give up the whole idea.

At last, Thea uncovered the sofa she knew was lying around somewhere in her bedroom. She could borrow Petal's sleeping bag and Toby could sleep in that.

Molly delivered Toby a little earlier than Thea was expecting. Although they were perfectly amicable, Thea sensed they were beginning to get bored with each other and hoped that she would be able to find some way of entertaining a small boy, given her complete lack of anything in the way of toys, games machines or experience. 'Hi, Toby. It's nice to see you. Do you want to come in, Molly?'

'No, I won't stop. I've got to rush home and have a bath before we go out.' She made a face. 'You know it takes me ages to get ready.'

Thea did know.

'Well, come in, Toby, and see my house. There's probably not much to do in it, but I dare say we'll have a nice time.'

Seeing her house through Toby's eyes was a little unsettling. He eyed the piles of clutter, the posters on the walls, the quantity of books lying in piles on the stairs, with eloquent silence. He didn't say anything, but it was obvious his own house was very different. Masculine and spare, was Thea's guess. All this artistic student mess would probably put Ben right off. He was, after all, related to Petal and Molly, who were always complaining about it.

'Now, Toby. Are you hungry? What would you like to eat?'

'Anything.'

'Could you be a bit more specific? I remember you're a vegetarian, so I could always do you a baked potato. But what about pizzas?'

'From the takeaway?'

'Well, no.' Thea was economising. 'From the frying pan.' Toby's eyes widened in incredulity. 'It's quite easy,' she went on. 'You make a scone base, flatten it into the pan and cook it on both sides in olive oil. It's not as good as a yeast base, of course, but it's quick.' Realising that recipes probably weren't what interested seven-year-old boys, she decided they should move on to the practical aspect as soon as possible. 'Shall we do that, then? You can put anything you like on top – as long as I've got it, of course.'

Toby had a whale of a time. It was possible he'd never cooked using raw, basic ingredients before, thought Thea, although he had told her that he could use the microwave. 'Microwaves are a safe way for children to cook,' she said, 'but sometimes it's fun to do things from scratch.'

She had cleared the table, swathed Toby and herself in aprons and got out the flour. Very soon the cooks, the work surfaces and the floor were covered with a fine dusting of self-raising. 'If you put an egg in the mixture it makes it a bit richer.' She handed Toby an egg.

'I've never cracked one before,' he said anxiously.

'Haven't you? It's not difficult. Here, do it in this little bowl, it's a bit easier. Whoops, that one's a miss, I'm afraid.' She scooped the raw egg which had gone over the edge of the bowl back in. 'Have another go. Right, now bung in some olive oil.' She handed Toby the bottle.

'How much shall I put in?' Toby was beginning to relax.

'Just a couple of glugs. That's right.'

It was fortunate that Toby was as enthusiastic a washer-upper as he was a cook. Thea set him to it while she scraped the table. 'We can cook the pizzas when we've got a bit of space, so just wash that bowl.'

'This is such fun!' said Toby, splashing water on the floor almost as fast Thea could wipe it up again.

'Don't you ever do cooking with your mum?' Thea didn't know much about motherhood, but she certainly used to cook with her mother, when she was little.

'No, she doesn't like mess, much.'

'Well, no one actually *likes* it – it just happens.' Thea scratched her nose with a floury finger. 'I don't suppose Ben is too keen on mess either.'

Toby shrugged. 'He doesn't mind it, I don't think, but we don't have much quality time.'

'Quality time? Oh.'

The flour on Toby, moistened with washing-up water, had now turned to glue. 'Mm. That's why we're down-sizing.'

'Downsizing? I mean, that's interesting.'

'Yup. He's going for this job in Bristol. He should be able to get home a lot earlier and we can get rid of Margaret. My nanny.' The word obviously embarrassed him. 'We should be able to find a nice little village where I could go to the local school rather than privately.'

Thea supposed it was the private education which made him so articulate. 'I see.'

'And it looks like Veronica's getting married again, so he wouldn't have to give her so much.'

'Veronica?'

'My mum. She doesn't like labels.' Toby frowned. 'I would quite like a mum, though.'

'You mean, you'd like your – Veronica – to be called Mum? But it doesn't really matter what you call someone, does it? If they're your mum, they're your mum. Surely?'

Thea had missed the point completely. 'No, I mean a mum like my friend Edward's. She only works part-time and is always there after school. I would have gone to stay with them this weekend, only they've gone to see their granny. She makes cakes,' he added.

Thea would very much have liked to probe further, to find out Ben's feelings on all these topics, but she knew it would be wrong. Besides, Toby had given away lots of information already, without her having to torture him at all. She felt he deserved a reward. 'Well, if I've got enough flour, we could make a cake, when we've done the pizzas.'

'Could we? Ace!'

Later, when Toby was watching *The Simpsons* – probably prohibited viewing for seven-year-olds – licking out the chocolate cake bowl and Thea was clearing up, she reflected it was a good thing he liked cooking.

'We have to wait until the cake's a bit cooler to put the icing on, otherwise it'll all fall off again,' said Thea. 'It's happened to me lots of times.'

'There's rather a lot of icing, isn't there?' Toby was a little embarrassed. As always happens, the icing had got too wet and by the time it was the right consistency there was enough for a small wedding cake.

'Don't worry. We can freeze the rest and either use it next time anyone makes a cake, or I can eat it frozen, when I've got a chocolate craving on and haven't got any.'

'Oh. OK. Do you think it's cool enough now?'

'Not really, but put it on anyway. I can't wait much longer. You do the icing. I'll make tea. You need tea with chocolate cake, don't you find?'

Toby had no opinion on this, took the palette knife and started spreading.

Later, teeth brushed, but no other obvious washing done, Toby pulled Petal's sleeping bag up over his shoulders and snuggled down on the sofa in Thea's room. 'Why are there so many black bags in here?' he asked.

'I'm halfway through sorting out all my clothes and getting rid of the ones that don't fit any more. I started before Christmas.'

'Oh. Veronica always does hers twice a year. Spring and autumn. She sends her clothes to an agency and gets money for them.'

'Oh.' Thea sent hers to jumble sales and, only if they were good enough, offered them to a charity shop.

'She says there's only any point in keeping really classic clothes that won't date.'

'You know a lot about it, Toby. Far more than me.'

Toby sighed. 'It's not very interesting, though, is it?'

'Well, different things interest different people. Will you be OK up here on your own? I should go back down and have another go at the kitchen. Molly will be over in the morning and you know how tidy her house is.'

'Mm. Our house is always pretty tidy too.'

Thea's spirits sank a little. She had really enjoyed Toby's company and his presence had made her forget about her money worries. It hadn't stopped her thinking about his father, though. They were so alike to look at. If only Ben were as easy to get on with as Toby.

Although grateful that he hadn't allowed her to cut herself off from his much needed assistance, she was still furious about him saying all that about relationships in the first place, as if he had to warn her off. It made her look like a groupie or something.

'Yeah, well,' she said now. 'I'd better get downstairs or I'll have to take a chisel to the flour and water paste.'

'It's good you've got the Harry Potter books. Veronica doesn't read children's books.'

'No, well, I think it doesn't matter whether a book is for adults or children; if it's a good read, it's a good read. Do you want the radio on, for company?'

'Haven't you got a television?'

'Not in the bedroom, no. But I'll put the radio on, it'll probably be news or something, but it may send you off to sleep. It always does me.'

At last Thea got herself away from Toby who, though sleepy, seemed reluctant to be left alone. If the kitchen hadn't looked like the television set for a chimps tea party, she would have found jobs to do upstairs, but with Molly coming in the morning she wanted to get it straight. Besides, Petal would tell her off dreadfully if she found the detritus of deep pan pizza making stuck to the table.

*

Toby woke in the night, just as Thea was deeply asleep. She struggled upright to check he could find the loo all right. 'OK?' she murmured, with only one eye open.

'I'm a bit cold.'

'Oh.' She thought about hot-water bottles and extra blankets, and balked. 'Toby, I'm really, really sleepy. Would you mind awfully just getting into my bed? It's a double and I can easily shift over.' She shifted, waking up a bit more as she reached the cold bit.

'Oh, OK.' Toby padded over and got into the space Thea had made. 'This is lovely and warm,' he said, and fell asleep.

Thea, convinced that in the morning she would be convicted of child abuse, decided she would worry about it when it happened and joined Toby in slumber.

Molly arrived promptly at ten o'clock as arranged. Seeing Toby sitting at the kitchen table eating pancakes, she looked at Thea. 'I hope you haven't been spoiling him.'

'Not at all. Toby and I like cooking, that's all. And I think it's important for men to learn the skills as well as women.'

As Molly had got through life perfectly well without cooking anything which hadn't come from Marks and Spencer's she lost interest. 'Well, can we go through to the sitting room? There's something I want to say to you.'

Typical, thought Thea. Most people who came into her house had to be prised from the kitchen with a crowbar. Just for this moment, her kitchen was as clean and tidy as it ever was, and Molly wanted to go into the sitting room, which wasn't.

Molly had already refused coffee, so Thea lead the way somewhat glumly.

'Now Thea, sweetie, I know you're not going to like this, but I've had an idea.'

Thea cringed into her favourite armchair, fearing what the idea might be.

'I want to put money into the gallery. Just until you're on your feet. Then, if you want to pay me back you can. Otherwise I can look on it as an investment.'

This was what Thea had been fearing and now didn't know how to answer. She was genuinely fond of Molly, but did she really want to be beholden to her, financially, when they hadn't even managed a week's holiday together without getting snappy?

'Derek said you wouldn't want to do it, but he also said' – Molly paused – 'that I was to tell you, that you were to tell him if I was getting too bossy.' She paused again. 'I know I can be.'

Thea suddenly felt overcome with gratitude and warmth. She went across to Molly and sat beside her on the sofa. 'Oh, Molly, it's so sweet of you. I don't know what to say.'

'I partly want to do it' – she cleared her throat – 'because I've decided to stop going on Tiger Tours. That thing with Gerald, it was because I was bored, really. I realised that when you and Rory – I mean – you didn't have an affair with Rory, did you? Because you knew that you needed a project. I really admired that. Because Rory was – is – gorgeous. To turn down someone like that because there was something more important – it taught me . . .'

'Oh, Molly –'

'It taught me that that was what I needed, a project I mean.'

'But what about Derek?'

'Derek said, "Go for it." After all, you need the money and I've got it lying around in an account that's not paying much interest. Then Derek said it would keep me out of mischief and I suddenly worried that he'd found out about Gerald.'

'I'm sure he couldn't have done. There wasn't much to find out, was there?'

'No, but I could have made the most God-awful fool of

myself.' Molly shook her head slightly. 'I won't interfere, I promise.'

Thea didn't ask how, if Molly wasn't going to interfere, it was going to keep her out of mischief, because Molly not interfering was like anyone else doing without oxygen, just not possible. But she still didn't know what to say, or what to think. In some ways it was the answer to her problems. She could move into the gallery immediately and start getting it ready. But Molly? Not an ideal business partner for someone, let alone for anyone who was so bad at saying no.

'Let me have a few moments to think about it, Molly.'

'You could have longer than that. You don't have to tell me in a hurry.'

'Yes, I do, if I'm going to get this gallery open. Just give me a couple of secs. I'll go and put the kettle on.'

By the time the kettle had boiled, Thea had had a short conversation with Toby about how to cook pancakes without getting them thick as planks and had made coffee, she had made up her mind.

She brought a tray back into the sitting room and, having moved a pile of NMEs, found space for it on a small table. 'I accept your very kind offer, Molly. It's really sweet of you and I'm very grateful.'

'But? I know there's a but, so you might as well tell me what it is.'

'I am going to be firm with you. I'm going to practise being businesslike. After all, it was because I was too naïve and trusting that I' – Thea paused – 'that I decided that photojournalism wasn't for me. This time I'm going to tell it like it is and say no if I think you're wrong.'

'Well, of course.' Molly was pink. 'I never thought you'd accept. I thought I was just too domineering for you. Derek says I should go on a de-assertiveness course.'

Thea handed her friend a cup of coffee, getting a sudden insight into her marriage; Derek probably let Molly do

155

more or less what she wanted, but it was him to whom she turned when she needed help.

'I was thinking of going on a course in "how to say no", but I don't think we're either of us going to have time.'

'You mean you'll let me help?'

'Of course! I need you to help, Molly, just as long as you do what I want you to. It'll be my turn to be bossy.' Thea sipped her coffee to hide her amusement at this notion. She could no more boss Molly than Molly could go to bed without flossing her teeth or applying expensive cream, with light, upward strokes, into her neck.

They were a good team. Thea signed papers and Molly signed cheques, and between them they put the fear of God into all the official bodies they had to deal with before Thea was given two sets of keys to what would be the gallery. She gave one to Molly as they drank a celebratory cup of coffee and Thea ate a celebratory cream cake. 'You'll need these. I'm planning to organise the lodgers to come in and help me clean and decorate. I'll have to pay them, of course. I'm not sure if Petal will do it, though. Unlike the others, she doesn't need the money.'

'Get her to organise the others. The way to deal with bossy people', said Molly, looking directly at Thea, but not changing her expression, 'is to channel their bossiness. Derek told me that.'

Thea had never really got to know Derek. She tended to do things with Molly on her own. Now, she liked Derek better the more she learned about him and mentally filed him away as a source of advice.

Later, she rang Rory and told him the good news. He was worryingly ambivalent. 'Rory, you're not going to let me do all this gallery thing, borrow hundreds – no, thousands – of pounds from Molly, and then just send your stuff to the States anyway?'

'Now, would I do a thing like that?'

156

His charm was less potent down the phone, but still evident. 'I do hope not, Rory, or I might have to fire-bomb your studio or something,' said Thea mildly. 'No one cares about your work as much as I do, except perhaps Ben. I'm busting all my guts, everything, to give you a completely fabulous space to show it in. I can't have you backing out now.'

'Now don't you go getting your knickers in a twist.' Thea winced at her least favourite expression. 'I'll let you have the first showing of my work, provided you've got space for it all.'

A finger of anxiety touched Thea for a moment, but she dismissed it. When Rory saw the gallery he wouldn't want his work shown anywhere else.

Molly was quite right about Petal. Once she was convinced that it was the right and cool thing to do (helped in her decision by her new boyfriend who, unusually for Petal, was hard up) she galvanised the troops wonderfully, making those without Saturday jobs give up their free day to Thea.

Molly, who had yet to shrug off entirely her previous existence as a 'woman who lunched', was just going to drop an estate load, which amounted to four students, at the gallery. Thea's car was packed with an enormous sound system which Petal insisted was essential if any work was to be done, as many of her old clothes as she thought would cover the workers, mugs, coffee, a huge chocolate cake she had made in the night when she couldn't sleep and a case of beers she planned to keep hidden until after the work was done. She also took her vacuum cleaner and Petal.

'You get them into painting gear while I make friends with the builder's merchants round the corner, and get paint and ladders and stuff. I've opened an account there, so that'll mean I don't have to go every time and pay.

We're going to be rigid about coffee breaks and only have them when we've seen real progress.'

Petal gave her a 'get a life' look, rolling her eyes, her expression saying 'like any of that's ever going to happen'. Thea frowned, wondering if she *could* fit in an assertiveness course, after all. Having dumped Petal and the contents of her car on to the pavement, she watched her organise a chain gang through her rear-view mirror.

It took ages to buy the industrial-size tubs of paint, sugar soap, soft brooms, stiff brooms, rubber gloves and all the other myriad items she and the man who served her thought she'd need. All the while more items were added to the list, or she took another docket to another window so she could pay, she consoled herself with the thought that Petal would have been making them get on. They couldn't do a lot, she realised, but they could start pulling up the carpet. Derek had put his tool kit into Molly's car.

She had forgotten that they were mostly art students. First, they had had enormous fun dressing up in Thea's old clothes. Then they had put the music on loud enough to threaten the glass in the windows and pranced about, exclaiming over the wondrousness of the space. They had also found the chocolate cake, though not, thank goodness, the beer.

Thea turned off the music, realising that either Petal had let her down, or that she didn't have quite enough of Molly's genes. 'Right, you lot!' she shouted assertively. 'I'll start paying you from the time you start work. We need to get this carpet up. And if this room isn't clear of carpet, walls and floor washed by five o'clock, no one gets paid and no one gets a lift back to town. Petal?'

She hoped no one heard the note of pleading, which to her was only too clear.

Chapter Twelve

At half past four Molly arrived, elegant as usual, to see if there was anything she could do.

Thea would have fallen on her neck in gratitude if she hadn't been so filthy. 'Take this lot away,' she pleaded quietly, so 'this lot' wouldn't hear. 'They've been wonderful, but they can't agree what music to play, and there's nothing more they can do apart from painting and I don't want them doing that – they're art students.'

Molly's estate managed to fit in Petal and the sound system, as well as the four who had come in it originally. Thea watched them drive past the window, waving madly, with a sigh of relief. They were nice kids. Two of them lived with her, one of them was Petal's boyfriend and one, a girl, was attached to another of her lodgers, but Thea had had enough young company. She wanted to have the place to herself, some calm, to give herself a rough idea how long it would take to get it into some sort of order. She couldn't do that with drum'n'bass beating in her ears at full volume. She only liked drum'n'bass through a couple of closed doors. Then it was fine.

The carpet was gone. The floor beneath washed, but otherwise in a bad way. She would have to hire a sander to get through the layers of dirt and stain. Then it would need lots and lots of coats of varnish. She'd have to find something that was fairly quick-drying.

Downstairs, in the basement room, they discovered the carpet was glued down. Thea had stopped them pulling it up until she found out if the glue would come off easily.

She didn't want people sticking to the floor, after all. The corner where they tried this indicated that only laborious scrubbing with a paint scraper would remove it, and with the prospect of varnishing the floor upstairs for days on end ahead of her, she decided to think of a plan B for the basement floor.

Now she was on her own she prowled around, exploring her territory. It felt good. It was still spacious and light, lighter without the carpet, and to her surprise it already felt like her space and she was happy to be there on her own.

She went down to the kitchen to make a cup of tea with the kettle donated by Molly. While she was in the kitchen waiting for it to boil, she explored the cupboards and found a door she hadn't opened before. It was a little room, beyond the kitchen. There was a window in it, but it was too small to use as exhibition space. It was like a bedroom, really. Then she noticed the washbasin in the corner and realised it *was* a bedroom. Why it was there she couldn't tell, but it might come in very handy – if the worst came to the worst she could let her own room at home and live here.

Back in the kitchen, where there was a desk, she opened out the envelope of plans she had been given, marking clearly what she had rented at such vast expense. There, beyond the kitchen, was the little room. Thea decided to bring a sleeping bag and pillow next time she came. Cheltenham seemed far away at the end of a long day and there would be many, many long days, though now, even if she'd had the sleeping bag and pillow, the call of a bath would have lured her home.

At home she was annoyed, though not particularly surprised, to discover there was no hot water when she felt the tank. She met Petal coming out of the bathroom looking pink and shiny, and irritatingly clean. 'I can't believe you lot have managed to use every drop of hot water,' snapped Thea.

She was usually much more philosophical about such small disappointments and Petal was affronted. 'Oh, sorry. We didn't think. We were all tired, so we wanted baths.'

'So did I!'

This was so unlike the easygoing Thea that Petal tried to placate her. 'We borrowed a bottle of red wine from you. Would you like a glass?'

Thea sighed. Actually she yearned for one of Rory's tumblers of neat whiskey, but more than that she wanted to rid herself of the grime. 'Later, perhaps. Did you let the water out? Of your bath?'

'Er . . . no. I was just going to clean it now.'

Yeah, right, thought Thea. Petal was wearing a very skimpy top and a pair of tight black hipsters, and clutching a pile of dirty underwear. She did not look as if she were about to wield the foaming cleanser and a sponge. Besides, her hair was wet and Petal had strong priorities.

'Then I'll get in your water.'

Petal shuddered at the thought.

Thea sighed and to soothe Petal's horror said, 'Thank you for getting everyone to work so hard today. You all did brilliantly.'

Petal smiled. 'We're sending out for pizza. Shall we order you one?'

Thea nodded. 'That would be great.'

A few moments later she was lying in a lukewarm soup of orange scented bath ballistics, baby oil and several other strange unguents with which Petal liked to anoint her body. It wasn't perfect, but it was wet and warm, and would do until she could have a proper bath.

The phone rang just as she had finished slooshing herself and the now empty bath with clean water. 'I suppose I couldn't just stop having a telephone?' she asked herself rhetorically. 'Would the world really come to an end?'

No one replied to her and, shivering, she waited to see if the others would answer it before realising that they probably couldn't hear it over the music. Praying that it wasn't Molly wanting to discuss tactics or anyone else who might be long, she wrapped herself in a towel and pattered across to her bedroom.

It was Rory. 'I'm about ten miles from you. I'm calling from a phone box.'

'Oh!'

'Are you at home to visitors?'

'Of course.' For anyone else she'd have said no, but Rory was different. Besides, she could hardly not invite him in the circumstances.

Quickly Thea washed her ballistic-stiffened hair, pulled on clothes and rushed downstairs, pulling at her hair with her fingers as she did so, in lieu of blow-drying. 'Hey, Petal! Rory's coming. Give me a hand tidying up this lot.' She indicated the table, littered with beer cans and glasses.

'Rory! Cool! Sorry I won't be here to see him. You really should put some mousse or something on your hair or it'll go all funny. Oh, and by the way, the hairdryer's not working. It's in my room.'

Thea glared at the door that Petal closed behind her. Still, at least Rory wouldn't mind the mess and by the time he'd got lost a few times she would probably have plenty of time to clear up. Her hair would have to look after itself.

'Thea! You smell like a flower garden and look even more appetising.'

Thea put her arms round Rory and hugged him, her affection for him heightened by red wine on an empty and tired stomach. He smelt of turf fires and Sweet Afton tobacco. He reminded her of clear, light air and silver seas. 'You got lost.'

162

'Sure. Your directions were hopeless.'

'They were not! Now come in and let me get you a drink and some pizza. Can you stay for pizza? Bought in, I'm afraid, but quite edible. Do you want to stay the night?' Quite where she'd put him she didn't know, as it was unlikely a sofa in her bedroom would satisfy Rory, but she'd sort something out if necessary. Then she became aware that Rory wasn't following her into the house with his usual confidence.

'I've got something in the car to show you, bring you, really.'

'Paintings?' At least now she had space to store them, although how she'd get them across to the gallery in her little car she would have to find out.

'Not paintings. I'm having those shipped. They should be here in a day or two. Puppies. And Lara. I need you to look after them for me.'

Rory moved to the back of the Land Rover. There was Lara and in front of her was a box of puppies. 'Rory! They're tiny! Although they have grown like mad. How old are they?'

'Can't you remember? You were there.'

It felt like several lifetimes ago. 'They can't be much more than a month old – possibly less.' Her heart leapt as she saw that all six were there; the little runt had made it this far. 'What are you doing dragging them all over the countryside? Bring them in before they get cold.'

Lara jumped down. She pattered down the road, then squatted and produced a wee the size of a garden pond.

Rory ignored this. 'It's May, you know, hardly the middle of winter.' He picked up the box of puppies. 'I'm off to London tomorrow. I'm hoping you'll look after them for me.'

Little black and white faces appeared over the top of the box, looking plaintively at Thea, who was staring at Rory in confusion and horror. Then she shut her mouth and ushered the party inside. The street was no place for a custody battle. 'Bring them down into the kitchen where at least we can talk.'

Lara went ahead and soon settled herself in front of the Rayburn which, because of the huge hot-water demands of the household, was kept going summer and winter. She grinned happily up at Thea, unaware of how unwelcome she was.

'I'll put the pups down here next to Lara.'

'Rory, I can't look after the puppies. I've just started work on the gallery. And anyway, they're far too young to be moved.'

'I know, but Susan's gone away somewhere and there's nowhere else I can leave them. I have to go to London. Sure, you wouldn't have me let them starve to death?'

Thea pursed her lips as she poured him a glass of wine. 'I don't suppose I should give you this. I'd better make some coffee.'

He took the wine. 'Ah, don't be cross.' He grinned maddeningly. 'Although you do look lovely when you're angry.'

'Rory! Don't you know saying that sort of thing is likely to get you something unpleasant and messy tipped over your head?'

'I thought I might get away with it with you, Thea.'

Thea couldn't be cross any longer. She was too tired. 'Well, let's get Lara fed. Then we can think what to do about the pups. Are they on solid food yet?'

Rory shook his head. 'I've no idea. Susan's been doing them up to now.' He pulled out a chair and sat down. 'Have you any more wine?'

'When are you going to London?' asked Thea, having retrieved her secret bottle from behind the bleach.

'I'm planning to drive through the night. I can't cope with London traffic in daylight.

That at least solved the problem of where he was to

sleep. 'Well, don't drink any more alcohol. If you've got to drive to London.'

'Stop fussing, Thea, and sit down and let me look at you.'

When Lara was happily eating her supper out of the washing-up bowl, Thea sat and poured herself another glass of wine. 'So, why are you going to London? I thought you had an aversion to the place.'

Rory didn't answer, but poured more wine into his glass.

'I don't want to sound like someone's mother, but there are laws against drinking and driving, you know.' If he drank any more, she'd end up having to offer him a bed for the night, which would involve all sorts of complications.

'I promise you, drink doesn't affect my driving at all.'

'You mean, you swerve all over the road anyway?'

'I do not and you know it.'

'So why are you going to London, Rory?' His body language made her wonder if he was hiding something from her.

'To visit family. There's a whole lot of cousins and aunts and things I haven't seen for years. I want to catch up with them all.'

It sounded a perfectly valid explanation. No reason why she should suspect him of anything. There were members of her own family she hadn't seen for ages. So why wasn't she quite happy about it?

'Tell me', he said, 'how this gallery's going. What are the chances of it coming off? Sixty-forty? Or only evens.'

'What? Rory, how dare you!' She was laughing, but she was genuinely incensed by his lack of faith. 'Of course my gallery is going to come off. I have been through hoops getting the space, that's all. Which meant borrowing money from . . . someone.'

She realised just in time that if she mentioned Molly he

would assume it didn't matter if Molly was paid back, because she was rich. 'I've spent all day pulling up carpets, washing floors, doing everything I can to make it into the most wonderful art gallery in the south-west, and you suggest to me that it might not "come off"?'

Rory sighed. 'Jesus, Thea, you know how to give a fellow a hard time.'

'I am not giving you a hard time. I am telling it like it is. So I hope you haven't even the inkling of an idea about reneging on our deal.' She put on her most landlady-like expression and then smiled. 'It was your work that inspired me. Your work which made me want to do it.'

Rory got up from the table, pushed past the chairs and put his arms round Thea. His hug turned to a kiss, chaste enough at first, but then he opened her mouth with his and kissed her properly.

Thea found herself responding. He was a wonderful kisser, his arms were firm and comforting, and she was tired, a little drunk and still angry. It was nice to be held and kissed, even though it was the cause of her anger who was kissing her.

He pushed his hand up under her shirt, caressing the skin of her waist and back. 'Come to bed with me.'

Thea reconnected with reality. 'No. You're an artist. A bloody good one, but I don't want to sleep with you.' She tried to pull away, but he wouldn't let her. 'Have you no morals?'

'I left them in my other coat. You're so lovely, Thea, and I want you so much. Give me one night in your arms and I'll take the puppies back to Ireland and let my family go hang.' He was getting more and more urgent, his hands up and down her body, running his fingers round under the waistband of her jeans.

Thea pulled away more determinedly this time. 'Rory! Sit!'

Lara, who had been watching the antics of her master

with interest, obediently sat. Rory looked like he wasn't going to. 'I'm warning you.'

He sighed and sank back down into a chair. 'Come on, it's a good offer, isn't it? You said you hadn't time to look after the pups. Sleep with me and I'll take them away.'

Thea watched him. Something about this situation wasn't quite as it seemed. She didn't trust him further than she could throw him – he would almost certainly make love to her, possibly several times, and then get in his Land Rover and carry on to London, and she'd still be left with Lara and the pups. No, it wasn't him trying to take her to bed that bothered her. There was something about this London trip which didn't ring true.

She gave him a friendly smile. 'You go to London and meet up with all the rich aunties who might leave you money. But don't think I'm going to take over your animals for ever. I'll want you back in plenty of time for the private view.'

He frowned. 'Sure, I'm not much cop at private views. Think of what happened last time. The critics might trash my work all over again.'

'No, they won't.'

'How do you know?'

'I don't *know*, but I do believe. I think you're the best, the most exciting artist I've seen for a long time. And so does Ben,' she added quickly, before he could remember that she had probably seen very little new art lately. 'He thinks you're very special, special enough to make it worth me mortgaging my house to finance the gallery.'

'What do you mean? Jesus, you never did that, surely?'

Thea didn't want to deceive Rory and she had nothing but a faint instinct that anything was wrong, but she felt she must stress her conviction that his work was worth enormous sacrifices and that she was making them. The fact that she hadn't actually mortgaged her house was only a technical matter. 'He thinks your work is worth me

167

giving up my life for, so I can create a space worthy of it. And I can tell you that his opinion is very highly respected in the art world.'

Rory was looking a little uncomfortable, although that could have been the hard kitchen chair he was sitting on. 'You're a wonderful woman and I'm truly grateful for everything you've done for me.'

To Thea, this sounded like she was being written off, but she produced a suitably modest smile. 'You're the artist.'

He nodded. 'You wouldn't have those slides you took about you, would you?'

Thea shook her head, secretly gleeful. 'I'm awfully sorry, Molly's sent them away to have postcards made. It takes ages, you see.' The lies tripped off her tongue like broken beads – they were only half-lies, anyway. They were going to have some postcards done and they probably did take ages. In fact, she'd better put it on her 'to do' list.

'Oh. That's a bit of a blow.'

'Why? So you could show your work to your aunties? You should have asked me, I could have got you another set done.'

'How long would that take?'

Thea shrugged. 'Hard to say. How long will you be in London?'

'I was planning on staying a month.'

'A month? That's not that much less than you gave me to set up my gallery from scratch. It's too long for a holiday, Rory. You can stay a fortnight, at the most, or' – she scooped up a sleeping bundle of black and white fluff – 'the puppy gets it.'

He laughed. 'You're a hard woman, Thea. Did I ever tell you that?'

Lara lay in front of the Rayburn, taking up almost the entire width of the kitchen. She stared resignedly under the sink, her puppies sucking away happily. The little one was still far smaller than the others, but he sucked strongly now and seemed to move about just as much as the others did.

Thea felt so tired she could have lain down on the kitchen floor next to Lara and gone to sleep. She decided that the puppies were doing well enough with their mother for now. If they needed solid food, they could wait until the morning. Lara had a bucket of water by her and was now lying on an old duvet instead of just the stone flags, and seemed content, although her master had abandoned her. She was like a child who had got used to being dumped in strange places. She just settled down and got on with things, rather as Toby had done.

Thea turned at the kitchen door and decided she'd better write a note for the lodgers, otherwise they might have funny turns when they saw Lara and the pups. And they'd definitely make enough noise to wake them up. Having done this, she toiled back up the stairs, thinking about Ben. Now if he had been making extravagant promises in exchange for a night in her arms, how would she have reacted? It was a little lowering to reflect that he wouldn't have to offer her anything, apart from the night in his arms. And she didn't know him as well as she knew Rory.

Just before she went to sleep, Thea realised that Rory had gone and not left her an address in London. 'I'm sure it'll be fine,' she murmured into her pillow. 'He's probably just visiting his aunties.'

Thea got up very early the following morning. The puppies all bumbled around while Thea showed Lara the tiny garden which was up a flight of rather narrow stone steps. Lara negotiated them easily, squatted and then made Thea send Rory messages of rage. How could he have left her with Lara and the pups when the dog did turds which wouldn't have shamed an elephant? She lived in a town, for goodness' sake! Pursing her lips and trying not to breathe through her nose, Thea rummaged in the garden shed and found a shovel. By the time she had dealt with Lara's offering she was seriously considering ringing the RSPCA. Lara and her pups would look lovely on *Pet Rescue*. When she'd washed her hands and gone back into the kitchen to give Lara her breakfast, she'd changed her mind. The pups moved slowly about like those giant blow-up puppets of sumo wrestlers, only in miniature.

The pet shop opened early. She bought a book and realised she'd have to look after the pups herself, even if she had to take them backwards and forwards to the gallery with her in the car.

The book told her that pups of three weeks should be started on solid food. Well, it was already too late for that. They should be fed in separate bowls to make sure they all got equal shares and they would need at least three meals a day. They would also have to be helped to eat. Thea saw herself spoon-feeding each pup, saying 'one for mummy' and playing aeroplanes. It would take hours out of her already completely full days. She put a jug of milk in the microwave, having not bought a proprietary puppy milk, hoping it wouldn't give them the threatened diarrhoea.

'If I'd wanted to become a dog breeder,' she growled to the absent Rory, when she'd finally got the cornflakes (all the cereal she had in the cupboard) to the right temperature, 'I wouldn't have chosen to do it while I was opening an art gallery. I'd have done it when I had absolutely nothing to do with my life except lie on my stomach and dabble my fingers in warm breakfast cereal.'

This sarcasm followed the many other curses she had sent to him over the ether. She cursed as she bought boxes of Weetabix and tins of puppy food, a proper water bowl and a set of new cereal bowls. Only at the last minute did she relent and let the lodgers have the new bowls, and use the old ones for the pups.

The lodgers were mostly delighted with Lara and the pups, even though it was only Thea who would clear up after her in the garden. Molly was very ambivalent. When Thea explained that she would have to take Lara and the pups to the gallery, if there was no one at home to give Lara her huge meals and the pups their little ones, she bit her lip. 'It's not that I don't love Lara' – she patted the huge head with some distaste – 'but an art gallery is no place for animals.'

'Tell me something I don't know,' Thea snapped, and then smiled to neutralise her irritation. 'But what can I do? Besides, if I did ever feel like sleeping over at the gallery, Lara would be company.'

Molly didn't approve of the notion of Thea sleeping at the gallery and so far the lure of hot water had always prevented Thea from doing it. But she could see that the drive home after a long day would seem like a dreadful slog, particularly in Thea's little car.

'I suppose so. And the pups are rather sweet.' One of them was chewing ineffectually at the toe of Molly's shoe.

Would she think they were sweet when those little baby teeth were big enough to do any damage to the Charles Jourdans? Thea wondered. 'The lodgers are very good at taking Lara round the park,' she said. 'Pete in particular. Although of course I can't persuade them to clean up after her, so I have to walk her first.'

'Clean up after . . . ? Oh, my God!'

'I shall leave them at home tomorrow, because I want to sand the floor and the noise will be dreadful, and Pete will be in to feed them.'

Molly, who had felt uncomfortably out of control when the talk had been of puppies and dog poo, swung into managerial mode: 'Thea, you cannot do that yourself. You must get someone to do it for you. It'll take you ages. I absolutely insist!'

'But I've booked the sander, now.' Thea actually hadn't been looking forward to being dragged about behind a large and noisy machine, but she was intent on doing everything the very cheapest way possible, which meant doing everything herself.

'Then leave it to me. I'll get someone to do it.'

'But Molly, we'll have to pay them. I'll do it for nothing.'

'Thea, I've told you, I'm happy to finance the gallery. Derek's happy. We've allocated an amount and you haven't even spent a third of it yet. Save your energy and your talent for things that only you can do. I've chased the shippers, by the way. The paintings should arrive the day after tomorrow. You can think about where to store them.'

Thea heaved a larger sigh than usual. Sometimes it was nice to be bullied. 'Most of them should fit in the little bedroom at the gallery and the rest can go in the passage.'

'Good,' said Molly. 'Then you can't sleep there.'

Chapter Thirteen

❦

The floor had been sanded and the pictures had arrived (after at least a dozen enquiries as to their whereabouts) but the floor still had to be varnished and Thea wouldn't allow anyone else to do it. She had not been pleased with the quality of the sanding done by Molly's 'little man' and what she'd said to Molly was, 'I'm damned if I'll pay anyone else to do the job badly when I can do it badly myself for nothing.'

She'd tracked down some quick-drying water-based varnish, which wouldn't poison her with fumes, and she planned to spend all evening and on into the night if necessary, putting on coat after coat until the floor would shrug off a diamond cutter, let alone the scuffing of hundreds of pairs of feet.

She had brought Lara and the pups with her, as there was no one at home to look after them. It was the first time, because until now someone had always been able to feed them and change the newspapers.

Thea had also brought a sleeping bag and pillow to the gallery, in case she felt too tired to drive back. With Lara and the puppies for protection, a radio for company and a little stash of goodies for comfort, she felt equipped for a marathon of varnishing.

Molly had offered to do it with her, declaring that she didn't mind getting her hands dirty. But as Thea knew this wasn't true and that the offer was made out of duty rather than a desire to get a repetitive-stress injury, she refused. Molly was proving a boon. Her bullying nature – or 'managerial qualities' as Thea now referred to them for diplomatic reasons – had come in very useful when it came to persuading magazines to accept their advertisements after their deadline, for wheedling important names and addresses out of people who couldn't usually be wheedled, and for giving the electrician hell when Thea was too nice to him. She was brazen about contacting people for publicity and persuaded several large local companies to sponsor the brochure in exchange for a very insignificant entry on the back page. So far, she and Thea hadn't fallen out and it was Molly who asked Thea what she intended to do or show 'after Rory'.

Up to now, Thea hadn't thought about 'after Rory'. Getting the gallery ready and his work into it was all she'd focused on. But Molly was quite right. Rory was only the beginning and she still had uncomfortable feelings about his commitment to the gallery. He'd rung her late one night, from a pub, and given her half an address, but he didn't sound like he was planning to come back any time soon.

'You need a theme, darling,' Molly had said, tentatively stroking Lara who had come upstairs into Thea's sitting room for some time away from her children. ' "Seascapes and sunsets", something like that.'

Thea mentally reached for her sick bucket, but took the point.

'Then you put in a call for work and people send you slides. The girl at the magazine was awfully helpful when I explained I – er – we were opening a new gallery. Students are always desperate for somewhere to show their work, she said, but we must be careful about quality and make sure we don't have anything too weird or it won't sell. I think we want some nice watercolours. People always like those.'

Thea picked a spot of white paint off her trousers. This was crunch time. This was when she had to explain to

Molly that her vision of what the gallery should do was quite different from what Molly obviously had in mind. 'Actually, Molly, I do want to show weird stuff, even if it doesn't sell.'

'But Thea! How on earth will we make any money if we can't sell the work?'

'We'll charge a fee for showing. Then we can show what we like – what I like. Otherwise we'll be just another art gallery selling Cotswold views. I don't want that.'

'But Thea . . . !'

'Molly, you very kindly lent me the money to open. I'm hoping that Rory's stuff will sell so well and so expensively that we'll get a huge amount in commission. If we do, I'll pay as much back to you as possible. If not, when I can arrange a mortgage' – she should have said, 'when I can persuade someone to give me a mortgage' – 'I'll pay you back. You've been wonderful, Molly. I've really enjoyed working with you. But if we want different things for the gallery we'll have to part.'

Molly absorbed this. She too had really enjoyed being involved. Before her marriage she had worked as a secretary to quite an important businessman when she really ought to have been in business herself. She left her job when she got married and since then her organisational skills had been confined to her husband and her committees. And her desire for adventure had been confined by the limits of Tiger Tours. Since she'd been involved in getting the gallery open, she had really felt fulfilled for the first time in her life. Her problem was going to be the awful rubbish that Thea might consider 'Art'.

'Very well,' she said at last. 'It's your gallery, after all. You can put what you want into it, but only if the people who exhibit pay a proper amount *and* we charge commission. Otherwise you'll never make more than enough just to cover your overheads. I've done some costings.'

Thea laughed. 'I'm so glad I've got you, Molly. I'd be hopeless on my own.' She had learnt a little about manipulation recently.

She had taken a glass of water upstairs and drank it, examining the task before her. It was impossibly hot. The first week in June had decided to live up to it's name and be 'flaming', purloin all the summer's heat for itself and discharge it that late afternoon when Thea was planning to work. She had opened the louvred windows in the one pane of glass which had in it anything you could open and she cursed herself for not getting the ventilators working. She had to be content with propping the street door open. At least the varnish was non-toxic.

When she'd given the pups and Lara a meal, and taken Lara to some waste ground for a sniff around, she stripped down to her bra, pants and old painting shirt, which just about covered her pants, and set to work with the roller.

She put Van Morrison on loudly and was well into the rhythm of both the music and her work when she straightened up to ease her back and noticed a section of ceiling which hadn't been painted.

She swore for a few seconds before deciding it would be better to paint it now than to depend on remembering to do it later. She didn't want to discover it unpainted when it came to hanging the pictures and if the floor wasn't absolutely hard, the ladder could scrape the surface horribly. With Rory's work being so enormous, she couldn't rely on people not looking up that high. Someone had advised Molly to buy a ladder which Thea didn't like very much, but according to Molly's adviser it was the most versatile system, which could be long or short, with or without a platform, in fact, could do everything except apply the paint.

Now, she set it up very carefully, working out which bit hooked over which other bit. It seemed to take for ever to assemble and she yearned for a straightforward pair of steps. Eventually it appeared to hold together and, gingerly, she climbed up it, her pot of paint over her arm, her paintbrush stuck down her cleavage. She couldn't run an art gallery if she was going to be pathetic about ladders. She had to be grown-up about it.

When she reached the top she realised that the wretched ladder wasn't quite near enough. She didn't like the fact that there was nothing to support her above her knees, and if she got down, moved the ladder and climbed up again, the whole grisly process would just go on longer. She knew it was silly, but she decided to get some paint on her brush, hang on for dear life and lean. With her painting arm outstretched, it might just reach.

She dug her brush into the almost solid paint. The pot was heavy and when she'd loaded her brush, she hung it on the ladder. Then, very carefully, holding on tight with one hand she leaned over the front, aiming at the bit of ceiling with her brush, praying her arm would extend far enough.

It did, just about. It wasn't the most perfectly painted bit of cornice, but no one would notice a few brush marks up there. She needed a dab more paint to finish the job. Her brush was just making a pleasing sucking sound as she dug it into the paint, when she heard a noise behind her. Startled, she jerked round and at the same moment that she saw Ben, she felt her ladder slip and begin to topple.

There wasn't time for her whole life to pass before her, but she did manage to wonder if she could jump free of the falling ladder, what on earth Ben was doing there and if she'd ever get the paint off the floor. One foot hit the floor first, sending a stab of pain to her ankle, then Ben caught her and she swayed downwards, unable to save herself. Her weight and the angle at which he caught her knocked him off balance and they landed on the floor together, breathless, she on one of his arms, the rest of him more or less on top of her.

For a moment neither of them moved or spoke. 'It's all right. Don't try to get up; just lie still and get your breath back. Thank God I managed to break your fall.'

Thea lay back. She felt strangely calm, considering that a moment ago she'd been confronting broken limbs or worse. She felt as if the elastic had gone in her arms and legs; they felt heavy and relaxed, as if she were in bed after a long night's sleep. Even the pain in her ankle subsided to a dull throb. Then she became aware that her shirt was halfway up her back and that Ben had moved off her a little. Also, that his hand was on her bare waist.

Questions flitted irrelevantly through her mind; when did she last wax her legs? Was there paint all over the floor? What sort of knickers had she put on that morning? Praying it wasn't one of the older pairs, she wondered why on earth Ben didn't get up. Was there some sort of medical reason why he should stay lying down too? Predominately, she acknowledged, she didn't want him to get up. She liked lying under him, half naked, with this strange feeling of lassitude making it impossible to do anything except stay there. Normally by now she would have jumped to her feet, frantically apologising, and started to mop up the floor.

'I must be squashing you to death,' he said, not moving.

Thea's brain was still on super-speed. She had time to realise that if he got up she might never get this close to him again. On the other hand her ankle hurt and she should really find out if she'd broken anything before even considering following up on this opportunity. 'Not really. I wonder if you could just have a feel of my ankle. It hurt as I fell. It's probably fine, but I'm a bit of a coward and I'd rather you checked if it was broken before I look. If I see it out of kilter I might be sick and this floor has suffered enough.' By now she could see paint, looking like yoghurt, splattered across the newly sanded wood. She had a horrible feeling she was lying with her head in it, too.

'I should get you up and have a proper look.'

'Just do a quick reccie. I'm afraid I'm one of those people who have to put the plaster on before I look at the cut.'

His hand on her leg and ankle didn't recoil from broken bone. In fact, it appeared to be telling her there wasn't much wrong at all, as it glided smoothly up and down. The feel of his warm palm on her leg was comforting, extremely pleasant.

It obviously didn't have the same effect on him. Here she was, practically naked, giving him the perfect excuse to get his hand above her knee and he hadn't done it. What could you do with a man like that? Just as well, she told herself, she hadn't fallen off the ladder and hurt her ankle on purpose, to get herself in this position.

'I don't think anything's broken, you've probably wrenched it,' he said. 'I'll get up so I can help you up.'

A whimper escaped from her.

'What's the matter? Have I hurt you?'

'No,' she breathed, looking into his eyes, wondering if he would ever get the message and kiss her. A lot of men would be smoking the post-coital cigarette by now. He was aware of her lying under him, he must be, and he hadn't got up himself either, but why hadn't he done anything else?

He sighed deeply and the corner of his mouth lifted in the beginnings of a smile. Thea closed her eyes, waiting – hoping – to feel his lips on hers, knowing she'd die of embarrassment if she didn't. She'd practically asked him to kiss her.

His lips brushed hers so gently that it was almost a tease. Then he applied just enough pressure for it to qualify as a kiss but no more. It dawned on Thea that he was kissing her out of politeness, to save her the embar-

179

rassment of lying underneath him, offered but unwanted. He took his mouth away maddeningly soon.

He could have saved himself the trouble. She doubted if she could have felt more hurt and rejected if he'd just said 'thanks but no thanks' and left it at that. She lay still, her eyes tight shut, hoping she wouldn't cry.

'I think we should get up. There's paint all over the floor. It's in your hair and everything.'

Just for that moment she didn't care about the paint, the floor or even the gallery. Because she'd realised that she'd fallen in love with Ben – at pretty much the same time that she discovered he didn't want her and had made it abundantly clear. She had him actually in her arms and she couldn't get him to do more than kiss her out of kindness. It was humiliating and heartbreaking. How could she bring herself to look at him again? She bet Petal never had this trouble – in fact, Petal's troubles were probably all the other way.

She allowed him to help her up, not looking at him, with her eyes closed, but as she stood upright she was aware that her ankle really did hurt. She squeezed her eyes tighter shut. Pain was a perfect excuse for a few tears, but she couldn't let herself shed them. Gingerly she put her foot to the floor, still clinging on to Ben. She bit her lip and inhaled sharply. 'Ow.' She wanted to say a lot more a lot stronger.

'Can you stand on it?'

'Probably.' She tried a little tentative weight-bearing. It was agony. 'Ow' no longer covered it. After a lot of inward breaths she said, 'Hurts like hell.'

'Do you think we should get you to casualty?'

'No!' Horror made it easy for her to look at him. 'I've got a floor to varnish, not to mention get the paint off from. I can't spend hours and hours in A and E reading old copies of the *Radio Times*. It's nothing to make a fuss about. It'll be right as rain in the morning. All it needs is a cold compress and a bit of a bandage.'

'Which you have in your first aid kit?'

'There's no need to be sarcastic. We can make a bandage out of some rags or something. Haven't you got any initiative?' He accepted her anger with irritating calm as if he knew the real reason for it. 'There's a dust sheet next door.'

Ben nodded. Then he bent and picked her up.

She was reluctantly impressed. She was a healthy woman and was probably heavy to lift, but he not only got her up into his arms, but carried her through to the next room. There, where there was a chair, he sat her gently down. Then he tore off the end of an old sheet Thea had been using to protect the floor and went to wet it.

He came back and lifted her foot. He was very gentle and she was reminded of the way he had handled the puppies when they were born. He probably saw her in much the same light: something which needed caring for and looking after, but nothing beyond.

'I wish I'd protected the floor next door,' she said, to give him a reason for her extravagant sigh, and to distract herself from the feel of his fingers on her foot and ankle. She had very sensitive feet and although her ankle hurt like mad, even the pain had a strangely erotic effect. It was no good having those sorts of feelings for a man who didn't want you. A tear got past her guard and trickled down her cheek.

She felt Ben stiffen, opened her eyes and saw that he too was angry now. 'I wish you'd just moved the ladder. How can you have been so stupid as to lean out from a ladder like that? It's incredibly dangerous. You should have known better. If I hadn't caught you, you could have been seriously injured. As it is, you've got what might be a badly sprained ankle.'

He sounded horribly paternal and, although he probably couldn't help it, she wasn't prepared to be treated like a naughty child by a man who'd just hurt her far more than any number of sprained ankles could have done. 'It's easy to be wise after the event, isn't it, and you've no right to talk to me like that.'

'If I think you've been incredibly stupid and careless I'm not going to hold back on the matter. Have you no common sense? Don't you know that people *die* falling off ladders? And here you were, all on your own, risking your life. You could have lain there for hours, unable to get help. I don't suppose the phone's connected, is it?'

It wasn't and her mobile was downstairs with her hand-bag. 'Oh, bollocks!' she said, hoping the word would offend him. 'What an overreaction. I probably wouldn't have fallen off the bloody thing if you hadn't come in and startled me.'

'Don't go blaming me for this. That ladder had started to go before I came into the room – otherwise I'd have caught you before your ankle hit the floor. God! If only it hadn't taken me so long to find somewhere to park.'

Thea suddenly remembered saying that you didn't get angry with people you didn't care about. And even if he didn't fancy her, he must be concerned for her welfare. She felt ashamed. He had tried to save her, he was now feeling the bones round her ankle very gently, she had no reason to shout at him. But she was not ready to forgive him entirely – her pride and her feelings hurt more than her damn ankle did, which was saying something. She hoped there was a special place in hell for men who refused the advances of nice girls, but still she summoned up some chilly dignity. 'I meant the compress and the bandage to be separate.'

'This'll do both jobs until we can get you home to a packet of frozen peas. Now,' he said, when he had finished binding her ankle with wet rags, 'where are the rest of your clothes so I can drive you home? You won't be able to drive yourself for a bit.'

There was an anxious silence while Thea realised what

he was saying, that she might not be able to drive, and she absolutely depended on being able to get to and from home at the moment. What with Lara and the puppies she'd never manage on public transport. Please God he was wrong. 'I'm not planning to go home, not tonight,' she told him, trying not to panic. 'I've planned to stay the night here, putting on coats of varnish whenever one dries, sleeping in between. I've got to get this floor done.'

'If you were varnishing the floor, what were you doing up a ladder with a pot of paint?'

'There was a bit of ceiling that got missed. I just thought I'd do it before I got to that bit of floor.' She summoned a carefree smile from somewhere. 'At least my hurt leg won't stop me varnishing,' she added brightly, if a little brittly.

He opened his mouth to say all sorts of sensible things, but fortunately had the good sense not to. Instead, he said, 'Then I'd better help you.'

She bit back a curt refusal: if she let her temper and her hurt pride get the better of her he might guess why, a woman spurned and all that. On the other hand he might just think it was hurting her ankle and spilling paint on the floor that was making her so touchy. 'You don't have to. I expect you've got somewhere else to go.'

He shook his head. 'No. I came to see you. I wanted to see how things were going.'

'But you didn't come all the way down from London just to chat?' She didn't let her heart flutter at the thought, although it wanted to.

'Not quite. I was in Bristol, having yet another interview, and I thought I'd catch up with you on the way home.'

Thea wasn't good at geography, but she was fairly sure that there were more direct ways back to London from Bristol than going via Stroud. He was probably planning to visit Molly, too. 'Where's Toby?'

'Staying with a friend. The friend he would usually have stayed with when I had to leave him with Molly.'

'Oh.'

'Thank you for looking after him that time. I heard all about you making pizzas and chocolate cake.'

'We had fun together. I really like Toby.'

A shadow of something, which might have been sadness or anger, flitted across his features.

Thea despaired. There was no pleasing the man. She couldn't even say she liked his son without some invisible code being violated. 'We'd better get on with this floor, then,' she said. 'I'll get started clearing up the paint. There are more rollers and things downstairs. Although you don't have to help if you don't want to. I'll manage.'

His eyebrow, raised infinitesimally, expressed his doubt. 'You said I could help – when I said I couldn't let you be without what little I can do.'

Thea looked away. She didn't want to think about that conversation, ever.

'And right at the beginning you were very clear about help including painting and decorating. You can't reject my offer now.'

She forced a laugh, ignoring the offer he had rejected. They would spend the rest of the evening and all night being offended and giving offence if they weren't careful 'Let's get to it then. By the way . . .'

It was too late. Before she could warn him, he had gone downstairs and she heard by his exclamations that he had met Lara and her puppies. Judging by the noises, Lara was very pleased to see him.

He came up a few minutes later carrying a roller and a couple of brushes. 'What the hell is Lara doing there?'

'Rory left them with me. He's gone to London, to catch up on family, he said.' She frowned slightly, still worried about it.

Ben looked intently at her. 'Bloody inconsiderate, seeing

how hard you're working to get a good space for him.' He frowned. 'Molly told me you're thinking about what to show after Rory. It'll be nearly time for the degree shows. You should scour the colleges for promising young talent. Have a graduate show.'

Most of the time Thea managed to avoid the reality, which was that she didn't know much about art; she'd had no formal training apart from what she'd learnt as a photographer and her exposure to modern art had been minimal. Now, her ankle was hurting, she was tired, Ben didn't want her and she might never get the bloody floor varnished. This whole art gallery thing was a crazy idea. 'Would I know promising young talent if it got up and bit me?' Her question sounded horribly plaintive, but she couldn't unask it.

'You recognised how good Rory's work was. I'll come with you. You pick who you like and I'll tell you if they've got talent or not.'

'You'd never have time to do all that.'

'I would if I get this job in Bristol. I'll be working from home quite a lot of the time, so I can be with Toby more, and I'll have far more autonomy.'

Thea allowed herself a sigh. It was still stinking hot.

'What's the matter?'

Thea bit her lip. 'Probably nothing. I've just got a funny feeling about this trip of Rory's to London. I'm worried he might back out. I didn't let him have the slides or anything, so he's got nothing to show – only his charm to work with.' She sighed again. 'But that's not inconsiderable.'

There was the subtle change of expression again; something she'd said was wrong. 'I think you're wise not to trust him completely. Which is why it's important to have a plan B.'

'Oh, fuck it!' she said. 'I can't think about all that now. Let's get to work. Put the music on and if you don't like my choice you can go home.'

At least the paint, being non-drip, hadn't spread too far, but the freshly sanded wood was thirsty and sucked it up. Thea had to scrub with sandpaper for ages to get the worst off and even then she suspected the shadow of her accident would remain on the floor for ever.

She was very aware, as she sanded, that Ben could well be looking at her bottom. Her shirt was long and she'd pulled it down as far as it would go, but she was aware that her by now filthy Sloggis, and certainly her thighs, would be on view for those who wished to see.

She had debated putting her jeans back on, but they were a bit tight and the weather was so hot that bare legs gave her much more flexibility of movement. Besides, if she put on her jeans now, it would make some kind of statement, implying she wasn't decently dressed before. She hadn't been, of course, but it was too late to worry about that now.

He had started applying the varnish with a roller. Thea had been worried about him getting his clothes dirty and had offered him one of the communal boiler suits. He had rejected them all as too small and, while she protested, she realised that she mustn't sound motherly and irritating.

She thought of the paternal nature of his anger to her when he thought she'd been foolhardy. He had been very cross, far more cross than the situation warranted. The thought gave her a little breath of hope.

Chapter Fourteen

❦

Thea managed to work well enough with her bad leg, although instead of standing and using a roller, she found it easier to stay on hands and knees and apply the varnish with a brush. By keeping on the opposite side of the room from Ben, she stopped herself worrying about her rear end and his attitude to it. The music kept them at it and they finished the first coat quite quickly.

'You can still see where the paint was, though,' said Thea sadly. 'Should I get the electric sander back in, do you think?'

'No – a few more coats and that patch will disappear into the rest of it.'

'It was a silly thing to do. Now,' she went on brightly, because she didn't want Ben to start telling her off again, and hiding her fatigue and the sense of anticlimax, 'shall we get a takeaway or do you want to go? You've worked very hard. You deserve something to eat.' Too late she realised she was talking to Ben in the same way she talked to her student lodgers: ever so slightly patronisingly.

His glanced flickered over her, not noticing her manner. 'I'll get the takeaway, seeing as you're not dressed. What would you like?'

'Whatever you can find, but you really don't have to stay. I can carry on on my own.'

'How will you get home? You're surely not really going to stay here all night?'

'I must. I've got to get that floor done and when I have, there are still two more rooms to prepare and that's not counting downstairs, where Lara is. I'm going to need every inch of space. I've got Rory's paintings but I'm still waiting for his drawings and sketches to come over from Ireland. The opening's less than six weeks away.'

She hadn't actually voiced her anxieties out loud before. She smiled, trying to pretend she had been joking. 'Actually, while you're here, you couldn't just take Lara out for me, could you? There's a bit of waste ground by the station.'

He stood looking down at her, where she sat on her chair, resting her ankle. She didn't look directly at him, but she was aware of his expression: exasperated, irritated and still a little angry. Eventually, he spoke. 'OK, fine. Have you got a lead?'

She nodded. 'And about a mile of kitchen towel in case she does anything.' *Do not explain about having to clear up after her*, she ordered herself. *He's a grown-up with experience of animals. He'll know that.*

'Right. While I'm gone, think about what you want to eat, but don't get up. Or you won't be able to drive tomorrow either.'

Thea smiled blankly, trying not to worry that in fact, now she was here, she might never get to leave the gallery. Thank goodness Molly had made her buy a mobile phone.

While he was away, she limped to the loo and bravely looked in the mirror. Her hair was curling wildly all over the place, but she knew that if she brushed it, it would either frizz completely or go flat. She pulled at it with her fingers, washed her face in cold water, then had to put Molly's hand cream on it, because it felt so tight. She had no make-up with her, nor any scent, and she was wearing painting clothes. 'Give up, girlfriend,' she told her bedraggled reflection. 'He didn't want you when you were practically lying on a doily underneath him. He certainly won't want you now.'

This reality confronted, she limped downstairs to feed

the puppies. Their little snuffling faces and scrabbling paws were incredibly endearing. It was nice to feel loved, even by things so small and young that didn't know any better.

After she had mashed their food and they had hoovered it up, she sat on the floor cuddling them. Who needed a man when she could have a puppy? She picked up Little Chap, the tiniest, and had a head-to-head conversation with him. After he had assured her that he was not going to die and was actually putting on weight, even if at a far slower rate than his chums, she lay down flat and let all the puppies clamber over her.

She was still lying there when Ben came back from taking Lara out. 'How did you get down here? I thought I told you to rest?'

The puppy therapy had soothed her prickles and she felt much more relaxed. She smiled up at him. 'I am resting. I'm just not alone. Oh! Don't do that, little one.' Her ear, which had been gently nuzzled, suddenly received an investigative nip. 'I had to feed them,' she explained to Ben. 'Or they'd have eaten me.'

'I could have fed them for you.'

'Yes, but you wouldn't have brought them all upstairs for me to cuddle. Isn't Little Chap adorable?'

'I'm glad Toby didn't see them. Or he'd nag me about that, too.'

Thea decided not to follow this up, since it would be bound to get her into trouble. 'What takeaway did you decide you wanted? My bag's in the kitchen. Take some money before you go.'

'I think I can afford to buy some fish and chips without contributions from you.'

'Oh, come on! You've been working so hard for me all evening, it's only fair that I pay for supper. It's your wages, after all.'

Thea tried to get up. It wasn't easy. After she'd got

herself free of puppies she struggled to her knees, but unfortunately she was too far away from the wall to go the rest of the way and had to accept a hand from Ben.

'I don't want wages.'

Thea didn't think she could offer him payment in kind in her present state of unloveliness so she gave up. 'Oh, well then, ask them if they do deep-fried Mars Bars, will you? I'll have one of them as well.'

He brought fish and chips and cold lagers.

'Didn't they do Mars Bars, then?' She'd never actually eaten a deep-fried Mars Bar and thought they sounded disgusting, but she couldn't resist winding him up.

'They did, but I decided you shouldn't have one.'

She was indignant. 'How dare you make decisions for me! I'm not a child.'

'He who pays the piper calls the tune,' he said and Thea realised she was being wound up in her turn. She decided it was probably a good sign that he felt he could tease her. She cuddled a puppy, pretending to pout. 'We'll never get to eat these if we stay down here.' Gently, he removed a pup who had decided the smell of salt and vinegar was irresistible. 'Can you go back upstairs again, or do you want me to carry you?'

'I'm not risking you suing me when you put your back out. I can crawl back up just fine, thank you.'

'Oh, good,' he said. 'Can I watch? I've got rather fond of the sight of your bottom.'

She found herself blushing. There was definite sexual innuendo in that remark. She contemplated telling him that if he were a gentleman he wouldn't look, but decided it might lead to all sorts of places she might not want to go. 'You take the fish and chips. I'll follow.'

'Are you sure? If I came behind, I could always give you a push if you needed one.'

'I'll give you a push if you're not careful,' she muttered.

It was more of a haul than a crawl, but at least he was well ahead of her. She wished she'd put on her jeans, until she got upstairs and realised how hot it was. It had been blissfully cool in the basement, but now the full heat of the summer night hit her. 'God, it's hot up here,' she said, collapsing back into her chair.

'But it's a dry heat. The varnish should go off quickly. Now, what do you want? Cod or plaice? I brought the salt and vinegar separately as I didn't know what you liked.'

'Give me a cold can and whatever's nearest.' She opened the can and took a long cool draught. 'That is so good! I feel like an advertisement for the stuff.'

'I felt the floor while you were coming upstairs. It's nearly dry. It'll be ready for another coat by the time we've eaten.'

'Oh, good. I'm aiming for about five coats eventually.' She ate a bit of fish and suddenly found she was hungry.

'And you were going to work all through the night?'

'I find it quite difficult to sleep in this heat anyway,' she said with her mouth full, 'and what with lying on quite a hard floor with only a sleeping bag, I didn't really think I'd do more than doze. I'd just listen to the World Service and lie there, picking my teeth. You're not eating. Was it something I said?'

He smiled and shook his head. 'Too hot.'

'What, the weather, or the chips?'

He ignored her question. 'You're very committed to this gallery, aren't you?'

She nodded. 'It's the first time in years I've really felt I'm doing the right thing. I mean, I loved doing the artistic side of the photography, but I was hopeless at the hard-nosed journalist bit. And even when I did it, it wasn't totally satisfying artistically. With this I feel I can really have fun.' She sighed. 'I just hope Rory doesn't pull out.'

'He might.'

'I know and he'd be perfectly entitled to. At the moment

I'm relying on him still hating the London art scene enough to stick with me.' She bit her lip and gave a little smile. 'Fingers crossed.'

'How would you feel if he did abscond, after all the work you've put in?'

'Terrible, but as it was me who wanted to do it, I can't really blame him. Which is why Molly and I've decided not to put all our eggs in Rory's basket.' She took another thirst-quenching sip. 'At first, he was the reason I wanted to open a gallery, but now I've started doing all this I've realised what a waste it would be. Even if I could pay Molly back on what I earn from Rory, we can't just stop there.'

'So how is Molly involved?' He was frowning. Did he disapprove of his second cousin once removed, or whoever she was, putting her money into a hair-brained scheme?

'I couldn't get a mortgage in time to pay the deposit and things, so she's lent me the money. But she's also a sort of partner, because she's doing all sorts of admin. She's brilliant at it.'

'You don't find her too domineering?'

Thea shook her head. 'Derek told me – via her, actually – to channel her energies. It works a treat. I did think we might fall out over what work we show. I think she wanted Cotswold views and wild flower watercolours. When she realised that I didn't and either she had to let me have artistic control or give up the gallery, she gave in.'

'It wouldn't have been a good idea to mortgage your house for something so uncertain.'

'Well, thank you for your confidence! Actually, I think I might sell it eventually, when I've got time to think about it.'

He frowned harder. 'But what about your lodgers? At least they're assured income.'

'You're such a pessimist. I could buy a house here, with

a garden, and have a couple of lodgers if I wanted. At least I wouldn't be traipsing across country to go home each night. And I'd have money over. Property is cheaper here. I should be able to manage to buy a nice little cottage with a garden and still have change from what I'd get for my present house. Anyway, I'm far too busy to think about moving at the moment. It probably won't happen until next year, although really, I should start doing it when the lodgers go home for the vac, only I've got the next show to sort out.'

'So how will you manage for money, when the lodgers go home?'

'You're very nosy.'

'Sorry. Of course, you don't have to tell me.'

She put down her fish and chip paper. 'Fortunately I'm not at all secretive and don't mind telling you, although if I started asking you such personal questions I expect you'd get very huffy.'

'I expect I would. So, how *do* you manage, without their rent money?'

'I used to have a job and I live cheaply. Not having them in the house saves a fortune in bills.'

'But you haven't got a job now.'

She smiled and made a sweeping gesture. 'I have my work.'

'But seriously –'

'Seriously, it's none of your business and you don't have to worry.'

'I worry about Rory letting you down. It would take ages for you to earn as much from anyone else.'

'But if I sell my house, I can pay Molly back.'

'You'd have to buy another house and you wouldn't have the income.'

'I do wish you'd stop fussing. I am going to make a great success of this gallery. People will flock to it. They will buy paintings and they will pay a fortune to show their work in it. And if I think Rory's going to back out, I will go to Kilburn or wherever it is he's gone to in London and sort him out.'

'How will you do that?'

'On a train, I expect. Although I could take the coach.'

He humphed. 'I didn't mean than and you know it.'

Thea tried to look insouciant. 'I have my ways. Now, I must go to the loo. Lager always goes straight through me.'

Aware that this was a little more information than he wanted to hear, she hobbled past him. Alone, she felt despondency creep in. Ben had only been saying things and asking questions that she'd asked herself. She'd thought of answers, so why was she letting anxiety rain on her parade? She decided it was because the loo was dingy and chilly. Once she was back in the gallery again she'd feel fine.

'What I need, of course,' she said a little later, getting into a corner with her varnish brush, 'is a rich husband.' The moment the words had left her mouth she regretted them. He would take them the wrong way whatever she said. 'I mean like Derek. He supports Molly in all sorts of mad projects.' She sat back and wiped her brow, adding to the layers of grime. That should make it all right, stop him thinking she was talking about him. 'I might advertise. Anyone would do, as long as they were rich and indulgent.'

'It could be very dull, being shackled to a man just because he was rich.'

'Then I'd take a lover, for entertainment.'

'Like Rory, for example?'

'Oh, yes. Perfect.' She paused for a few moments, wondering how she'd managed to talk herself into this situation. 'It's funny about fish and chips, about twenty minutes after I've eaten them, I always want them surgically removed. You wouldn't have a Rennie – or some sort of mint – about your person, would you?'

Later, they drank tea. Thea was beginning to get drowsy and wanted to lie on her sleeping bag and doze, but what would she do about Ben? 'Are you sure you don't want to go home?'

'I was going to be staying with Molly and it's too late to disturb her now. Why, do you want to get rid of me?'

'No, I just wanted to rest for a bit. We can't put on another coat for a couple of hours.'

'I'm tired myself.'

Thea exhaled in exasperation. 'OK, let's share the sleeping bag. It's in the little bedroom downstairs, but we'll have to tiptoe or we'll wake the puppies.'

Thea had opened out the sleeping bag and had laid it in the corner of the room. She had brought a light blanket to put over her as she didn't want her limbs confined when it was so hot. Now, when she looked at it with Ben at her shoulder, she realised it looked like a love nest.

'I'm not sure I can share that space with you,' he said.

'Why not? It's a bit hard, but it'll do for a couple of hours.'

'I don't know how to put this . . .'

Thea wasn't going to help him out. She wanted him to say he wanted her, even if he didn't do anything about it.

'I don't have casual affairs.'

Thea was indignant. 'You told me you don't have the other sort, either. Well, neither do I!'

'You don't get it. I can't lie down there with you and not want to make love to you. Christ, Thea, you're half naked. You have been all night. I'm only human.'

'I'll put my jeans on. It's chilly down here anyway. Would that help?'

'Only marginally.'

'This is silly. Surely we can lie down on the floor next to

each other without' – how could she put it without sounding coarse? – 'anything happening. Petal's lot often share beds platonically.'

She was suddenly too tired to go on arguing, and she was also too tired to fetch her jeans, which were in the bathroom upstairs. She flung herself down on the sleeping bag, in the space nearest the wall, and pulled the blanket over her. 'You can do what you like, wander around all night watching the varnish dry, or lie down and rest, but I'm having a nap.'

He looked undecided.

'I don't know why you're making such a fuss about sharing a bed with me. Toby did and he didn't come to any harm.'

'Toby did! What did you say?'

'What you thought I said. When Toby stayed the night with me he got cold and lonely, and he got into my bed. I know that may make me some sort of monster, but I promise he went back to sleep the moment he was warm.'

Ben stood looking down at her as if indeed she were either a child molester or a wicked seductress, but as he couldn't decide which, he couldn't accuse her of either.

'It's no big deal. He was in a strange place, with someone he didn't know very well –'

'He knew you well enough to get into bed with you.'

'He's a child! He only wanted a little warmth and company. Don't make things so bloody complicated. Now either get in, or stay up, I don't care, but I'm going to sleep.' She turned on her side and pulled up the blanket, suddenly exhausted. Ben could take a running jump if he liked, as long as he didn't disturb her.

She awoke and was aware of his dormant presence by her side. She lay still for a few moments, relishing his solidness and the sound of his breathing. She realised that actually she wouldn't have felt happy sleeping in the gallery by herself. It was a big space, but only part of a much larger building that was all offices. During the day the building felt busy and welcoming. At night it was extremely quiet. It was a shame she needed the loo and would have to get out of bed, and somehow manage not to disturb him.

The easiest way would be to stand up and step over him, but although her ankle felt a lot better, she realised that if she tried to stand, she'd quite likely fall on top of him. She could crawl down to the bottom of the sleeping bag and creep along by his feet. As long as they weren't sensitive this might work.

Her indecision must have disturbed him because he suddenly turned over and put his arm round her waist.

She froze, forbidding herself to relax into his hold. It felt so good, so comforting, all she had to do was to shuffle backwards a bit and she'd be totally embraced. It would have been so easy, and lovely, and one thing would lead to another.

She hesitated just too long. He pulled her closer and nuzzled into the back of her neck.

It wouldn't do. She wanted him to make love to her while he was conscious, doing it on purpose. While he was asleep, thinking she was someone else, would not count. And his guilt would be unendurable.

By now his hands were on her ribcage, pushing upwards under the shirt. She'd undone her bra some time during her nap and he'd reach her breasts any second. For her, that would be the point of no return. She cleared her throat. 'Ben. It's me, Thea. We're here varnishing the floor, remember?'

For a second of two he was bleary and confused. 'Thea? What? Oh, my God, what did I do?'

'Nothing, it's all right. I'm just going to the loo.'

'Can you manage?'

'Of course.'

When she came back he said, 'I am so sorry. I thought you were someone else.'

'I know. Don't worry, it's a mistake anyone could make.' She smiled to hide her hurt. All cats are grey in the dark; it's easy to mistake good old Thea for someone you really fancy when you're asleep. 'I'm going to put another coat on,' she went on. 'You stay here. If you're still sleepy you might as well sleep.'

'OK.'

Thea crawled back upstairs, wanting to cry, she felt so pathetic. Rejected by Ben and now doing the floor all by herself. It would take for ever and it would be no fun.

She'd just realised how like Petal she was sounding in her thoughts when he joined her. 'I couldn't go back to sleep after all. Where's my roller?'

They didn't go back to bed again. They just worked through. They had four coats of varnish on by morning and Thea felt exhausted, more from the awkwardness between them than from the work and lack of sleep.

'So, shall we load up Lara and the puppies now?' he asked. He'd already walked her round the waste ground and between them they'd watched the puppies have their breakfast.

It was still early. Thea's ankle was hurting, although not as much, and she badly wanted to be at home. On the other hand, because she was tired, and despondent and irrational, she didn't want Ben driving her. She didn't want him forced into helping her up the stairs, into the bath, or whatever. It would be so intimate and yet so detached.

'Actually, Ben, I've got one or two things to do in town. I might as well do them while I'm over here. I'll give Molly a ring later.' She glanced at her watch. It was still only seven o'clock. 'She'll come and give me a hand, if I find I can't drive. If you go now, you'll be in London before the worst of the traffic.'

He looked at his watch. 'Hardly. I might as well stay and see that you're all right.'

'I *am* all right.' She forced a smile to reinforce her words.

'I'm not happy about leaving you here like this.'

'You don't have to be happy about it. Just do it. I'll be fine. Really I will.' A whole lot more fine than if you stay looking down at me like that, as if I were a delinquent schoolgirl.

She resolved that she was definitely going to wean herself off Ben. It was just no good loving a man like him when you had morals. She could have let him carry on what he'd started when he'd been three-quarters asleep. Many a good man had been trapped by more devious means. But unless he wanted her while he was wide awake and conscious, he couldn't have her at all.

'Very well. But you've got to promise me you'll be more careful. No more climbing on ladders if you're here alone. You could have been seriously injured and no one would have known anything about it.'

She wanted to hit him. Now he was treating her like a delinquent geriatric. Thea put on an expression of mock contrition. 'Yes, Daddy.'

A spark lit the back of his eyes in a way she hadn't seen before. Too late she remembered that he was also tired and possibly frustrated. She had to force herself not to step back and risk falling over.

'Daddy!' he whispered dangerously quietly. 'Daddy, is it? I'll show you.'

His kiss was suitably punishing, hard, intense and intrusive. Thea closed her eyes and went with it, even though it was anger that had motivated it. It was still extremely effective. When at last he was satisfied that she was sorry, he pulled away.

'Mm, that was nice,' said Thea foolishly. Then she did step back, aware that she should have kept silent or at least been less flippant.

He glared down at her and Thea sensed from his expression that he wanted either to smack her or make violent love to her, or both – one false move from her and he'd flip. She also knew that he blamed her entirely for making him feel such primitive emotions.

Neither of them dared to speak. He sent a few volts of silent fury at her and then flung himself out of the door. Thea watched him march down the road, half wishing she'd had the courage to push him beyond the limits of his civilised boundaries. She closed her eyes and fantasised about it for a moment, before she realised that their coupling, or however it could be defined, would have been taking place in what amounted to a shop window. Unless, of course, Ben threw her over his shoulder and carried her downstairs – where they would be joined by Lara and six puppies.

A reluctant smile forced its way past her frustrated passion. 'Come on, Thea. Go and deal with the dirty news-papers, and then see if you can get those puppies upstairs on your own.'

Chapter Fifteen

❧

Two days later Thea received a telephone call. It was Ben, as brisk and as 'nothing whatever happened between us' as possible: 'How's your ankle?'

'Fine. I managed to drive myself home the other day and it's been getting better ever since.'

'Good. Now the reason I rang is I've got a couple of days winding up business with clients and as it happens I have to go to, or near, quite a lot of places which have art colleges. You'd better come and see the graduate shows that are on. Some places have their shows quite early.'

Oh, to be a man and able to compartmentalise one's life so simply! What had nearly happened in the gallery was obviously filed under 'momentary aberrations'. That went in the top left-hand pigeon-hole, next to 'nanny' and 'gas bills'. Looking at graduate shows with Thea probably qualified as 'charity work', which was way down on the bottom row in the corner. Quite separate.

Thea put on her new assertive voice. She hadn't perfected it yet, but she hoped it would work all right down the phone. 'I really haven't got time to go gadding about the country looking at art. I've still got to do something about the floor in the basement –'

He made a sound which could have been a chuckle. 'You haven't got time not to come. You won't have another chance to see so much work all at one go. You need to be thinking about your next show.'

'Oh. OK. I suppose you're right. But it doesn't involve

any overnight stays, does it? I've got no one to look after Lara and the pups.'

'Will Molly come in and see to them during the day?'

'I expect so.' *She would if you asked her, Ben,* she said silently, hoping he could hear. 'She's not really a dog person, though. And the puppies make an awful mess.'

'I'll have a word. If I explain how important it is for the gallery she won't mind.'

Yes! He might be an insensitive brute in some ways, but in others he was perfect.

Although, when Molly rang her later to confirm details, Thea wondered what on earth Ben had said. 'There's nothing funny going on between you and Ben, is there?'

Thea went hot and cold, and ended up guarded. 'What do you mean, "something funny"?'

'Nothing specific, it's just when he mentioned you he sounded a bit – well, brisk.'

'He always is, isn't he?' Brisk was OK. Molly couldn't read anything into brisk.

'Well, I don't know. But honestly, Thea, you mustn't do anything to annoy him. We really need his contacts and his advice.'

'I'm sure I'd never do anything –'

'Not on purpose, perhaps. But he's a very organised, controlled sort of person and you're –'

'I'm not?' Thea helped her out.

'No, you're warm and spontaneous and –'

'Beautiful?' She helped out again.

Molly ignored this. 'But you're not Ben's –'

'Type?' This diffidence was unusual for Molly. Normally Thea couldn't get a word in edgewise and here she was, having to finish all Molly's sentences for her.

'Mm.'

'I see. I was wondering why you threw every unattached man you knew at my head and didn't produce your home-grown cousin.'

'Thea! I never did anything –'

'It's all right. I'm only joking.'

'And OK, I did try to find you a nice man, but to be honest, when you first came down here Ben was still in the last stages of a very tricky divorce . . .'

'And I'm not his type?'

'Not really. When his wife was there their house made mine feel I had to rush out and get in an interior designer.'

Thea laughed, her good humour restored. Molly did have the same feelings as everyone else, she just reacted to them differently. Most people would feel they had to rush out and buy a pot of emulsion, or make some new cushions.

'And after the first girlfriend he had tried to mother Toby, which really annoyed Ben, he's never gone out with anyone who's remotely maternal. Or over a size eight,' she added.

Well, that's me put in my place, size fourteen if I'm a day and desperately maternal, even if I haven't got any children of my own. Aloud she said, 'Well, enough idle chatter. Do you mind coming in to see to Lara and the pups on the days I'm away all day?'

'No, that's fine. My cleaning lady's going to do it. She loves dogs and is very obliging, and she can do extra hours for me.'

Ben picked her up at ten o'clock two days later. It was pouring with rain. 'I've got a list of what degree shows are on. There's one in Winchester you ought to visit. I've got a couple of clients to see, so I'll drop you off at the art school and you can have a look around.'

Thea's resolution to be nothing but businesslike failed before they'd even said hello. 'But Ben, I don't know anything about art. You were going to help me choose. You said!'

'I seem to have said a lot of things I don't mean lately.'

Thea didn't have time to work this one out. 'You definitely said you'd help me choose work. You can't let me down. This is the gallery at stake here.'

Ben concentrated on getting his car across three lanes of traffic. 'I don't want to let you down, but when it comes down to it, it has to be your taste.'

Thea realised, not for the first time, what an enormous undertaking she had made. 'But I might choose all the wrong people; we might never sell a thing. Oh, God! Why did I have this stupid art gallery idea in the first place?'

'Something to do with Rory?' He glanced across at her, somehow implying that Rory had charmed her into it. 'But now you have had the idea you've got to persevere with it a bit longer, if only to keep Molly happy.'

How like a man to treat a momentary exclamation as a serious statement. He'd been just as enthusiastic about Rory's work as she had been. Now he was implying there was something personal in it.

'I'm *not* doing it just for Rory and it's *not* just a whim. I really want this gallery to work and not only to keep Molly happy, either.' Her resentment at his implication that her gallery was some sort of distraction for idle women bubbled up. 'But if ever you find giving us advice and support too much trouble, just say. We can manage perfectly well without you.'

Ben frowned through the windscreen. 'I never meant to imply I objected to helping you. I just want you able to do this on your own, without being dependent on anybody.'

Thea sighed. 'Well, that's what I want too. And you're quite right. I've got to make my own mistakes and learn from them.' Even if Molly does go broke in the process.

'Tell you what, when you've chosen all the artists you're interested in – and you won't be able to get hold of some of them, and others will balk at paying a fee, however small – I'll have a look at the postcards, or the slides, or whatever you've got with you.'

'I'm going to take pictures of anything I like, to make sure I don't only choose one type of work.'

He glanced across at her and smiled the rare, wonderful smile, which transformed his whole persona. 'You're not a complete idiot, are you?'

Thea decided not to comment. She'd only say something she'd regret.

Ben left her in a strange street in a strange town and told her the art school was on the corner to the left. He'd offered to park the car and personally escort her, but she'd refused to let him. She regretted this independence as she fought her way through the traffic. Eventually, she reached it and a girl on the desk gave her a map, showing her how to get to the exhibition.

It took her a while to negotiate the staircases and corridors, but at last she found herself in the middle of the building: a huge, galleried space, full of works of art.

There were not many people about, only a couple of students minding the shop, who just glanced at Thea and went back to their discussion about whether the latest Oscar-winning film was really all that great.

It was nice to be able to wander round on her own, though at first she thought she didn't like anything. She worried that she'd lost her pleasure in art because now she had to like it. Then, suddenly, she turned a corner and found an installation which made her laugh out loud.

It was a kitchen, cooker, fridge and microwave, only everything was made from tooth-rot-pink plastic, and covered with sequins and diamanté. Lace curtains served as the microwave's door, the cooker's hotplates were made from doilies, but on inspection it turned out that they were ceramic. The longer she looked, the more surprises she found – the black velvet washing-up gloves with fingers covered with rings, a lurex washing-up brush, plastic goldfish floating in the washing-up bottle, which was filled with glycerine soap, and cooker knobs made from icing. She was chuckling to herself, searching for a comments book, or some indication about how she could get hold of the artist, when a tall, elegant, extremely pretty girl appeared.

'Is this your work?' asked Thea. 'I absolutely love it! I want to show it in my gallery.'

The tall, elegant, pretty girl threw herself into Thea's arms.

Cheered by this, Thea went round the rest of the show having decided that unless the work made her respond as strongly as the Barbie Kitchen had she wouldn't consider it. She had to feel passionate about everything in her gallery. Even if she didn't particularly like it, she had to admire it and feel it really was good.

She slept as Ben drove her home. She had a bag full of artists' postcards, business cards and addresses, and three rolls of used film. She had picked far more than she would need from just one art school, but she wanted to have plenty to choose from the first time.

She slept because she was very tired, and because it would save her having to talk to Ben about what she'd seen and chosen. At the beginning of the day she'd wanted him to be with her and take responsibility. Now she didn't want him disparaging her selection. When she'd got all the work in, she might show him. Or she might not.

He commented on her reticence two days later, when he took her north to Leeds. 'At first you wanted me come in with you to hold your hand. Now you won't even tell me about the work.'

'Once I'd realised you were right about me needing to decide on my own, I didn't want anyone else's opinion clouding my judgement.' She bit her lip and turned away so he wouldn't see her smile. That'll teach him!

Their last trip was to Cornwall. Ben had stayed the night with Molly and collected Thea very early in the morning. 'I wasn't expecting you to be ready,' he said, when Thea appeared, brushed, made-up and eager to go. 'I thought no woman could get dressed in under two hours.'

Thea gave him a disparaging look. 'You don't know many real women, do you, Ben? We were in Ireland together; surely you noticed that my time spent in the bathroom was minimal.'

'Sorry – I thought that was because you were sharing it with Molly and Petal, but I apologise for my assumption.' He glanced at her. 'Two hours or ten minutes, the effect is . . . charming.'

Well, it was a compliment of sorts, but 'charming'! Couldn't he have said 'ravishing' or 'gorgeous' – or something sexier? Later she decided he'd only said it out of politeness and that actually, even 'charming' was beyond her.

It was a shame that although Ben kept himself so aloof and dignified, which maddened and frustrated her, he didn't get one jot less attractive. In fact, he got better looking every time she let herself peep.

By the end of Thea's three forays into the world of art she had a huge folder full of contacts, names and addresses, their slides, her own slides, catalogues and postcards. The minute she had Rory's show up and running she would select them, or possibly even before. Then she'd get Molly to tell them that while they would be exhibiting in a really lovely space, they would have to pay a small fee for the privilege.

She was very grateful to Ben for taking her round the country. 'It would have been really difficult for me to get to all those places on my own, when I'm so short of time, so please accept this bottle of wine as a small thank you.' Aware that she sounded as if she were addressing a public meeting, she added, 'Derek chose it. So it should be OK.'

Ben took hold of the bottle as if it might explode. He looked at it without seeing it. He didn't speak for such a long time that Thea wondered if she should just get out of the car and go in. Eventually he said 'thank you', but the words seemed weighted with a whole lot of other things he wanted to say but couldn't.

A couple of days after their last trip together, Thea was determined to have an early night. Her house was now a student-free zone, until one of them decided he missed his girlfriend too much, or that home life was too confining, and needed to come back for a bit.

She had just put an egg on to boil – a vain attempt at something resembling 'a proper meal' – when the phone rang. She looked at the timer and at the phone, and silently cursed. It was probably not even for her. She let it ring a few more times and caved in. Rather than hear her own voice on the answering machine she picked it up. She would get whoever it was to ring back. It might well be Rory. Apart from the one garbled phone call from the pub, she hadn't heard a thing from him. Fine father of puppies he was! Not even a single tin of dog food had he sent for them. Leaving her in sole charge was bad enough; she wasn't going to have to eat an over-boiled egg as well.

It was Toby. Although he announced his name it took her a moment to work out who this rather high and breathy voice belonged to. When she did, she panicked. 'Toby! Are you all right? Is anything wrong?'

'No, no, I'm fine.' There was a short pause. 'Dad's out. I've got a babysitter. We've been watching videos.' Another pause. 'I just wanted a chat.'

'It's a bit late, isn't it?'

'Sorry.'

'Oh, well, I suppose it's Friday. But can I ring you back? I'm just boiling an egg and I hate them too hard?'

Thea mashed up the egg on to the toast and cut it into bits so she could eat it with one hand. She felt dreadfully clandestine dialling Ben's number, because she was quite sure Ben would be furious if he knew Toby had rung her. After what Molly had told her about him hating maternal women, this would make him hit the roof. It was probably because she and Toby had had such a good time together that Ben was so aloof.

But on the other hand she and Toby had a relationship which was quite separate and a lot more satisfactory than hers with Ben.

Toby was quite a long time coming to the phone. Thea was beginning to think the babysitter had come to her senses and sent him to bed. The answering machine cut in and Thea was about to leave a quick message and ring off when Toby picked up. 'Oh, hi,' he said.

'It's me, Thea. What can I do for you, Toby?'

'Nothing really, I just wanted a chat.'

'What about?'

'Oh – er nothing much.'

'Shouldn't you be in bed? I know I should be.'

'I always find it really hard to get to sleep when Dad's out. He's with a woman.'

It sounded awful, as if the woman were a prostitute or something. 'You shouldn't tell me things like that; he might not want me to know.' *And I don't want to know about the size ten models he's escorting round London, either.* Particularly when he'd told *her* that he didn't have either relationships or cheap affairs with women.

'Oh, but I must. We've just been watching this film where a little boy rings up a radio station, trying to find a wife for his dad.'

'I know the one.' Thea's heart sank. If Ben found out about this that babysitter would never work again.

'Donna said I should ring you.'

'Well, you shouldn't. I mean, of course you can ring me for a chat, but you mustn't start matchmaking.'

'What's that?'

'Trying to get people together with other people. Your

Aunt Molly does it with me and it drives me mad. People want to find their own people. You probably wouldn't like it if someone said, "Go and play with Tommy, he's a really nice little boy and you've got lots in common."'

'Teachers do that all the time.'

'Oh. Well, isn't it irritating?'

'Yes, but this is important. I mean Dad goes out with these women that he chooses and they're *crap!*'

'Toby!' It was probably the babysitter again. They had a lot to answer for . . . she seemed to remember one in the film Toby had just watched.

'He doesn't choose anyone I like.'

'Why should he? He's a free agent.'

'What?'

'I mean, he can go out with who he likes. You don't have to like them too.'

'But I do if they're going to be my stepmother.'

'Well, of course, that would be different –'

'And the women he chooses would be crap as mothers.'

Thea, not at all certain of the parentally approved way to proceed, cleared her throat. 'You have a mother, Toby, and she's special to you. No one your dad went out with, or married or anything, would ever be as good as her.' Thea was proud of herself. She sounded adult and sensible, like an agony aunt.

'But my mother's no good as a mother. I mean,' he went on quickly, before Thea could protest again, 'she doesn't make cakes.'

Thea took a bite of toast and crunched it to give herself time to plan her reply. 'There's a whole lot more to being a mother than making cakes. Even I know that.'

'But we have cake sales at school. I want to bring a cake to one.'

'There's nothing to stop you making your own cake, Toby,' she said, wondering how Ben would feel about it. 'I could write down a recipe for you. If Ben's not keen on clearing up the mess, you could do it when you've next got a babysitter, if she liked cooking too.' *It would be a lot more sensible than watching sentimental films and picking up unsuitable language,* she added silently.

'It's not just the cakes. It's the being there when I come home from school. My friend's mum is always there at home time. It's cool!'

'It probably is, but lots and lots of mothers work. They have to –'

'I want you to be my mother . . . stepmother.'

Thea couldn't decide whether to be angry, sympathetic, or sad. She aimed for something in between all three. 'Toby!'

'But I would! You're *cool*. I want to have a mum who *cooks*.'

It would have been far more flattering if Toby had said he wanted a mum who was a raving sex symbol but, she supposed, even more complicated. 'But I don't cook all the time,' she explained. 'Lots of times I just do boiled eggs.' She took another bite of hers. 'And lots of people would like to have a mother who was beautiful and had a glamorous job, who took you to nice places, stuff like that.' As she knew very little about Toby's mother it was hard for her to stress her good points, but she did her best.

'But I want a motherly mother as well.'

Exasperation was creeping in. 'That's greedy. And lovey, even if you had me as a stepmother, it wouldn't all be cooking pizzas and chocolate cake. It would mostly be all "do your homework" and "have you brushed your teeth?". I may not know much about parenting, but I do watch *Neighbours*.' Trying to divert him a little, she added. 'What does it mean when they say "you're grounded"?'

'It means you can't go out.'

'Well, there you go. That's what sort of a stepmother I'd be, learning how to do it from Australian soap operas.'

'Why are they called "soap operas"?'

'It's a long story. Years and years ago, in America . . .'

But Toby had lost interest. Thea heard a muffled conversation going on in the background. The babysitter doing her duty at last and putting him to bed. 'Donna says', said Toby loudly, 'the important thing is, do you like my dad?'

Thea was tired. She'd done her best and, with half an ounce of luck, Toby wouldn't read anything into it. She sighed. 'Yes, Toby. I like your dad. He's a very nice kind man who's helped me a lot.' Hoping this sounded suitably platonic, she tried to end the call, but heard more whispering.

'Do you like him "like that"?'

'I really don't know what you mean, Toby. Now it's late and I do think you should go to bed.' Hoping she sounded a sufficiently cruel stepmother to make Toby feel glad she wasn't his, she added, 'Now, good night. Oh, and Toby –'

'Yes?' He sounded a little hurt and Thea felt dreadful.

'Don't tell Ben about this conversation. I really don't think he'd like it.'

He didn't like it. And it hadn't helped that most of it had been recorded on the answering machine. He was furious when he rang Thea the following night. 'What do you mean by encouraging Toby in this nonsense about a step-mother?'

'Excuse me! I didn't encourage him. I made it very clear that although we'd had a very nice evening together, it wouldn't be like that all time.'

'Did it occur to you that you shouldn't have discussed it with him at all?'

'Yes – no –' Thea exhaled sharply. 'What was I to do? Toby wanted a chat. I didn't know what he wanted to chat about and when I did, I tried to stop him – or explain.' Aware that he'd heard her conversation more recently than she had and that she'd forgotten the detail of what she and Toby had discussed, she floundered to a halt.

'Well, you shouldn't have let him carry on.'

Ben was really angry. Thea was tempted to tell him about the babysitter and the video, but if he'd listened to all the tape he'd know about her and she didn't want her to get into more trouble. On the other hand she was damned if she'd apologise – she hadn't initiated the call. 'I did my best.'

'And does your "best" include telling my son to deceive me?'

'I never –'

'Oh yes, you did! It's on the tape quite clearly. "Don't tell Ben about this, he wouldn't like it." '

'Well, I was right there, wasn't I?'

She slammed the handset down. She had to be in the gallery early the following morning as they were coming to put the phone in. Then she indulged in a glass of wine, a few tears and a packet of chocolate biscuits. It didn't help at all.

While Thea had been waiting for the telephone man, she made the decision to rip up the carpet in the room downstairs, although originally she'd decided not to. By now the puppies' presence had begun to be apparent, even when they weren't there, and she didn't feel the odour of puppy wee was quite what an up-and-coming young gallery needed.

She'd got half of it up and was wondering if she'd ever fit it into her car to take to the tip, when Petal called down the stairs, 'Hi! Are you there? I've brought Dave over to have a look at the space. He's in the third year, so he'll want to be in your next year's graduate show.'

Oh, the confidence of youth! Thea wasn't certain of anything happening next year, except perhaps Christmas. 'How nice.'

'And the phone man's here. And I brought a letter for you from home. It's from Rory.'

Thea dropped the length of carpet she was holding and went upstairs. She snatched the letter from Petal as she passed and greeted the telephone man.

Only when he was happily muttering about junction boxes and extra lines, and Petal had made tea for everyone (she would have made it just for Dave, but her sense of fair play kicked in) did Thea take out the letter and open it. A cheque fell out of it.

'Shit! Shit! Shit! Shit! Shit! Shit!' she said loudly. 'Oh, sorry, everyone. But this is *dreadful*. Fucking – sorry Petal – Rory!'

'What? What's happened?' Petal was worried. Thea rarely swore and hearing her do it now was alarming.

'I can't believe it! I'll read it to you! It says,

Dear Thea,

I'm sorry if this is disappointing news for you, but I've decided that I really must show my work in London first. I've got a gallery really interested and they've advanced me some money! I enclose a cheque and I'd be grateful if you'd arrange to have my pictures sent to this address asap.

And the address is just for someone's house, not a gallery, so I don't know where he's intending to show.'

'What does asap mean?'

'As soon as possible. He seems to have forgotten that he already owes me money for the framing and stuff! This is intolerable.'

'You mean, you won't have a show?'

'Exactly. Because f—bloody Rory has decided to show in London first, in spite of promising me –' Then she remembered the promise had been rather dragged out of him and she'd always known he might take his work away from her. 'What I want to know', she went on more calmly, 'is how he managed to get a gallery so interested when he didn't have any slides.'

'But he did have slides,' said Petal, surprised. 'I sent them to him.'

'You *what?*'

'He rang one night – can't remember when – and said you'd said you'd put them in the post, but as he hadn't had them, he thought you'd forgotten.'

'Forgotten on purpose. I didn't want him to have them!'

'Oh. Well, I didn't know that. I thought I was being helpful when I posted them to him. They were of his pictures, after all.'

'They were my slides! Thank God I can get copies. But anyway, why didn't you tell me you'd sent them?'

'I forgot.' Petal's mouth began to quiver. 'I didn't know I'd done wrong. I'd thought I'd done you a favour. He said you'd promised.'

Thea dimly remembered some conversation wherein she'd said she'd send slides when they were back from the printers, but she'd never meant to do it. Apart from Lara, whom she didn't think he cared about, they were her only bargaining chip. Now she'd lost it. 'It's all right, Petal, it's not your fault. I should have told you I didn't want Rory to have the slides.'

'But why didn't you?' asked Dave.

'Because I want to show his work here first. If no one in London knows how great he is or, at least, only have his word for it, I've got a better chance of keeping him.'

'So, is the show off, then?' asked Petal. 'Aren't you going to have a gallery now?'

Thea took a breath so she wouldn't take a swing at Petal. 'Yes, I *am* going to have a gallery now. I have not gone through all this time and effort, and Molly's expense, setting it up, not to have one now. And what is more, Rory's work is going to be on show on the appointed night.'

'But if he wants to show in London –' said Dave.

'What he wants isn't relevant.'

'But how will you stop him?'

'I've got his paintings. If he wants them, he's got to come and get them!'

'But he's sent you the money to send them. You can't just keep it!'

'Yes I can.' She glanced down at the cheque. 'He owes me far more than this.'

'So, what are you going to do?' Petal's expression became a little pained.

'I'm going to go to London and sort that Rory out!'

Chapter Sixteen

✦

Petal told Molly about Thea's decision to go to London with a sort of shocked awe. Molly looked at Thea for confirmation of this mental aberration. 'You're what?'

'Going to London to find Rory. I can't just sit here without at least trying to get him to change his mind.'

'Sitting? Here? Precious little of that! You still haven't decided what to do about the basement floor and if you only use upstairs there won't be nearly enough room. We're tight for space as it is.'

'But Molly, unless we get Rory's work it won't matter what we do about the basement floor, because we won't need to use it. The graduate show isn't until August.'

The silence with which Molly greeted this told Thea she hadn't really taken in the significance of Rory's defection. 'Oh, shish-kebabs!' she murmured.

'Exactly,' said Thea, although her own expletive had gone on a lot longer and had been a lot less genteel.

'I'm going to have to leave you in charge of the gallery, Molly. It's only for a few days. Will that be all right?'

'Of course.' Thea could already see that Molly was beginning to relish being in sole occupation and could only trust that the power wouldn't go to her head.

'Now my only problem is what to do about Lara and the pups.'

Molly and Petal seemed to physically retreat. Petal was happy to spend hours cuddling them, but faded away like dew on a sunny morning if their newspapers needed changing. 'Well, I'm going home,' she said quickly.

'Mummy's been on at me for ages. She doesn't understand why I haven't gone before.'

'Well, could – could . . .' Thea struggled to remember the name of Petal's current swain and failed – 'your boyfriend stay here and keep an eye on them?' He was local, which was why Petal hadn't gone home for the vac.

'Oh, no. He's coming home with me.'

Thea spent a few moments tussling with thoughts of murder and dismembering. By dumping Lara and the pups on her, Rory had not only made it possible for him to zoom off to London but impossible for her to follow him.

'You're not going for long, are you? I'm sure Mrs Jones, my cleaning lady, wouldn't mind popping in . . .'

'It's not just a matter of feeding them. They need exercise and company, they can't be in the house on their own all day and night. It would be dreadfully cruel. Does the RSPCA do respite care, do you think?'

Molly and Petal looked bemused. Thea was always something of a mystery to them, now she was completely incomprehensible.

'I mean, if you have a handicapped child, or an elderly relative that you look after and you have to go away, you can sometimes get them into a home for a couple of weeks. It's called respite. That's what I need for Lara and the puppies.'

Molly and Petal exchanged anxious glances; Thea had obviously really lost it this time.

'Leave it with me,' said Molly. 'I'll think of something.'

'Would you, Moll? I'd be so grateful!'

'Only if you don't call me "Moll" – it's a name always preceded by the word "gangster's".'

Trusting that Molly would be able to bully or blackmail someone into being a resident dog-and-puppy sitter, Thea picked up the phone and rang her friend Magenta, who she hadn't seen since she left London and spoke to only rarely.

After a lot of 'why haven't you been in touch?' and

explanations of busyness, Thea cut to the chase: 'Can I come and stay for a few days? My star attraction has disappeared and I'm very much afraid that he's found somewhere better to exhibit than my gallery. I don't know how that's possible, but there it is.'

'Better than a gallery in . . . in . . . whatever godforsaken corner of the country you ran away to? Impossible.'

'Magenta, I did not run away and my gallery is not in a godforsaken –'

'OK, OK, no need to be so touchy. Of course you can come and stay. I'll take you round all the hot galleries and pick up the gossip. We'll soon track him down.'

'Thank you. You're a star! I'll ring you from the train to give you an idea what time I'm arriving and take a cab to your place.'

Thea was staring into her wardrobe, trying to decide which of her clothes were the least shabby, when Molly phoned to tell her she'd found the perfect puppy solution. 'Well, almost perfect, anyway. It's two young men.'

'What?'

'Pet sitters,' she declared. 'They come into your home and look after your pets, water your plants and things. These two like to come together, apparently.' There was a tiny pause. 'I didn't dare ask if they were gay. It wouldn't have been politically correct.'

'No. And not really relevant, either, as it's out of the question. It would cost an arm, a leg and the whole damn torso besides.'

'Don't be disgusting and I'm paying. It's the only sensible solution. Who else could you get, for goodness' sake?'

Thea sighed. 'I do realise it's not easy. I've been racking my own brains and come up with a big fat nothing.'

'Well, then. The firm do stringent police checks and things, so they should be utterly reliable.'

'As long as they know what they're taking on.'

'Oh, yes. Apparently they're quite used to puppies and large dogs. In fact, they've just lost a Great Dane and will adore Lara. It's perfect.' Molly sounded more than usually pleased with herself.

'Not quite.'

'Well, what's wrong with it? Your dogs are going to be given first-class care. What's your problem?'

'It means I've got to tidy my house. If I had a student to do it for me, I could just pack up and go!'

There was a short pause. Molly possibly thought this was good news but was just tactful enough not to say so. 'Mm. Well, you must admit your house could do with a bit of a going over.'

Thea fumed, silently but passionately. This might be the moment when she fell out permanently with her friend. But somehow she held back. 'I have been busy. And what will they expect? With a litter of puppies in it? They're not called "litters" for nothing, you know.'

'But the puppies don't go into the bedrooms, do they?'

Thea wasted several minutes jumping up and down in fury. Trust Molly to put her in a situation of having to clean her house when she wanted just to dash up to London to save the gallery. She decided she'd clean for an hour and anything that wasn't cleaned in that time could just stay dirty.

She set the kitchen timer and swooped and swiped and banged the hoover about, stuffed things under cushions and flung bedspreads and tablecloths over piles of boxes. The timer eventually pinged just as she'd blocked up the hoover, trying to vacuum up a sock. 'Oh, well,' she said, switching off the offending appliance and kicking it into the cupboard under the stairs, 'if they need to use it, they'll have to sort it out first.'

Her packing was necessarily speedy, while she longed to be one of those women who just threw the Armani section of their capsule wardrobe into their Louis Vuitton weekend case and leapt on to the train. Although rushed, Thea had plenty of time to regret the clothes she'd given away before she'd left London. Those black jersey trousers, for instance, which gave her freedom of movement and relative smartness.

Deciding Petal could be useful, if absent, Thea went into her room and raided the carrier bag full of discarded clothes. There was a pair of trainers in there which might be the very thing. Comfortable feet were definitely essential if she was going to spend the next few days tramping round art galleries. And Petal's trainers, unlike Thea's, had the advantage of never having been used for anything more sweaty and energetic than retail therapy, which Petal did with great concentration and not much speed. The trainers were the only thing of Petal's that Thea could fit into.

When she'd dealt with her packing as well as she could, she dithered over whether she should bring the file of material for the graduate show. It would be great to discuss it with Magenta, who had a good eye and a better idea of what was current, or 'hot'.

But it was of Ben she thought, as she flattened her carefully ironed clothes with the folder. What would he think of that video?

She'd fallen in love with it. It was of a large patch of white willowherb, and the seeds had turned into silken fluff. Every so often a puff of wind would blow the seeds high up into the air, sending them up and around, catching the light as they flew. But it was probably completely off track.

Molly had been very sniffy about her having a video at all. 'But who will buy them?' she had asked, sensibly enough, when Thea had got a copy and shown her.

'No one will buy them. But the artists might be asked to do an MA somewhere, or win a prize. This gallery isn't only about making money, you know.'

'As if,' said Molly, sounding very like Petal.

The two young men were charming. They admired the original features in the house, didn't look sniffily about at the traces of student, which were everywhere, and fell in love with Lara and the puppies. They exchanged meaningful looks. 'I know it's mad, but maybe, perhaps, one of these might be what we need to fill the gap Lorenzo left. He was a Great Dane.'

The other said, 'It's a bit soon to be thinking about getting attached to another animal, but you never know.'

'Well,' said Thea. 'If you and the puppies get on OK, and you think you might like one –' She left her sentence unfinished. 'It's not going to be easy to find homes for mongrels that size. The little one I shall keep myself.'

'We've never had a mongrel before. We used to breed Great Danes and show them, but they die so young they break your heart.'

Thea glanced at the kitchen clock. 'Is there anything else you need to know about anything? The washing machine works fine as long as it doesn't get coins in it. There should be loads of hot water and the telly works OK, only it doesn't get Channel 5.'

'Don't worry about Channel 5, dear. We prefer Calvin Klein anyway.'

After a moment Thea laughed. 'And you've got Molly's number if anything domestic goes wrong.'

'Molly? Oh, yes, *charming* lady. She came to our house and interviewed us. Though I don't think she really appreciated dogs like we do. *So* stylish, though.'

Thea left them lying on the kitchen floor bonding with the puppies, happy that her charges were in such good hands, and delighted at the thought of Molly as a gay icon.

Once on the train, after cursing herself for forgetting her mobile phone, Thea found herself feeling quite excited about her trip to London. She'd been back very seldom since she left and, although she was furious with Rory for defecting, she would never have taken time off at such a critical time at the gallery without a really good excuse. The thought of a little time away from the combined pressures of the gallery, the puppies and her confused emotions put her in a 'let out of school' mood, which she hadn't felt for a long time. It was also a good opportunity to catch up on some much needed sleep.

Magenta was waiting for her at the end of the platform.

'Darling! You didn't need to meet me! I could have just got a cab. Or even the tube –'

'Honey, you haven't been in London for a long time, have you? You've forgotten about the Northern Line. And why didn't you phone?'

Ignoring Thea's protests, and apologies, Magenta ushered her into a taxi. The two women settled back into the comfort of the leather seats.

'Now,' said Magenta. 'Tell me, do you just want to concentrate on finding this Rory guy, or do you want to see some art as well? I mean, you didn't have much time to research this gallery idea. Perhaps you ought to see what other people are doing.'

Thea was tempted. She desperately needed to find Rory, but it would be silly to waste all her time in London's hottest art galleries looking for that ingrate. It would be nice to take the time to look at a few pictures as well.

'I tell you what,' said Magenta, checking her purse for change. 'I won't take you anywhere that will be of no use at all, but I will drag you to some of the more up and coming places that are really important, even if it's unlikely to be there.'

It seemed easier just to let Magenta take charge. What was it about her personality, she wondered, that made people want to organise her? Molly, Magenta, Petal, they were all at it. 'Fine.'

'I'm glad you decided to go with what I've planned. I've got a fabulous schedule, which will blow you away. Have you got comfortable shoes on?'

Thea only needed a very short time to change into Petal's discarded trainers, brush her hair and demolish half a litre of fizzy water, so they were back in another cab less than half an hour later. When she protested about the expense, that she was living on money she didn't have at the moment, Magenta would have none of it.

'I'm working. I'll set the cab fares off against tax.'

'But what are you working *at*, Magenta?'

'Giving you a crash course in contemporary art. What else?' She obviously knew the London art scene very well, She was up to date on all the new shows and new galleries, and she seemed to be personally connected to all the important people.

'I had no idea you knew so much about all this. I'd have been picking your brains the moment I thought of having a gallery of my own.'

'You didn't tell me you'd decided to open an art gallery until you rang me. I thought you were still mothering students.'

'Well, of course, I still am.'

'And too busy to keep your old friends up to speed. But in a way it's a good thing. It might have damaged your confidence, knowing too much about it, and possibly stopped you having your own original ideas. I probably would have come down and taken over the show.'

'Even though you hate the provinces?'

'Oh. Yes. I'd forgotten that.'

Serious again, Thea asked. 'But supposing my ideas aren't original at all? When I started out all I had was fabulous space and Rory. Now I haven't got him any more, I've only got a lot of white walls and some sanded floors. '

'Garbage! Did you bring your portfolio?'

'If you mean that folder with a lot of postcards, Rory's slides I showed you and some brochures, and a dubious video, then yes. Although I left it in your flat.'

'Good. I've got a friend you can show it to tomorrow. If he approves, you know it's OK.'

Thea looked down at her feet and examined Petal's trainers. 'I thought I had a friend like that, too.'

'But you haven't now?'

Although Thea had deliberately made it impossible for Magenta to see her expression, she must have betrayed something in her voice. 'Well, I expect I've still got him as a friend. In fact, he's been great. Really helpful.'

'But you'd like something more than friendship, right?'

'Mm.'

'Tell me about him. We've got a while before we arrive at number 506. It's out near the Dome.'

'It won't take long. He thinks I'm a complete idiot.'

'Where did you meet him?'

Aware that she'd had no one to talk to about Ben, Thea relaxed into it. 'In my kitchen. I was standing in a dustbin at the time. I think it set the whole tone of our relationship.'

'So, when did you fall in love with him?'

'Well, I didn't know it at the time, but it must have been when I saw him deliver a litter of puppies.'

'Thea! I'll never leave you to your own devices again! What in hell have you been up to?'

'Not as much as I would have liked.'

'I hate to say this,' Thea eased off her shoes and eased her hot feet on the cold marble. 'But I think I'm galleried out. How many have we seen?'

'Only half a dozen and I'm afraid I'm going to have to leave you to do the last couple on your own. I've got a hair appointment.'

'Lucky you. Can't I come with you? I've seen so much

art, so many galleries and not a sniff of Rory.' Thea was very tired and on the verge of becoming deeply depressed. 'It might be best just to forget about him and carry on with the degree show.'

'You can't give up now! I'm really into this guy now you've told me so much about him. And even though I only had time to glance at his slides, they seemed great.'

'Mm. Imagine them twenty times the size, or whatever. But I'm shattered.'

'I know. We'll pop into the Wallace Collection for a bit of therapy.'

After so much contemporary work – some of which Thea found intensely stimulating and exciting and some about which she just wondered what the point was – the Wallace Collection was a haven. Time seemed to have stood still there for centuries and Thea was quite happy to stand still with it. 'I'd forgotten there were so many old masters here,' she whispered to Magenta.

'I know, and while the National and the Tate have them too, they're not so easy just to step into and wander.'

Thea stood in front of each painting for ages, staring at fur you could almost run your fingers through, at velvet so soft and dense you wanted to drape yourself in it, and pearls more real than anything she had ever actually worn in her own life. 'Can people still paint like that?' she murmured to Magenta. 'Nothing we've seen today implies that they can. Perhaps it's a skill that's been lost.'

'I got the impression from the slides that your Rory could.'

Thea turned to her friend. 'You're right. I thought it was just the subject matter, landscapes so bright and vivid they're like winter sunshine after months of fog and rain. But it must have been the quality of the painting that made them like that.'

She cast her mind back to when she first dragged his paintings out on to the Irish hillside and saw them properly. The same prickles of excitement she had then stirred the hairs at the back of her neck. No, it had to be she who brought his work to the eyes of the world. She'd earned the privilege.

'Let's go and find him.'

Chapter Seventeen

※

Thea was quite relieved that Magenta had left for her hair appointment. She wanted to slip into the last gallery for the day on her own and just be an ordinary punter looking at art. She could ask questions later.

She found it quite easily, down a side street at the back of Harrods. From the outside she thought it looked far too small for Rory's work, but Magenta had said that the curator was a big name and a good contact.

Once inside, the space was much larger that it had appeared, and wonderfully cool after the heat and dust outside. The weather had been getting hotter and more humid; thunder seemed inevitable. Thea decided she must make sure she was in a cab and on her way home before the storm broke and everyone wanted one.

She heard voices and, glad to slip in unnoticed, followed the sign to the exhibition upstairs. She could investigate the ground floor and find the owner later.

It was, she realised, the first gallery of the many they had seen that she actually envied. She had very little confidence in her abilities as a gallery owner, but she knew that none of the other spaces, or the way they had arranged the work, inspired her like this one. In some ways it was a relief. She had been beginning to think that she was too jealous of other galleries to judge them fairly. In this, she knew she was looking at true class.

It helped that she really liked the work. It was an eclectic mix of paintings, ceramics and three-dimensional work. She didn't like all of it by any means, but she did respect it and felt that if art had been required always to please the eye it would never have progressed beyond tasteful paintings of children playing with puppies. She wondered, briefly, how her own puppies were getting on.

Some of the work she loved. There were wonderful paintings composed of the purest pigments, red so intense that from some angles it looked black, scored with a slash of a palette knife so the paper beneath was revealed. Others were blue-black, the night sky distilled and intensified into a three-foot square.

As she wandered around she realised that this was the standard she was aiming for and that she didn't want anything less good in her gallery.

The voices still murmured on but she decided to go downstairs anyway. Her curiosity about what might be there lured her on.

She couldn't see the speakers because they were through in another section, where the gallery obviously extended into the building next door. At first, she ignored them and just gazed at a very complicated textile hanging piece, but then she heard a familiar laugh and knew she'd found her quarry. All day, she and Magenta had hunted him, asking questions, picking up snippets and bits of information accidentally let fall; now here he was, in person.

If this was the gallery Rory had found there was some sort of comfort in the fact that he had chosen such a wonderful one to abandon hers for. If he'd just gone for a good address, with no substance behind it, she'd have been incredibly hurt. While she was still hurt, not to mention bloody furious, at least she'd been left for a class act.

She had to think carefully how to approach him. After all, what could she say? Stamping her foot and telling the gallery owner that it wasn't fair, Rory had promised to show in her space first, wouldn't cut any ice. Especially when he asked what or where her gallery was. He was probably like Magenta and despised 'the provinces'.

It was her passion for Rory's work and the memory of her first sight of it that gave her the courage to pursue the matter. That and the fact that she'd committed herself so far, and potentially made such a fool of herself anyway, a little embarrassment in a gallery she would never visit again was neither here nor there. But what argument could she possibly offer Rory to make him change his mind?

She was about to go and confront him, hoping something halfway sensible would come to her, when another woman came in. She walked straight past Thea to where Rory and the owner were talking. Damn! Pratfalls were all very well, but Thea would have preferred to take hers without extra spectators.

The woman obviously knew Rory. Thea could hear the air kisses from where she was. Rory laughed again. It was, she had to acknowledge, a very sexy laugh and, judging by the laugh the woman gave in return, she thought so too.

Thea moved closer. She was well within sight, so it wasn't really eavesdropping. She was invisible in any case, because she wasn't anything except a slightly dishevelled woman in her thirties, looking at works of art she obviously couldn't afford.

'So, Rory, when are you going to let Edward have the paintings? He can't plan a show properly without them. Can you?' the woman said.

The man murmured something and everyone laughed again.

Thea wished she'd got a better look at the woman, or could see her now. But at least she knew that this was indeed the gallery in question, and it gave her some satisfaction that the pictures they wanted were in hers. Possession, after all, was nine-tenths of the law. In theory, anyway.

'I did explain.' Rory sounded apologetic. 'It is a little difficult. I promised this woman I'd show with her first.'

'You really don't need to worry about that,' the woman was soothing yet adamant. 'After all, she isn't anybody. No one would expect you to keep your word made in those circumstances. I mean, she may have got you to show your work to her, but that doesn't give her any rights to it whatsoever.'

'Well –'

'She didn't buy any of it, did she?' This time the voice was edged with irritation.

'She did pay to have the drawings and sketches framed.'

Well, thank you, Rory, for remembering, thought Thea.

'Then all you need to do is pay her back for the framing. A cheque will do it. You don't have to hide your work away as well.' Her voice became cooing and Thea was willing to bet she was now holding on to Rory in some way.

Thea began to shift about uncomfortably. She was definitely eavesdropping now. Rory didn't know she was there and he was talking about her. If she didn't reveal herself soon, it would get to the stage when she couldn't.

Just as she was plucking up the courage to say something ingenuous like 'Oh, hello, Rory, I didn't know you were here', to her enormous surprise she saw Toby and a young woman approach the door of the gallery. This was somehow a greater shock than coming across Rory. In the nick of time she stepped behind an elevated circulating fridge and avoided being seen. What the hell was Toby doing here? Surely not just looking at art with his nanny.

Toby moved to the woman and said in a polite but strangely unenthusiastic voice, 'Hello, Veronica.'

Thea's heart started jumping in her chest. She felt blood rush up through her body and sweat broke out at her hairline. Suddenly she seemed like the victim of some horrible plot. *Don't panic*, she ordered herself. *Veronica could be anyone; she doesn't have to be his mother. It's quite a common name – probably.*

But 'Veronica' put out her arm and pulled Toby to her. 'Hello darling. I see you're wearing that new shirt I bought you. It might look better tucked in.' There was no doubt. Only a mother or a teacher would tell a boy to tuck his shirt in.

This was the moment. She moved from behind the suspended fridge and cleared her throat. 'Hello,' she said, wishing she could think of something less banal.

'Thea!' said Toby and Rory at the same time.

It was Toby's presence that kept Thea calm. She couldn't shout and scream and throw things with him there. It wouldn't be fair.

'I'm sorry? Do I know you?' asked Veronica icily.

'This is Thea, the woman who made me get my work out of the shed,' said Rory. He seemed extremely put out to her and was shuffling about like a schoolboy caught investigating his sister's underwear.

Thea glanced at Toby. After his initial delighted greeting, he now seemed reluctant to look at her. Thea began to feel more and more certain that something very untoward was going on.

'Oh!' said Veronica. 'So you're the one.' She came forward, hand outstretched. 'I've heard such a lot about you.'

Thea took the hand, which was cool and hard, and at the same time took a good look at its owner. She was aggressively thin, attractive, though not pretty, and had that high-maintenance gloss which made it hard to tell her age. She had probably looked as she did now when she was eighteen and would go on looking like it when she was fifty.

'Sorry,' said Thea, 'I don't know your name.' *Even if I do know, perfectly well, who you are.*

'Veronica de Claudio. I discovered Rory.' Veronica smiled. She smelt strongly of some sophisticated perfume and her clothes were the sort Thea wouldn't know how to wear, even if she could fit into them; layers of silk, trousers, a floor-length waistcoat and a sort of embroidered panel across her concave stomach which showed her hips were no more than six inches from point to point.

'Oh, really?' Thea inclined her head graciously. 'I thought I did that.'

Veronica's eyes narrowed with pleasure. She gave Thea the sort of smile people give when delivering bad news that actually delights them. 'Oh, I was way ahead of you. I saw Rory's graduate show and his subsequent exhibition. In Cork Street.'

'Oh?' The implications of this announcement were many and Thea's stomach was beginning to churn alarmingly, but just now, she wanted Veronica's take on Rory's fatal exhibition.

'It was stunning, absolutely stunning.'

Rory had turned away and was trying to engage Toby in conversation about one of the sculptures. Whether he was embarrassed to hear his work described as stunning or felt bad about what happened afterwards Thea could only guess. Knowing Rory, the former seemed rather unlikely.

'I thought the critics panned it,' said Thea.

'Oh, they did. And rightly so. Rory's work was far too immature and his behaviour at the show even more so. I told Maxim . . . you know? Maxim Applozzia? You must have heard of him – he's got three galleries in New York and is opening here next year.'

Thea nodded, hoping her ignorance wasn't as obvious to everyone else as it was to her.

'I told Maxim to take it all down, close the show. Rory just wasn't ready to exhibit.'

The nausea which had been threatening now seemed a

real possibility. She didn't trust Veronica remotely, but parts of her story were probably true – possibly all of it was. But why in God's name had Ben never said a word about her part in Rory's downfall? If she'd known where the loo was, she'd have escaped to it. As it was, she could only stand her ground and hope her body wouldn't let her down. 'Oh, really?' she said tightly. 'I'd heard Rory's story, of course, but he didn't mention your part in it.'

'Oh, he probably wasn't aware of my part in it.' She laughed gaily. 'The poor boy was in no state to be aware of anything –'

'Except that his show had been taken off and the critics had completely disparaged it.'

Veronica decided to take some time with this woman, who obviously was a little slow but if she was ever to be got rid of she would have to have a few things pointed out to her. 'Darling, Thea? Interesting name. I don't think you quite understand. The critics may have given Rory a very hard time, but that doesn't mean they didn't admire his work. They just thought it immature. I knew that in a few years he'd mature beautifully –'

'Which? Rory, or his paintings?'

'And of course, while we're terribly grateful that you found him for us in Ireland, you were only just a few steps ahead of us. Edward and I had put out a lot of feelers and were about to track him down.'

And the 'feeler's' name was Ben Jonson, no aitch, like the poet. Thea began to shake, aware that she was suffering from shock.

Veronica went on, 'Of course, we will give you a credit in the catalogue, won't we, Edward? That would only be fair.'

Thea knew she had to get out of there and soon, or she'd vomit over Veronica's Manolo Blahniks. 'I think I need to talk to Rory about being fair. Would you give me a moment, Rory? Outside?' Her teeth were beginning to chatter and the air-conditioning suddenly seemed far too powerful.

Rory, looking shifty and embarrassed, was only too willing to follow Thea into the street.

The sweet, dirty smell of a city when it's about to rain was refreshing after the powerful odour of Veronica's scent. Thea stood for a few seconds, breathing deeply, trying to fight the physical symptoms of shock which seemed to linger long after her brain had accepted the situation; she had been totally and utterly shafted by everyone. At that moment she could have suspected even Petal and Molly of being in on the act.

'Where would you like to go?' he asked.

'I don't want to go anywhere! I just want you to tell me why, when you never intended to show in my gallery, you let me go to all the trouble and expense of setting one up.'

He looked down at her and put his hand on her shoulder. 'Would you like to go to a pub or something? Somewhere we can talk.'

'No. I have to stay in the fresh air for a bit.'

'If you call this air fresh.'

'For Christ's sake! It's all there is.'

'Let's find a park or something.'

'God, Rory! Can't you just tell me you've sold me down the river here and now? Or, being an artist, do you need some goddam sylvan setting?' She set off down the street so fast that she could hardly avoid the oncoming pedestrians.

Rory hurried after her. 'OK, forget the park. But slow down, please.'

Thea couldn't slow down. She had to work off the adrenalin she could feel rushing through her veins, filling her with panic.

Eventually Rory managed to get alongside her. He took hold of her arm in an effort to calm her.

Thea ignored it but let it stay. 'So tell me. Did you ever mean to show with me?'

Just then a terrific clap of thunder deafened the world and rain, warm and hard, came down on them.

'Jesus, Thea, this is ridiculous! Come inside somewhere.'

'No! Why don't you just tell me the truth? After all, I know it already. I just want to hear it from you, personally, the artist I've turned my life upside down for!'

They were both drenched remarkably quickly. Thea was only wearing a long cotton skirt and a little vest top. In seconds even her underwear was soaking and she watched Rory's magnificent torso appear as the rain plastered his T-shirt to his body. 'Well?' she demanded.

Since the storm, she no longer felt the need to hurl herself along at breakneck speed. She stopped on a street corner, ignoring rain and hurrying people alike.

'It wasn't like it seems! I'd –'

'*Thea!*'

As she turned she realised the plaintive little voice had spoken before.

'Thea! You went so fast I could hardly keep up with you!'

'Toby! Darling!' He was drenched, his fine hair plastered to his head and he was shivering violently. To crouch down and wrap him in her arms was entirely instinctive. 'What are you doing here?'

'I wanted to stop you running away.'

Thea, huddled on the pavement, still holding the shaking child, wanted to cry. She had been so wrapped up in her problems that she hadn't even noticed Toby chasing after them. Anything could have happened; he could have been run over, knocked into the road, or even kidnapped.

'I wasn't exactly running away, I wanted to talk to Rory, but it must have looked like that.' It had felt like that, too: escaping from Veronica's cloying scent, her glamour, the elegant gallery which had seemed to mock everything she'd done in the last two months.

'I'm so glad I've found you. Dad would have been so cross if you'd got lost or anything.'

Thea straightened up, still keeping hold of Toby's hand. She didn't think Ben would give a toss – if he could betray her as he had done, why would he care if she took a few wrong turnings and ended up miles from anywhere? 'Well, I haven't, so that's all right. Now, which way back to the gallery?'

Rory shrugged. The rain was still beating down and they were all shivering.

'Which way, Toby?' Rory asked. 'You're the Londoner.'

'I don't live in Knightsbridge,' Toby said.

'I can't believe this!' Thea said. 'We've only been gone a few moments. We can't have got so far away that we can't find our way back.'

'You were going at a hell of a lick, Thea.'

'So we are lost, after all?' asked Toby after they had all looked up and down the streets, searching for clues as to their whereabouts.

'It certainly seems that way, only not just me, but you and Rory as well.' She sighed. 'Well, never mind, we'll get a taxi and give the gallery's address. It's not really a problem. If we walk up to the crossroads, we've a better chance of getting one.'

'It's always hard to get a taxi when it's raining,' said Toby, after trying to spot an orange light on top of the many taxis that sped passed for several minutes.

'We could go to the underground station,' suggested Rory. 'At least we'll be dry while we look and Knightsbridge tube is quite close to the gallery. I'll know the way from there.'

'OK, you find the nearest station, then.'

South Kensington Tube station seemed to be several miles away, although it was probably because they took so many wrong turnings finding it. In her London days Thea always carried about a tattered *A to Z*. It had since fallen apart completely and, because she was going to be with Magenta, who had a perfect sense of direction, she hadn't bought a new one. It made her feel incredibly vulnerable.

While they joined hundreds of others waiting for the tube, Thea had a belated thought. 'I suppose we should ring the gallery and tell them we've got Toby. His mother will be out of her mind. Have you got a mobile, Rory?'

'No. Haven't you?'

She bit her lip. 'No. I left it at home. I was in a hurry to get to London.'

'So, why did you come to London?'

'Why do you think?' she hissed, clutching Toby's hand like a lifeline. 'And I can't talk about it now!'

Eventually a tube came and they stuffed themselves on to it. Belatedly, Thea realised it was the rush hour, and they'd have a very squashed journey. She felt Toby's hand become sweaty in her own, but she wouldn't release it. It was her fault he was lost and she couldn't risk it happening again. 'I expect we'll start steaming soon,' she told him. 'Like in a rainforest.'

It was still raining when they emerged and the warmth they had felt in the tube was washed away. 'OK Rory, we're in your hands. Which way?'

Rory lead them to the gallery quickly enough, but when they got there it was closed.

Thea rattled the door in frustrated disbelief. 'They can't just close it. They must have known we'd come back with Toby. Veronica must be beside herself with anxiety.'

'My nanny will be more worried, I expect.' Toby began to look nervous himself.

'It's all right, Toby,' Thea soothed. 'We'll sort it out. Where's Ben at the moment? Up here, or down in Bristol?'

'Here.'

'Were you going to go home with Veronica?' The thought of Toby spending time with that harpy made Thea shudder.

Toby shook his head. 'No. She's too busy to see me this weekend, which is why we visited her at the gallery.'

'Then why didn't she stay there? Now we must think what's the best thing to do.'

'Get out of the rain,' said Rory.

'Should we go back to your house, Toby? Or Veronica's?'

'Mine, but it's miles away.'

'Then why in God's na—I mean, then why did you visit Veronica at the gallery if it's miles away from where you live?'

Toby shrugged. 'I think she thought it would be fun for us, coming on the bus.'

'You don't remember which bus, Tobe?' asked Rory. 'We could get one back.'

'We had to change. It took ages.'

'Well, I've had enough. I'm going to lie down in the road outside Harrods until a taxi stops.'

'But Thea,' protested Toby as he was pulled along behind her, 'they won't see you if you're lying down.'

'Well,' said Rory a few moments later. 'I was a bit shocked by the way you pushed that old lady aside, Thea.'

'I didn't push her aside and she wasn't old. She was warm and dry, and had just indulged in a lot of retail therapy. Our need was the greater.'

'It'll cost an awful lot to go by taxi all the way to my house,' said Toby, who had given the address to the driver.

'Too late to think about that now, old man.'

'And even if it wasn't,' said Thea, 'I'd have still got in. I've had enough of the underground for one day. Even if it was only one stop.'

239

Toby sighed. 'Do you think everyone will be dreadfully cross?'

'I expect so. People always are when they're worried. But it'll be all right. They'll be so overjoyed to see you. Veronica will probably buy you a mega present.'

'I don't expect she'll be there. She never comes to our house. She and Dad don't get on.'

'I expect that's why they got divorced,' said Rory.

Just as the taxi drew up outside Toby's house, while Thea was calculating the tip, a car drove up and tried to park in too small a space opposite the taxi. Thea was still fiddling around in her purse, hunting for pound coins and didn't notice, but Toby said, 'Oh. It's Dad. It's early for him to be home.'

Thea didn't want to see Toby's dad, unless she had a blunt and heavy instrument about her person with which to batter him to death.

The taxi pulled away at about the same time as Ben managed to park his car. He got out, slammed the door, his expression matching the weather, which was still thunderous.

'Dad!'

'Toby!' Ben seemed to cross the street in a single stride. 'Thank God you're all right. What in hell's name happened?'

Toby released himself from his father's embrace, avoiding his gaze.

'It's a long story,' said Thea defensively. 'It's not his fault.'

This time Ben's rage was not tempered by relief. He turned it on Thea at full force. 'Of course it's not his fault!'

Rory cleared his throat. 'Would it be a good idea if we went into the house? It's still raining cats and dogs, and Toby here is drenched. We all are.'

Ben thrust his hand into his pocket and gave his keys to Rory. 'Take him inside and get him a hot drink if his nanny's not there. You' – he took hold of Thea's shoulder in a vicious grip – 'you, come with me and give me an explanation!'

Chapter Eighteen

It took all Thea's strength to rid herself of his hand, clamped to her shoulder, and she didn't manage it until Toby and Rory had gone into the house and he slackened his grip.

'Now, what the hell do you mean by running off with my son? What have I ever done to you to deserve that?' he demanded.

'What?' She was as angry as he was but also confused. 'What do you mean, "running off"? I haven't done anything of the kind. It's you who's totally and utterly betrayed me! God! I thought it was bad the first time it happened to me! But this . . . it's . . . worse.'

'Veronica told me Toby had been kidnapped.'

'Kidnap—I don't believe it! You're out of your mind. Where on earth did she get that idea from?'

'So how would you describe removing my son from the custody of his mother and his nanny, and disappearing into the streets of Knightsbridge, then? A little gentle exercise in a thunderstorm?'

Thea shook her head to clear the rain from her eyes. He was now as wet as she was though, in a suit, was a little better protected. 'You are mad,' she declared. 'Stark, staring, fucking mad! Why on earth did you think I'd kidnapped Toby? And if I did, why did I spend a small fortune on a taxi taking him home?'

Ben shrugged dramatically. 'I don't know! Nothing you do ever seems logical.'

Thea's eyes flashed to rival the lightning. 'Well, let me

explain! I took him home to you because that's where he said he wanted to go. Although it was bloody miles away and, as I said, cost me a fortune in fares. Don't you think you should be inside, comforting him, instead of shouting at me, who's done nothing whatever to be ashamed of?'

'Don't tell me how to look after my own son!'

'I wouldn't dream of it! Though just one tip: tell your wife and your nanny that it's a good idea to stay where you last saw the child, rather than disappearing into Greater London!'

While Ben now realised that Thea had done nothing wrong, he was still upset. 'Don't stand there shouting. Tell me what happened.'

Thea was incredulous. 'I think you mean, "I am so sorry, Thea, I don't know how I could have been so stupid!" Only don't bother to apologise, because what you've done to me is so much worse than you just being a dickhead about Toby.'

The expression broke through his anger. 'Look, I'm sorry, I obviously got completely the wrong idea, but tell me what did happen.'

It was better than having to confront him with his perfidy, so Thea obliged. 'I was talking to Rory – or trying to – in a pigging thunderstorm and Toby followed us. By the time he'd caught up with us we were all lost. It took us ages to get back to the gallery, and when we did, everyone had gone. I just cannot believe it! How could a mother just swan off when her son is missing in the middle of London?'

'She didn't swan off. She went back to her flat, in case Toby had gone there. They rang me at the office and said Toby had disappeared.'

'So naturally you all assumed I'd kidnapped him. And you accuse *me* of not being logical?'

Ben sighed. 'None of this is very logical. Let's go back to the house and get you warm and dry.'

243

'No! I'm not going into your house, Ben Jonson, and I wouldn't if yours was the last house I could find sanctuary and a band of thugs were after me. Now I'm going to get a taxi.' Then she remembered she'd just spent almost all her money on the taxi they'd recently got out of and would be lucky if she had enough left for a bus.

Ben took hold of her shoulder again. It still felt bruised from last time.

'Let me go, you ape!'

'Not until you tell me why you won't go into my house. Rory and Toby are there. You'll be quite safe from my lust.'

This unfortunate choice of word reminded Thea of when they'd been together varnishing the floor. She blushed hotly at the memory. 'I doubt if you know the meaning of the word,' she muttered, remembering her bitter humiliation.

His mouth hardened and his grip tightened. 'Then what is it?'

She put her chin up and her shoulders back, losing his hand as she did so. 'You should be able to work it out for yourself, but as you're obviously incredibly dense I'll spell it out for you. You let me go to all the trouble and expense, worry and hard work, of setting up an art gallery, when you knew bloody well your wife was going to make Rory an offer he couldn't refuse and I'd be left with a gallery but no star artist . . . and no chance of making any money.'

'What?' He frowned in puzzlement.

'Oh, come on, don't tell me you're deaf as well as stupid!'

Ben was obviously still angry too, but was better at hiding it than Thea. 'I'm not deaf and I'm not stupid, and because I'm not stupid we're going to carry on this conversation in the house.'

'No. I said I refuse –'

He didn't argue. He just picked her up in a fireman's lift,

carried her back down the road and up the steps to the house. Thea found she couldn't kick him, though it wasn't for want of trying. Battering his back with her fists hurt her more than it seemed to hurt him. He pulled her down so she was on her feet when the nanny opened the door. 'Thank you,' he said to her. 'Now, you.' He turned to Thea. 'Upstairs and into the bath.'

Thea was torn. She'd been wet and cold too long not to yearn for the comfort of hot water. On the other hand she was damned if she'd take orders from Ben, even if it was more for her good than for his.

'I'm not listening to any arguments,' he went on. 'You can use my bathroom; you'll be quite private. But when you come out, you're going to tell me what the bloody hell you're talking about.'

Thea made a rapid plan. She would appear to comply, go upstairs, run the bath and, when he was out of the way, she'd tiptoe back downstairs and out, and run away. His behaviour was monstrous, almost as monstrous as his betrayal had been. She was damned if she'd explain anything to him, and get his calm and logical answer in reply.

Thea's plan didn't allow for Ben actually running the bath for her, giving her a towel and a robe, and ordering her to get out of her clothes. Not that it was quite an order, more a suggestion it was hard not to comply with. 'If you give me your wet things I'll put them in the tumble-dryer.'

Thea bit her lip. 'Oh, all right.' She snatched the thick towelling robe. She might as well avail herself of the facilities, but she really didn't want a confrontation. She was too tired and angry to guarantee she wouldn't get emotional. Tears would just add to the many humiliations she had suffered recently.

The bath, she decided, was the nearest thing to heaven you could experience this side of the Pearly Gates. Forget sex, or chocolate – hot, deep water when one is really chilled has to be the best. She sank down so only her head was above it, abandoning her plans for a quick dip and escape. After all, she might as well stay in the bath until her clothes were dry.

Once the heat had penetrated every chilly cell and pore, she washed her hair, using Ben's herbal shampoo, which smelt expensive and slightly medicinal. She sat up a bit and examined Ben's bathroom – knowing he'd betrayed her even more badly than Conrad had didn't affect her curiosity.

It was a very male bathroom, black and white tiled floor, shiny white suite, white tongue-and-groove panelling and a small mirror. It was also extremely tidy. No rogue bottles of shampoo, conditioner or body wash littered the edges of the bath. No hair-filled Ladyshaves, cracked soap or crumbling bath bombs either.

Mentally she doubled the size of the looking-glass, placed a large, spectacular shell in front of it and added some real sponges or large beach pebbles, something to provide a little cheer without making it feminine. Some big, square bottles would be nice, too.

She sighed. She could tell herself, quite convincingly, that her own bathroom was full of clutter and rubbish because of Petal and her other students, but she knew it wasn't true. She was a cluttered sort of person and Ben wasn't. Even if his betrayal hurt her far, far more than Conrad's had done, even if he were the kind, sexy man she'd once thought him, they were totally wrong for each other. They'd drive each other to distraction.

Draped in towelling from head to foot in the form of Ben's bathrobe and the towel he'd given her, Thea went downstairs and found the kitchen. She'd already gone into Ben's spartan bedroom, telephoned Magenta and brought her up to speed, Thea thought, remarkably calm about it all.

Now, Thea didn't feel very calm and she did feel rather

foolish. She hadn't been able to find anything even distantly related to moisturiser in Ben's bathroom cabinet and her face felt tight and shiny. Without even a trace of make-up to soften the effect, she probably looked like a sunburn victim. Still, what did it matter if she looked a fright? She just needed her clothes back.

Toby was sitting at a completely clear pine table, eating a plate of pasta. His nanny, whose name Thea couldn't remember, was leaning against the equally uncluttered work surface, drinking a glass of wine. There was no sign of Ben or Rory.

'Oh, hi,' said Thea.

Toby looked up and grinned. The nanny detached herself from the worktop and asked, 'Would you like a glass of wine? Ben will be back in a moment, but I've got to go home, now. You might as well have one while you're waiting.'

'Are my clothes dry, do you know?' Thea accepted the glass of cold white wine.

'Nearly, I think. But now you're here I'll pop off. That's OK, isn't it, Tobe?'

'Fine,' said Toby with his mouth full.

Thea sipped the wine. It was not all right with her. If the nanny wasn't here she couldn't just get dressed and slink off, as she had planned. She'd have to stay with Toby. She couldn't abandon him without a responsible adult. And it was a nuisance to have lost Rory again. Still, perhaps it was for the best. If she was going to have to seduce him into showing with her, she'd prefer to be dressed for the event. With Ben's robe gathered round her, she looked like the Michelin Man.

'Before you go, where's the tumble-dryer?' If she delayed the girl a little, Ben might come back, and in the changeover period between nanny and father, Thea could make her escape.

'Oh, it's here, in the utility room. Just open the door and

it'll stop and you can get them out,' said the girl casually, unaware how badly Thea wanted to get into her clothes, damp or not. She put in her hand and felt the clothes as they stopped. 'Another ten minutes or so I'd say. Sit down and drink your wine. Ben'll be back in a minute anyway, and he might give you a gin and tonic or something before supper. He's gone to get some things from the 8 till Late.'

Supper. That sounded terribly like a meal, terribly as if Ben was planning that they should slug it out over a salmon en croute after Toby was in bed. Not long ago – yesterday, even – this would have sounded lovely, she and Ben alone, with no distractions. Now it seemed like torture. Ben would be calm and logical, and explain he'd acted in Thea's best interests, and she would weep with frustration and possibly attack him with a fish knife. No, she couldn't let it happen.

She debated putting on her clothes as they were and making a run for it, while the nanny was still wiping the perfectly clean worktop with a perfectly clean cloth. But Thea badly needed to know if Rory had said anything before he'd gone. No, however unpleasant, some sort of confrontation with Ben was essential.

Toby had gone upstairs to play on his computer, having assured Thea that his bedtime wasn't yet and that Dad wouldn't mind. Thea, dressed and made-up with the nanny's emergency supply, planned what to say to Ben.

She tried to look surprised when he arrived in the kitchen, although she'd heard him come in, talk to Toby and come downstairs.

'Hello,' he said. 'I've bought some supper.'

'Nice for you.' *Don't be rude, Thea. If you're rude he'll guess how much you care. Keep it calm, polite and unemotional.*

'I hope it's nice for you, too.'

'Well, I think that's unlikely, don't you?' Good resolutions abandoned, Thea turned on him. 'Do you really think it's possible for me to sit opposite you and chat as if nothing had happened? As if your wife hadn't purloined Rory, just before he was going to show with me? Where is he, by the way? Did he tell you?'

'Thea, I do wish you'd give me a chance to explain a few things, before you let your imagination go completely haywire.'

'What things would those be? Like why you watched me, *helped* me even, set up an art gallery when you knew from the beginning Rory wasn't going to show there? Was that why you were so keen on me setting up a graduate show?'

'Could we eat first? I'm starving and I'm sure you are too.'

'No, we couldn't. Tell me!'

He sighed, but switched the oven on before turning round to face Thea. 'I didn't know Veronica had any plans for Rory.'

'Yeah, right! You didn't come all the way to Ireland with Toby because Molly asked you to. You did it to track Rory down for Veronica, so she could put on the show he should have had first time round.'

'Veronica doesn't have a gallery. She's a patron, she collects artists, but she doesn't have space of her own.'

Thea made a dismissive gesture. 'Well, whatever, you knew Veronica was interested in him, which was why you went to Ireland. What I want to know is why the *fuck* you let me set up the gallery?'

'I tried to stop you. I pointed out the pitfalls.'

'You're pathetic! You didn't try to stop me at all. You know bloody well that if you'd told me Rory was destined for Cork Street or wherever, and wouldn't show with me, I'd have gone back from Ireland to my lodgers and my part-time job, and taken up a hobby!'

'I've told you I didn't know Veronica had plans for Rory and I don't believe she did until she heard about your gallery – and before you accuse me of telling her, she heard about it from Toby.'

'Hide behind your son, would you?'

Then she winced as she watched his reaction. His rage seemed to fill him like an implosion of explosive gas. Frightened, she prepared to duck or run as surely he would direct his anger at her.

Seeing her hover, prepared for flight, enraged him more and his eyes glittered. He thumped his fist on the worktop and the glasses in the cupboard above clattered together.

Thea kept her weight on the balls of her feet, but held her own. Her fear had insulted him further and as much as she hated him, she wished she hadn't shown it.

'I am not hiding behind my son,' he said in a dangerously quiet voice. 'I am telling you the truth. If you don't choose to hear it and prefer to write your own little scenarios about what happened, don't let me stop you. But I'm not going to defend myself to you any more.'

'Fine.' Her voice was shaking. She no longer felt like slugging it out with words. She didn't believe him, not because she didn't want to, but because it just didn't seem credible. Why on earth would Veronica only have become interested in Rory again when she heard about Thea's art gallery?

'I think we should eat,' said Ben.

His voice was shaking too and Thea wondered how near he had actually been to hitting her.

'Would you like a drink?'

'Yes, please.'

He got out two glasses and a bottle of whisky. He'd poured one huge measure when he stopped. 'Where does the friend you're staying with live?'

Thea's mind went blank. She had it written on a piece of paper which was in her bag. Her bag was probably still in his once immaculate bathroom. 'I can't remember. I've got it upstairs.'

'I'd better not have anything if I've got to drive you home.'

'I can easily take a taxi.' Thea felt that half her life had been spent in taxis just recently.

'I'm sorry to mention this, but Toby said you spent all your money on the one from Knightsbridge.'

'When I wasn't kidnapping him, you mean?'

'I'm sorry about that, too. It was Veronica who suggested you'd kidnapped him. It was how it seemed to her, you see.' A rueful grin disturbed his serious demeanour. 'Look at it from her point of view – you left her favourite gallery with her pet artist and her son. It did look quite like theft.'

Thea sighed. She could see that from Ben's point of view it had its funny side, but while in time she might see the incident as amusing, her life was nevertheless in tatters: she'd still lost her artist.

She sipped the drink he handed her. 'I think I'd like to go back now and not eat first.' She made a rather pathetic attempt at a smile.

'Thea –'

'I've got a lot of thinking to do.' She put down her glass. 'I'll go upstairs and get my bag.'

He was in the hall when she came down, holding his car keys.

'I'll just go and say goodbye to Toby,' said Thea.

Ben nodded. 'He's in there. I've asked my neighbour to pop over for a few moments.'

'Oh, I'm sorry. I didn't think. I'm not used to looking after children.'

'You don't do too badly.'

The moment was full of confused emotions, things unsaid. There was too much between them and too little. 'I'll say goodbye to Toby now.'

He opened the door to the sitting room without speaking.

'Hi, Toby.'

Toby pressed something on his console and got up.

'I'm off now. Ben's taking me home. We've had quite a day, one way and another, haven't we?'

Toby came over to Thea. 'It wasn't Dad's fault, what happened.'

Thea put her arms round him. 'No, of course it wasn't. It was just a silly thing that happened. It wasn't anyone's fault.'

'So you will go on being friends with him?'

Thea was about to say that of course she would and why on earth did he think she wouldn't, when she realised he might well have heard them quarrelling. 'Relationships get very complicated when you're grown up, Toby. But whatever happens, we can still be friends.'

Toby shook his head. 'That might be quite difficult, actually.'

Thea nodded in agreement. 'We could try, though. Molly would help us.'

Toby suddenly smiled. 'Yes, she would, wouldn't she?'

Thea had to bite her lip very hard not to cry as she gave Toby a last hug. They both knew they probably wouldn't see much of each other in future and Thea felt she'd lost someone she loved very much.

Magenta gave Thea a large vodka and orange juice. Thea sank back into her soft, cream-coloured sofa in relief. 'It's been such a long day. I'm completely shattered.'

'But you found Rory, which was the object of the exercise.'

'And lost him again, though I do know where to start looking, which is something. But Mags, that gallery! It's to die for and at a really swish address. How am I going to get him out of there and into the sticks?'

Magenta raised a perfectly groomed eyebrow. 'You mean, "How you gonna keep 'em down on the farm, now that they've seen Parree"?'

Thea had to laugh and nodded.

Magenta's answer was food: 'What do you fancy to eat?'

Pleased to be let off the hook, Thea considered. 'Toast and Marmite or pasta. I want comfort.'

'You shall have it. And I've got a box of truffles in the freezer, kept for emergencies.'

Thea had no energy left for talking. After they'd eaten pasta with a cream and smoked salmon sauce, and half a box of truffles, all she felt fit for was the futon in Magenta's spare room. She brushed her teeth, smeared herself with Magenta's expensive night cream and fell into bed, praying that sleep would prevent her thinking too hard about her shattered dreams.

In the morning, well rested and lured out of her pit by the smell of fresh coffee and the sound of Magenta's electric juicer, she felt different. Yes, she was still heartbroken about Ben's defection, for however much she wanted to believe his story, logically she just couldn't. After all, she thought, who would you support? Your ex-wife and mother of your adored son, or some zany friend of your second cousin once removed?

But now, she told Magenta brightly, she was going to fight for Rory tooth and nail. 'And as I don't care about my nails one-tenth as much as Veronica cares about hers, I'm bound to win.'

'Well, I'm glad you're feeling so upbeat about things this morning,' said Magenta. 'Have a multi-vitamin.'

'I don't feel upbeat, actually. I feel as if I'm trying to sort out world peace single-handed, but I'm also too angry not to try my very hardest to succeed.' Thea took a sip of orange juice and swallowed the pill.

'But don't forget,' said Magenta. 'You have Rory's pictures and they don't.'

Taking vitamins and feeling angry was one thing. Actually fronting up at the gallery demanding to know

Rory's home address required the loan of a beautiful linen skirt and a good squirt of some scent Magenta guaranteed would bring men to their knees. After all, strong perfume hadn't appeared to do Veronica any harm.

Thea went in and crept around the exhibition as she had done the day before, quietly, without announcing her presence. When she had stored up enough little snippets about the work to sound intelligent and informed, she approached the desk where Edward, the curator, was sitting. He was in his early sixties, still very good-looking and immaculately dressed.

'Hi!' She gave him a warm, slightly apologetic smile. 'I sort of hope you don't remember me, but I was in yesterday.'

He smiled graciously back. 'Of course I remember you. How could I forget? Such turmoil you left behind you.'

'I'm so sorry. Was it very dreadful?'

'For a while. Veronica blamed the nanny and the nanny blamed Veronica and tried not to show it. It was awful. I had to calm them all down with nips of brandy.'

Thea laughed. 'Well, it wasn't really anyone's fault, expect Toby's, sort of. But he's under the age of criminal responsibility, so no one can pin anything on him.'

Edward laughed. 'Now, what can I do for you?'

'Well, I've already hugely enjoyed this exhibition. And it's a lovely space . . .'

'Thank you. I selected the work and arranged it, and I also created the space. So what can I *really* do for you?'

Thea bit her lip. This was the hard part. She could spend all morning flirting with this attractive man, but it wouldn't get Rory back for her. 'I want to know where Rory's staying. I really *do* have to talk to him. Our conversation yesterday was cut short by Toby and a thunderstorm.'

'Now tell me, my dear, why should I give you the address of one of the most exciting young artists I've seen for years, when I know you're going to try and take him away from me?'

It was a fair question. Thea took a deep breath. 'Because my chances of getting him to come to me instead of staying with you are so infinitesimal that it wouldn't be fair of you not to give me the opportunity to at least try.'

Edward nodded. 'True, but you're a very charming young woman. Your chances might be better than you think. Can I risk that?'

'I was a charming young woman when Rory abandoned me for you, so to speak. I've got to give it a last try because I've worked too hard and committed too much of my partner's money to give up. But I will probably have to admit defeat.'

'What will you do? Abandon the idea of a gallery?'

'Good Lord, no! I'll have my graduate show and resign myself to never making a penny. I'll have to work in a bar in the evenings to keep myself, but it'll be worth it. It is a fabulous space, you see. I think it could be a really good gallery.'

Edward became thoughtful. 'Have you got any pictures?'

'Of the space?' Thea was cautious. The fact that she was getting on so well with Edward didn't mean he had ceased to be the enemy. 'I've got all my slides and stuff for my graduate show at my friend's flat and I think there are a couple of shots of the gallery as well. I was a photographer in my past life.'

'Have them biked over.'

'What?'

'Get your friend to ring a courier and get them sent here. I'd like to see what you've found in the graduate shows that really excites you.'

Still Thea hesitated. It would be an expensive exercise and what good could come of it?

'I'm not planning to steal all your young hopefuls,' said Edward, laughing. 'I just want to get an idea of how good your eye is. I might just need someone like you in my life.'

Chapter Nineteen

By the time the work arrived, one and a half hours later, there was only one other person whose opinion Thea valued as much as Edward Grampian's. And as she planned never to speak to Ben again it was what Edward thought that made her anxious as she slit the parcel tape on the package.

She couldn't bear to be present while he looked. This degree show might have to be her start in the world of gallery owning and if what she'd chosen was no good, she'd either have to learn very fast or give up. She prowled around Harrods Food Halls for an hour, trying not to imagine what a distinguished gallery owner might think of the Barbie Kitchen or the video of willowherb seeds swirling up into the sunshine.

Eventually, she forced herself back to the gallery. Edward was sitting at the desk, a very distinguished pair of gold spectacles on the end of his nose. He looked at her over them.

'Well?' she demanded. 'Shall I give up my gallery and take up knitting instead?'

'Oh, no. I shouldn't think you'd be any good at knitting.'

'Edward!' By now she felt they were old friends. 'What do you think? Don't keep me in suspense. I'm on pins here!'

'I think you've got the makings of a very good show. I think you need to add something a little more mainstream, so you don't antagonise the more conventional members of the public, but you don't need to go too far. A half-decent painter would do the trick.'

'Not easy to find. I looked and looked, but it's just not in fashion at the moment.'

'It will be. When Rory's had his show.'

There was a silence between them. For a while they'd forgotten they were in competition for the same ground-breaking young artist. Edward had Rory and Thea had the paintings. Thea felt that having Rory put Edward ahead, because she knew she wouldn't be able to keep the paintings against everybody's will. But Edward might not know she had them, which gave her a smidgen of advantage.

'Edward, about Rory's show.'

'Yes, Thea?'

'If you told him he could show with you afterwards, at some time in the future, he might well do the decent thing and stick with me.'

'He might. And while I probably would always be happy to show Rory's work, when I've got the space, I've no intention of telling him that.'

'But why not? You know how hard I've worked for this. You know I discovered Rory in a shed in Ireland!'

'You forget, I saw Rory before he disappeared. I was an admirer long before you were. By the time you found him he was easy to appreciate. He'd refined his art, done years of concentrated work. I saw the talent behind the rawness.'

Thea sighed deeply and tried again. 'But you're an established gallery. People will come here and buy from you whatever you put in it. You don't need the recognition like I do.'

'I have a reputation to keep up. People buy from me because they trust me to know what's good, what will appreciate in value. You can afford to fail. You've only money to lose. I have my integrity – far more precious, I assure you.'

That's the trouble with being fair-minded, thought Thea despondently. *I can see Edward's point of view perfectly. I know all about integrity, how important it is, how hard it is to acquire, how devastating to lose.*

Possibly sensing her surrender, Edward went on, 'But I will give you Rory's telephone number. If you can persuade him to show with you and not me, I won't hold it against him in future. Though I should warn you, Veronica has a lot of influence and she won't use it to your advantage if you take Rory. She's a scalp hunter and she won't be able to display Rory's if he shows with you first.'

This was something of a blow. She had, up until now, felt she had enough against her; shortage of capital, time, having her artist threatening to leave, without malicious interference. But if Veronica had nearly ruined Rory the first time round, she could do it again and ruin her at the same time.

'Just as well I haven't got a towel about my person, then, isn't it? Or I might be tempted to throw it in.'

She met Rory at the pub he stipulated. It was not in a part of London she knew and Thea felt a little awkward going into a busy pub on her own, when she had no confidence in Rory's punctuality. But she went in and searched the crowd for Rory.

He was at the bar, entertaining a couple of young men with Irish jokes. 'Hey, Thea! Over here! What are you having?'

'If you're paying, a large one.'

'Of course I'm paying. Jimmy, a large Paddy for the lady.'

Thea almost changed her order to a mineral water, but then decided a bit of Dutch courage, or in this case, Irish courage, might not be a bad thing. 'Rory,' she said firmly, when she'd thanked him for her drink. 'I do need to talk to you. Can we go and sit down?'

'I suppose so, Thea, but I don't think you're going to like what I'm going to say when you've said your piece.'

'Probably not, but I've got to say it. I've got to try and make you do the decent thing. I mean, do you really want Veronica, who pulled the plug on your first show, getting the credit for discovering you?'

'I wouldn't if she had. But she says she always stuck up for me. She says she tried to persuade everyone to lighten up and let my show run its course.'

'And you believe her?'

'I have to believe her. She got me a show in one of the best galleries in London. Edward cancelled a retrospective of a really famous artist, so I could show.'

Why hadn't Edward mentioned this to her when they were discussing whose right to Rory was the greater? Was Edward not telling Thea everything? Or was Veronica lying to Rory? 'Who was that, do you know?'

Rory shook his head. 'Forgotten. Someone terribly important. I'm going to have to bone up on contemporary artists. I know nothing about them.'

Thea smiled, not really amused. 'You must ask Edward as soon as possible. In case you need to give a lecture on them.'

'That was a low blow, Thea.'

'You deserved it.' It wasn't so much a blow as a hint. If Rory did ask Edward, he might learn that not everything Veronica told him was true. She tried one more appeal to his sense of fair play. 'So I can't persuade you to do the decent thing?'

'Not if I value my life. Veronica would kill me if I changed my mind now, after she'd gone to so much trouble to introduce me to Edward and set up the show.'

'Oh! So you're not worried about *me* killing you? For pretty much the same thing? Only in my case it wouldn't be so much murder as justifiable homicide! I put my own money, Molly's money and the sweat of my brow into my gallery! Weeks of hard labour! Not to mention looking after your dog and your puppies so you could come to London and leave me stranded!'

'No,' he said baldly, unimpressed. 'Because you're not that sort of person. You wouldn't sabotage a vicar's tea party out of spite, let alone someone's career. Even if that someone happens to be me. Veronica wouldn't think twice about it.'

'I could learn to be that sort of person,' she muttered, wishing it were true.

Rory put out his hand and cupped her cheek in it. It was warm and comforting and trustworthy, quite unlike its owner. 'No you couldn't. And that's why I love you.'

She looked at him, startled.

'I mean the word in its widest sense,' he added. 'I'm afraid I've come round to thinking that you and me are a beautiful relationship that was destined not to happen. But don't worry, I'm not completely brokenhearted.'

Thea suddenly felt tears spring to her eyes. She bit her lip. She was tired and had gone through a lot in the past twenty-four hours. Despair, which she had kept at bay with every trick she knew, suddenly seemed very near. She took a large sip of whiskey. 'Oh, God,' she murmured so quietly he couldn't hear her. 'I wish I could say the same.'

It was dispiriting to have to take the train back to Cheltenham to tell Molly that her mission had failed. Rory had not promised to change his mind and come back to Thea's gallery. He hadn't even promised to think about it. He had refused. The only good news was that Edward Grampian was seriously talking about giving Thea a job that she could do and still run her gallery. It would be hard work, but she would scout around the country for work which wouldn't usually come his way. He might even offer exhibitions to artists who'd previously exhibited with her.

This, she hoped, would be enough to stop Molly getting too downcast. But it wouldn't stop her railing against Rory and his perfidy. Thea could have done quite a bit of railing herself, but there was no point. She just had to move on and look forward to the graduate show.

She decided not to tell Molly about Ben's part in it all. It wasn't fair to her – it wasn't her fault, but as his relation she'd feel bad about it. And worse, she'd probably feel obliged to stick up for him, to explain away his actions as being 'for the best'.

To her surprise, Molly was waiting on the platform with Petal as the train drew in. She must have come home for some reason, Thea thought, as she struggled to open the door through the window. *I just wish I had some good news for them.*

'Hi, you two!' She stepped down on to the platform, her bag preceding her. 'How lovely of you to come and pick me up. Save me having to get a taxi.' She kissed Molly and was about to kiss Petal, when she saw the expressions on their faces. 'What's the matter? It's not the pups, is it? Lara? Oh, no, don't tell me. I couldn't bear it. Not Little Chap, the one I've been hand-feeding?' *That's why Petal's here*, she thought distractedly. *So I won't be alone in the house.*

'The dogs are fine,' said Molly. 'Or they were when I picked up your keys half an hour ago.'

Thea's heart, which had begun to race, took a moment to realise all was not lost. 'Then it must be the gallery. A flood. Oh, my God, not a fire! Not all Rory's pictures!'

'Thea!' said Molly, irritated. 'What has got into you? Why are you imagining all these disasters?'

'Because you two have got faces which could announce the outbreak of World War Three. What's happened?'

'Ben rang and told us *everything*,' announced Petal.

'What?' *What 'everything' could Ben have possibly told them?*

'We can't talk about it here,' said Molly. 'Let's get in the

262

car and go back to Thea's. There's a lot to discuss. Though I must say it's very disappointing.'

'Can't argue with that,' Thea agreed. 'You get in the back, Petal. I've got all my stuff.'

'You could put it in the boot,' suggested Petal, who liked the front seat best.

'Oh, just get in, both of you,' snapped Molly.

Home was much tidier and cleaner than Thea had left it, in spite of her high-speed attack on the dirt. The hall smelt of polish and air freshener, and the floor shone as it never had before. Even the kitchen was surprisingly orderly. The newspapers on the floor had been used, but they hadn't yet been ripped and rumpled by puppy games.

Thea picked up Little Chap and then the kettle. 'So, what did Ben say, to make you both look so miserable?' She managed the kettle and puppy together, filling one and cuddling the other. She wished she could have the place to herself, to have a quiet cup of tea, see to her dogs and plan a strategy.

'He told us that Rory definitely won't be showing with us,' announced Petal. 'Because Veronica – that's his wife – has found a really wonderful exhibition space for him.'

'Well, I knew that.' She put down Little Chap so she could deal with mugs and tea bags.

'But you don't seem to understand the implications,' said Molly, sitting down.

'Or you wouldn't be so cool about it,' broke in Petal. 'It's all been a complete waste of time. I may as well go back to Surrey!'

'Well, there's no point in weeping and wailing and gnashing my teeth. Rory's not the only pebble on the beach.'

'But this was our big chance to make a name for ourselves as a gallery,' protested Molly, as if Thea must have forgotten. 'We were going to get so much publicity and interest from the art world. Rory would have put us on the map.'

'I know. His paintings are wonderful, but I've got a really good degree show lined up. And we'll have a bit more time to get ready for that. We weren't ever going to be a one-show wonder, Molly. We'll just have to make our reputation a bit more slowly, without Rory's help.'

'I still don't think . . .'

'Would you like tea, Molly?'

'Yes, please. But I don't see why you're not tearing your hair out over this. I mean, the whole reason for you dashing off to London was to convince Rory to change his mind and you failed. We know you did, because Ben told us.'

'Ben doesn't know everything,' said Thea airily. 'Ben doesn't know that I showed my slides and stuff for the graduate show to the owner of the gallery where Rory's showing. He liked them a lot. He thinks I have a good eye and he wants me to be a scout for him. So there!' She could have added a lot more, but didn't, for the sake of discretion.

'Oh. And this proper gallery owner actually liked that ghastly pink kitchen and those weird videos?' Molly was at once appalled and disbelieving.

'Yup. You see, we don't need Rory.'

Petal sighed. 'I was really looking forward to his show, I must say. I don't know if I'm really into the gallery now.'

'Well, honestly!' said Thea. 'A fine friend you are! Take away the crumpet and only leave the art and you lose interest. Perhaps I should point out that some of the graduates are fairly gorgeous, too.'

'It's not that,' said Petal, making it clear that it was.

'Well, have a cup of tea, both of you. And then, now I know that the gallery hasn't been burnt down, or been flooded, or anything, I would like to unpack and sort out my washing and stuff.'

They took the hint, drank their tea and left.

Thea spent the rest of the day at home. Somehow she couldn't face the gallery just yet. Although all her cheery statements about its future were true and she did believe them, she was more bruised by Rory's defection than she wanted Molly and Petal to know – probably because of Ben's part in it all. If only she could believe him when he said he hadn't gone looking for Rory for Veronica's sake. If only she hadn't fallen in love with him, or even if only she could fall out of love with him now she knew he was the root of all her troubles. It was a shame the heart didn't work like that.

She went to bed early and fell asleep immediately, aided by hot milk with whisky in it. She was in the middle of her deepest sleep when the phone finally penetrated her dreams enough to wake her.

It was Rory. He sounded drunk. 'Is that you, Thea? It's me, Rory. I'm ringing from a pub.'

'I guessed. What do you want?'

'I was just ringing to tell you that I've decided to show with you after all.'

'What?' Thea sat up in bed to make sure she wasn't still asleep.

'I said I'm going to show with you after all. It means you can keep the pictures. I'll be down in a few days to tell you where to hang them.'

'What? Why? What changed your mind?'

'I decided not to let my life be ruled by that bitch. I'll show where I want to show and let Veronica go hang. Let her try and ruin my career all over again!'

'Calm down, I'm sure she won't do that.'

'Yes, she will. She told me. But I don't care. And now I'm ringing off. Goodbye.'

Thea stayed sitting up in bed, wondering if she could allow herself to be pleased, or if Rory would have forgotten about his drunken telephone call in the morning.

Fortunately, because it had taken a while to wake up, most of the call was recorded on the answering machine. For a moment the thought drifted through her head that, should she have to sue him, she could actually produce the tape in court.

Far too wide awake now to be able to go back to sleep, she lay in bed for a while, mentally placing the pictures and wondering if it would be worth disturbing the puppies to make a cup of tea. If she went down, they'd all think it was morning. She'd have to heat milk and give them Weetabix, and take them out into the garden. If it had been four or five, Thea would have done this to get a head start on the day. But it was only half past one.

Eventually she decided she'd never get back to sleep if she just lay there, listening to the news on the World Service. She got up, braved the puppies and took a cup of tea back up to bed. Typically, it was half past five when she finally dozed off.

Dragging herself out of bed at seven, Thea felt terribly groggy and short of sleep, but knowing there were hungry pups, lakes of wee and piles of poo awaiting her, she pulled on her dressing gown and threw herself in the direction of the stairs.

If only she'd put on shoes. She put her foot in a puppy poo the moment she opened the kitchen door. She swayed about for a moment or two, debating whether to scoop up newspapers and deal with the other poos first, and then try and hike her foot into the sink in the scullery, or vice versa. It was the thought of balancing on one leg after so few hours of sleep that unnerved her, but then again, walking about with poo between the toes was worse than unnerving. She limped to the sink.

When her foot was at last clean, she emptied out her wellingtons and put them on. By the time the kitchen floor was swabbed, all the puppies had raced around the tiny garden for a bit and had eaten their breakfast, she realised that there was a definite bubble of cheerfulness developing within her. She would hold Rory to his promise, and if she had to threaten to cut his pictures into pieces and send them to him bit by bit, she would do it.

'I can't understand it! Ben definitely said that Rory *couldn't* show with you because Veronica would use all her influence to ruin him!'

Thea tucked the phone under her chin and picked up a puppy. 'Rory obviously felt differently. Perhaps he's not as frightened of Veronica as Ben is.'

The sarcasm floated past Molly. 'Oh, Ben's not frightened of her. But he has had to fight hard to keep on good terms with her for Toby's sake.'

Thea sighed, her broken night suddenly catching up with her. 'Well, anyway,' she said, 'Rory *is* showing with us, so we can get back on track and organise it all.'

'He can't change his mind again, can he?'

'No. I'm going to weld his pictures to the walls quickly, so there's no question of it.'

'But Thea! You can't do that! You'll never get them off and we'd have to redecorate all over again.'

'Only joking, Molly.' Really, by this time she shouldn't have to explain all her jokes to Molly. Gently, she set the puppy back on its feet.

'Are you going to ring Ben and tell him the news?'

'Nope,' Thea said firmly. 'If you think he needs to know, you ring him. Personally I think he could just find out when he gets his invitation to the private view.'

'Thea! What have you got against Ben, all of a sudden? I thought you liked him.'

'Did you? Oh, well. You tell him if you want to. I really don't mind one way or the other. Now, lovey, I've got a million things to do. I'll see you at the gallery in about an hour.'

Chapter Twenty

The gallery seemed larger, whiter and brighter than it had done only a few days ago. The sun, shining through the massive windows, added to the impression of a huge light space. One of the big windows still had to be blocked off, to make extra space, but now Thea just enjoyed the sense of airy joy the place gave her.

She went downstairs to where Rory's pictures, shrouded in bubble-wrap, were stacked in the passage. She hadn't allowed herself to look at them when she thought they might be denied to her. Now she dragged one of them into the big gallery and undraped a landscape.

It took her straight back to Ireland. She could almost feel the cold air on her face, the bright sun in her eyes. She knew the feel of the sea against her ankles if she went down to the shore and took her shoes off.

She propped it against the wall and dragged out another. Molly would be here in a minute, full of bustle and questions about the private view. Should they serve canapés, what sort of wine? Now, she wanted a really private view, just her and the paintings, with no one else around.

Her reverie was pitifully short. Molly arrived, as Thea had predicted, the party for the private view her chief concern. She barely glanced at the paintings.

'I think we should serve things to eat, otherwise people will just lap up the free wine and get plastered.'

Well, she certainly didn't want Rory getting plastered – perhaps food was a good idea. 'OK, Molly, what sort of things do you think? Sandwiches, sausage rolls? Little quiches?'

Molly looked appalled; working with Thea could be very difficult. The poor girl had *no idea* what was what. 'I was thinking blinis with caviar, a little sushi, perhaps. Maybe smoked salmon, that sort of thing?'

'That sort of thing won't stop anyone getting drunk and it'll cost a fortune. And who's going to make it? I've got more than enough to do without spending all night stuffing cherry tomatoes!'

'We get a caterer! I know a lovely girl who'll do it all for us. She'll even provide waitresses.'

'But how much will it cost? Financially, we're running on empty with this gallery. Until we start earning, we can't afford unnecessary luxuries like that.'

Molly stuck out her chin. It was what she did when Derek said they couldn't afford something and it always worked.

'It's too expensive,' said Thea.

'I'll pay,' said Molly.

Thea's own chin went out, rivalling Molly's.

'Oh, please let me! Just for this show.'

Molly's disappointment was more effective than her pouting. 'We should start as we mean to go on.'

'It's just that Ben has –'

'What?' Thea hadn't told Molly of her falling out with Ben, but Ben must have said something or Molly wouldn't have halted in mid-plea.

Molly started picking at a spot of paint on the light switch. 'He said he wanted to invite all sorts of people from London.' She turned to Thea. 'He really wants to help the gallery, Thea, whatever you think.'

'It's all right, Molly. If Ben wants to invite a few of his friends, he's welcome. If he thinks they'll come all the way out here.'

'That's my point!' declared Molly. 'If they do come, I

don't want to look like a small-town gallery that doesn't know what's what.'

Thea didn't either, but the thought of spending the equivalent of several pictures' worth of commission in case Ben's arty chums turned up to patronise her did not appeal. 'I'll compromise. No food, but I'll book a table at the Chinese for afterwards. At least that way we won't be buying food that won't get eaten.' She resolved to make sure Rory ate several large stodgy sandwiches before the opening, to line his stomach.

'The Chinese!' Molly couldn't have been more horrified if Thea had suggested going on to a strip joint.

'The Chinese Dragon is really elegant. Have you been there? It's just like a proper restaurant. I went there with friends when it first opened. It's fab, honestly. I'll book a table for ten or so and hope some of them pay for themselves.'

'OK, that sounds quite fun, but I want canapés!' The stamped foot was implicit.

Thea caved in. She had other, bigger battles to fight. 'Oh, all right, Molly, but only for Rory's show. When things are normal we'll just have wine, and charge them for the second glass.'

Molly hissed in horror, as if Thea were suggesting she charged people for sherry in her own house.

'Well, you don't actually charge them, that's illegal, you just ask for contributions. It's what people do, honestly. I found out when I was in London.' This was a lie, but if Molly could stamp, she could bend the truth.

'Very well, I'll let you know best on that one. But for our very first party – I mean show – I want to do things properly.'

Thea shrugged. 'She who pays the piper gets the sushi.'

Molly smiled, but then became serious. 'Ben's quite worried, by the way.'

'Oh, dear. Poor Ben.'

'No, really – about Rory suddenly changing his mind.'

'Changing it back, you mean.'

'It did make me wonder if we really ought to let Rory show here. Veronica can be so spiteful and according to Ben she was spitting tacks when she heard.'

The phone calls must have been flying to and fro across London like nuclear missiles. 'I don't think anyone could ruin Rory's career now. Edward, the gallery owner in London, thought very highly of him. And although Veronica seemed to take the credit for getting the space, Edward would have shown him anyway. I really don't think she can hurt him.'

'I think Ben was more worried about what Veronica would do to this gallery than to Rory.'

This did pierce Thea's confidence a little. 'Why? Why would she do anything to the gallery? What could she do? Fire-bomb it?'

'Don't joke! She's a very influential woman! The wrong word from her and people will stay away in droves. She's never liked me and –'

'And what?'

'Ben says she thinks you kidnapped Toby.'

'Well, that's totally ridiculous. No one could possibly be so stupid as to think that. For God's sake, Toby followed us out of the gallery. She must have realised that. If she ever cast a glance in his direction she'd have seen him leave.'

'Well, I don't know, at least, only what Ben tells me. And he did tell me that Veronica's livid with you.'

'Because she thinks I kidnapped Toby?'

'Oh, I think there's more to it than that. I think she's peeved because you got on so well with Edward Grampian, who Ben tells me is very important in the art world. And she doesn't like it if Ben gets interested in a woman. She doesn't want him herself, but she doesn't want anyone else to have him.'

'She needn't worry about that. Ben is not interested in me. Not in the slightest. Now, do you think we could stop gossiping and get on with some work?' Then, realising she shouldn't have shouted at Molly, Thea went on, 'Sorry. I am a bit stressed by everything at the moment. And I do think Ben should have made it clear to Veronica that he and I aren't even good friends.'

'Aren't you?' Molly was so unaccustomed to seeing the easygoing Thea in this mood that she couldn't think of a better answer. 'He's renting a house in Bristol, you know, to make it easier for house-hunting.'

'Oh? Well, I hope Toby won't mind leaving all his London friends.' It then occurred to Thea that perhaps it was her friendship with Toby that had made Veronica jealous.

'I expect Ben'll end up sending Toby to prep school. It is easier for a single parent.'

The thought of Toby going to boarding school brought sudden tears to Thea's eyes. 'I thought that was why they were moving, so he could go to a local school. What's the point of uprooting him if he's going to be sent away anyway?' Then she got a grip. 'Anyway, it's none of my business,' she said, trying to sound brisk. 'So, when is your pet man coming to fill in the window? Or shall we tackle it ourselves?'

'Thea! I wouldn't have an inkling of how to start! I know it's good to be economical, but really, there are limits to DIY.' She said the word as if it were strange, very coarse slang and unfit for a lady's lips.

Thea managed to laugh. 'Only joking. We'll have your Handy-Andy.'

'He's not called Andy.' Molly looked worried. 'He's called Bob.'

'Just be a doll and give him a ring, Moll—ee.'

Molly shook her head. Sometimes she found Thea completely incomprehensible.

A lifetime later, at home, Thea sorted through the post, the puppies fighting with her ankles as she did so. Apart from the junk mail there was one letter. She opened it. It was from Toby. He had typed it on his computer.

Dear Thea,
   I'm writing to say sorry for causing all that trouble. I heard Dad on the phone to Veronica and I know he doesn't think you kidnapped me. I just hope you and Dad go on being friends. Please tell me you are.
   Love,
      Toby.

This rather formal communication was decorated with stars and space ships. Thea bit her lip. There was no point in her getting sentimental. Toby wanted her and Ben to get together, so he could have a proper mother. Now she'd met Veronica, Thea could see his point. She might not know the first thing about child-rearing herself, but at least she genuinely enjoyed Toby's company, which she doubted Veronica did.

She just hoped Ben didn't know how Toby felt. It would madden him. Relationships were difficult enough without having your son trying to influence your love life. Ben would never marry anyone Toby didn't like, she knew that instinctively. In the same way that she could now accept that if he said he didn't go looking for Rory for Veronica he probably hadn't; it was all a horrible coincidence.

Not that it would have made any difference. If she'd said, OK, I believe you, when Ben had first told her that it wouldn't have warmed his tepid feelings into passion. The only passion he ever felt in connection with her was anger – not an emotion to build a relationship on. But still, if she got an opportunity, she would like to tell him that she no

273

longer thought him capable of such a massive deception. Perhaps, if he came to Rory's private view, there might be a chance then.

Which still left her with Toby's letter, which she would have to reply to, and quickly, or it wouldn't reach him. She didn't want to find herself obliged to ask Molly for Ben's Bristol address – it would promote a torrent of probing questions that Thea had no answers for.

Later, she sat at the kitchen table with a lined pad, thinking what to write. She had a nice card she could copy it on to when she'd finally thought it out. So far, she hadn't got beyond 'Dear Toby'.

Eventually, after much crossing out, starting again and making balls of paper for the puppies to chase, she came up with,

> *Dear Toby,*
>
> *Adults don't always behave logically and sadly, I don't think Ben and I can go on being friends, quite.* [The 'quite' was because in spite of everything, she couldn't absolutely close her heart and mind to the idea.]
>
> *But that doesn't mean that we can't be friends separately. You can come and stay with me any time. Molly would arrange it.* [She hoped this didn't sound furtive, or like custody arrangements.]
>
> *I do hope you and Ben are happy in Bristol, and that you don't miss your London friends too much. The good thing is that Bristol is quite near me, so you can come and see the puppies, or make chocolate cake and pizza whenever you like.*
>
> *With much love,*
> *your friend, Thea.*

She decorated her letter with drawings of Lara and the puppies, chasing each other round the page, leaving puddles behind them. By the time she'd done all this she realised it wouldn't fit on the card, especially if she wanted to re-create the drawings, so she just folded up the letter and sent it as it was. Toby wouldn't criticise her for writing on lined paper and if Ben did, well, he always had dis-approved of her terribly.

As she walked Lara to the postbox later, she resolved to put Ben completely out of her mind. There was so much still to do before the show that she wouldn't have any spare thought capacity for him anyway.

The rhythm and pace of Thea's life became hard and fast. She kept her wellington boots by her bed and leapt out of bed at six o'clock, straight into them. Once she had swilled out the kitchen and fed everyone, she took Lara for as long a walk as she had time for. Then she checked that whoever was detailed to come in and see to the brood at lunchtime was aware of their responsibilities, got in her car and drove off to the gallery. Thea discovered the sad fact that the more people she had to help her, the longer every job seemed to take.

The main picture hanging, which Rory insisted on attending, took two days and included an over-indulgent evening at Thea's house, where Rory stayed.

It didn't take so long because he and Thea argued about what should go where – in fact, their ideas were sur-prisingly harmonious – but because there was such a lot of work to be fitted in and it was difficult to decide exactly where on the wall to hang each one. It was only when they started the process that they discovered that half the walls weren't true and had little unsuspected bulges.

'Rather like when you put on a clingy dress,' said Petal, who was helping. 'You find bumps all over the place.'

Thea and Rory regarded Petal, a perfect size ten. 'But in your case,' said Rory, 'the bumps are in all the right places.'

Arranging a lighting system took another two days and more money than Thea could bear to contemplate. But in

the end they had one which was flexible, easy to change –
provided you could cope with climbing ladders – and
made the work look sensational.

Thea said as much to Rory who was offended. 'I mean,
your work is sensational if you see it in a garage with the
door shut. But a lot of the artists I have may need a little
assistance with the lighting. It's very important. It's the
same as good framing. It makes all the difference.'

Rory laughed. 'Sure, I was only teasing you. I know it's
important.'

Ben, who kept away from the gallery, occupied her
thoughts only when he had a genuine reason to be there,
like when she was wondering if the painted hardboard
floor, laid directly over the carpet, was all right. Or if she
should have the prices discreetly stuck up next to the
paintings, or on a sheet, to be handed to each person. Was
Little Chap really thriving and catching up with his
siblings, or was it just wishful thinking on her part? In fact,
she reckoned wryly, she only thought about him twenty or
thirty times a day. That's practically over him, she told
herself.

The days flashed past and gradually the gallery began to
look like a gallery. The ladders and dust sheets were
moved out; the fine dust which had covered everything
when the floors were sanded was no longer discovered in
unlikely places. Thea even got to the stage of redecorating
the little room beyond the kitchen, in case they had to
expand into it. Sadly, painting over the walls did nothing
to erase the poignant memories she had about the room.

Molly began to do some serious PR, telephoning
everyone she could think of to tell them about Rory and
the exhibition. But the response was disappointing. The
moment people heard that the show was out of London
they lost interest. Molly started to despair. 'If we're not
careful it'll end up just being a social event for our friends.'

'Well, that's all right, isn't it? Isn't it nicer to entertain your friends than a of lot of London media types who'll just turn their noses up at the whole thing?' Thea was beginning to think that obscurity was better than success. If she was going to fail, she wanted to do it quietly, with no one looking.

'You don't think it's anything to do with Veronica, do you?' demanded Molly.

'That's paranoid. Why should she bother to sabotage us?'

Molly regarded Thea but, for once, didn't say anything.

Then, four days before the private view, when Thea was about to resort to ringing round her friends to make sure they at least came, things changed.

The first time the phone rang and it was a London paper, Thea was thrilled. She called Molly immediately and told her about it. Molly, who'd planned a trip to the beauty therapist in preparation for the big day, cancelled her appointment. 'Just so that I can be there if it happens again.'

'Showing your usual confidence in my PR skills I see?' said Thea light-heartedly.

'Of course not, Thea – oh honestly! I'll be over in an hour.'

Thea had dealt with three more calls when she heard the gallery door open while she was scribbling down some details. 'Thank goodness you're here. The phone hasn't stopped all morning and I'm desperate to go to the loo. What kept you?' She looked up and saw not Molly, but Ben, who stood in the doorway, hesitating. 'Oh. You're not Molly.'

'No. Sorry.'

Thea's mouth was suddenly dry and she stopped feeling like a gallery owner creating interest in London, and felt gauche and foolish, uncertain what to say. 'Well, come in, then,' she managed.

He came into the space and looked around. 'I wasn't sure how welcome I'd be.'

Thea smiled a little stiffly. 'Perfectly welcome.'

He looked very tired and formal, and more attractive than Thea had thought it possible for any man to look. She wanted to fling herself at him and hold on to him so tightly that he would never escape. Against her will, her mind went back to the last time he had touched her, gripping her shoulder, manhandling her into his house. Instead of anger or indignation, she just wanted to feel his touch again, even an angry touch.

'I came to make a confession.'

Oh, not now, thought Thea. *Don't tell me anything dreadful now*. 'Is it really necessary? I'm sure you'd never do anything really terrible.'

'Are you? Last time we met you seemed to doubt that.'

It was odd. A little while ago she'd have given much to have the opportunity to tell Ben that she knew he hadn't betrayed her. Now that it was presented to her she felt reluctant to do so. Was it spite? Did she want him to suffer a little of what she'd suffered? 'Well, I'm sure you can't blame me for doubting it. It was a little hard to accept that you really didn't know Veronica would snap up Rory the moment you found out where he was.'

'I do see that and I don't blame you for doubting me.'

'So what have you got to confess now?'

'I decided I had to do some damage limitation.'

Thea frowned. 'Oh?'

'Veronica was very bitter about Rory changing his mind.'

'Was she?'

'So that she didn't manage to convince everyone that your show wasn't worth crossing the street for, let alone visiting the wilds of Gloucestershire, I decided to take action.'

'What action? Oh, excuse me, there's the phone again.'

It rang again, twice, before she had a chance to carry on her conversation with Ben, by which time Molly had arrived. 'What is going on?' she asked. 'And what are you doing here, Ben?'

'I came to warn you both. I asked a friend of mine to do a press release and ring up a few of her contacts. She knows absolutely everybody.'

'Oh.' Thea felt ambivalent about this piece of information. She should be thrilled to have so much publicity and interest in her gallery. But she also felt she should have been consulted. 'Shouldn't I have written the press release?'

'I'm sorry. I would have consulted you, but writing press releases is a fairly skilled art. You have to capture the attention of a lot of very bored journos who are unlikely to have any interest in art unless there's a story attached.' He paused. 'And I didn't want you to tell me *not* to do it, because I knew it was important that I did.'

'Oh.'

Molly, aware of uncomfortable currents flowing between Thea and Ben said, 'Well I'm sure I could have managed something.'

'Molly, I know you're really well connected but my friend truly has an enormous number of contacts.' Ben sounded apologetic.

'Oh, well, could you at least show us a copy of the press release?' asked Thea. 'So we have some idea what the story is?'

'Sure.' He put his briefcase on the desk and took out a sheaf of papers. He handed one each to Molly and Thea. It read:

There are pots of gold at the bottom of rainbows in Ireland, but something even more exciting has been discovered in the far west of County Mayo. A young man, whose work hasn't been seen since just after his graduate show, has been working in private on a series of landscapes that is creating enormous excitement in the art world. Offered a show in London by the Edward Grampian Gallery, he decided instead to exhibit at a brand-new provincial gallery, opened by one time girlfriend [Thea coughed] Thea Orville, who created the gallery just to show his work. Why he should make his debut in a completely unknown location instead of in a well-established London gallery is a mystery, but the art world will be flocking to see. The fact that he happens to be 'a ride' is just a bonus.

A photograph of Rory staring out over Clew Bay, which she remembered taking herself, shared the page. Thea had to admit that he looked as beautiful and romantic as possible.

'Well,' she said, feeling very ambivalent, handing back the page. 'It's obviously done the trick. The phone hasn't stopped – oops, there is goes again.' After she had dealt with the call, she turned back to Ben. 'But I'm not at all sure it's ethical. I've never been Rory's girlfriend and it's his work they should be talking about, not what he looks like and whether or not he happens to be "a ride".'

'What does that mean, anyway?' demanded Molly.

'I think it's what Petal would describe as "well-fit", in Irish,' said Thea. 'And I haven't time to keep answering the telephone to journalists who are more keen to know whether or not Rory and I were an item than about his work.'

'Well, are you? An item, that is?' asked Ben.

'What has that got to do with the price of fish?' demanded Thea, furious with him for asking, especially in front of Molly, so they couldn't have a proper row.

'Possibly nothing. It's just helpful to know the facts. From a PR point of view.'

'Oh, really? Going on what I've just read, you just make it up. Facts have nothing to do with it.'

'Oh, stop bickering, you two,' Molly snapped. 'How are

we going to cope with the phone when we've got so much to do? I've got a hair appointment. There are some extra postcards to collect and goodness knows what else.'

'And I've one or two things to do myself,' Thea added, thinking of her 'to do' list, which got longer and longer as every hour passed.

Ben's eyebrows flicked upwards. 'Get Petal back to do it for you. Tell her exactly what to say about your and Rory's romantic status, and when the private view is.'

'Molly's insisting on canapés, so we have to know how many people are likely to come.'

'Many more than you've invited, that's for sure. Have you made a list of which papers you've spoken to?'

'Yes,' said Thea, crossing her fingers behind her back, hoping that, if she was quick, she would remember and could make one.

'I'd better get on to the caterer,' said Molly. 'I hope she can manage the extra numbers.'

'But first, can you ring Petal and ask if her father can bring her over? I can't keep racing back up the stairs every time the phone rings and I've got things to see to down there,' Thea pleaded.

'You need a portable phone that you can carry around with you.'

'Yes, I know. But right now I need Petal. Please, Molly –' The phone rang again.

'I'll use my mobile,' said Molly, as Thea picked it up.

'I'll have a look round,' said Ben. 'If you don't mind.'

Thea was on the phone, so she couldn't tell him that actually, she minded very much. She wanted to show him round herself.

Chapter Twenty-One

꧁ꕥꕥꕥ꧂

The next time the phone rang Thea made Molly answer it and went down to see what Ben was up to. She felt terribly cheated that she hadn't been there to show it to him, to see his face when he saw the paintings properly hung for the first time.

He was downstairs in the large gallery, with the painted floor laid over the glue-covered boards. He turned when he heard her come in. 'It's fabulous. They look wonderful. You've done a brilliant job.'

'I only got the pictures up on the walls. It's Rory who's brilliant.'

He shook his head. 'The setting is important and it's worked out just right.'

Thea bit her lip. She'd so yearned for his praise, but now that she'd had it she didn't know what to say.

'Thank you for writing to Toby,' Ben said. 'He was thrilled to get the letter.'

'Oh, good. You know he wrote to me? I felt I had to answer.' What she really wanted to know was whether Ben had read her letter to Toby.

'It was kind of you to think of a small boy when you've got so much else on your plate.'

Thea smiled. 'It wasn't a small boy, it was Toby! That's quite different. He and I are friends.'

'But you and I can't be?'

Oh. So he had read the letter. 'Well, what do you think?'

He sighed. 'No. I've got plenty of friends and they're none of them like you.'

'But I hope it won't mean Toby and I can't see each other. I'd be really sorry not to. I love him.' The words came out on a sigh. It was true, she did love Toby, but she also loved the man she was talking to. It was like blowing a kiss in the wrong direction.

Ben nodded.

'Thea!' Molly called downstairs. 'Petal's father's driving her over now. But you'll have to come and mind the phone. I've got to see the caterers and pick up the postcards. Oh, and Rory rang to say he's coming.'

Ben gave a wry smile. 'Well, I'll go now. I've got a house to have another look at.'

'In Bristol?'

'No. Near here, actually. So you and Toby can carry on your relationship.'

Thea spent a few seconds trying to find an appropriate response.

'It's in Goldenley,' Ben went on when she failed.

'Oh. Lovely views up there.'

'I know. It's why I bought it.'

'I look forward to seeing it some time.'

'I'm sure you will. Molly will make me have a house-warming party.'

If Thea hadn't been so ferociously busy she'd have wept.

Rory was wonderfully uncomplicated and when he appeared in the gallery doorway, Thea went to embrace him. His strong arms were comforting and she clung on to him, wishing they belonged to someone else – someone not comforting at all.

'Hey, Thea! Put me down!'

'I'm just so pleased to see you.'

'Well, I'm not staying long. There's a woman over towards Gloucester I've got to see. Now what's happened? You're not usually so keen to put your arms round me.'

Thea laughed, feeling better. 'Nothing's happened,

exactly. It's just the phone is ringing constantly and until Petal arrives to answer it I've got to. And Molly is stressing about your statements. She says if we're to get them typed, copied and laminated, she has to have it now. Or yesterday, for preference.'

'I'm not writing a statement.'

'Not even one? Molly wants one for each picture.'

'Well, she can't have it. They're a load of shite.' He grinned. 'Or, at least, mine would be.'

'I could help you write it. If you're not so hot on the written word.'

'Why is it, for Christ's sake, that artists, who communicate visually are expected to become writers? It's like asking novelists to illustrate their work, or paint pictures for their covers.'

Thea laughed. 'That sounds like a well-rehearsed argument. You'd better polish it up for when Molly gets back from the printer's.'

'I'm back now,' said Molly from behind a pile of boxes. 'What argument?'

'No statements, Molly,' said Rory firmly. 'They're shite and they interfere with the work on the wall.'

'They wouldn't be on the wall. They'd be in lovely shiny folders, on laminated sheets. Look!' She produced a folder of impeccable glossiness from the bag which hung over her shoulder.

'Oh, Molly! More money!' Thea wailed.

'They're only samples,' she said to Thea and then turned back to Rory. 'People like to know what they're looking at.'

'They can see what they're looking at,' Rory told her. 'They're landscapes. They're not abstracts; they don't have any secret codes in them. What more can they possible need than a bloody great picture, eight foot high?'

'I've visited a lot of galleries just lately to find out what they do and I like to have something to read.'

Rory laughed. 'Shite galleries, if you'll forgive the expression.'

'Oh, don't apologise now,' snapped Molly. 'You've already used that word several times.'

Thea put her hand on Molly's arm, to make up for the fact that she was on Rory's side in this matter. She'd visited a lot of galleries with Magenta and mostly she found the statements embarrassing. 'Rory's right, Molly. His work doesn't need any explanation and I like things simple. People should be able just to wander around and enjoy themselves without having to carry a huge book to refer to.'

Rory, who'd made his stand, was getting bored. 'So, when you've got the rest of the prints up it'll be finished, with a whole day to spare. You've worked miracles, Thea.'

'We have,' Thea agreed. 'But we haven't got a day to spare. Have you seen the state of the lavatory?'

'I suppose I must have done. I've certainly used it.'

'Then you'll realise it needs decorating.' Thea had hoped they'd get away without doing this, but when Molly pointed out that 'Kim luvs Simon' and other far less acceptable graffiti was clearly visible, she was forced to capitulate. 'You wouldn't like to do it for us? I'm sure you've got time before your hot date. I can lend you a boiler suit.'

'Sure, I'd love to help you. But you know I told you I've got to see a woman about –'

'*Please* say it's about a dog, or even a whole pack of them. I'd let you off painting the john for that.' Thea, who was still going home to soggy newspaper and piles of poo, had given up hope of Rory ever taking responsibility for Lara and her pups again.

'Thea, I promise you I'll sort out Lara and find homes for all the pups very soon.' He grinned. 'But actually it's about a television programme she wants me to make. Talking about art through the ages. They saw my picture and thought I'd be perfect for it. Something to do with my cheekbones.'

Thea and Molly exchanged glances but didn't comment. 'Well, as long as you're back here tomorrow by five thirty at the latest – sober! I've got all my photography friends coming to take pictures. I'll need you – or at least your fabulous cheekbones.'

'Bitch,' he said fondly, 'of course I'll be back. I might even beg a bed for the night tonight.'

'You know which your room is. It's still got your sheets on it. And if you're home before I am, see to the puppies, will you?'

After he had gone, Molly and Thea exchanged glances. 'Well, I hope he's better at art through the ages than he was on Cézanne,' said Molly.

'He was so crap!'

Molly frowned. 'I know you've been spending a lot of time with Petal, but do you have to raid her limited vocabulary?'

Thea shrugged. 'Crap or not, as he's not going to paint the bathroom I'd better do it while you're here to man the phones.' She yawned. She'd been keeping very late hours recently.

'Did I tell you I've got my cleaning lady to come in tomorrow and give things a final polish? It's so important that everything is *gleaming*.'

'Molly, love, I despair of you. We're supposed to be running this gallery on a shoestring. I'll let you get away with it this time, for Rory's show, but after this we're going to have to wield that vac ourselves. Do you think you can manage that?'

Molly made a face. 'I was a chalet girl once, you know. I can do cleaning if I have to.'

'Oh, good. What about the windows? Newspaper and vinegar puts on a lovely shine.'

Molly's expression was so horrified that Thea relented.

'It's all right. I've got one of the boys booked. He did window cleaning as a Saturday job. He's got all the gear and he's coming first thing.'

'What are you going to wear for the opening?' Molly asked Thea nervously, as she watched her climb into the boiler suit she had offered Rory. 'Not that, I hope.'

'Oh, I thought I would. I thought it would be cool and funky, a sort of urban statement.'

'Thea, really, I don't know . . .'

'It's all right, I'm joking again. You should know me by now.'

'So, what *are* you going to wear? I'm willing to bet you've nothing suitable in your wardrobe.'

'And nothing suitable in my bank balance, either, so it doesn't matter that I haven't time to buy anything new.' Thea chewed her lip. This problem had crossed her mind a few times, but as she couldn't think of a solution to it she just let it pass right on through.

'Thea.'

Molly was so stern that Thea put down the paint she had just picked up. 'What?'

'I am begging you, please, please, please let me take you shopping to buy something. You are the human manifestation of this gallery. It is essential that you look absolutely beautiful.' She held up her hand before Thea could even draw breath, let alone speak. 'Yes, the work will speak for itself, but when half the art world think you and Rory are having an affair, you don't want them wondering *why*.'

'Oh, my God! They don't, do they?'

'What? Think you and Rory are having an affair? Of course they do! And so do most of your friends, for that matter.'

'But –'

'*I* know you're not, of course.' Molly gave Thea a sidelong glance to check she was right about this. 'But I'm willing to bet all those arty London types will assume it. Why else would he show here?'

Thea had been entertaining a tiny hope that it was because of the beautiful space, but that had been deflated and now she couldn't think of a single reason. 'Why indeed?'

'So it's essential that you look *so* drop-dead gorgeous that it seems perfectly logical.'

It seemed anything but logical and totally impossible. Thea tried to protest. 'But I want the gallery –'

'No. You're not having them come through the door, take one look at you and think, my God, those rumours can't be true.'

'But –'

'Good God, woman! Have you no feminine pride? Apart from anyone else, there's Ben!'

'What about Ben?'

'The women he's been toting around like Lulu Guinness handbags! There was a family party last week and he brought this . . . woman.' Molly obviously couldn't think of a word bad enough for her. 'She was a size ten, or possibly eight. She looked about nineteen, but it turned out she was twenty-five – hardly any better for a man Ben's age – and she smoked almost continually.'

'What has this to do with me and what I wear for the opening?' Thea asked, trying to match her expression to the casualness of her words.

Molly looked discomfited. 'Oh, nothing really. I just think it's time Ben settled down and not with someone Toby will be having the hots for by the time he's eighteen. Honestly, Ben has no sense when it comes to women.'

'Really.'

'But none of this is to the point. We need to get you a dress. I'll give you two hours to paint the loo, then I'm taking you away. I know a lovely shop in Cheltenham. It's

288

a good thing you've lost a little weight recently.'

Molly had left the gallery before Thea could protest that it *wasn't* a good thing. It was because she hadn't time to eat properly during the day and was too tired to cook anything when she got home. All her calories at the moment were derived from chocolate, orange juice and the occasional portion of chips. Thea did not approve of society's requirement that all women should be stick thin and certainly didn't want to subscribe to it. But on the other hand it was hard not to feel just a tiny bit pleased to have dropped a dress size.

Reluctantly, two hours later to the minute, Thea handed her paint roller over to Petal's boyfriend who had appeared simultaneously with Petal. 'If you don't do a good job you'll never show here,' she said earnestly.

'Don't worry, I'm an artist. I can paint.'

Thea let this pass. 'Don't forget, we don't want any contrasts of texture, or experiments with perspective. We just want plain white walls.'

'You've done one coat already, I'll just go over where you've been.'

'I'll see that he does a good job,' Petal promised. 'Now, you just go shopping with Aunt Molly.'

Reluctantly, Thea climbed out of the boiler suit. In fact, she'd rather have finished painting the lavatory. There was something very soothing about white paint.

Once in Molly's car, a leather-seated, power-steered automatic that had cost the equivalent of a small house, Thea felt glad to get away. Molly was a stylish driver and just now the gallery was full of noise and chaos, and the moment when she could declare it ready seemed like winning the lottery: wonderful, but very unlikely to happen.

'I think you'll like the shop where I'm taking you. It's run by such a talented woman.' Molly overtook an artic and a tractor with one swift movement. 'She knows what suits one better than one does oneself.'

'I'm sure it must be horrifically expensive.'

'An investment. But I promise you she won't let you buy anything you're not happy with.'

The shop was terrifyingly tiny – the sort you could never go into on spec, because you'd be too embarrassed to leave without buying anything. However, once over the threshold in Molly's company, Thea found it a pleasant space and the owner an extremely attractive woman who was fifty if she was a day. It was a huge relief. Thea might not feel she was nearly as good-looking as this elegant person, but knowing she was fifteen years younger did give her some advantage.

Molly and the owner kissed each other fondly. 'Caroline, this is Thea. I've brought her to see you because she needs something absolutely stunning. We're ... she's opening an art gallery tomorrow.'

'Oh! Is that the one I heard about on local radio this morning? With the new Irish artist? It sounds so exciting.'

'I hope it will be,' said Thea somewhat glumly. The enormity of what she'd taken on suddenly seemed a terrible mistake and now it would be a public mistake. Like the Millennium Dome, it would be a spectacular failure.

'Of course it will be! With Molly on your side it'll be smashing. Now, what do you feel comfortable wearing?'

'Jeans.'

'So, trousers, then.'

She shook her head. 'No, I've got thighs.'

Caroline asked a lot of questions and then said, 'Right. You two sit down and have a glass of wine, while I find a few for you to try on.'

'She didn't ask me what size I was,' whispered Thea anxiously.

'No need. She can tell at a glance. Most of the women

who come in here have got personal trainers,' Molly went on.

'Personal trainers?' Thea was awestruck. 'Does that mean no one else can wear them? How lovely!'

Molly opened her mouth, and then closed it again. 'Oh, you're joking. Sorry.'

Thea wondered if it was the wine on an empty stomach, or whether she really looked as good as the mirror in front of her told her she did. She looked svelte, a word she thought she would never be able to apply to herself – not in a million years. 'Crikey,' she said.

The dress was black, strapless, short and close-fitting. But it was so well-cut and well-boned, so carefully, subtly ruched, that instead of feeling like a streetwalker, Thea felt like a minor film star on Oscar night.

'That's the one,' said Caroline.

'It's *fabulous!*' said Molly.

'I bet it costs a fortune,' said Thea glumly, 'and I'm not going to have many opportunities to wear it. The cost per wear is going to be horrendous.'

'Usually' – Caroline poured more wine into Thea's glass – 'I'd agree with you totally about the cost per wear. This dress is never going to be truly cost-effective. But I always say that some occasions are worth more than others. After all, a wedding dress, which could cost several thousand, is only worn once. But for that particular *occasion*, it's worth it.'

'And this isn't several thousand, after all,' Molly argued.

'And I'm not getting married, nor likely to be. So this could be the equivalent dress. Expensive but exquisite. How much is it, by the way?'

'Don't tell her!' Molly put up a silencing hand. 'Darling, this is a present from me and Derek – we're so grateful. I've had such fun and he's had such peace and quiet. Buying you a dress is the least we can do.'

'But it's not the least you have done! You've already . . .'

'That was all boring stuff; this is fun.' Molly dismissed the matter of cost with an airy wave. 'Now, Caro, what have you got for me to wear?'

The three photographer friends who, unlike Magenta, hadn't had a hand in her present existence, arrived half-way through Saturday afternoon. Fortunately, when they saw Rory, the work and the space, Thea didn't have to spend too long convincing them she'd made the right decision about her life at last.

'Magenta told us the work was fantastic. She didn't say anything about Rory,' said one.

'She only saw the slides of his work, not him,' Thea explained. 'We spent all day looking for him, but I didn't come across him until after she'd gone off to the beauty parlour.'

'Foolish Magenta! I think this is a great gallery and much better for you than being a landlady. I bet those students walked over you.'

Petal, who was running a cloth over the skirting boards – her gesture to manual work – was within earshot and she looked up indignantly.

'Well, some of them did. Not you, Petal, of course.'

Petal made a face. Unlike her aunt, she knew when Thea was being sarcastic or making a joke.

The photographers set up their equipment and snapped happily. They all took conventional photographs of the work, and roll after roll of film of Rory, Petal and Thea doing things.

'Did I tell you that a journalist pal is arriving soon? She wants to do an article about you for one of the gossip mags.'

'Oh, my God! All I need now is for someone to tell me that the *Sunday Sport* are coming to photograph me and

Rory topless. I think everyone else has already been in touch.'

'That would be fine by me,' said Rory, who had climbed down from the ladder where he had been posing. 'I like the idea of Thea topless in front of one of me daubs.'

'Well there are going to be pictures of your pecs all over the press,' said Thea. 'Satisfy yourself with that thought.'

'Seriously,' Magenta put in. 'You should be really grateful for all this publicity. It's not easy to get and it's very hard to get started without it.'

'It was Ben,' said Molly proudly. 'He arranged it all.'

'Who's Ben?' asked one of the women.

'He's connected to one of the London galleries,' Magenta said, protecting Thea from probing questions. 'Bloody useful, too.'

'He's also my cousin,' Molly added, not wanting to miss out on any reflected glory that was going. 'Now, Thea, when are you going to get changed?'

Thea looked desperately at her watch. 'It's only four o'clock!'

'I'm not saying you have to do it now. I'm saying you have to leave enough time to go home, change and get back.'

'Oh, I'm not going home.' Thea laughed at this suggestion. 'I'd never have time to do that! I'm going to change . . .'

'In my hotel room.' Magenta still looked like a model. 'It's just across the road. I'm going to do her hair and make-up.'

Thea started on the 'Oh, no you're not' but saw she was outnumbered and closed her mouth again.

'Oh, good,' said Molly, referring to her ever-present clipboard. 'That's one thing off my mind. Now, where are we going to set up the bar?'

*

At five to six Molly, Petal and her crowd, Rory and Thea were all ready. They were all nervous, although Rory refused to acknowledge it. He was impossibly good-looking in his casual suit, clean shirt and new shoes. No tie, of course, and although the clothes were all designer, he hadn't lost his rugged manliness. Thea was aware that every woman who saw him would metaphorically fall at his feet.

'Well, we're all here,' said Rory, 'and the champagne and smoked salmon are here. Let's forget about the punters and just have a lovely party!'

Too late Thea remembered she'd resolved to fill him up with stodge, so the alcohol wouldn't go straight to his head. 'Rory, can I have a word with you?' She drew him through into another room. She gathered a plate full of miniature tartlets filled with caviar and stuffed quails eggs. 'Before you drink anything you're to eat these. I'm not having you jeopardising your second chance because you got drunk again. Apart from anything else, it would do for my gallery before it's even had a chance.'

'It's all right. No need to panic. I drank a tablespoon of olive oil before I came, which is what the Russians do to line their stomachs. I forced down a pint of water, so I'm too full to drink much and I've learnt my lesson after last time.'

'Well, that's a weight off my mind. I thought I'd have to be following you about, counting every glassful, smacking your wrist if you had too many.'

'So you're not going to do that now?'

'Well, no, not if you've decided to be sensible.'

'What a shame. I think I would have rather enjoyed it. You know you look sensational, don't you, Thea? You knock those other women, who are not at all bad-looking, right out of the frame.'

'Really?' She didn't believe him for a minute but his flattery was lovely.

'Yes, really, and I might break my resolution not to try my hand at getting you into bed again. Now that would be worth staying sober for.'

Thea laughed. 'You're a terrible man, Rory Devlin. Let's go and join the others.'

Chapter Twenty-Two

Although desperate for a drink to relieve her nerves, Thea had decided not to have anything alcoholic until it was all over. She couldn't risk even the tiniest lapse of concentration.

Petal, who had a stream of beautiful girlfriends as well as copious male friends, had turned two of each into waiters and waitresses.

Molly had wanted the catering company to provide staff, to reduce the risk of the waiters getting drunk, or getting into artistic arguments with the art critics, but Thea had stood firm. 'We're only having champagne and canapés as a special dispensation. I draw the line at paying for waiters.'

'Oh,' said Petal, who had been listening keenly. 'Aren't they going to get paid, then?'

'Of course,' Thea backtracked. 'But you're family. I'd rather pay you lot than strangers.'

Molly gave her niece a look which promised eternal hellfire if anyone she had brought along for the work let them down.

Now Rory said, 'Right, let's open a bottle and have a stiffener before the hordes arrive.'

'I'll have an orange juice,' Thea said. 'And I hope they do arrive.' She opened the gallery door and looked anxiously up and down the street.

'They're not due until six thirty,' said Molly. 'I'm sure someone will come.'

'Oh, my God!' Thea was still doing her 'Sister Anne,

Sister Anne, is there anyone coming' impression. 'A massive black car has just drawn up.' She ducked back into the gallery. 'I don't want anyone to come now. I just want it to be us. And the girls.'

'The girls', who objected to this name in a casual way, were all still in the hotel opposite getting ready. Once they had dispatched Thea, looking as glamorous as any model and a lot more beautiful, back into the gallery, they had their own ablutions to make.

Rory put a glass of champagne into Thea's hand. 'Here, one drink won't knock you over and it'll help keep the smile on your face. Ah, here are the lovely ladies.'

Thea's friends exchanged glances. 'Do we object to that more than "girls" or less?' asked Magenta.

Having decided it was a moot point, they helped themselves to champagne. 'Lovely party, Thea. Here's to you!'

Thea was still clutching her glass, as yet untouched, when the contents of the huge black car entered. She walked forward to greet them and found herself wrapped in a cloud of Eau Savage. 'Thea, my dear, this looks fabulous!'

'Edward! You came!' Thea returned his embrace heartily, forgetting how important and influential he was, and thinking only how pleased she was to see him. 'Come in and have a drink. Let Rory show you the work.'

'Oh, Rory's here, is he? How did you manage to keep him in line when so many of us have failed?'

Thea laughed and asked quietly, 'Do you think Veronica will come?'

'Darling, I don't think she could keep away.'

To her relief, there were a few serious art journalists among the gossip columnists and photographers. They fought their way to Thea who had just discovered she was mistress of the soundbite. Deliver a few snappy sentences with confidence and people actually think you know what you're talking about. You even got to believe it yourself. She decided to put Veronica to the back of her mind. If she did come, she might not spot Thea, or better, Thea might not spot her.

But even while talking to genuinely interested people, she found her eye constantly flicking towards the door, looking for Ben and Toby. She had sent Toby a personal invitation, adding in pink pen 'promise you'll come'. She had had a sweet note back from him promising that he would.

Her expensive dress, which was causing a minor sensation among her friends who were more used to seeing her in jeans, had been for Ben's benefit. In her private heart she knew that. As was the make-up, the hair styling, in fact, everything that wasn't directly concerned with the gallery. If she hadn't been hoping to prove to him that she too could be attractive and glamorous, she would never have let Molly talk her into any of it. She wanted Ben to see her at her shining best and wonder why on earth he had let her get away. It was petty, childish and about as unfeminist as it was possible to be, but it was human and she couldn't help herself.

It seemed several lifetimes had passed spent talking, introducing Rory, smiling and having her photograph taken, before at last she saw Ben's tall figure appear in the doorway.

Toby wasn't with him, but two thin, glamorous women were. One was Veronica, wearing a twist of fuchsia-coloured silk and a diamond choker; the other was a much younger woman. Ben was holding the younger woman's elbow in a very protective way, probably guarding her from Veronica.

Thea's simple black silk sheath, which had seemed so expensively perfect, felt far too hot. How on earth should she greet Veronica? As if they were old friends? And did she still believe that she'd kidnapped Toby? She suddenly felt in need of a bit of protection herself. She looked wildly around and spotted Rory. For the moment he was unattached, probably looking for a drink. 'Hold my hand, Rory, quickly, please,' she whispered urgently.

Without asking for an explanation, Rory obligingly put his arm round her and rested his hand on her bottom. 'Will this do?'

'Perfect. Veronica's just come in, with Ben.'

'Veronica! Oh, my God! She'll be out for my blood – and that's only the mentionable part she'll be after.'

'We'll just both be very cool and very polite. Use your charm, but subtly. For God's sake, Rory, if you can't charm the pants off a woman like Veronica you're not the man I thought you were!'

'I never managed to charm the pants off you.'

'Oh, stop being silly and let's go for it. We'll go up to her and Ben, and say hello like we really want to see them. Come on.'

She didn't actually push through the crowds to get to them, but she did manoeuvre herself and Rory so Ben and his party would notice them quite soon.

Ben spoke first. 'Hello, Thea. You're looking very . . . thin.'

She decided against kissing him. She had kissed everyone else in the room, man, woman or child, but she couldn't kiss Ben like that.

'Oh, Ben, hi,' she said, 'and Veronica! How kind of you to come. I've been hearing how influential you are and I'm so grateful you've slogged all the way out here to see the show.' She squeezed Rory's hand to make him say something.

'Veronica!' He released Thea and embraced Veronica for long enough to make sure someone got a picture. 'Will you ever forgive me? You do all that for my career and I ship out at the last moment.' He looked down into her eyes in a way that Thea recognised. If Veronica had a speck of oestrogen in her body she'd have to respond. 'Come with me to find some champagne. I want to drink it from your slipper.'

'Silly boy!' Veronica allowed herself to be lead away, aware of the envious glances of several other women. 'I'm wearing sandals.'

Somehow Ben was still there, silently demanding attention. Now Veronica was out of the way, Thea felt free to ask him a question. 'Where's Toby? He promised to come to my show.'

'He wanted to, very much. But private views aren't really the place for children, are they?' said Ben's companion. 'He'd be dreadfully bored.'

Thea was hurt on Toby's behalf. He'd want to be here for her sake, if not for the sake of 'Art'.

'He can always come and see it another time,' said Ben. 'Oh, sorry, I haven't introduced you. This is Poppy Jacks. Thea Orville, the director and creator of the gallery.'

Thea waited in vain to be told that Poppy Jacks was terribly important in the art world, which would also tell her that Ben had only brought her to be useful, not because he had anything to do with her.

Poppy Jacks extended her hand. 'Hi! I think it's terribly brave what you're doing. Opening an art gallery against all the odds. Ben told me how much effort he's put into it himself, just so it wasn't a complete flop before it even opened.'

For the first time that evening, Thea found herself without a suitable soundbite, or indeed anything to say at all. Eventually she managed, 'I've got a hundred people I must talk to. Ben, why don't you show Poppy round?'

'Who's Ben with?' demanded Molly. 'I saw Rory working on Veronica. I must admit, when he chooses to use it, that man has the charm of the devil.'

'And the cheekbones of an angel,' said Magenta, scooping a glass of champagne off a passing tray. 'I've got some fabulous shots. Must go. See you later.'

'So?' Molly hadn't had her answer yet.

'You could ask him yourself, but she's called Poppy.'

'So is she the one who did all the PR?'

'You're the one who knows all about Ben's private life. Why don't you go and get an update?' Thea smiled to soften her crispness. 'Now I must find Edward Grampian and make sure I've got his seal of approval.'

Molly found Thea a little later. 'It's not the PR woman. She's that one over there, talking to Rory now. Poppy's just a popsy. Oh! I've made a pun. I think.'

'We're going now. It's been a wonderful show.' Ben kissed Thea's cheek.

'Yes,' Poppy added. 'It's been such fun. Now we're going to eat. Edward has taken Veronica on somewhere, so we're off the leash.'

'That's nice,' said Thea. 'Are you eating in town? We're all going to the Chinese Dragon, if you'd like to join us.' Watching Ben flirting with Poppy all night would be torture. The thought that she might never see him again if she let him escape was even worse.

Poppy laughed. 'Oh, no. Ben's promised me something a little more sophisticated than we can get here.'

Thea's jaw clamped down on the words 'The Chinese Dragon is very sophisticated'. She was extremely tired and a sense of anticlimax threatened to overwhelm her. If she wasn't careful she'd burst into tears in a very messy way.

'Poppy doesn't like Chinese food,' said Ben.

Thea forced her mouth open. 'So, what are you going to do instead?' She wouldn't have asked, but as Ben was just standing there, Poppy tugging on his arm, instead of getting the hell out, she had to say something.

'Ben knows a little place near Chipping Norton.' Poppy almost clapped her hands in anticipation. 'Sounds wonderful!'

'Sounds a long way away,' said Thea.

'So what are you going to do again?' Ben asked.

Why was Ben was still there when, if he'd had an iota of tact, he would have left Thea to allow herself a short, violent display of emotion? As it was, she had to keep up with the small talk. 'I said the Chinese Dragon. Rory and I are going to get rat-arsed. I think we deserve it, don't you?'

There was a flicker of something in Ben's expression, but it was probably just shock that she'd used such a vulgar expression. He didn't speak again, but steered his woman out of the gallery into the warm summer night.

There were nearly twenty of them in all at the Chinese Dragon, although they had only booked for twelve. Several of the party were drunk on Molly's champagne. There were a few men who'd been at art school with Rory, a couple of journalists who, being young, now wanted to drink on and get to know the star, and several other men and girls Thea couldn't connect with anyone. The Chinese Dragon was courteous and welcoming, and moved tables about, found chairs and chopsticks.

Thea didn't sit next to Rory, although he invited her to. He was very excited, high on his success, which had been extraordinary by any standards. The art-buying public, most of whom had been at the show, had, in Thea's opinion, lost their heads completely. Once the first red sticker went on, others followed, everyone desperate to get a piece of this exciting new talent, notwithstanding the enormous prices Thea and Rory had decided on. It was doubtful if most of the buyers really loved the pictures as Thea felt they should be loved, but they saw them as an investment. Not one of them objected when Thea told them that the paintings were possibly to be shown in London, and that they might not be able to get their hands on their prize for months. This was after Edward had told her he still wanted Rory to exhibit and would she not let any of the work be taken away before he'd had a chance to decide what he wanted.

Rory would always be able to make his living from his work from now on, especially as the television producer he had met had been so impressed. Thea had met her too and had wondered if she should give a few hints that Rory might not be a great presenter. She decided against it. Rory could probably read an autocue and could be trained into being more relaxed in front of an audience.

Thea had no appetite. Her heart was thumping, she felt she had drunk twenty cups of strong coffee when all she'd had was the single glass of champagne that Rory thrust on her and several pints of mineral water. When people eventually began ordering, she just agreed to share a set menu someone else had decided was good.

Rory was the young lion, the centre of attention, charming the socks off everyone present. Thea was glad she wasn't at his side. She didn't want them to be seen as a couple. It wasn't fair to him when he probably wanted a woman to end the evening with. No matter how charming he was, how appropriate their ending the evening together might have been, she wasn't going to let him think anything like that would happen with her. But there were several other young women in the party, possibly not encumbered by scruples and damaged hearts, all hungry for his smile or anything else he might be giving away.

She sipped her mineral water. All she wanted to do was to drive home, on her own, and go to bed. She was so tired she could have slept where she sat and was just slipping into a state not far removed from sleep when she was aware of someone calling her name.

She looked up and saw Ben. 'Thea,' he said. 'Can I have a word? In private?'

He spoke very urgently and Thea wondered what on earth could have happened. She got up immediately. 'What's the matter? Is it Toby?'

He shook his head ever so slightly, but lost nothing of his urgency. 'Bring your bag and coat.'

Thea looked at Molly who seemed not to have noticed Ben's appearance. Rory was Blarney-stoning one of Thea's photographer friends and hadn't noticed either. Thea picked up her jacket from the back of her chair.

Once in the street, he took her by the shoulders. Suddenly wide awake, she felt angry. 'This is getting to be a habit, manhandling me in the street! Tell me what the problem is and let me get back to my friends.'

His fingers bit into her skin and he looked intently down at her. 'I'm sorry. I hope I'm not hurting you. But I have to know. Are you really going to sit with that lot all night and get "rat-arsed" as you so elegantly put it?'

'And why shouldn't I?'

'There's something I want to show you.' He made as if to push her along the road.

She forced him to stop, although he didn't release his grip. 'What is it? I can't just walk out on everybody. I have responsibilities.'

'Most of them are drunk and Molly will see to anyone who isn't.'

'But I don't *want* to walk out on them!'

This time he turned and took hold of both shoulders, staring down into her face intently. 'Don't you really? Haven't you had enough of braying women and sycophantic men, all wanting to know your private life and whether there's anything in it for them?'

Honesty fought with pride and won. She shrugged.

'Then come with me. I promise you, you won't regret it.'

'But where's your friend? Popsy – Poppy?'

'I put her in a taxi. Now, will you come with me or not?' He didn't wait for her answer. He just took her wrist and pulled her along the road to where his car was parked askew across a double yellow line.

Thea had about two minutes to decide whether or not to go with him. It took her five seconds. When he unlocked the car door for her she got in. Just being away from all the noise and activity seemed sufficient reward for being so passive. Now she'd been taken from all the heat and hubbub, going back would seem like re-entering hell.

He drove up and out of the town to a valley Thea didn't know. She stared out of the window at the beauty of the summer darkness. The moon had risen, bathing everything with light, casting strange shadows. The trees stood out against the sky. The hills took on the shapes of enormous mythic beasts and honeysuckle-scented hedges were dotted with bindweed flowers, strangely white. It was the kind of night when maidens of old performed strange rituals and laid their linen smocks on the grass to bleach in the moonlight. She didn't let herself think about where she was going or why, she just hoped the drive would go on for ever. At the moment it was perfect: she didn't have to speak and she was with Ben. The minute they had to talk they'd start misunderstanding and fighting with each other again.

He took his car down a drive to where a house sat silhouetted in the twilight. There were no lights on and it looked empty. Roses, in dire need of pruning, grew almost across a leaning wooden porch. A 'For Sale' sign, with an 's.s.t.c.' band stuck across it, stood by the front gate.

Ben stopped the car and got out. Then he walked round and opened her door. 'Come on.' He lifted open the gate for her to go through.

Reluctant as she was to spoil it all by opening her mouth, she had to protest. 'Ben, we can't call on people at this time of night. Not when I don't know them and they've only just moved in. Or are they about to move out?'

He didn't answer; he just manoeuvred her up the path to the front door. They were standing very close together and she was intensely aware of his physical presence. She was only wearing a pair of briefs underneath her dress and she yearned for him to catch her mood and take her in his arms. He didn't. He held back the roses, so she wouldn't get scratched, then produced some keys and unlocked the door. 'There.'

She stepped past him, away from his disturbing nearness, and looked about her.

The house was obviously empty and had been for some time, because there was dust everywhere. Thea stood in the entrance, trying to make out the details in the moonlight.

The door opened directly into the front room, which was large and had probably been two rooms at one time, judging by the beam that ran across it. She could make out a massive fireplace at one end and a staircase at the other. There was a window almost opposite the front door through which Thea could see a garden and tree-covered hills beyond. The house was enchanting, unrestored, probably bristling with original features. Thea would almost have put money on there being an old Cotswold privy outside. It must have cost a small fortune.

'It's amazing,' said Thea. 'But I don't understand. You kidnap me – and you really did kidnap me – take me away from all my friends and important contacts to show me a house you could have shown me at any other time.'

'I couldn't wait any longer. I couldn't risk it. If I hadn't taken you away when I did, you'd have gone to bed with Rory.'

'Oh. Why did you want to stop me? You've got Poppy, after all. You've never shown any interest in me, so it can't be jealousy.'

'Jealousy! If you knew what I'd gone through. What do you mean, I've never shown any interest in you? You must know by now how I feel about you.'

'How was I supposed to do that? By ESP? There certainly haven't been any other indications! You've only ever kissed me when you've been angry and couldn't hit me.' Suddenly she found herself smiling and was glad he probably couldn't see. 'You're angry now, aren't you? You want to hit me again.'

She heard him laugh softly as he walked towards her. 'Well, yes, but not quite as much as I want to kiss you.'

He swept her into his arms, crushing her expensive dress and her with the same ruthlessness. His mouth came down on hers as if drawn by a magnet, his fingers pushed up into her hair at the back of her neck. She couldn't move, could hardly breathe and wanted to stay there for ever. It felt as if all the kisses he'd never given her were concentrated in that one kiss. He kissed her as if he were never going to stop.

Eventually, breathless, he released her mouth, but kept hold of her body. It was as well he did, otherwise she'd have fallen over. 'So,' he said, breathing hard. 'Now can I ask you to marry me? And don't say it's all so sudden, because it isn't and you know it isn't. I've been in love with you since I first helped you step out of a dustbin. We may fight like cat and dog, but we're destined for each other and you know it as well as I do.'

Thea swallowed, trying to get her breath and her balance back. Her mind was a little quicker to recover. While she wanted nothing better than to go on kissing Ben for the rest of her life, she had to get a few things straight first. 'What about those other women? That Molly told me about? Like handbags?'

'What are you talking about?'

'Always another pretty girl dangling off your arm. Molly told me about them. You took one to a family party.'

'Oh, her.'

'Yes, her. She wasn't Poppy, I assume, or Molly would have recognised her.'

He laughed again. For possibly the first time since she'd known him, he seemed boyish and carefree, like Toby making chocolate cake. 'Cilla was just to stop the family gossip and Poppy was a smokescreen so Veronica wouldn't guee I cared about you.'

'I don't think she knew that was her function! You used her!'

'She's used plenty of people in her time. It'll do her good to be useful for once.'

'You are a bastard!'

'Thea, have you any idea how utterly terrifying it is to realise that the woman you love could be seriously harmed by the woman you once loved? If Veronica had got an inkling of how I felt about you she'd have sued me for custody of Toby.'

'She wouldn't have got it, would she?'

'I don't know, but she'd have gone for it. And what would that have been like for Toby?'

'Oh, God!'

'And if I'd gone to a family party without a woman, they'd have pestered me with questions about this woman that Toby likes so much. Word would have got back to Veronica and she'd have had her knives into your gallery so deep you'd never get them out. Now, can we please stop arguing?'

'I'm not arguing. You're doing it all on your own. And if you liked me so much, why didn't you ask me out, like a normal human being?'

'I've told you. Because of Veronica.'

'Well, Veronica's still alive, isn't she? Why is it all right to bring me here now?'

'Because now your gallery will be a success whatever she does. And no judge would give her custody of Toby when they hear Toby tell them how much he wants to live with us.'

A horrible thought struck her. 'Ben, you're not doing all this because of Toby, are you? I mean, I really do love him, but I'm not going to marry you just to make him happy.'

'What about making me happy?' he whispered. 'Or

you?' He caressed her cheek with his hand. 'Would marrying me make you happy? Because that's the most important thing.'

She couldn't speak. She knew that if she tried she'd burst into tears.

'Listen, why don't you come and sit down? Your feet must be killing you in those ridiculous heels.'

Glad that he was back to criticising her, she said, 'They're not ridiculous, they're essential to go with this dress.' She turned to him. 'Don't you like it? It was very expensive.'

'It's wonderful, but I can't stop thinking about what you'd look like without it on.'

'Oh.'

'I'll give you two seconds to get to the door, but if you don't run I'm very much afraid that I'm going to have to make love to you.'

She gave a petulant little sigh. 'These heels are all very well, but they're hell to walk in.'

He growled and came towards her, picking her up with terrifying ease. She started to giggle. 'This is terribly romantic, Ben, but where are you going to take me? This dress cost far too much for me to make love on top of.'

'Shut up and let me worry about that.'

She was giggling and he was panting as he carried her up the dusty staircase, along a moonlit corridor to a bedroom. He kicked open the door and revealed a double sleeping bag, some pillows and some carrier bags.

He lowered her to her feet, suddenly diffident. 'It's not very romantic at all. In fact, you may want to change your mind. We could easily go to a hotel, somewhere with a proper bed.'

Thea turned to him and pushed her arms round his body under his jacket, feeling the heat of his skin through the fine cotton. 'Whatever you think is best.' She burrowed into him, inhaling his scent, trusting he wouldn't take too long to decide that a sleeping bag could be just as romantic as a honeymoon suite with en suite bathroom and complimentary basket of fruit.

He hesitated just a second too long for her liking. She took hold of his hand and put it on her breast, under the top of her dress.

'Oh, God, Thea,' he breathed and seconds later her dress had rustled to her feet, leaving her in her high heels and her briefs. 'You are so beautiful. I could look at you for ever.'

She sighed, tutted and kicked her dress out of the way. 'Not if I have anything to do with it, you couldn't. Now get your gear off – you've pulled.'

At first they were so urgent and hungry for each other that there was no time for tender caresses or subtle movements. It was only after they fell apart, sweating and panting, that they had time really to enjoy each other.

'I didn't realise sex could be like that,' said Thea, still out of breath.

'I'm a bit surprised myself. Would you like a glass of champagne?'

'What?'

'What I said. I may not be able to offer you a goose feather duvet, but I did get in a few essential supplies.'

'Ben, what are you talking about?'

He sat up, his muscled torso highlighted by moonlight, and reached for one of the carrier bags. 'Two bottles of champagne, originally ready chilled, but possible warmer now. A tin of foie gras, some Bath Oliver biscuits, a few tomatoes and some cheese. Oh, and some chocolate truffles for pudding. I hope you like them.'

He rolled off the sleeping bag and crossed the room to where his trousers were lying in a heap. From the pocket he produced a Swiss Army knife.

Watching him move, Thea longed to have a camera with her, to capture for ever the sight of his beautiful masculine body as he moved about in the moonlight. Then she remembered she didn't need a photograph of it after all. It was hers to look at whenever the moon was full. 'I think I'm going to like being married to you, Ben,' she said when he handed her a biscuit loaded with pâté.

'I'm going to make absolutely sure you do.'

His kiss tasted of champagne.